THE MERRY BAND

The Plot Bandits Quartet

The Disposable

The Merry Band

The Narrative

The Taskmaster

THE MERRY BAND
Copyright © 2021 by Katherine Vick.
Cover design by Nada Orlic.

Thinklings Books
1400 Lloyd Rd. #552
Wickliffe, OH 44092
thinklingsbooks.com

For Kerry,
my own Merry Band,
with the Quest from the first page

And for my parents,
just for being themselves

The Plot Bandits, Book 2

THE MERRY BAND

by

Katherine Vick

Thinklings Books, LLC
Wickliffe, OH

Still mourning the loss of poor Gort, Erik and his
companions pursue Sleiss's brother Vagg into a grim
and miserable forest, harried by vile bat-winged
creatures in the thrall of those who would stop them.
A mysterious old crone points them in the direction
taken by the villainous thief, but warns them of a
monstrous dragon that lives in the hills and hungers
for the taste of human flesh. As they head into
ominous forests and pass through a ruined city, they
are attacked once more by the creatures and lose each
other in the harsh mountains.

It was a place that nightmares were made of.

The contorted, gargoyle-like trunks of towering trees more dead than alive twisted out of the harsh, boggy ground, balancing precariously on a web of sinuous roots that burrowed into the rotting leaf litter and knotted pits of brambles like hungry worms. Tangled, claw-like branches arched and scratched their nails towards the sky, the few leaves that clung to their wild, pitted, blackened bark dancing like spectres on the wind. In the shadow of these hideous, monstrously deformed shapes, a puddle of black, foul-smelling goo bubbled cheerfully away by itself.

It was a forest with character. A forest with threat. A forest that whispered of the terrible fate that lay within its clutches; a forest of dark creatures and vile monstrosities; a forest that would chew you up and spit what was left of you out to moulder forgotten forever.

Erik hardened his chin grimly. It was the perfect hiding place for those who sought to rip the world asunder.

His mind shuddered at the thought of the events of the last few days. Poor brave Gort, their loyal dwarfish companion felled by the cruel swing of an enemy soldier's sword. Zahora wounded to the edge of death, the power of Elder's healing magic all that kept her too from an early grave. Torsheid—brother of noble, slain Halheid—sent to his death at the hands of an unnatural, chain-mail-clad wench mere moments after joining them. The Ring of Anthiphion, the greatest and most powerful magical object in the history of the Six Kingdoms in the hands of a

1

common soldier, a servant of the dead High Lord of Sleiss—a soldier
who, through some means inexplicable to even the mind of the great
sorcerer Eldrigon, had found a way to bypass the constraints of blood
descent and use the Ring's power to whisk himself and his foul allies to
this gods-forsaken forest. Prince Tretaptus, supposedly an ally against
the darkness, had been exposed as a raving madman and the mastermind
behind their present misfortunes. And as for the Prince's kidnapped
betrothed, the beautiful Princess Islaine...

Islaine.

Erik's mind fell into a frantic whirl at the memory of that pale,
beautiful face lying stricken beneath waves of gold-red curls, her gentle
breath, her delicate form. He remembered her agonised scream as foul
Tretaptus and his allies had dragged her by means of stolen magic to this
vile wilderness where who knew what atrocities might befall her...

No. He could not let that happen. He would not let it. Not to her.
Not to so pure and so perfect a being as Islaine...

"We must hurry!" Erik's voice rang boldly through the twisted tree
trunks. "Slynder! Which way?"

The thief glanced up from his crouch as he examined the unhealthy
ground for signs of their quarry, Erik's sudden energy rushing through
him in a vibrant burst. "This way!" He pointed into the shadows as he
grabbed hold of his saddle and vaulted agilely onto his horse. "Yes, yes!
I see a trail!"

"At last!" Sir Roderick's eyes gleamed in the shadow of his visor.
"We must rescue my lady Islaine!"

Erik could relate to that. "Then let's go!"

Fired with fervour, his companions whipped their reins with his; and
together, they ploughed into the insidious forest: Elder, his white beard
streaming, his eyes deep in distant thought; Zahora, warrior maiden, her
armour glinting in what little light crept through the shroud-like canopy;
Sir Roderick, his face a mask of resolve; and Slynder, riding at the front
as his stare picked out signs from the dirt beneath that none but his eyes
could read. The world blurred to a heartbeat as Erik ducked and wove his
loyal horse between the perilous trees, searching desperately for that hint
of gold-red, a glimpse of porcelain skin, just to know, desperate to know

she was safe...

And they rode and they rode, ground pounding beneath the horses' hooves, the sky stolen from view as shadows loomed around them, empty and threatening and—

"This is ridiculous!" Zahora's exclamation and the abrupt reining-in of her horse brought their frantic, tumbling ride to a sudden halt. "What are you even following, Slynder?"

Slynder glared at her with blazing affront. "There is a trail..."

"What trail?" Zahora retorted violently. "I can track also, and I see nothing!"

Slynder's expression was pinched and harsh. "Perhaps the blow to your head from that wench did more damage than Elder could fix!"

Zahora's eyes flared. "I see perfectly! And I see we are wasting our time! We cannot keep riding in circles!"

"What choice do we have, Zahora?" Elder's bearded face was an irritable mask. "We know that foul Tretaptus and the men of Sleiss who aid him fled somewhere in this direction. We have traced them as far as we can, but the trail is cold! What more do you suggest?"

"We need a plan!" Zahora sounded frustrated, and Erik could understand, but this halt was helping no one. "I cannot stand to act so pointlessly!"

"Neither can I!" No one could thunder out a sentence quite like Elder. "Zahora, we have had this debate time and again today! Can you not find something useful to suggest?"

"We need a plan!" Zahora repeated hotly. "We need direction!"

"What direction?" Sir Roderick intervened moodily. "Do you know of something we do not?"

"Of course not." The warrior woman glared at the knight briefly before switching her gaze back to Elder. "But is there not some magic we could use, some spell or incantation?"

Elder actually rolled his eyes. "If there were, do you not think I would have used it before now? Your moaning is utterly unhelpful! Why can you not be still?"

Zahora's expression was incandescent with rage. "How *dare*..."

From the concealing shadows of the nearby trees, Strut the Officious Courtier, the Taskmaster's taskmaster, assigner of duties both epic and mundane and the official unofficial voice of the instructions, shook his head and sighed.

It was degenerating again. There was no question about it. The Narrative was running out of ideas. The frustration of foiled plans and repetitive, unproductive searching was leaking from the characters it guided.

No Quest had ever been so stymied. The world had never been so wrong.

It was almost unbearable.

He could feel the urge growing within him, the powerful, desperate urge to reach out and grab the world and shake it and shake it until it hauled itself back into neat, proper, regular order and it tugged at his soul and shredded his nerves that he couldn't. Out of control! Never in all his life, in all the Quests he'd spent as the bringer of the Taskmaster's instructions, had he ever felt anything but in total control of his situation. The Realm had been his to order, and order it he had, fitted it to the instructions without another thought because the instructions *had* to be obeyed, and that was that. In this Realm, under the thrall of the Taskmaster and the call of the Quests and The Narrative, that was all in life that mattered. It was all that anyone had ever needed to know.

Until now.

Because the last few days had brought Strut's tidy, orderly life crashing down around his ears. The instructions had fallen apart. The Quest was in chaos, and every confused-but-hopeful face seemed to be looking to him to solve the madness and bring back structure and sanity. And though it pained every fibre of his being to admit it, even to himself, he didn't have the faintest idea of how to make things *right* again.

But he would. Of that there was no doubt. Because whatever other insanity was being preached by mad, rogue elements, there was no room in Strut's soul for anything but order. There *had* to be order. Because if there wasn't...

His mind flashed in an instant to *that* room, to *those* shapes. He shuddered to his core.

Quickening...

No. *Order.* Nothing could be allowed to risk that. *Nothing.*

Strut felt his teeth clench so hard his jaw strained. Those damned Disposables.

Why? *Why?* Why were they doing this? How were they doing it? It made no sense. How were they defying the will of The Narrative? It was their guide, their guardian, their everything, moulding the minds and words and actions of those within it into perfect characters. It was undeniable. It was *everything.*

So how was it that two rogue Disposables, an Interchangeable Barmaid, and a rebellious Royal prince had managed to reject its commands and defy The Narrative not once but several times? It was an act that had never before been done, that no one had ever even dreamed of doing: suddenly one Ordinary Disposable, instead of allowing himself to be slaughtered as was his expected duty, had turned upon the Merry Band themselves, slaying Thud the Barbarian against instructions decreeing that he would live and kidnapping the princess that the Merry Band was supposed to have rescued.

Without the plot-crucial Princess Pleasance, The Narrative had, for the first time in memory, been forced to improvise: the Taskmaster had restored Thud as his own twin brother and realigned the plot to allow for the kidnap of the princess. As long as Pleasance was to be retrieved quickly, Strut had known, things would have been returned smoothly to normal.

But she hadn't been. And it was then that Strut had learned just how serious the situation was.

For this Disposable, this Fodder, had dared to ask why they, mere Ordinary commoners, were never allowed the lead in Quests and had *even* questioned why it was the Taskmaster had to be obeyed *at all.*

The very thought was enough to make Strut shudder. What kind of a warped mind could think in such a way? It was *sickening.* But worse was to come, for it quickly became clear that he wasn't content merely to *talk* of such things. He wanted to turn the very world itself upside down, abandon all convention, all tradition, all the rules. The appalling man would not be content until he brought the Quest itself to a halt!

The fool! He had no idea of the forces he was playing with, of what his stupid game might do. He'd never seen *that* room and *those* shapes;

he'd never heard the stories of the incident of Quickening all those Quests ago. So very few had. The Courtiers had passed the knowledge down, and the pixies remembered, and both had more sense than to tell of what they knew. The world was not ready.

They were fortunate in that most people had more sense than to listen to this Fodder's nonsense and it had felt as though the matter would soon be quietly squashed when Pleasance had managed to escape from them and return to her family.

Until the traitorous Prince Dullard intervened.

It had come as a genuine shock when Dullard, a Principal player no less, had turned against his own and aided the rebels in Pleasance's recapture. And then... Strut shook his head painfully at the memory of the disaster that had followed in those woods and that *escape*. It shouldn't have worked. It *shouldn't*. But somehow, it had. Fodder had scooped up his friends and poor Princess Pleasance and whisked them away to somewhere in the Wild Forest, beyond The Narrative's grasp. If it wasn't for the fact that the other Disposable had been beheaded by Clank in the skirmish, it would have been a total disaster.

True, a beheaded companion would not stop them. But it would slow them down. Damage inflicted In Narrative could only be fixed via the ministrations of Squick the Duty Pixie and his healing dust and Strut had quickly ensured that orders were issued banning any help for the rebels on that front. And if his forces moved fast, scoured the Wild Forest, and relocated the troublemakers soon, perhaps things could even be returned onto course in time for the rescue of the princess from the Dragon....

Strut shook his head. The Dragon rescue should have been chapters away. Everything had to move so much faster than the more leisurely pace of the average Quest and great chunks of Narrative were being eaten up by nonsense. Even the instructions, the precious instructions, were becoming more and more disordered, hurried, vague. Strut's order that the Taskmaster's instructions from the Golden Tome be passed on to him and his fellow Courtiers verbatim had felt a wise precaution at first, a way to cut through the nonsense. But it had only made matters worse. Never before had their instructions contained *ifs* and *buts* and *as long as*. And, much as it seared Strut's brain to think it, the treacherous thought had snuck into his head:

The Taskmaster was *struggling.*

In the beginning of the crisis, Strut had admired the smoothness with which the Taskmaster had countered the rebels' crass attempts to thwart the Quest. Thud's imminent introduction as his own *triplet* to break up the monotonous, unfruitful search was stretching even Strut's vast wellspring of credulity.

Was this how it had begun before? Was this the way in which things fell apart at the Quickening incident? Was this the beginning of the end?

No.

Never. Not on his watch. Not again.

This needed to end and end quickly. And a way had to be found to ensure that no one would ever dare risk trying the same thing again. The threat of a lifetime chained in the dungeons of the Grim Fortress had made no impact at all on these rebels. Something more was needed, something more frightening, an example to others, a punishment of horror that would cause any who came after to shrink in terror at the very prospect of sharing their fate...

A gentle tinkling and a glow of gold interrupted Strut's grim musings. Reaching down, he pulled out the small book in which his instructions from the Taskmaster appeared. His eyes skimmed the first few lines and for the first time in several days, he felt his tangled nerves unravelling. How had he ever lost faith? For there, in the Taskmaster's familiar script, was the answer.

```
Elder is quick to find a solution to his foe's unex-
pected magical prowess...
```

Strut smiled grimly. Perfect. All they needed was the chance to use it.

"Strut! *Strut!*"

Strut turned sharply as a dishevelled and foliage-battered young Priest stumbled out of the forest to his right. The Priest staggered and then withered beneath the weight of Strut's glare.

"Do not shout," the Taskmaster's taskmaster hissed. He gestured to the vivid glow of light through the trees from which raised voices still echoed. "The Narrative is in earshot!"

"Sorry!" was the contrite whisper of reply. "But it's urgent!" The Priest's eyes were wide. "A Trapper saw them, three of them at least, just up that rise! They didn't see him, and they're close! We've found them!"

Strut felt a rush of anticipation. Oh yes, soon this would be dealt with, order would be restored, and as for punishment...

Well, imagination wasn't his strong point. But he had a good idea whom to ask.

"Lay a trail for Slynder to find and be quick about it!" he snapped at his breathless subordinate. Order would be restored. Order *would* be restored.

No matter what the cost.

* * *

Rebels.

There was a certain cachet that went with a title like that, an oddly dangerous glamour and wild authority that struck a strange kind of romance into the souls of those who heard it. Pictures would swim into the mind of bold men and women with shiny swords and twanging bows, standing in proud defiance, vastly outnumbered by the forces of a greater enemy but undaunted and unbowed, for their cause was righteous and their souls were true. But no one had ever bothered to mention that it might make a bloody mess of your *boots*.

"You know, I don't think it's going to come off."

Fodder of Humble Village, former Disposable and accidental rebel against every value and belief that his Realm held dear, scraped as best he could at the tar-like coating of black gunk that had secured itself to his feet when he'd inadvertently stumbled into a cheerfully bubbling pool of goo a short while before. Impossible as it seemed, the sticky blackness felt as though it was wrapping itself more intently around the scraping stick whilst clinging to his boot for comfort.

From slightly above, braced on her narrow perch on a branch of the rotten, hollow old tree, Flirt the former Barmaid and most emphatically *not-wench*, glanced down at him with an expression that contained little in the way of sympathy but a lot in the way of amusement.

"Well, I said you should watch where you're going, didn't I?" she called down softly as she turned back to rake her eyes over the canopy once more. "And if you hadn't turned back to me to say you were doing perfectly fine, you wouldn't have gone stumbling straight into that gunk and fallen flat on your arse in the first place."

Fodder pulled a face. "Flirt, I have a dent the size of a fist in the side of my head." Abandoning the stick as a bad job, he reached up and carefully pushed back his helmet, gingerly fingering the edges of the gaping wound concealed there. The too-familiar tingling, itchy sensation of a Narrative wound gnawed persistently at his broken skull. "That kind of thing doesn't do much for your orientation."

"Don't pick at it!"

Fodder snatched his hand away obediently at the tone of Flirt's voice.

"And don't you start banging on about being disorientated." She released her breath in a gusty sigh laced with overtones of irritation. "I've had it up to here with that! Why do you think I volunteered to come and scout for The Narrative in the first place?"

* * *

"A *trail!*" Slynder's voice was rich with sudden excitement, and the sound of his voice set Erik's frayed nerves ablaze with sudden adrenaline. "Here, look here! The marks of feet heading towards that rise! It is them; we have found them!"

"Then we have no time to waste!" Elder's ancient, wise eyes flared. "Ride!"

* * *

Fodder's sigh joined Flirt's as he pulled himself to his sticky-booted feet. "Why do you think I volunteered to join you? If I have to listen to one more round of 'woe-is-Shoulders,' I'm going to snatch his head off him and chuck it down the nearest sinkhole."

Flirt rolled her eyes. "Almost two days. I wouldn't have thought it was possible for someone to moan solidly for almost *two days*. And if you say anything—if you offer advice, try to help out, or, heaven help you, try and be sympathetic like poor Dullard did..."

Fodder allowed himself a quiet groan at the memory of Shoulders's relentless screeching that Dullard could keep his sodding pity to himself. Time and again, the prince, driven by some strange, deep-held conviction that kindness would breed kindness, had ventured back into the muddy, peril-strewn waters of Shoulders's post-beheading paddy; and time and again, the headless Disposable had capsized his boat, set fire to the life raft, and unleashed the sharks.

"You've got to admire his bravery." Fodder shrugged slightly, hoping that the strange warmth he could feel around his gunky ankle was only in his imagination. "Mind you, anyone who can try and befriend Princess Pleasance probably has nothing left to fear in the world."

Flirt snorted. "When it comes to Pleasance, a sinkhole would be *generous*, wouldn't it? I like Dullard and I respect him but there's nice and there's *stupid*. Volunteering to look after Pleasance: you see, that's nice but stupid. And volunteering to help Shoulders find a better way to carry his head? That's nice but *suicidal!*"

"We have to try *something*." Fodder shook his head. "Shoulders's huffs and stumbles and hissy fits are slowing us down. If The Narrative catches up with us while he's in that shape, he'll be a dead weight and we'll be buggered. And if that was an AFC you saw scouting…"

"I'm pretty sure, aren't I?" Flirt squinted through the crack once more, surveying the tangle of the Wild Forest's canopy below them. They'd chosen this hunk of rotting wood because the prominent rise draped in yellowing grass upon which it stood offered the best vantage point for miles around. If The Narrative or any accompanying search parties were closing in on them, this would be the best place to spot its light from. "It was grey, it was flying, and it had gangly limbs. And I don't think they'll be able to do us any more favours if they actually *see* us, and it wouldn't be fair to expect any. They won't get away with any more *singsongs* or *pretty birds in interesting trees*, will they?"

Fodder allowed himself a brief smile at the memory of a band of claw-fingered, scaly, toothy monstrosities belting out a beautifully harmonised rendition of a charming love ballad. Whatever happened from now on, it was a recollection to treasure.

Fodder shook himself back to business. "Any sign of The Narrative out there?"

* * *

The trees flew by, low branches causing frantic ducking, brambles slapping at his tender skin; but Erik cared not, for they had direction, they had a purpose, the target was all but in their grasp…

Islaine. My Islaine. I am coming for you!

* * *

Flirt pulled a face. "It's hard to tell, isn't it? The canopy's so thick and tangled that The Narrative can't see the sky. Unless something leaks through, it could be anywhere down there and we wouldn't have a clue."

Fodder twitched his sticky foot. It *was* getting warmer; he was sure of it…. "We need to know if they're close," he muttered, nearly to himself. "We daren't go near the Pixie Patch with The Narrative right on our tail. It'll be hard enough persuading Squick to help us as it is."

Flirt's voice was strangely quiet. "You really think he will?"

Fodder shrugged wearily, trying to ignore the persistent itch of his head and the spreading warmth at his ankle. He scraped absently at his sticky boot with his spare foot. "What choice do we have? Shoulders's neck and my head have serious Narrative damage, and only Squick and his pixie dust can fix that. We'll be at a huge disadvantage In Narrative if we don't get patched up and fast. And besides—do you want to find out just how long Shoulders can keep moaning for?"

Flirt shuddered. *"Don't.* But are you sure he won't turn us in? The pixies work for the Taskmaster, and they've hardly done us any favours this far, have they? Remember Higgle's waterfall?"

"Squick didn't turn me in that first night." Fodder was clinging to the memory. It was his one hope for getting Shoulders fixed and his itchy, broken skull patched up before he was forced to throw his old friend's head into the nearest sinkhole out of sheer irritation. "He could have, but he didn't. If we can find him, I think he'll help us."

"I hope you're right." Flirt glanced down briefly before resuming her scan of the woods. "I don't think I can take much more of Shoulders otherwise. It can't be that much further to the Pixie Patch, can it?"

Fodder grimaced. "I don't think so, but it's hard to say. Squick told me they do tend to move it if it might get in the way of The Narrative, and the Merry Band is bound to be heading this way after what they heard me say."

"Wonderful." If sighs were rationed, Flirt would have run out hours before. "I wonder why the Duty Pixies live in this forest. Like Dullard said earlier, it's hardly the most *wholesome* of places, is it?"

"The Pixie Patch itself is pleasant enough." Fodder's mind flashed back to his brief visit to Squick and his fellow pixies' home several Quests before, when his new liver had been made while he waited. "It's a wildflower meadow with a clean pond and a cottage carved into the trunk of a big oak tree. Squick told me it was built for a mystic fairy haven before any of us were born and that the pixies were so taken with it, they decided to keep it afterwards. They have to hide it, though, and the Wild Forest is one of the quietest places in the Realm, so..." He shrugged. "They keep it here." He hesitated briefly. "Somewhere."

Flirt fixed him with an icy look. *"Don't* let Shoulders hear you say 'somewhere' like that. If he thinks you don't know the way for sure, he'll go up like a climactic volcano, and that's all we need, isn't it?"

Fodder permitted himself a shudder. "I know. But I'm as sure as I can be. The last time, I followed the Winding Trail to Cackle the Crone's Hovel, and the Pixie Patch was about a half mile to the east of it." He sighed deeply, his eyes drifting once more to his ruined boots. "I need to try scraping at this with something stronger than a twig. How about your sword?"

Flirt's hands flew protectively towards the intricate handle of her blade. It had been forged by Dullard, whose many hobbies had unexpectedly turned out to include sword-smithing, and was, in fairness, less a sword and more a beautifully crafted and perfectly balanced work of art.

"My sword?" she repeated incredulously. "Use your own!"

"Yours is stronger." It was true. Dullard had a knack with metal that meant his blades had even defied The Narrative's attempts to break them.

Flirt's expression darkened to almost the shade of the gloop. "This sword is a magnificent weapon designed to reap terrible damage upon any who cross my path. I am not using it to scrape black crap off your shoes!"

Fodder glared. "Well, we've got to try something! This stuff is hardening! It isn't coming away, and it's getting tighter!" He tugged violently at his boot for a moment, confirming his worst fear. "See? I can't even get it off now!"

Flirt gave his ankle an appraising glance. "I could chop your foot off."

"That's *not helpful.*"

* * *

The ground began to rise, a low ridge coated in foul, rotted trunks heaving up before them, and the trail blazed towards its crown. Erik clung to the neck of his horse as he hurtled after Slynder, drawing upon every ounce of his strength and his resolve, for he would not let his Islaine down again—no, never, ever again—and he would reap a terrible vengeance on those who had tormented her…

* * *

"Oh dear. You are in a bit of a state, aren't you?"

Fodder glanced up sharply as a familiar, lanky figure ambled out of the twisted trees nearby, his quizzical gaze fixed on Fodder's gunked-up feet. Prince Dullard of the Other Kingdom, Rejected Suitor and Quest Principal, was a man of distinct intelligence, unexpected battle prowess, and surprising insight wrapped up in the body of a hopeless buffoon. But none of these talents, Fodder felt, could ever quite match his gift for polite understatement.

Flirt glared at him. "What are you doing here? You're supposed to be keeping an eye on Shoulders and the princess."

"I found a cave near the bottom of the rise." Dullard's thoughtful stare remained fixed on Fodder's feet. "They'll be safe enough out of sight in there for the time being."

Flirt snorted. "I meant you've left them alone together. Only one of them will come out of that cave alive, won't they?"

"I'm sure they'll be fine," Fodder lied blatantly, but the prince's curiosity had set light to a beacon of hope in his heart, and the last thing he wanted was him rushing off to break up a potential fight. Not when Fodder was losing feeling in his toes.... "I don't suppose you know how to get this crud off me, do you?" he asked, hoping his voice didn't sound quite as desperate as he felt.

The prince examined the sticky black mass that had consumed his boots with a clinical expression and then smiled. "Oh yes, it's really quite straightforward. You just need the leaves of the Viscous Ivy. Did you want me to—"

"*Please.*"

Flirt cast down a disdainful look from her lofty perch. "We're being pursued by an enemy we can't see, hunted by our former friends, and there's a damn good chance our lifelong friend and our hostage are going to rip each other to pieces. And all you care about is your *feet?*"

"I care about keeping them," Fodder retorted irritably. "A damn good sprint may be the only thing that stands between me and capture, so if you don't mind..."

"And I wouldn't worry about Shoulders and Pleasance too much," Dullard added as he scoured the trunk of a nearby tree. "Shoulders is rather too preoccupied with his own woes to pick a fight. And Pleasance..." He sighed, his expression vaguely troubled as he plucked at the dank foliage, gathering a handful of dark-coloured leaves in his hand. "She doesn't seem in the mood to argue."

"And that's a problem?" Fodder remarked casually as Dullard picked up a flat stone and set to work grinding the leaves against a nearby root. The princess had not spoken a word to anyone since her request that Shoulders's head be removed from her lap two days before. Fodder had regarded the respite as a good thing.

Dullard sighed quietly, an odd look flickering across his face as he picked up a nearby stick and poked at the oozing, foul-smelling paste that had emerged from the leaf grinding. Absently, Fodder wondered if he needed to be alarmed when the stick started to blacken. "I think that rather depends."

"You didn't answer my question, did you?" Flirt called down pointedly. "Why are you here?"

Dullard was staring blankly at the steaming stick as he scraped it around, coating it in the unpleasant paste. "I was hoping to talk to you both. Try to hold still, please. It would be best not to get this on your skin." Dullard raised the stick, crouching down as he leaned over towards the sticky black mass on Fodder's boots. Gently, he began to tease it through the mass of blackness as steam drifted up from Fodder's ankle in a slow curl.

Fodder stared at the tangle of thick branches overhead—it was better than thinking about what might be about to happen to his feet. "And you couldn't have done it this morning?"

"I wanted to wait until Shoulders wasn't listening." Dullard's eyes never left his task, but his expression was alarmingly distant. "I'm not sure he should hear what I have to say."

* * *

The crest was closing, the trail growing fresher by the instant—Erik could see Elder gripping his staff in anticipation of some great magic—and Zahora, her face awash with the need for vengeance, palmed her bow. Sir Roderick's sword was already to hand and one of Slynder's knives glinted in the palm not clinging to the reins as he scoured the ground at speed to keep them on their path. Was it his imagination that he could hear voices carried on the wind?

Close. They were so close.

* * *

"Which is?" Fodder ventured.

The prince didn't seem to hear, lost for a moment in his own world. The curl of steam was rapidly becoming a surge.

Abruptly, blessedly, the black gunge that had enveloped Fodder's boot peeled away in a steaming heap on the rough ground, an instant relief of pressure bringing the immediate sensation of pain as the numb pins-and-needles wore off. Biting his lip, Fodder massaged his stinging foot against the rough earth.

"Thanks, mate," he said to Dullard; but to his surprise, the prince didn't seem to register the words, his eyes lost in distant thought. Then, with suddenness, he snapped back to reality.

"I've been thinking," Dullard declared, his head bobbing like a drinking bird's. "And I came up here to talk to you about it because I thought it was very important we discuss this before any further Narrative encounters. It's about The Narrative, you see, and how we defy it. Do you remember I asked if we could discuss it sometime?"

Fodder nodded. "Of course."

"Good." Dullard tutted to himself. "Because now I've experienced it myself, I have been thinking the matter through. And I've had something of a thought."

Fodder regarded the uncertain prince with interest. "What kind of thought?"

"Well..."

"Are you two done having your chat yet?" Flirt interrupted. "Only, you do remember we're in dreadful peril here, don't you? And we're supposed to be scouting for it!"

Fodder sighed. If he was honest, dreadful peril over the last few days had been in pretty short supply compared to discomfort and vast amounts of moaning. Other than a passing AFC, they had seen few signs of pursuit, and he'd felt less in danger wandering in the concealment of the forest than he had done in the chase-strewn days before.

In a way, it was almost disappointing. A touch of dreadful peril would break up the day.

Please tell me I didn't just think that.

Fodder allowed himself the appropriate moment of contemplation such a doom-laden statement could provoke. But when no thunderbolt was instantly forthcoming, he moved on.

"Flirt, this chat may be important." He understood her edginess, but it was starting to feel unnecessary. "We haven't seen a hint of The Narrative or anything but an AFC looking for us in two days, and for all we know, he was passing through. I don't think we're in imminent dang—"

The vivid light smashed out of the trees, blinding his eyes like a spit of fire. He tried to stumble backwards, to hide or to run as he heard Dullard's gasp and Flirt's yell of horror, but there was nothing, nothing he could do as the glare filled his world and pulled him...

In...

"—er!"

"There!" Slynder's screech of triumph was music to Erik's ears, and yes, there they were, the soldier of Sleiss and his treacherous royal master staring in blank shock at their tumultuous approach. Already Slynder was high in the saddle, one knife raised for a lethal throw.

"Oi!"

Two feet swung like an axe from the tree above, scything into Slynder and hurling him from the saddle as the chain-mail-clad woman swung down from the branches, dangled awkwardly for an instant, and then dropped to the ground, her eyes wild.

"Run!" she screeched, grabbing her companion and their lord by the arms and hauling them towards the concealment of the trees.

"Get them!" Zahora's arrow was already on a string, singing from her bow as it hurtled like a force of nature towards the fleeing backs of their enemies. The woman gasped and stumbled sideways, careening into her companions and causing all three to stagger. The arrow whisked past, missing the prince's ear by less than an inch before it buried itself quivering into a tree trunk.

"Die!" Sir Roderick's sword was a silver blur over his head as he charged towards the unsteady trio through the awkward, narrow confines of the trees. Erik, his own short sword drawn, rode a hoofbeat behind. Rage and fear were burning through his veins. Where was Islaine? What had they done with her?

"We need them alive!" Elder's voice bellowed through the woods as magic crackled on the breeze and fire danced on his fingers. "Wound but do not kill! We need to know about the princess and the Ring!"

"We need but one to talk!" was Sir Roderick's harsh retort.

"Oh, lord!" This time it was Tretaptus himself who laid hands upon his lackeys, grabbing both by the head and hurling them and himself to the ruined earth as both Roderick's sword and Elder's lance of crippling fire arced narrowly over their heads. As a nearby twist of half-dead mistletoe ignited like a fiery torch, Erik reined his noble mount in sharply and pitched around, his sword seeming to glow and grow as his anger channelled itself into the steel, feeding on the flames nearby and dancing with a metallic fire of its own.

"Mysterious powers!" Tretaptus's voice was a traitor's screech. "Quickly! This way!"

Scrambling like animals on their hands and knees, the unwholesome trio scrabbled with little dignity to their feet and dived forwards towards a heavy, broad knot of rotten, fetid briar that clung to the far side of the rise like some vegetative pustule. Even as Erik turned, his glowing sword raised like an avenging beacon, they plunged into the sordid mass and...

Out...

"Ah!" Briar thorns scraped at Fodder's face and arms as he battled his way to the tangled centre of the mass of branches, out of sight but sure-as-hell not out of mind of The Narrative. Flirt had yanked her sword from its sheath, slashing them a semblance of a path as she winced and grimaced. Without any armour, Dullard was taking the worst of it, his face scratched and bloodied as he stumbled in Flirt's wake.

"We can't stay here for long!" Flirt's eyes were wild as she staggered to a halt, staring back at the hint of light poking through the tangled branches. "Maybe they can't get horses in here, but they can get in on foot, can't they?"

"Not to mention with magic." Dullard dragged a handkerchief from his pocket and wiped his bloodied face with a wince. "In fact—"

"*Malis fieratorum!*" Magus the Sorcerer's voice thundered with the weight of Narrative power. With a creak of pain, the briar about ten yards behind them burst into flames.

"Oh dear." Dullard's lips twisted, and he shied from the gathering inferno. "I was rather hoping it might take them longer to think of that."

"Surrender yourselves!" The voice of Clank the Knight, as noble Sir Roderick, echoed over the creeping shimmer of flames. Fodder pulled a face. It was always strange, hearing the voices of Narrative characters from outside The Narrative itself—though they lacked the echoing emphasis of words heard within the grasp of the light, they always carried a certain, underlying weight that made them sound distinctly unnatural. "We have surrounded your pathetic hideaway! Emerge now, and we will consider letting you live!"

"Now *that's* an incentive, isn't it?" Flirt's anxious face matched Fodder's pounding heart as she glanced around, her sword gripped in her hand as though to battle back the rising fire. Her voice was muffled as she shielded her nose and mouth with her hand. "Consider it, my arse!"

Sweat pooled on Fodder's brow as the flames licked closer and higher, the heat pulling at his breath as smoke teased at his eyes and nostrils. He coughed sharply. "We'll have to make a run for it," he choked. "What else can we do?"

Dullard had pulled the top of his doublet up over his mouth as he waved ineffectually at the smoke swirling round his head. The crackling of burning briar grew louder.

"Fodder," he gasped. "What I was saying earlier, about The Narrative? Well, I have something of a theory and—"

Fodder had often wondered if Dullard lived in quite the same universe as the rest of them. But this… "Dullard, no offence," he interrupted sharply, "but we're trapped in a burning briar patch surrounded by pissed-off Principals. Do you really think this is the time for Narrative bloody philosophy?"

"But I think it might be important." Dullard's eyes were alarmingly sincere. "I need your opinion. If you could give me a moment to explain—"

"Your time is running out!" This time, it was Magus as Elder whose voice pounded over the roar of the flames. "All we want are Princess Islaine and the Ring of Anthiphion! Give them to us, and we will consider mercy!"

Flirt's eyes widened like saucers. "How stupid are we? Fodder, we've got the bloody Ring of Destiny! If we nip into Narrative, you can do whatever you did last time and get us out of here!"

Fodder's eyes widened. The Ring! In the frantic rush of the sudden attack, he'd forgotten about the strange circumstances of their last escape. But still… "What about Shoulders and the princess?"

"We can come back for them, can't we?" Flirt's face was alive with impatience. "We don't have to go far, just far enough!"

"And what if they're ready for that?" Doubt flooded through Fodder's mind like a wash of the smoke surrounding him. "I'm not even sure how I managed it last time!"

"Actually," Dullard intervened anxiously, "that was rather what I was trying to—"

"Not now." This time it was Flirt who cut the prince off. "Fodder, stop blathering and get on with it, will you?"

"All right!" The heat was becoming intense, a sting against his skin that whispered of a vastly unpleasant experience mere yards away from arriving. His hand slapped down to the rough pouch where he had stored the Ring and—

Found nothing.

His hand slapped again. The pouch failed to be forthcoming.

He looked down, his eyes streaming, and found the remains of a broken string clinging to his belt. The pouch it had held was gone.

Along with its contents.

There was only one thing to be said. "Bollocks."

"Fodder?" Flirt's muffled voice was dangerous, and Fodder opted to get to the point.

"My pouch is gone!" he declared. "I've lost the Ring!"

Flirt's expression was more deadly than the flames around them. "What? You mean it's out there? In The Narrative?"

"It can't be!" Dullard injected. "The Narrative would have seen that in an instant! Fodder, when did you have it last?"

Fodder tried to cast his mind back, although surrounded as he was by smoke and ash and the raging heat of the approaching wall of fire, it was tricky trying to concentrate.

"I had it when we set out!" he exclaimed. "I remember seeing it right before I..."

Oh.

He glanced down at his stained boots. He glanced back up.

"Fell..."

Flirt's smoke-stained face hardened. "Oh, don't tell me. That damned pool of gunk." She shook her head. "Right, you and Dullard head straight there, find it, and *don't* lose it again. I'll see you there. And when this is over, I'm getting you a better pouch."

Fodder blinked at her. "And how exactly do you expect us to get out of the encircled inferno?"

Flirt's features, blackened as they were, were rich with determination as she pulled up her chain-mail hood and tucked away her hair. "Because the Merry Band are about to get distracted, aren't they?"

"By what?"

"Me doing *this!*"

"Flirt!" He read her intention a moment too late. Even as he lunged, trying to grab her, trying to stop her from her immense act of suicidal bravery, the ex-Barmaid charged through the part of the briar not quite in flames and burst out into the light of The Narrative.

"Here! Oof!" As Fodder staggered back from the sudden invasion of Narrative light, he caught a glimpse of Swipe the Thief slamming to the ground on his backside as his horse reared sharply and pawed the air with its hooves. There was a flash of chain mail as Flirt bolted into the trees, and the Narrative light surged and congealed in her direction.

"Come on!" Dullard's smoky face was anxious as he grabbed hold of Fodder and hauled him through the suddenly less vivid gap Flirt had left behind. "Before they come back!"

And then they were running. In the trees to their left, Fodder could see splinters of Narrative light arcing through the gaps in the trees, could hear the echoing, weighty voices of the Merry Band as they bellowed their lines in pursuit of Flirt, the pounding of hooves and the breaking of foliage and a very promising-sounding screech of indignation from Harridan. The Barmaid seemed to be holding her own—and so much for the good because if she pulled a stunt like this only to get herself chopped up, he was going to bloody *kill* her.

An arc of light burst through, searing into the ground inches ahead. Screeching to a startled halt, Fodder grabbed the back of Dullard's doublet and hauled the prince unceremoniously behind the large, bulky trunk of a rotting tree. Light surged around them like an ocean, licking at the narrow peninsula of their shadowed concealment with greedy fervour. But for a corridor of shade too narrow to traverse, they were surrounded.

"Which way did he go?" Harridan's voice, alarmingly close, echoed with rage. "How could you lose him?"

"He cannot be far!" Clank, on the other hand, sounded reassuringly anxious. "The man of Sleiss will not escape us again!"

Anxiety flooded Fodder's mind. Had they seen him after all? Had The Narrative touched him without his realising? But it dawned on him: Flirt had pulled her mail hood up. Her hair had been hidden. The Merry Band hadn't realised whom they were chasing.

Knowing he wasn't the one in slightly more imminent danger didn't make things any better. His stomach knotted with concern for his friend. *Bloody Flirt! Why did you bloody do that?*

"We must split up!" Magus thundered, as he ever did. Fodder sometimes wondered if the man was capable of speaking without injecting echoing volume into every syllable. "And keep your eyes alert! We cannot assume Tretaptus and that foul wench perished in the flames! They too may be at large!"

Split up. Great. Fodder caught Dullard's eye as the two of them pressed harder against the tree that provided their only shelter from a world of Narrative trouble; and he saw his own fervent, silent wish reflected in his friend.

Please, please, please, don't let them split up this way.

Hooves scattered against the ground. Light licked down the sides of the tree, shimmering, hungry as the Narrative dispersed with its splintering characters. Closer, closer, getting closer...

"Erik!" Clank's voice bellowed from farther away. "Stay with me, boy! We would not have you ambushed!"

Oh, thank you, Clank. Fodder had never expected to think that. Indeed, if Shoulders ever learned such a thought had crossed his mind, his life would be reduced to a miserable pit of endless moaning as punishment. But The Narrative's default point of view was Bumpkin as Erik, and Clank's call had made Erik turn another way. The light he carried with him flickered and began to dim as he moved in a different direction.

Fodder breathed out. It seemed appropriate.

"Fodder." Dullard's voice was soft. "About my theory."

Fodder could feel a sigh building but he politely stifled it. "Really now?" he whispered back wearily. "You can't let this wait?"

Dullard shook his head. "I don't think so. If we are planning to enter The Narrative and use the Ring—"

"All right." The Narrative light faded and died; apparently, Bumpkin had moved out of sight. "Talk as we go. But keep your eyes peeled. The Merry Band are in the forest, and we don't have The Narrative to spot them by. It only takes one glimpse from them to call it over."

"I know." Dullard nodded. "Believe me, I will be paying attention."

Quietly, carefully, both sets of eyes scanning the forest around them, Fodder and Dullard moved out from behind their saviour tree and made their way cautiously ahead.

"Go on, then," Fodder breathed, as he peered through the dark, impenetrable gloom ahead, trying to remember the route he and Flirt had taken that morning from their overnight camp to the ridge. They had been in that clearing with that big, ugly hollow tree at the centre and the pool of gunk he'd tumbled through had been in the shadows at the edge of it.

"Well." Dullard looked thoughtful even as his eyes raked the forest. "Defying The Narrative. How do we do it?"

"Because we want to." Fodder squinted. Was that a hint of movement? In the distance, he was certain, he could hear hoofbeats, but they didn't sound so frantic. He could only hope Flirt had gotten herself out of sight. "Because we're strong enough to resist it."

The prince bit his lip. "That's what I'm not so sure about. The thing is, I don't want to damage your confidence at all. And it shouldn't be damaged!" he hastened to add at Fodder's expression. "Please do bear in mind the astonishing things you've done already. This theory is more about...well, me, really, but Flirt and Shoulders too, and maybe even Pleasance and what I've found from having experienced The Narrative without being a character whilst—"

"Mate, no offence," Fodder cut in sharply. "But we are on the run here. Could you get to the point?"

Dullard pulled a contrite face. "Right. Sorry. Well, the point is, I've come to the conclusion that defying The Narrative isn't so much about the will to defy it." His features creased as he searched for the right words. "I think it may be more about...ourselves."

"Ourselves?" Fodder glanced up from his search of the path ahead as a strange, inexplicable bell gave a hearty clang in his mind.

"Mmmm," Dullard assented wordlessly. "About knowing ourselves. You said yourself that The Narrative works best with our willing participation, which suggests that our input, be it as characters or as ourselves, is important. I think the key may be to enter The Narrative confident in who you know yourself to be." He hesitated uncertainly. "What do you think?"

Various rogue thoughts tumbled together in Fodder's head, falling into place. He glanced around but other than a distant hint of voices, he saw no immediate danger. He tried to fight off the brief but potently unpleasant thought that that might be because they were concentrating on Flirt. "I think you're onto something," he said; and that was true, that was right, that fitted neatly into his head, into everything he'd done as though a hole had been waiting for the words to fill it. "It was when I realised and admitted to myself that I wasn't happy with my lot that I found I could resist The Narrative. I was honest with myself for the first time that night."

"Yes, exactly!" Dullard nodded. "In that moment, to put it rather philosophically, you found yourself. You stripped away the lies you told to keep you from unhappiness and admitted the truth of who you were and what you felt you were worth. And I was watching Flirt, both earlier and when she was fighting against Thud." He paused a moment. "Is that—"

"Down!" With unceremonious abruptness, Fodder slapped his hand across the prince's mouth and dragged him behind a clump of brambles an instant before the head of a horse loomed from behind a stand of twisted trees about twenty yards away. Peering through a gap in the thorny tangle, Fodder caught a glimpse of the unshaven face of Swipe the Thief, his eyes scanning the darkness as he wove his horse between the trees, squinting into the grim woods in search of them. Without the Narrative glow to illuminate his features, he looked strangely ordinary.

The horse and rider moved closer. Fodder released Dullard, and they shrank into the shadows. The gentle thud of the horse's hooves rebounded against the earth. They could hear the jingle of its tack, and its light snort and the heavy breathing of Swipe, who was apparently not as fit outside The Narrative as in it. The shadow of their combined shape loomed over the brambles before trotting slowly past. As they headed off into the trees beyond, Fodder heard Swipe muttering rude words under his breath.

"Bloody waste of bloody time, stupid, bloody Disposables, stupid bloody prince…"

The muttering and hoofbeats faded. The horse and its rider were swallowed once more by the shadows.

"You know," Fodder whispered as he pulled himself tenderly to his feet. "I don't think he likes us much."

"I would tend to agree." Unfolding his lanky limbs, Dullard too pulled himself upright. "Which way?"

Fodder sighed. "The way *he* went. So move slowly and stay alert."

Dullard nodded. "Of course. Now, as I was saying, about Flirt…"

As he started forwards, straining his ears for the sounds of danger, Fodder had to admire the prince's single-mindedness. Even if it was an unpleasant reminder that Flirt's current situation was still unknown. "Okay, go on."

Dullard did. "Flirt found herself in the fight, in the chance to stand up for herself and not take the treatment Thud and his ilk had hitherto meted out to her," he declared, picking his way past the brambles and towards a fallen log in pursuit of his companion. "It's like making the magic work. The Narrative creates events out of belief. If you believe in yourself, you can *be* yourself within it. But those who believe it can only do as they are told because they do not believe in who they are and their own will to be that person. They believe only in their character. That's why when a person doesn't really believe in their character, that character doesn't work. And if they don't believe in themselves, they do only as they are directed."

Something inside Fodder's head clicked as the reason Dullard had wanted to have this conversation away from their headless companion flashed into clarity.

"And Shoulders doesn't believe in himself and so Clank keeps chopping his head off, right?"

Dullard sighed. "Yes, his situation is a pity—he expects the worst and, in such a scenario, the worst is what he will receive. I don't think he knows what he wants. I talked with him the night before the waterfall, and a fairly substantial part of him doubts that this is the right thing to do. He's too afraid of the risks to see the benefits. You saw him in The Narrative—he was torn both ways, and that indecision left him helpless, neither fully obedient nor truly free. And until he can know his own mind..." He pulled a face. "We can't tell him any of this—he may start to believe in his own failure and only end up making it worse." He added a sigh to the expression. "Oh dear. Though it's satisfying to have reasoned this out, I can't help but feel it could be more problematic than helpful."

Somewhere in the heavy woods ahead, Fodder heard something large and heavy making its way through. Catching Dullard's shoulder, he pulled him to a gentle halt. "But why? If we know how it's done, then surely it'd be easier to teach others to join us..."

His words tailed off at the look of quiet resignation on Dullard's face. "Can you imagine if someone like Poniard was able to sober up enough to find himself? Can you imagine how he'd be and what he'd do?"

Fodder winced as he pictured the psychotic Assassin, whose fervent death wish was directed firmly at the rest of the universe. Poniard considered Squick the Duty Pixie's constant fixing of his victims as a personal affront. "Too bloody easily."

"But at the other end of the spectrum, there's you." Dullard smiled. "Because what you've found in yourself is the desire to make the world a better place, not just for you but for everyone. And the more you take that determination and belief into The Narrative, the more it will drive you. The more it will let you do."

Fodder stared at the leather straps that made up the remains of the pouch at his waist where he'd earlier stowed the Ring of Destiny. His mind was settling this...not *new* exactly, but *realised* information into place. "And so the magic worked."

"Indeed." Dullard's smile lingered. "And that's why it will keep working as long as you want it to. You see why I wanted to discuss this before you tried using the Ring again?"

"Hmm." Fodder nodded, allowing the thoughts to settle in his head as he felt a sudden surge of determination. *So the magic will work if I believe, and so I have to keep on believing. I have to believe more than anyone else...*

As long as we get the bloody thing back.

"Let's go try it out." The rustling noise ahead was lessening as Fodder started forwards. "Come on, let's find Flirt, get that ruddy Ring and—"

"Wait!" This time it was Dullard's turn to yank his companion back, hauling him down behind the fallen log where they had paused. Fodder caught a glimpse of a lithe, shadowy black shape vanishing through the trees ahead.

Fodder breathed out. "Who the bloody hell was that?"

Dullard shook his head. "I only saw the shadow. I didn't see his face." He frowned slightly. "He didn't look like one of the Merry Band."

"Great. More people hunting for us. That's all we need." For what felt like the thousandth time, Fodder dragged himself to his feet. "The clearing isn't far. Let's get this done, find Flirt, and get out of here."

"AWWwwwwwooooooooo! *AWWwwwwwoooooooooo!*"

The sudden, harsh cry of a wolf startled Fodder to his core, for he recognised a signal when he heard one, especially knowing as he did that the Realm's trained wolf pack had been evicted from this forest by Squick for crapping on his begonias. Even as he and Dullard wheeled, Fodder saw the triumphant-looking outline of a Trapper, one of the Realm's hard men of the hills, lurking instead in the forest as he grinned fiercely at the men who had become his quarry. "Oh, I'm getting big lines for calling down on you two!" he exclaimed, his voice the standard woodsy rasp as he stalked forwards victoriously. "A whole scene! Hah! They'll be coming!" A heavy cudgel thudded in his palm. "And you'll be waiting for them!"

"Bollocks!" Fodder dived to one side as the cudgel thudded into the log. Kicking out, he heard a satisfying grunt as his foot impacted the man's knee. The Trapper staggered, but only for an instant—even as Fodder dragged himself up yet again, he had wheeled on Dullard, advancing on the prince who, to Fodder's great alarm, made no move to draw his sword but simply backed away and raised his hands in a placatory manner.

"Now, I don't want to hurt you," he said anxiously. "So if you'd please..."

The cudgel swung. Fodder, darting forwards, knew he would be a moment too late but miraculously, Dullard dodged the blow, ducking under his swing as, with an expression that melded discomfort with apology, his reluctant fist lashed out into the man's face.

The Trapper stumbled backwards, and this time Fodder was ready, snatching a rock from the ground and smashing it over the man's head. Even as the Trapper collapsed, groaning and grabbing his skull, Fodder wheeled to find Dullard wringing his knuckles painfully against the air.

"Oh my!" he exclaimed. "That really does hurt quite a bit more than it looks!"

There was no time for sympathy; Fodder could hear hoofbeats and see a trace of light through the trees. "Just run!" he yelled, and Dullard obeyed, rushing to his side as the pair wove through the forest floor. It was as though the air itself had suddenly grown heavy, as though the world about had thickened, tightening around the trees through which they bolted like a closing trap. They were coming.

There was no more talk, no time to talk; they simply ran, juts of ragged wood scratching at their faces as they plunged through the trees, clawing past undergrowth, stumbling over roots and rocks. The whole time, the heaviness in the air was growing, the sense of closing light, breaking twigs snapping in the distance as their pursuers honed in. The light ahead grew, but naturally; the trees thinned and parted. The two men stumbled out into a clearing familiar to Fodder, yellowed grass draped over a low mound upon which a lone, hulking, hollowed-out tree of some size was rotting to itself in the cloudy light, its broken and twisted branches reaching towards the sky as though to scratch it into shreds. A pool of foul-smelling black gunk was bubbling cheerfully between its ragged, jutting roots.

"There!" Fodder hurled himself forwards, scanning the ground desperately for some sign of his pouch. It had to be here; it had to be close to where he could see the scuffed earth that he had scrabbled up as he'd tumbled, the broken-off root that had snagged his belt as he'd struggled to pull out his feet...

Wait, that root, the root he'd yanked himself free from so violently, the one right over the sodding pool...

Oh *bloody hell*.

"I don't see it!" Dullard exclaimed, powerfully stating the raging obvious as they skidded to a halt beside the tree. Fodder noted absently that his scratched face was bleeding a touch. "Is this where you fell?"

Fodder shook his itching head. "I think the damned thing's gone *in*. I caught my belt on that root when I was getting up...."

The air was rich with Narrative syrup as light glimmered in between the trunks of the trees. Footsteps and hoofbeats were closing in fast—how could they kneel down and ferret about in a pool of gunge right now? They needed to hide.

There was no time to lose. The mound itself would probably offer enough cover to make a break for the trees away from The Narrative's line of sight, and they could only hope that the brief ponce around for the inevitable description of such an interesting feature as the lone tree would provoke, would give them enough time to find somewhere better to hide. But an exposed tree likely to draw down a description was no place to be when The Narrative swept in.

Dullard was staring at the pool with alarming thoughtfulness. "We'll need a branch or a twig—something to root around with."

Voices drifted through the trees, familiar voices sharpened around their edges by the strength of The Narrative. The vivid Narrative light spread up the sides of the mound, engulfing it slowly but surely in the weight of descriptive glory as the point-of-view holder neared the edge of the trees. One touch would be all it needed to drag them to a place where retribution would be swift and punishment eternal. Horses' hooves thudded on the earth a dozen yards away.

They were out of time. There was only one chance left.

"Not now!" Fodder yanked at the prince's doublet as he jerked his head towards the trees on the far side from the glow. "We have to get out of sight before—"

The quiet, concealing trees towards which he had been yearning burst open as a mailed figure staggered out, gasping for breath with wild eyes fixed upon them. Flirt's expression was horrified as she stared at Fodder standing in the open, fighting off the conflicting urges to collapse in relief that she was fine or to bawl her out for her stupid overblown heroics that had scared him so much in the first place.

"Get out of sight!" she hissed, belting towards them. "Swipe's right behind me! He didn't see me but...bollocks!" Her sentence died as her gaze was caught by the glow on the far side. "In the tree! Quick!"

This was a bad plan. Fodder knew this was a bad plan. The badness of this plan was almost overwhelming. Unfortunately, alternatives were unforthcoming. Gritting his teeth, he obeyed, darting through the large and distinctly unconcealing crack in the rotten tree's trunk. Dullard, a step ahead of him, flung himself against the woody innards of the trunk to the left-hand side. Bundled along with Flirt's momentum, Fodder tumbled, half off his feet, to the right, dragging himself and his Barmaid friend into the rotting core as the Narrative light swallowed up the peeling bark around them. Even as they collapsed in an uncomfortable heap against the inside of the trunk, the light without intensified sharply. The Narrative swallowed the tree in what Fodder could only assume was a lovingly vivid description.

But they couldn't hear it. That was what mattered. As long as they couldn't feel what The Narrative had to say, then The Narrative couldn't feel *them*.

He stared at the man-sized split in the trunk through which they had crawled. It would only take one glance from a passing Principal...

Light gleamed through a peephole slightly above. Fodder was under no illusions: some eagle-eyed Merry Bander would spot any eyeball that ventured to use it, just as they would catch any stray whisper—it was hard enough to swallow the heaviness of his post-chase breathing.

But they had to get away from the entrance. He turned his head to where his friend lay crushed and rather disgruntled-looking beneath his supine body. Gently, he laid one finger against his lips. He judged, from the raised eyebrow he received in return, that Flirt had already found the need for silence to be self-evident. Ignoring this unspoken sarcasm, he gestured carefully upwards with one hand. Thankfully her eyebrows made no riposte, and, as carefully as she was able, Flirt hauled herself out from beneath the weight of Fodder and climbed on soft feet onto the lower reaches of the tree's decaying innards. Keeping her head ducked beneath the peephole, she offered Fodder her hands—and with a grimace, managed to haul him upright. Digging his fingers into the crumbling wood, Fodder pressed himself against the hollows by Flirt's feet. At least he would be in the shadows....

"He came this way! I am certain of it!"

Horses snorted and reins jangled and hooves ground to a standstill at Harridan the Warrior Woman's words. Fodder grimaced. Oh, wonderful. The Narrative, it seemed, had chosen this nice, impressive location to hold a scene.

Stop wasting time! Go search for us already! Where's your sense of urgency?

Fodder's thoughts unfortunately made no impact.

"I saw no one pass this way!" Swipe as Slynder proclaimed. Oh great, they were converging.

"Nor I this!" intoned Clank as Sir Roderick. "The figure we pursued cannot have escaped from this glade. They must be concealed somewhere close by!"

Oh, you choose now *to grow some intelligence?* That was cheating as far as Fodder was concerned, and Dullard's expression, in the shadows beyond, implied a similar opinion.

"Be careful!" Magus the Sorcerer, in his incarnation as Elder, wise and noble guardian to young Erik, spoke with all the raging pomposity that could be mustered within a single human form. The long white beard had always helped in that respect. "Foul Tretaptus has trained his soldiers well—these men of Sleiss who aid him show unexpected slipperiness. They are…"

He could hear their voices, hear the scene, the argument as it played out, but Fodder was no longer listening; it was as though a bucket of cold water had been hurled over his head. Foul *Tretaptus?* The men of Sleiss who *aid* him?

That was just…*just…*

Typical!

It wasn't anger, exactly, that he could feel spiralling within him. It wasn't exactly anything other than that same strange emotion that had swallowed him that first night, in those few days forever ago when he'd first defied the wishes of The Narrative and turned against everything that mattered in their world. But after all that had happened, after he had kidnapped the princess and killed Thud the Barbarian's first character, after he had escaped their trap at the Grim Fortress and stolen the princess again from within the walls of their own Palace, and after he had, in defiance of injury and the laws of the Quest, used their own magical Ring of Destiny against them, The Narrative still referred to him as nothing more than "a man of Sleiss" and gave the credit to *Tretaptus*. After all his efforts, all their toils to prove a Disposable could make a difference, The Narrative had given the blame squarely to the only Principal character involved.

He glanced at the prince and saw at once from the shadowed but distinctly apologetic look on his face that Dullard hadn't missed the implication either. And it wasn't Dullard's fault. He'd simply been brave enough to stand up with them, and the day he tried to take credit for someone else's hard work was probably the day the universe would shudder and come to a stop. But, helpful as he'd been to their cause and as much as Fodder liked him, there was no denying his presence had changed the game.

The Taskmaster was clever; Fodder couldn't deny it. Deep inside, he was sure that the all-powerful controller of the Realm and The Narrative knew exactly who was responsible for starting and maintaining the chaos going on in this hitherto obedient world. The Taskmaster knew who had taken the princess and utilised the magic. But the Taskmaster had taken advantage of the presence of a Principal to maintain the status quo, and as far as the Quest was concerned, Fodder was still a Disposable—a persistent one perhaps, but still a lackey, a henchman, there to fight and to die in the name of Sleiss or Tretaptus or whomever. In spite of everything he'd done, the Taskmaster was refusing to grant him a promotion.

And that showed no *respect.*

If Fodder had had the Ring, he would have been tempted, almost drawn to lay into the Merry Band with a surprise burst of magic, to bring the Quest to a desperate, shuddering stop. But the itch of his skull and the scrap of broken string at his waist were enough to bring him back to earth with a thump. Taking on The Narrative at full strength was one thing. Taking it on with a hole in his head and no mystical powers to draw upon was quite another.

The time would come, though. On their terms or on his, he was going to be ready.

They were going to need a new plan. Killing the princess In Narrative remained on the cards, but...

The not-quite-gentle nudge of a boot against his shoulder broke his chain of thought. Flirt was staring down at him, her expression quizzical but her glare pointed. His absent gaze had not gone unnoticed, and the message was clear. This was no time to daydream. Pondering could wait.

Gritting his teeth, Fodder turned his attention back to the events beyond the protection of the trunk, and—

"Look out!"

The echoing, bloodcurdling screech made Fodder jump, and the slap of Flirt's boot against his cheek and the not-quite-inaudible gasp from Dullard implied they had also been startled. The sound of leathery wings clawing at the air overhead mingled with the whistle of drawn weapons and the horrified whinnying of the horses as Fodder battled a groan.

Oh, no. It wasn't only a scene. It was a *fight.*

And what happened in fights? AFCs got thrown against trees....

"A creature! Arm yourselves!" Clank, quick on the ball as always, shouted out the obvious. Swords sang in the air as grunts and cries battled with the screeches and screams of the winged, grey beastie attacking them. Fodder struggled not to pull a face. For goodness' sake, it was just the one AFC. They had a Sorcerer's magic and the mysterious powers of a Boy of Destiny, so what on earth were they waiting—

"Die! Die, foul creature!"

Oh, no.

Fodder saw Flirt tense. And this was not the mere contraction of a few muscles; this was the spasmodic freeze of a whole body in the instant before it launches into a vicious, frenzied attack. Her face locked into a terrifying glare of death, her eyes virtually glowing in the darkness. One hand slapped against her sword hilt.

There was a leathery thud. The attacking AFC gave a terrible, gurgling death rattle, wings flailing in the air and—oh no—getting closer as he struggled to stay airborne through his final death throes. There was no escaping the thought that he was going to crash into the tree and yes, glancing upwards, Fodder could see grey AFC limbs flailing against the hilt of the axe buried in his chest. The creature pitched towards the open split above them, getting nearer and nearer as the light from The Narrative began to creep like a sunny shadow into the crack in the trunk...

"Not here!" Dullard breathed. "Don't land here!"

And the AFC's ears twitched.

Their hearing. They have brilliant *hearing...*

The AFC had *heard* him.

"*Arrrrkkkkkkaaaauuuuugguuuuuuhhhhhhh!*" With a final, hideous, drawn-out screech, the AFC gave a nearly impossible lurch in the air and flung himself forwards. Even as Fodder's head swung round, he saw the grey, scaly body thump down amongst the roots inches from the crack through which they'd climbed, twisting and writhing with his eyes tight shut as he clawed at the axe within his chest. With a final roll, his wings flexed out and thumped back against the trunk.

The Narrative light that had been creeping around the edges of the crack cut off like a sudden eclipse. The AFC's leathery wings had completely obscured The Narrative's view inside.

Fodder felt the breath he was holding release in a wave. Bless the AFCs. Perhaps they had no interest in joining Fodder's side, but they weren't exactly going out of their way to help the Taskmaster either....

He had no idea to whom he was grateful; Fang, Gibber, Chomp, and their fellows were too indistinguishable to readily identify one from the other. But Dullard was rather better read on the spotter's guide.

"Thank you, Fang," the prince whispered.

A scaled, sharply clawed hand poked underneath the leathery concealment. Finger and thumb formed an acknowledging O.

But Flirt's icy face told Fodder that in spite of this assistance, there was no safety to be found. Her teeth were gritted violently, and her hand was massaging her sword hilt as she listened to the Merry Band member she loathed above all others finagling his way back into The Narrative's glory for the third time.

"...was not aware our noble Halheid had so many brothers," Magus was saying. "But nonetheless, master Svenheid, your assistance was timely."

There was something distinctive about the swaggering footsteps of Thud the Barbarian as they, well, *thudded* their way up the mound towards the body of the creature he had Narratively slain.

Please don't pick him up; leave the foul brute to rot where he lies.

"I was seeking to join my brother Torsheid and aid him in avenging our poor Halheid." Thud's voice was close, too close for comfort as he stomped his way to his victim. Fodder laid a careful, restraining hand on Flirt as her eyes glittered with rage. He could see her mouthing the word "bastard" to herself repeatedly.

"I considered it my honour and my duty to come to my two womb-mates' aid." Thud gave an abrupt and unconvincing sob. "Imagine my distress to learn I have lost two brothers, one to a foul rebel and one at the hands of a wen—"

Fodder was not sure he had ever moved so fast. Thrusting out both hands, he slapped them down over Flirt's ears with as much careful hurry as he dared, shaking his head frantically as her face flared with infuriated rage. He could see her body flexing, could see her biting down on her lip as she fought with every fibre of her being to prevent the precipitous action that the word "wench" inevitably invoked. But her common sense won out, albeit very marginally, over her temper. The desire for vengeance, however, glittered in her eyes.

Fodder didn't rate Svenheid's chances of making it to the end of the Quest much more highly than his brothers'. Thud had slapped Flirt's backside one too many times.

"...do not rate a female warrior, my lord Svenheid?" Harridan had waded in with an arch response. If Fodder hadn't known she was destined to fall in love with whatever Barbarian brother happened to survive to the end of the Quest, he probably would have appreciated the intervention on Flirt's behalf. But he knew, just knew what was coming.

"I rate any warrior who can prove themselves in arms, lady." Oh no, there was a bearded smirk on Thud's face; Fodder could smell it on the breeze, and the suggestive tone in his voice told as much as volumes' worth of indecent illustrations. He didn't need to see the Barbarian's attempt at swaggering appeal to know the horror of it. "I will happily cross my weapons with yours at any time."

Fodder's eyes met Flirt's. And then, as one, their faces crinkled with disgust.

Blessedly, the exchange ended there as a noisy squelch signified that Thud had retrieved his axe. "I shall leave this foul brute where he lies," the Barbarian proclaimed, much to Fodder's relief. "He shall serve as a warning to the others of his kind that strafe these skies. Let them come, and they shall share his doom!"

"Alas, we have no further time for such pleasantries," Magus proclaimed in his best proclaiming voice. "We have but lately been in swift pursuit of the foul villains who have so decimated your family. At least one of them, and perhaps two others, lurk around us in this foul waste as we speak; and we can but assume poor, kidnapped Princess Islaine is concealed somewhere nearby. Will you help us find them?"

"Of course. I am at once at your disposal." Thud always sounded far too smooth In Narrative—it really didn't work for anyone who'd ever heard him the rest of the time.

"We must split up once more." Harridan's voice was intense. "We shall comb these woods from end to end, survey every brush and tree limb! We shall not be thwarted again!"

"Agreed." Magus projected the word with unnecessary vigour. "Spread out and search every nook and cranny you can find. They shall not escape us! Away!"

Away was good. Fodder was all for awaying, and his relief was palpable at the sound of horses turning and hooves pounding against the earth, the sharpened voices of the Merry Band retreating as the thick, vivid light faded once more into hints and an air of heaviness. The Merry Band might have departed the immediate vicinity, but it hadn't gone very far.

Great. Oh, great. Now what do we do?

He glanced at Dullard, but the prince's expression was still creased with concern as he remained flattened uncomfortably against the trunk on the far side. Above, Flirt looked pained as she struggled to balance. But going anywhere was hardly an option, even if the immediate danger appeared to have passed. Their saviour, the bloodstained owner of the leathery wings, managed to clamber to his feet whilst keeping said wings in a suitable blocking position. It was fortunate he did so.

"That's a deep gash you've got there, Fang."

Fodder's eyes widened. *Squick!*

His mind raced. Squick was here? Maybe they wouldn't need the Pixie Patch, if they could persuade Fang to look the other way and—

"Repair his damage quickly, Squick. We require as many Assorted Freakish Creatures as can be obtained for search duty. The renegades must be found."

The voice, dripping with acres of superior condescension, was unmistakable. Strut, the Taskmaster's taskmaster, organiser of the hunt for them and mouthpiece of the Taskmaster, was no more than six feet away.

"Aye, I'll do me best." The pixie's voice sounded vaguely weary. "But yon AFC lads have been taking a lot of axes these last few days, and I'm fresh out of hearts for them. I'll have to take Fang up to yon Patch for repairs."

"See to it." The dismissal was abrupt and, to Fodder's ears, slightly edgy. "Primp!"

Dullard winced noticeably as a scurry of footsteps implied a new arrival and, as Fang the AFC reluctantly stepped away with Squick, Fodder caught a glimpse of one pair of skinny, hose-lined legs appearing beside another. Dullard's uncle Primp, the Officious Courtier responsible for the AFCs, had apparently joined his superior.

"Yes, Strut?" If Strut had sounded edgy, poor Primp sounded positively harried. To judge by Strut's stern tone, it was no wonder.

"What happened?" Strut, usually so composed, snapped viciously at his inferior. "The attack and Svenheid's introduction should have been delayed as I instructed. They were supposed to wait!"

"I *tried.*" There was a note of apologetic pleading to Primp's tone, the voice of a man who knew he was under the cosh. "But do you know how difficult it is to get a message to someone in the air? Fang was told to wait above this clearing and attack when the Merry Band entered. As far as he knew—"

"I'm not interested in your excuses." Strut's tone made it abundantly clear that this was the truth. "What about Thud? I asked you to keep an eye on him until it was time for him to go back in. Why did you let him proceed when you knew we were mid-pursuit?"

"He wouldn't be stopped!" There was no doubt that Dullard's uncle was having an extremely bad day. "I did tell him, but he wouldn't listen to me! He was so impatient to get back into The Narrative, and he knew that was supposed to be his cue…"

"Enough." Never had so much dismissal been crammed into one word. Nor indeed had so much disdain ever been crammed into the sigh that followed. "Are your Creatures searching? Did they see where the rebels went?"

"I spoke to Gibber during the chase. They report having seen no sign of them. The forest canopy is too thick."

Fodder couldn't help but grin, wondering how many pretty birds and interesting trees that feat had taken. The AFCs' senses were good enough that they should have been able to hear the passing of footsteps from well out of sight, and Fodder doubted, from Fang's performance, that they owed their ongoing freedom entirely to their own efforts. This didn't surprise him, given the fairly ad hoc nature of those efforts thus far.

Strut did not appreciate this. "That is not good enough, Primp. Your Creatures have already let us down with their carelessness in allowing the three Disposables to escape, not to mention this fiasco." Fodder saw Primp's leg twitch, presumably recalling the twenty-second head-start he had allowed them on the grounds that one of the fugitives was his nephew. It seemed the Officious Courtier was being made to regret his generosity. "I offered them this chance to redeem themselves, and I expect them to take it."

"They are working very hard, Strut." There was a vaguely resentful ripple underlying Primp's tone. "They've barely rested in days."

"I have no doubt they are. But effort is useless without *results.*" Strut paused for a moment, allowing the strident word to fade. When his voice came again, it had regained a little of the lost composure. "The rebels need to be found quickly. We cannot proceed to Cackle the Crone's cottage until we are certain of their direction. The incident with the Dragon may be our last chance to reinsert the princess seamlessly enough to effectively conclude the story, and we cannot afford to waste it. I want every Freakish Creature airborne and searching. You have your instructions for Maw?"

"They have appeared in my book, naturally." There was no doubt about it: Primp was definitely not enjoying being told how to do his job. "I will inform him as soon as the Taskmaster needs me to."

"Be ready. Given the"—Strut paused a moment, almost seeming to choke upon the following word—"*unpredictable* nature of current events, we may have to act quickly, and the scene with the Dragon is everything. Understood?"

"Of course." The legs were moving away, two sets of footsteps retreating around the mound.

"Good." Strut's voice dropped to a hush. "You know how important this is, Primp. You know what is risked by failure, just as I do."

Primp's voice was apprehensive. "You mean the incident at Quickening?"

Fodder's ears pricked. Incident at Quickening? Wait. Where had he heard that phrase before?

"Silence!" Strut's exclamation was fierce. "Speak not of it! Or must I reprimand you as I had to Hauteur?"

"Indeed not," Primp said hurriedly. "I'm sorry. I forgot myself."

"From now on, remember better," Strut snapped. "Now, we must—"

An unholy and very familiar squelch put pay to the rest of Strut's sentence. Fodder heard a foul sucking noise as down below, he suspected, a Courtier's curled shoe was retrieved from a cheerfully bubbling pool of black goo.

"What…is…*this*?" Strut's clipped voice could have laid waste to empires.

"I believe I've heard it referred to as 'gloop.'" Primp's matter-of-fact tone didn't quite hide the edges of amusement creeping through it.

Strut did not speak, but his angry sigh could have seared through metal. With a squelching tread, their Courtier footsteps retreated into the trees.

For a moment, there was only silence. Fodder rested his head gently against Flirt's leg as he let out a fresh and better-timed breath of relief.

"Bloody hell," he muttered.

"I second that." With a groan and mutterings about cramp, Flirt pulled herself down and out of her snug hidey-hole and poked her head very cautiously around the edge of the crack in the tree. She sniffed at the air in an animal-like fashion before ducking back inside.

"Bugger," she whispered eloquently. "They're still close by; I can feel it in the air, and there's light off in the trees not far from here. We're going to have to be bloody careful, aren't we? And we can't randomly blunder into the open." She frowned. "So where's the Ring?"

Dullard groaned as he unfolded his lanky body from the tense position in which it had been pressed. "We aren't entirely sure," he admitted quietly. "We didn't exactly have time to look before—"

"We reckon it's in the gloop." Fodder decided to cut to the bad news.

"Oh, that's magnificent, isn't it?" Flirt rolled her eyes expertly. "This day keeps on giving. *Back!*"

A shaft of Narrative light arched briefly across the edge of the mound before fading once more into the trees. It was definitely not a good time to be rummaging in gunk.

"I think we may have to stay here for a bit." Dullard once again displayed his talent for stating the obvious as he unpeeled himself from the inside of the tree trunk. "With the Merry Band and the Trappers combing the woods for us, I'm not sure we'd get far enough to even search the gloop, let alone back to the cave." Disconcertingly, he smiled. "Mind you, we've got plenty to talk about."

"We do?" Flirt looked slightly alarmed.

"Well, that conversation between Strut and Uncle Primp was rather interesting. Given how much they were emphasising the importance of the Dragon scene, I wonder if there is some way we could use that to our advantage. If it's so important to them, perhaps we could turn it another way or even sabotage it altogether?"

Fodder nodded. "It's a thought. We do need a new plan and a good one."

"If we ever get out of this tree." Flirt's voice was irritable, but she was looking thoughtful. "But about that chat: I was more interested that Officious Courtiers are talking about an incident at Quickening again. That's the second time that's cropped up, and that makes me curious, doesn't it?"

Fodder's attention was caught. "You've heard that phrase before too?"

Flirt nodded. "Hauteur said it, didn't he, when me and Shoulders were eavesdropping on him and Cringe. And he shut up pretty sharpish when he realised he had. It sounds like it got him in trouble." She glanced at him curiously. "You've heard it as well, have you?"

"Somewhere." Fodder racked his brain. "I was trying to..." He snapped his fingers. "Preen! Preen mentioned it that first night when he was talking to Strut, and Strut cut him off with a glare of death. I had enough other things on my mind not to think much of it, but now..."

"But now it's got something to do with what we're doing." Flirt's expression was thoughtful. "What do those Courtiers know that we don't?"

A thought struck Fodder. "Hey, Dullard, have you ever heard of this incident-at-Quickening thing? Has your uncle ever said anything about it?"

It was Dullard's turn to shake his head. "I'm sorry, I'm afraid not. It's not something I've come across before."

Fodder frowned. "I guess that's no great surprise. The way Strut reacts when it gets brought up, it seems to be restricted knowledge."

"We could ask Squick," Dullard suggested. "The Duty Pixies have seen every Quest there's ever been. Whatever this incident was, he or one of his family might have witnessed it. And given we were heading to see him anyway..."

Fodder nodded. "Good thought. Though I reckon we should concentrate the early parts of the conversation on getting Shoulders's head fixed. Preferably before he drives us insane."

"I'll bloody say," Flirt seconded at a whisper.

"Indeed." Even Dullard conceded the point. He clicked his tongue. "I do hope he and Pleasance have managed to stay out of sight. I'd hate to think anything had happened to them."

The light beyond their concealment began to thicken once more. Almost wearily, for there was no denying the relentless pressure of this hunt was pretty knackering, Fodder tensed and pressed himself back away from the crack as Narrative light danced once more over the mound outside, accompanied by the distant sound of Erik's voice.

"But Islaine was not with them! Noble Elder, surely she must be our greatest priority..."

The light faded once more, the voices retreating. Dullard sighed profoundly.

"Well, it would seem they haven't been found," he muttered. "That's something to be grateful for."

There it was again. Fodder had spotted the odd tone, the strange expression on Dullard's face when Pleasance's behaviour had been mentioned earlier.

"She's still giving you the silent treatment?" he remarked carefully. The Rejected Suitor nodded.

"Very much so." He paused, his features creasing gently. "To be honest," he added more softly, "I'm growing a little concerned about her."

"Concerned" was not the word that Fodder would have chosen. With Shoulders's constant griping, the princess's silence was more of a blessed relief than something to worry about.

Flirt's snort implied she agreed as she edged past Fodder and dug her foot into his shoulder, hoisting herself up to the peephole above as she scanned the clearing for signs of The Narrative. Fodder winced but, given the situation, he let the matter go.

"She's sulking, isn't she?" the Barmaid said, her eye pressed to the gap as she balanced precariously above. "Let her. It's much better when she's not being such a pain in the arse."

Dullard said nothing, but the slight frown that crossed his brow as he glanced up at her was the equivalent of a blazing rebuke from pretty much anyone else.

"I can't say I miss the screaming," Fodder suggested more diplomatically. "Or the kicking. Or the biting."

"I know, but..." Dullard leaned back against the tree, his eyes staring blankly upwards. "Perhaps I was wrong, but I couldn't help but feel that back in the boat, before the trouble with the waterfall and The Narrative... Well, I thought that maybe she was starting to come round. But she won't even argue with me."

Fodder shrugged slightly, earning a brief tap against the top of his head from Flirt for affecting her balance. "I thought you hated arguing."

Dullard pursed his lips. "It was more of a debate. And at least we were communicating."

Fodder was surprised to see a hint of genuine distress on Dullard's face. *Blimey. She kicked him and called him names and bit him on the nose, but yet* he really is *worried about her.*

Fodder had to admit that he hadn't had much time for Pleasance since he'd kidnapped her. She'd been an irritating, inconvenient means to an end. Recruiting her had never even crossed his mind, and Dullard's efforts to win her over had always seemed to him a pointless waste of time, something to keep the prince busy and the princess riled.

But that moment on the boat, when the matter of marriage to Bumpkin had been mentioned—oh, that had been a nerve strike and no mistake, a chink in her defiant armour. When the rope had threatened to drag Dullard off into the water, it had been Pleasance who had saved him. And Fodder could have sworn in that moment in the woods when she hadn't been gagged, that her eyes had been open. Yet she hadn't screamed for help, so how could that be true? But surely, trying to win her over remained a lost cause.

Didn't it?

"Maybe that's why she's clammed up." Fodder wasn't entirely sure that Dullard's campaign was one he should be encouraging, but nevertheless, he opted to speak up. "I think you struck a nerve on the boat, you know, when you mentioned marrying. Maybe I'm wrong, but I got the feeling she might not be young Bumpkin's biggest fan."

Dullard nodded. "I got that feeling too. Did you see the look on her face when she fell into Narrative and saw him?"

Fodder shook his head; he'd still been woozily coming to his feet, groping for the Ring that had spilled from Flirt's chain mail when Pleasance had made her big entrance. "Not pleased to see him?"

"Maybe I mistook it, but from where I was lying, *horrified* would be closer." Dullard's look was intense. "I don't think she finds the idea of being Islaine to his Erik so appealing anymore. And I'm sure she must have been awake when I left her in the woods to react to Shoulders's head as she did. But she didn't scream for help before that." He shook his head. "Maybe if I could get her to open up to me about it, we could get somewhere. But she won't even talk to me."

"I think you're barking up the wrong tree there." From above, Flirt chipped in once more with a distinct lack of irony for their current situation. "Even if she doesn't fancy Bumpkin, she's too keen on the glory. I think she'd take him on for her shot at being Heroine, don't you?"

But much as he hated to admit it, Fodder wasn't sure he agreed with Flirt's blunt assessment. He could see where Dullard was coming from. Something had changed in the princess since their encounter with the Merry Band.

"I don't know," he hedged. "I think she wants the glory—Flirt's right there. It's if she wants it enough to stomach Bumpkin."

"That's just it." The Rejected Suitor stared at him. "I really don't think she does. But if she won't talk to me…"

It was Fodder's turn to sigh. "Maybe you need to keep trying," he suggested diffidently. "She probably needs time."

Dullard's eyes were distant. "I'm sure she was awake on the beach too," he murmured absently, as though he hadn't heard what Fodder had said. "The Narrative wanted her awake, and yet she stayed unconscious. Was it because Bumpkin was there? Did being near him make her realise…?" His voice trailed off.

"Well, you never know." In the wake of the overwhelming negativity Shoulders had spent the last few days throwing around, Fodder decided to risk a touch of positivity. "Having the princess on our side would certainly scupper The Narrative. As prospects go, that's not so half tankard."

Dullard's brow creased. "Half tankard?" he inquired.

Fodder grinned wryly as his mind popped back to that near-but-so-distant day out on the road when this mess had started. Shaking his head, he explained the reference.

To his surprise, Dullard looked oddly thoughtful rather than dryly amused by the story. "It probably wasn't such a bad idea," he said pensively. "Perhaps if it had been better executed? Ah well…"

"Right, I've had enough of this, haven't I?" Fodder winced as Flirt once more utilised him as a ladder to clamber down from her perch. He gave her a resentful look, which she completely ignored. "I'm not sitting in a bloody tree with you two for the rest of forever debating whether Pleasance is less of a bitch than she clearly is and whether Shoulders's bad ideas aren't so bad. It looks quiet out there and the air doesn't feel so bad, does it? I'm going to look around."

"Oh, no." Fodder wasn't going through this again. "I'm setting a ground rule, Flirt, here and now. No more death-or-glory charges from you. This isn't The Narrative, and there'll be no noble sacrifices while I'm around, okay?"

Flirt snorted once more. "Sod noble sacrifices. I don't intend getting caught, do I? Come on, the pair of you. If we can find that Ring, we can risk making a break for it, can't we? Because if the buggers catch up with us again, at least we'll be able to get away."

Fodder shook his head as he looked at the dark-haired Barmaid in her chain mail and armed with her magnificent sword. They'd come such a long way from the old days, mere days ago, in Humble Village, abandoning their petty roles to try and prove they were worth as much as any Principal. Had it been so short a time since Flirt was inflating her bosom to order and handing out tankards of ale?

"All right," he conceded. "Let's get on with it."

It felt odd to step out of the protection of the hollow tree, like breaking free of a concealing cocoon and stepping into the firing line. But Flirt was right—the heavy taste of the air was distinctly less, and there was no shout of watching eyes from the trees around. For the time being, no one had seen them.

"Fodder, you keep an eye out." Flirt was scanning the shadowy trees. "Given your history with this gloop stuff, let's keep you apart, shall we?"

Fodder opted not to deign this with a response, concentrating instead on searching the dark, tangled forest surrounding their clearing as he strained his eyes and ears for the sound or sight of anyone at all. He squinted, pausing beside a particularly gnarled-looking specimen lurking at the glade's edge. Wait. That shape, that shadow beneath that branch—was it watching them?

No. It was just a shadow. Nothing alive was that still. Fodder's gaze moved on.

Beside him, Dullard was already scanning the ground. "We'll need a stick, something to feel around with—I wouldn't recommend rooting around in that pool with bare hands. Maybe if we—"

"No need." There was a sardonic twist to Flirt's voice. "Your intensive search failed to check under this root right here, didn't it? With your astounding powers of observation, is it any wonder I put you on watch?"

Fodder glanced back, a mixture of relief and chagrin flooding his stomach as he saw Flirt hold up his missing pouch, gunkless and clean. He hurried over, snatching it from her as he pulled open the drawstring. The gaudy outline of the Ring of Destiny glinted back at him.

He could defend himself again. Properly. And he knew all he needed to do was believe.

The surge of determination he'd felt earlier upon hearing of his demotion In Narrative whispered through his veins with renewed vigour. "Come on," he muttered, glancing through the shadows once more but finding no more than he had already noted. "Let's get the others. Then we can find Squick and the Pixie Patch and get out of this dank forest for good."

"Nice plan," Flirt agreed. "But we need to watch our backs, okay? The Merry Band haven't gone far." She groaned gently. "Gods alive, we've got to try and move discreetly with Shoulders in tow. How the hell are we going to pull that off?"

"I'll try to help him again, if you'd like," Dullard offered with fool-hardy optimism. "I'm sure I can think of something. That half-tankard business…"

Moving as quickly and quietly as they could, the three companions crossed the clearing and plunged back into the concealment of the forest. And from the trees, in silent stillness, the shadow watched them go.

* * *

"The Winding Trail."

With a sigh, Fodder gestured to the almost invisible thread of clear ground that zigged and zagged through the monstrously deformed trees. Being here was a risky move—the Trail was the best-known route through the Wild Forest and a common passageway for the Merry Band to use In Narrative—but it was also the only decent landmark in the area and the only sure signpost Fodder had to lead them to the last place he remembered seeing the Pixie Patch. It wasn't a safe place to be, but this wasn't a safe time to get lost.

Beside him, Flirt looked doubtful. Their unashamed sneak back to the cave to collect Shoulders and Pleasance hadn't been without incident—there had been a close call with a Trapper, and Clank had ridden within sighting distance twice as he'd circled the area—and the idea of abandoning that caution to walk along a Narratively-known thoroughfare was not sitting comfortably.

"Do we have to follow it far?" she asked grimly.

Fodder shook his head. "For an hour or two, maybe; I'm not exactly sure. If Cackle's Hovel and the Patch are both where I left them, we should be there by sometime this afternoon."

"Thank goodness for small mercies." Flirt grimaced. "Because any more from the headless wonder and I'm going to—"

"Will you watch where you're putting your hands, you clumsy oaf? That's my bloody nostril! I don't need your help!"

It was all Fodder could do not to grit his teeth as he slowly turned his head to where he could see his friend hunkered against a jagged tree trunk, the rawness of his severed neck mercifully concealed beneath a grubby scarf. His clumsy fingers pawed awkwardly through his scruffy blond hair, struggling to extract the twigs that had become tangled there in an earlier drop of his head into the undergrowth. His brows were knitted and his face aglow with rage against the world but more specifically in that moment, against Dullard, who was staring at the glowering Disposable with dangerous amounts of sympathy in his eyes. The prince's personal philosophy of unthinking kindness wasn't doing him any favours.

Fodder sighed. Shoulders was one of his oldest friends. They'd known each other as Urchins, grown up together, joined the Disposables on the same Quest—but after two days, two long, epic, solid days of listening to the nasal sound of his voice going on and on and on in that same harsh, whingeing tone, Fodder had reached the point where he would have cheerfully thrown Shoulders's head up the nearest tree and walked away without a qualm. He'd already planned the tune he would whistle as he sauntered off, leaving that voice to fade into blessed, blessed silence.

It wasn't that Fodder wasn't aware that Shoulders's situation was, well, not that pleasant. He had been in the same boat himself once or twice, albeit only briefly, and was very much aware of how difficult it was to manoeuvre a body that was no longer in physical contact with the part of it giving orders. And he would have been quite prepared to be helpful and sympathetic if it wasn't for the fact that neither of those things made the slightest bit of difference. All Shoulders wanted to do was moan, and no force in the universe was going to stop him.

Dullard, unfortunately, had yet to grasp this. A few days' acquaintance was nothing on a lifetime, and Fodder barely managed to gesture in time to forestall his parting lips. Another platitude from the prince at this juncture would only end in tears.

Fortunately, Flirt got in there first.

"Will you keep your voice down?" she hissed sharply. "In case you've forgotten, we're being hunted, aren't we?"

Shoulders turned his hands sharply in order to glare afresh at her. "Oh, I'm so sorry if my crippling decapitation is an inconvenience!" he retorted mordantly.

"It's more the crippling sound of your voice, isn't it?" Flirt snapped in return. "Asking you not to moan is like asking the sun not to shine; I know that, don't I? But can you moan *quietly?*"

Shoulders huffed loudly but did not reply. Dullard cleared his throat. Although his expression remained uncertain, the weight of hidden explosive potential in the air was enough to guide him to prudence. He stepped away from the angry Disposable and over to where Fodder and Flirt were waiting.

"Did you get any further helping him carry his head?" Fodder asked softly.

Dullard winced slightly. "I'm working on it. Perhaps a little longer…"

Flirt shook her head. "We don't have any longer, do we? We're exposed enough as it is, and we aren't stopping *here.*" She sighed, shaking her head. "We'll just have to leave him as he is and live with it. Get the princess, and let's go."

Fodder frowned as he glanced over at the messy blonde bird's-nest that had once been the perfectly coiffured ringlets of Princess Pleasance of the Noble Kingdom. The gag she previously had worn as a matter of course had, at Dullard's insistence, not been replaced after the incident at the waterfall, although her hands remained firmly bound. She was staring absently, all but blankly, down at the line of the Winding Trail a few yards away from her, her porcelain brow creased in thought. She had still not spoken a word since they had returned, but having spent several hours alone with Shoulders, the blankness of her mood seemed to have the slightest edge of annoyance to it.

"Pleasance, are you ready to go?" At the sound of Dullard's voice, Fodder saw Pleasance start abruptly. Her jaw locked as her fingers clenched around each other.

"And maybe we could have something to eat as we walk?" The prince was rummaging around his pack, pulling out one of a cluster of wild apples he'd picked before breakfast that morning. "We need to keep our strength up. Fodder, Flirt, would you like one?"

"Might as well." With a shrug, Fodder accepted the small piece of fruit, downing it in a couple of bites. Things didn't grow well in this forest.

Flirt declined with a shake of her head but lowered her voice abruptly. "Not Shoulders, okay? Do you want another repeat of last night's rant on the unpleasant nature of food consumption for the headless? I don't know about you, but I've heard quite enough about the *gap swallow*, haven't I?"

Dullard's expression grew pained. "Perhaps not," he conceded prudently. "Please hold on a moment while I see if Pleasance wants one before we get going."

Fodder watched as Dullard approached the disconcertingly silent princess and offered her a wild apple. She took and ate it grudgingly, but with a lack of comment that was vaguely alarming. When this meal, such as it was, was done, Dullard made some brief, passing attempt to engage her in conversation; but with only a couple of distinctly half-hearted glares, Pleasance made it clear his company was not required. With a sigh and a shrug, the prince moved back to join Fodder.

"Still nothing?" Fodder asked softly.

Dullard simply shook his head. "I'll keep trying."

"Right." Flirt was scouring the forest. "We won't walk on the Trail, only off in the trees to the side. Keep your eyes open and your voice down, and if you see anything, say so discreetly, and we'll hide. We'll have to move carefully and—"

"Wait a minute." Shoulders's eyes darted sharply in the Barmaid's direction as he tuned in to the last sentence spoken. "What about my head? I already told you I can't go on like this!"

"Stay here then," retorted Flirt flatly. She had definitely reached the end of her tether. Hours of solid grouching would test all but a Dullard-like patience.

The patient prince himself was examining Shoulders with the same thoughtful gaze he'd worn since the half-tankard discussion as he helped the silent princess to her feet. "There has to be something we can do," he mused, tapping one finger against his chin.

"Well, there's not!" With an echoing huff, Shoulders lifted his head up to glare at them, frowning features angled outwards and rife with both frustration and truculence, enhanced by Flirt's virulent "Shush!"

"Voice down!" she hissed again.

Shoulders glared but did obey. "I can't do it!" he snapped at them irritably but softly, his head bouncing a touch as his chin worked around the words. "I can't stomp along and hold up my head at the same time! Do you have any idea what that's like? Well, I'll bloody tell you! Your balance is shot to buggery because your arms can't move with you! You can't see where you're going because you have to manually angle your head the whole time! And your elbows will bloody kill you!"

Dullard's lips were twisted as his face continued to show a certain amount of sympathy. "Perhaps it might be worth trying holding it under your arm again?" the prince suggested tentatively. "It might offer some relief and more stability than—"

Shoulders's ill-tempered growl cut him off. "Weren't you listening earlier?" he retorted fiercely. It crossed Fodder's mind that there had been a lot of listening to endure in the long, drawn-out trek that counted as *earlier,* but since saying so would certainly not help matters, he kept the thought to himself. "You know, when you said you'd help and came up with bog all?"

Dullard gave an inoffensive shrug. "I did offer suggestions," he ventured. "If you recall, you simply didn't approve of any of them. I do think under your arm is the only—"

"I can't see properly from down there!" Shoulders's interruption was dismissive. "It's too disorientating and too, too, too…*cliché!*" He folded his arms untidily, resting them on the crown of his own head as accompaniment to his glare. "I am not doing it!"

"Well, what do you want to do instead?" Flirt snapped. "Because you've not come up with a better way, have you? You won't hold your head up, you won't hold it under your arm, you won't put it in a sling or let us carry it! All you do is moan! You need to pick something, Shoulders, pick something and live with it! It's not like it's forever, is it?"

"There may be a way." Dullard's quiet statement thankfully cut in before Shoulders could launch into a fresh tirade. "Hmm…I wonder…"

The result of Dullard's wondering was one of the oddest sights that Fodder had ever seen. In a remarkably short space of time, Shoulders's helmet had been carefully replaced onto his loose head and helmet and head together balanced onto the severed stump of his neck. Leather straps taken from the climbing equipment Dullard had brought along had been secured to the helmet. Holding the two parts of the neck in place were two halves of a tankard from their pack, split, bent out, and knotted and bound in place with twine.

Shoulders looked stranger than he did decapitated, and he was constantly forced to correct his lolling, sliding head back into place as he tried to walk, but at least the moaning was notably lessened. It appeared having his head back in some semblance of the right place indeed made a difference.

Not that there was silence. That would most likely have heralded the end of the universe.

"I look ridiculous."

"Yep." Fodder decided to be honest.

Unable to turn his head and face his friend, the best Shoulders managed was a kind of sideways glare. "What if someone sees me like this?" he demanded irritably. "I'll be a laughingstock!"

"If anyone sees us, being a laughingstock'll be the least of your problems, won't it?" Flirt remarked pointedly. "We'll get you to Squick and he'll fix you. The only people who'll be mocking you is us, and we can't be bothered."

"Speak for yourself," Fodder added with a grin.

"I think I can refrain." A few steps behind them, Dullard was eyeing the contrivance he'd created. "I'm sorry it's so unwieldy, but it really was the best I could come up with. We do have limited resources, unfortunately..."

"And limited safety." Flirt shook her head. "Can we *please* go now?"

They could. With Dullard trailing behind with the silent princess and Flirt scouting from the front, Fodder reluctantly sacrificed himself in the name of friendship to walk with Shoulders, who, despite his improved situation, was happy to maintain a low-grade grumbling about his inability to turn his head and search for danger. Keen to drown this out, Fodder strained his eyes and ears, searching the shadows for a hint of pursuit and praying he would not find one.

A squeal from behind caught his attention at once. As he glanced back, he saw the princess stumble in a muddy hole, staggering briefly before Dullard's hands rushed out, catching her carefully as she reeled, her bound hands yanking as she squeaked. Gently, he eased the princess upright.

"Are you all right?" he asked with a friendly smile.

Pleasance's lips worked for several seconds, apparently torn between a lambaste and a thank you. In the end, she settled for neither, clamping her lips together as she turned her face resolutely away from her escort once more.

Dullard sighed quietly. "I do wish you'd tell me what I've done wrong," he said almost plaintively. "Other than the obvious kidnapping and all that, I mean, but... Oh goodness, I know this isn't a situation you'd like to be in, but I was hoping we might find some way to make it more palatable for you?"

Fodder could see the glow in the princess's eyes, could see her clamped lips yearning to part and let her captor know exactly what she thought of *palatable*—but yet again, she restrained herself. An odd shiver passed across her eyes.

Fodder frowned. Dullard was right; something was definitely going on behind those petite features that hadn't been there before.

"Oi!" Shoulders had halted just ahead, half-turning awkwardly. "Are you abandoning me?"

"Sorry." Fodder returned to his friend's side, but his ears latched on to the one-sided conversation afoot between the figures following him.

"I was hoping we could talk about what happened when The Narrative came." Dullard's voice was soft and serious. "It's just...you *must* have been awake. Nothing else makes sense but..." He sighed again. "I'd forgotten your gag but...you didn't cry out. And I was really hoping you might be willing to tell me...*why?*"

There was no reply. Fodder hadn't expected one, but there was something profound about this particular lack of response, rich with unspoken words. Ducking under a low-hanging branch, he risked a glance back, but the brief glimpse he got showed Pleasance's face to be a determined mask.

"I'm sure you must have had a reason. I know it must be an extremely good one, to keep you from returning to The Narrative." Dullard's voice was oddly soothing. "And...well...I am aware it's probably none of my business. But I know you're somewhat alone here with us, in a manner of speaking, and while I'm certain that I'm probably not your favourite person, I am the one person available to hand who is most likely to listen and understand." Fodder sensed rather than saw the smile. "Possibly out of those *not* available at present too. Because although you are technically a prisoner here, I don't want you to feel you can't talk to me if something's bothering you."

Fodder suspected that what was bothering Pleasance most at present was the prince himself. There was something relentless about Dullard's gentle interrogation. It was like sitting under a fountain of liquid toffee—harmless and not necessarily unpleasant, but slowly the sticky weight would grind you down.

Fodder heard Dullard take a deep, careful breath. "Perhaps I'm being presumptuous," he offered quietly. "But I did wonder... Perhaps in regards to Bumpkin, whether you—"

"Oh, for *pity's sake!*" The sudden explosion of high-octave sound from Pleasance shook the craven branches around them. "What part of my not wanting to talk to you is so hard to understand? I am *not* going to reply! There will be no words! So will you *please* stop jabbering on at me?"

"Oh, *she's* allowed to yell?!" Shoulders swivelled indignantly. Pleasance was breathing hard, her normally pale cheeks flushed and her eyes hard as sapphires as she glared up at her wide-eyed interrogator. For his part, Dullard looked a little surprised by the outburst, but Fodder could practically see the victorious cogs clunking into place at this successful if unintentional rise.

"Well," Dullard ventured with a lopsided shrug. "Forgive me but... Just because you aren't talking to me, I wouldn't have thought that would preclude me talking to you. And anyway..." He took his life in his hands as he risked a smile. "Aren't you talking to me now?"

"You...I..." The princess worked her mouth furiously for a moment, a cocktail of indignation, anger, and frustration doing war behind her eyes. *"Why?"* She flung the word into his face, but in spite of the fury that laced it, it sounded to Fodder almost like a plea. "Why are you doing this? Why must you blather on and on and on at me and pretend to be my friend? You are my jailor! A traitor! Why would I possibly want to confide in you? Why can't you *leave me alone*?"

Dullard cocked his head slowly to one side. A lone eyebrow softly rose.

"Would you honestly want me to?" he asked, the words gentle but devastatingly earnest. "Really?"

Pleasance was breathing heavily, her chest heaving as she stared up into his face with something akin to fear. "Just...*stop it!*" she screamed. "All right? Shut up! Leave me alone!"

Dullard was staring at her sadly. "Very well," he replied. "If that's what you want."

"Oi!" Flirt appeared abruptly beside the two Disposables. "Will you lot keep the noise down? We're not that far from the Merry Band, are we?" She glowered at the princess. "If she yells like that again, that gag is going straight back."

"It's fine." Dullard's hands came up reassuringly. "I do believe Pleasance has finished."

Flirt looked unconvinced. "One more shout..." she threatened grimly, waving a finger in Pleasance's direction before turning and heading back out to plot their route parallel to the Winding Trail once more.

With Shoulders muttering at his side about how easy Pleasance got off for shouting, Fodder turned quickly back as the two resumed their walk once more; and this time, as he had said, Dullard made no further attempts to engage the princess in conversation. The sound of their footsteps seemed to echo in the void left by the lack of conversation, the weight of the silence pressing down like a pall. Fodder tried to ignore it, tried to concentrate on the silver back of Flirt that he could see glinting in the trees ahead and upon avoiding the vast quantities of low-hanging branches designed to snag his helmet and catch on his mail, but the quiet rose up and dominated everything around it, reverberating, almost echoing. It was that most illogical of things—a silence that roared.

It was nearly unbearable, and it lasted a good fifteen minutes before one of the participants finally cracked under the pressure of it.

"You're doing this on purpose, aren't you?" This time there was no explosion, no screech or scream—Pleasance's voice ventured stiffly into the muddy quagmire of the silence as though terrified of its footing. "This is some kind of petty revenge."

"You asked me to leave you alone." From any other lips, Fodder suspected that sentence would have emerged wreathed in sarcasm. But from Dullard, it was a quiet statement of fact. "I thought that was what you wanted."

Pleasance huffed slightly. "But I didn't think you'd actually do it."

Dullard mulled this over for a moment before replying. "So you really don't want me to shut up then?"

"I didn't say that."

"But you don't like my being quiet."

"I didn't say that either."

"I am terribly sorry but…that isn't something you can have both ways."

"I'm aware of that, thank you."

Yet again, the pause from Dullard was brief but profound. "Forgive my presumption, but…I don't think you really want me to leave you alone, you know."

"I don't."

"There now! You see? That wasn't so hard to—"

"I meant I don't forgive your presumption."

The tight sentence stamped ruthlessly over the brief elation that had flared in Dullard's voice. He sighed briefly before continuing.

"I do wish you could learn to trust me. I know it must be hard…"

"To trust my kidnapper?" Pleasance retorted sharply. "To trust the man who tricked me into the hands of my enemies? I wonder why that might be?"

"But I do think if you could find it in yourself to get past that—"

"Hah!"

"—that you would find it of benefit to your own well-being." Dullard ploughed on with scant regard to the venom fervently filling the air around him. "Because I think I'm starting to understand why it is that you didn't cry out when you were awake In Narrative."

"I didn't cry out because I wasn't awake, you pointless buffoon!" Pleasance's tight chilliness was rapidly melting into red-hot fury once more, though fortunately not at any great volume. "If I had been, you and your stupid friends would be locked safely away!"

"...And if I'm right," Dullard pushed on obliviously, "I think you know that it isn't something you can confide to anyone else. But I will listen. And better than that, I will understand. I promise you that. If you can—"

At a hiss, Pleasance ignited. "You don't understand anything! How can you?" She hauled in a deep, angry breath. "You're just...you've... You have got to be the most irritating excuse for a human being I have ever met!"

There was another heavily loaded silence. This one had all the tonnage of a baby elephant that badly needed to diet.

"Irritating?" Dullard's voice, when it came, sounded genuinely perturbed. "Really?" He swallowed hard as Fodder, distracted by the war behind, fought a brief and lively battle with a hanging twig that had tangled itself in his chain mail. "I haven't been trying to annoy you, honestly. I only want to help."

"I know." Pleasance ground out the words. "That's the most irritating thing. You mean it." Fodder could virtually hear her teeth gritting. "It's harder to despise someone when they mean it."

"So." Dullard lingered briefly on this opening syllable. "You...don't despise me?"

"I said *hard.*" Pleasance's voice had dropped back into chilly stiffness. "I didn't say *impossible.*"

Dullard stared down at her for a moment. "That's a shame," he offered sincerely, "because I really do feel like under other circumstances we could get along, you and I. I believe you're a better person than you let yourself be. And in spite of you yelling at me and arguing and biting my nose...I...well...I *like* you."

Never had so harmless a sentence killed a conversation so completely. Silence fell once more with emphatic certainty.

"Fodder!" Abruptly, Shoulders's elbow contacted with Fodder's chain-mailed ribs, jerking him back to the immediate vicinity. "I need to go for a pee."

Fodder regarded his friend with all the potential horror this statement might contain.

"You don't want me to help or something, do you?" he exclaimed. "Because there's friendship and there's—"

"Oh, thanks for that disturbing mental image!" Shoulders's moderately lopsided head pulled a disgusted face as he stumbled to a halt and turned to face his friend. "I can still do a ruddy pee by myself!" He grimaced slightly. "But wait for me, okay? I..." He sighed. "I don't want to be out here alone. Not with The Narrative about."

Fodder's mind flashed back to his earlier conversation with Dullard about Shoulders and his Narrative difficulties. Decapitation would hardly prove a boost to his confidence in that regard.

He nodded. "'Course, mate. I'll be right here."

As Shoulders stepped awkwardly into the undergrowth, Dullard and Pleasance arrived at Fodder's side. The prince looked at him quizzically.

"Call of nature," Fodder explained, noting the revulsion that flashed across the princess's face as he did so. "You two carry on; we'll catch up in a minute."

Dullard nodded, moving with Pleasance towards where Flirt was scouting a path. Fodder hoped that she'd spot their destination soon. They'd been going for nearly an hour following the path of the Winding Trail and, given the number of times they'd headed through the trees to cut off its trademark zig-zag corners, he could only hope that Cackle's Hovel would soon...

"Fodder! *Fodder!*"

Shoulders's frantic hiss cut off his musing instantly. "Shoulders?"

His friend came staggering back out of the undergrowth, his eyes wild. For a moment Fodder wondered if his lack of co-ordination had caused an accident, and there were some pretty big thistles knocking around in...

"Back there! In the trees!" Shoulders was gasping—breathing proved to be tough when one's windpipe was in two pieces. He grabbed Fodder's shoulder for balance, leaving him to subconsciously resolve to wipe his chain mail down the first chance he got. "I saw...I don't know! A shape! A shadow or something! I think someone's following us!"

Fodder was instantly alert. "Where?"

Shoulders tried to shake his head, but the result wasn't pretty. "I can't see it now, it's gone! But it was there, I'm telling you! There's someone there!"

A part of Fodder was inclined to dismiss this confident declaration, especially given Shoulders's renowned paranoia and the fact that his own frantic scanning of the shadowy trees produced no results. There were so many creepy, gnarled stumps and branches lurking about that were so easy to mistake for a man.

But they had to be sure.

"Go get Flirt," he said quietly. "I'll take a look."

Fodder had done many stupid things in his life. Going back alone to investigate a possible stalker wasn't one of the most highly rated, but it had the potential to be up there. As Shoulders stumbled off, Fodder slowly drew his sword and made his way carefully back the way they had come, his ears peeled for the slightest snap of twig, his eyes seeking the remotest scrap of movement. Branches around him shifted in the wind, creaking and teasing him as his head whipped from side to side, searching and searching as painful minutes crawled by like hours. A looming stump offered a damned good impression of a crouching man; creeping ivy had a scary stab at being a reaching hand. There was no hint of light, no heaviness to the air. That was good, but as he and Dullard had so unpleasantly discovered, there were Trappers lurking in these woods—wiry, deadly hunters who would betray them in a heartbeat for a couple of Narrative lines. He had to be alert, he had to be ready, he had to be—

A hand touched his shoulder. Fodder swung with a stifled screech, his sword whipping up to find Flirt staring at him with eyebrow raised. Pointedly, she slapped one finger against her lips.

Fodder glared at her, but she shrugged. "Very vigilant, aren't we?" she mouthed.

Fodder let the insult pass. "See anything?" he mouthed in return.

Flirt shook her head. "Only you," she whispered as she jerked her head back the way they had come. "And no tracks I can see. Come on."

Quietly, carefully, still searching the undergrowth, the pair made their way back to where Dullard, his sword drawn, was waiting with the pale princess and the very anxious Shoulders.

"Well?" the Disposable hissed. "Did you get him?"

Flirt shook her head. "No one there. You probably saw that tree stump, didn't you?"

Shoulders's eyes flared with paranoid glory. "Tree stumps don't move. I'm telling you we're being followed."

Flirt rolled her eyes. "By the Merry Band and every other helping hand they've been able to drag into this forest to look for us. We *know*, Shoulders."

Shoulders rolled his eyes right back. "I know that. But it's more than that. I saw a shadow."

Flirt sighed. "Yeah, you don't get many of them in the shadowy woods, do you?"

Shoulders glared openly. "A *specific* shadow. *Following* us."

Fodder decided it was time to step in. "Mate, no offence, but you didn't seem that sure when you told me about it. You said you thought you saw a shape."

"Which had turned into definitely a man by the time you got to me, hadn't it?" Flirt rested her hands on her chain-mailed hips. "Once your imagination had smoothed out the edges."

Shoulders flared indignantly. "I'm not making this up!"

"No one has said you are," Dullard intervened soothingly. "But everyone's eyes play tricks, especially when they're afraid."

Luckily, Flirt got in before the rising fury on Shoulders's crooked face could manifest at this affront to his courage. "Shoulders, if we were being followed, The Narrative would be on top of us already, wouldn't it?" She glanced at Fodder. "That Trapper that caught you and the prince out made a wolf-call to summon it, right?" Fodder nodded as Flirt continued. "Well, I've heard no wolves. And if it was a Merry Bander,

The Narrative would flash straight to their point of view. It's not here, so we're not being followed right now and if we keep our heads and our voices down, they probably won't find us at all. Okay?"

Shoulders looked deeply disgruntled. "I know what I saw."

Flirt nodded calmly. "I'm sure you do, and we'll keep our eyes open. But at the moment, we've other things to worry about. The end of the Trail is about two hundred yards ahead, right at Cackle the Crone's Hovel. We've made it."

"Is Cackle at home?" Fodder asked at once. "Only it's a long way through nasty undergrowth if we don't pass through her dell."

"Yep." Flirt dashed his hopes with a simple word. "Or she was right before I came back to let you know and found Shoulders telling me you were in mortal peril. She was outside it along with three elves."

"Elves?" It was Pleasance, surprisingly, who was first to join in this conversation. "They've no right to be here! They aren't needed for this Quest!"

"Just because they aren't needed doesn't mean they aren't some-where," Dullard pointed out gently. "People who aren't In Narrative still have to exist. They don't disappear into nothingness."

Pleasance glared at him but there was something oddly forced about the effort. "Shame. I've been hoping you'd disappear for days."

Fodder chose to ignore the exchange. "What are they doing there?"

"It looks like Cackle's been darning their socks for them and doing some laundry." Flirt wrinkled her nose. "It needs doing, to tell you the truth. They don't exactly look their usual stylish selves. Come on and see for yourselves."

They moved quickly, following Flirt's lead to a cluster of thick bushes overlooking a swampy glade, where twisted logs and cadaver-ous-looking dead snags overhung a burping, sluggish quagmire of greenish gloop. All but surrounded by this uninviting bog was a cottage that more closely resembled a rotting log pile than living quarters, a crooked hovel built of roughly woven dead wood, slanting under a creeper-swamped roof of ragged thatch. In defiance of this grim scene, however, red-and-white-checked curtains hung in the windows, a vase of daffodils perched cheerfully on the windowsill, and a washing line that hung between two dead snags displayed a beautifully laundered collection of elegantly embroidered tunics in various shades of green.

Under the eave of the crooked doorway, the owner of the Hovel herself was holding out a pile of socks to three tall, long-haired, pointy-eared figures who were staring down at her as a starving man might regard a ten-course banquet.

Fodder had only met Cackle the Crone a couple of times. She was precisely what one might expect from a mysterious old woman living alone in a savage forest: her nose was large, bulbous, and sharply hooked; her skin was pockmarked and punctuated by numerous shapely and impressive warts; and one eye socket gaped noticeably larger than the other. Her fingernails were long, broken, and jagged; her back was bent; and her voice was a cackling wheeze. But for Fodder she had been a good laugh when she'd been required to unexpectedly defeat them as they'd charged in to rescue the princess she was holding captive and had given them tea and biscuits whilst Squick fixed them up. And when Clunny had respectfully asked her why she lived alone out here between Quests rather than moving to the comfort and companionship of the Magnificent City, Fodder recalled her insistence that the other folks living out in the forest needed her and that the poor dears wouldn't be able to cope if she was gone. He'd wondered vaguely at the time what she'd been talking about, but it suddenly dawned on him that the Mystical Forest, home to the soaring treetop homes of the land's elfish population, was only a mile or so over the ridge to the north of Cackle's Hovel.

The grateful, almost reverent looks on the faces of the three elves as they accepted their socks from the professional Crone had told Fodder clear as day that they could only be the "poor dears" she had been referring to. Indeed, they did very much look in need of her care. Every elf that Fodder had crossed paths with In Narrative had been a tall, graceful, immaculate figure with perfectly honed, smooth features and beautiful, flowing hair. And whilst the three clustered before Cackle did indeed possess the familiar exquisite looks and pointy ears, their long hair was snarled and mussed, their faces were scratched and muddy, and their clothes were battered and smeared with browny-greenish stains that looked very much like bark. In short, they looked like they'd fought a war with the undergrowth and lost.

"Thank you *so much*." The leading elf was gazing down at Cackle with an adoration that was frankly embarrassing as he passed the socks back to his companions. "You are the most..." He shook his head as he stared at the warty vision before him with love in his eyes. "You are the *only* person I've ever met who really understands how hard it is to live up a tree!" he exclaimed. "Oh, it's all very well when The Narrative's there to send you gliding through the branches, but no one ever thinks about how tough it is for us balancing around up there when it's gone! Twigs in your backside, leaves in your hair, bark-burn! Birds in your face and insects down your tunic! Only two days ago, poor Windblossom slipped on a wet branch, fell twenty feet, and landed on a badger! It's a nightmare!"

"There, there, Leafstar dear, I know." Nodding with understanding, Cackle leaned forward and patted one warty hand against the elf's wrist. "But I'll always be here to wash your tunics and darn your socks for you. There's nothing them trees can do to you that I can't fix, don't you worry! And...well..." To Fodder's surprise, the Crone's eyes drifted slightly coyly towards the earthen floor. "If it gets too much for you, you'd always be welcome to...use my spare mattress...for a few days...?"

The elf called Leafstar stared at her for a moment. Suddenly, to Fodder's astonishment, he blushed a solid scarlet and began an intensive examination of his shoes.

"That's..." he stammered awkwardly. "Lovely of you to offer... I wouldn't want to impose... So generous...but...maybe I could...think about it?"

His perfect green eyes drifted up and caught Cackle's uneven gaze. The look lingered a smidgen too long to be comfortable for onlookers.

One of the other elves gave a none-too-subtle cough. Leafstar and Cackle both gave a noticeable jump as they tore their eyes apart.

"Anyway!" the elf exclaimed sharply. "Must be going! Thanks again, so much for the socks and doing our washing and well..." He let out a long breath. *"Everything."*

There was a definite hint of pinkness to Cackle's sallow face as she ducked back into the shelter of her Hovel. "Always ready and waiting to help, my dear," she murmured in reply. "Always waiting."

Leafstar gave a hurried nod and, together with his two companions, gathered a handful of socks almost lovingly in his arms and set out across the marshy ground towards the edge of the trees to the left of Fodder's clump of bushes. Instinctively, the Disposable ducked lower as the three elves wound their way closer, but the bushes did not mute the quiet conversation as they approached.

"You are *so* in there."

The voice presumably belonged to one of the other two elves, and judging by Leafstar's abrupt response, it was not a welcome observation.

"Don't be so stupid, Moonbright!"

"I agree with him," the only female elf chimed in. "Trust me, Leafstar, she was giving you the eye."

"But..." Leafstar gave a gusty sigh. "That's ridiculous! I mean, for goodness' sake! Look at me! Look at this smooth, characterless skin! Look at these sculpted, regular features! Look at my pointlessly long limbs! What have I got to offer to a woman so...so...*amazing?*"

In the shadow of the bushes, Fodder caught a brief glimpse of the look on Shoulders's face. His eyebrows had risen so violently that Fodder was surprised they didn't knock his helmet contraption off and send his head rolling away.

"I mean, those knobbly hands of hers!" The note in Leafstar's voice had sped straight through the waters of wistful and emerged emphatically on the coast of veneration. "Her shapely features! Her face is just so...so unique! So interesting! And she's so kind and makes such wonderful tea and...and..." Through a gap in the leaves, Fodder caught a glimpse of his shaking hands as he cradled his cargo of socks like a precious thing. "And she can *darn!*"

He shook his pointy-eared head despondently. "What have I got to offer her? She could have any man she wanted. Why would she want a boring specimen like me?"

"But she does!" The appropriately musical voice of the female elf was insistent as the trio of elfish perfection began to fade into the trees in the direction of the Mystical Forest. "Don't waste this chance! You'll never meet a woman like her again!"

"You are so lucky," the male called Moonbright chimed in. "What I wouldn't give to have a woman like Cackle giving me those kind of looks…"

Their voices faded into the forest as they wound their way back home. A moment later, they were lost to the wind. In the glade, Cackle lingered a moment longer, looking wistfully in the direction the elves had departed. With a sigh, she turned into her cottage and pushed the rough-hewn door closed.

There was a moment of silence. And then, with a shrug that made his head pitch sideways, Shoulders snorted.

"Bloody nutters!" he muttered. "Too long up a tree, that's what it does for you. It makes you go blind."

Although his expression remained typically amiable, Fodder couldn't help but notice that there was something a bit tight about the set of Dullard's shoulders.

"Actually, I found their attitude quite refreshing," the prince commented mildly. "Having lived most of my life in an environment where looks are valued far more highly than good character, I thought it a pleasure to see that elf was able to appreciate the lady for who she was rather than what she looked like."

Despite the fact he was struggling to readjust his head into a useable position, Shoulders nonetheless managed a grin.

"Well, you would say that," he remarked with no little mockery as his eyes raked Dullard's impressive profile. "Being so *interesting* yourself."

Fodder saw Flirt sit up sharply at Shoulders's insensitivity even as his own lips parted, but to the astonishment of all concerned, it was another voice that cut in first.

"How *dare* you? You're hardly an artist's dream yourself, you weasel-faced oik! And after he went to so much trouble to help you too! Just because a person isn't some gallant pretty boy like Bold or Valiant doesn't mean…that they're…not…"

Pleasance's voice trailed away as four pairs of eyes fixed upon her in astonishment. Her eyes widened in horror. Her lips closed with a snap.

"He…he's *Royalty*," she stammered shakily, her glare both tremulous and defiant as she took in the faces of her captors, her chin jutting stubbornly by instinct. "I won't tolerate a commoner speaking to a fellow Royal like that." She swallowed hard. "Even one I *loathe*. *Heartily*."

Dullard's sigh was barely audible but noticeably there. "Well," he said with a hint of a smile. "Thank you all the same."

There was an odd, awkward silence as Pleasance glared furiously at her own shoes and Dullard stared curiously at Pleasance. Shoulders, whose grouchy insult had sparked off the unexpected exchange, carried on trying to readjust his head without looking the slightest bit contrite, and Flirt exchanged a look with Fodder that was both pointed and surprised. Perhaps there was something to be said for Dullard's gentle approach after all.

"Well." It was Flirt who was the first brave soul to sally forth into the air of awkwardness. "Now what? Do we try and sneak past the Crone's Hovel without her seeing us, or do we go looking for another way?"

Fodder shook his head as he pulled off his helmet. His damaged skull was still itching and tingling and the rub of the metal against it wasn't helping. "There isn't another way. The forest around here is designed to push folks in this direction. We'll have to sneak and hope for the best."

"And if she sees us?" Shoulders inquired acerbically.

"We tell her we're here to get our livers serviced or something." Fodder gave a weary shrug. "We don't exactly have much choice."

"And if she doesn't believe us?" With an unpleasant judder, Shoulders finally managed to ratchet his detached head back into some kind of upright position.

Fodder sighed, battling not to snap in the face of overwhelming pessimism. It was a hard fight. "We'll have to hope it doesn't come to—"

The loud creak of never-oiled hinges broke into Fodder's sentence. The door to Cackle's Hovel swung open, and the Crone herself, her hooked hands dripping with soapy water, came staggering out into the dell. Her arms grasped a basket piled high with tiny but clean leather jerkins and little cloth hats in a variety of colours. They looked freshly laundered.

"Poor wee dearies!" she muttered to herself. "Never time to wash their own clothes, and they do such messy work. I do hope they haven't run out of underwear yet."

Balancing the basket on one hip, Cackle pulled the door to her Hovel closed and headed with deft care across the marshy ground. A few moments later, she slipped into the shadow of the trees and out of view.

"The pixies!" Flirt exclaimed. "Those were their clothes, weren't they? If we follow her, we'll find the Pixie Patch!"

Shoulders was already half on his feet, one hand shooting out to stabilise his lolling head. "What are we—"

Pleasance's sharp, horrified squeal cut the rest of the sentence dead. Even as Fodder wheeled, he saw Dullard fly backwards and tumble into the undergrowth in a flurry of limbs, saw Flirt freeze, her hand on her sword hilt, saw Shoulders stumbling to try and turn around. And then, he saw the princess.

And more particularly, he saw the blade pressing violently against the soft skin of her throat.

Uh-oh.

A dark leather glove grasped the knife hilt, its fellow wrapped around the bonds that already restrained her, yanking her back to press tightly against their owner. Black leather shrouded the lithe figure, his face shadowed by the deep depths of his hood, but there was something there, something in the shape of the features, something in the hint of the eyes.

But it couldn't be... Please, it couldn't be...

"Poniard?" Fodder breathed.

The hooded face turned sharply towards him and he knew. It *was.*

But this was not the drunken, unshaven, scruffy Assassin that he and Dullard had accidentally fired up back at the Rowdy Tavern. Worrying amounts of sobriety glittered in his gaze, lit up by a disturbing level of intensity. There was something in those eyes...

If he sobered up, he'd only be morose; that was what the Artisans had said. But he didn't look morose at the moment, and the use of him as an example of how bad things could get in terms of finding oneself in his earlier conversation with Dullard was looking alarmingly close to the mark. Had he taken their words about killing the princess to heart after all? If so, that would be to their advantage, but not if he did it right here and now.

"What do you want?" Fodder asked quietly, distracted slightly as Dullard, more scratched and battered than ever, staggered out of the bushes, his eyes widening with horror as he too reached the same conclusion. "If this is about what we said..."

"Shut up!" The Assassin's wild tone was enough to suggest that sobriety had not helped Poniard much in the sanity department. His eyes darted from one face to the next with frantic abandon as his knife hand tightened at the princess's throat. She gasped and only Flirt's hurried hand against his chest stopped Dullard, his expression full of concern, from starting forwards.

"You know, don't you?" The Assassin's voice was a hiss. "You know where he is, don't you, hmmm? Back at that clearing, I was watching you; I heard you say it! Why do you think I've been following you?"

Clearing...*oh*. Fodder felt a coldness tighten in his chest as he remembered the shadow he'd seen lurking, the shadow he'd dismissed as nothing.

"Following...I *told you* I saw something!" Shoulders erupted. "I told you, but it was all, 'Oh *no*, you paranoid sod, you spotted a bloody *tree stump'*..."

"Shoulders!" Flirt hissed through her teeth. "Be smug *later*, will you?"

"I've been combing these woods for days now, days!" Poniard's breath was coming in short, frenetic bursts. "D'you think I can find the winged bastard? No, nowhere, nowhere to be seen, but you know! You know where I can find him, and once I've got him and dealt with him, the world will be mine to slaughter, you hear me? *Mine!*"

Shoulders was staring at the raving Assassin incredulously. "What the bloody hell is he talking about?"

"Squick." Fodder felt sick. Had they done this? Had he and Dullard put this madness in his head? "He wants to kill Squick. He thinks no one will respect his work unless his victims stay dead."

"But he keeps fixing them!" Poniard butted in. "Keeps destroying all my fine work with a flick of his happy dust! Well, no more! Not once I'm done with him!" His eyes flared. "And you are going to take me to him! Otherwise, we'll see what we can do with your fancy miss here!" His eyes, made grim in the shadow of his hood, went momentarily misty.

"You know I know six hundred and seventy-three different ways to kill someone? Six hundred and seventy-three! But a slit throat—that's always been my favourite. So simple, so elegant, so *graphic.*"

"Ummm." Flirt tilted her head cautiously. "Just to point this out, but...we aren't In Narrative here. You do know anything you do here won't kill her, don't you? It'll sting a bit and make a mess of her dress, but..."

The reminder, whilst timely, was unwelcome. Poniard's eyes flooded with resentful rage. "Maybe I can't!" he roared angrily. "But a damned good maiming, that would be a good start! And you know, The Narrative's not far from here, is it, hmm? I've seen it! How's about I go chop her up in there?"

"Be our guest!" Shoulders intervened encouragingly. "In fact, go ahead, you'll be doing us one hell of a favour."

"Shoulders!" Dullard's tone actually contained a trace of shocked annoyance. "Stop that!"

But the Disposable was not alone. "Actually," Flirt offered, "he has a point, doesn't he?" She turned to the confused-looking psychopath and smiled. "You take her and carry on. We'd appreciate it, wouldn't we?"

Dullard blinked at them in horror. He wasn't the only one. Princess Pleasance's expression transformed from one of rampant fear to sudden irritation as it became very clear to her that her rescue from a grisly fate was not a priority; her jaw hardened like a clamp as she glared.

"Fine!" she hissed.

And then, like a lunging snake, she struck.

Poniard gave an unmanly screech as Pleasance's teeth sank violently into his knife-wielding fingers; the blade tumbled from his hand in shock as his helpless prisoner turned on him with indignant rage, one heeled foot lashing out with a deathly accuracy that sent him reeling away from her. As the still bound-up princess staggered clear, Dullard rushed forwards, his sword whistling free of its sheath as he darted between them.

Teeth gritted in sudden rage, Poniard's head whipped up. "Why, you—!" he rasped.

A voice, sudden and really not well-timed, echoed out of Cackle the

Crone's glen behind them. "Cackle? Lass, are you about?"

Fodder went cold. *Squick!* Mere minutes ago, he'd have been ecstatic to hear that voice, but for him to show up here, now of all times...

"Passing by, I was!" the oblivious pixie's voice continued. "Thought I'd drop by and collect me smalls! Anyone home?"

Poniard's smile was frenzied. With a howling scream, he ripped out a cutlass to grasp in one hand and snatched up a bolas in the other. *"Time to die, you little bastard!"* he screeched.

"Squick, *go!*" Fodder cried out at the top of his voice, but Poniard had already plunged forwards, crashing through the undergrowth, ploughing into Flirt and Shoulders as he did so and sending the pair of them flying in a heap to the ground. Fodder scrambled after him, with Dullard hot on his heels, and he caught a glimpse of a green-and-purple flying blur as Squick took good advice and attempted to vacate the area at speed. But it was already too late.

With a roar, the Assassin released his bolas. The weighted cord snaked through the air and smacked against the flying blur with a loud *whack.* Fodder caught a brief glimpse of Squick's potato-like face before the Senior Duty Pixie dropped like a stone into a bubbling pool of marsh water.

"No!" Fodder was wrenching his sword from its sheath, but Dullard was two steps in front of him, his elegant sword ready as he launched himself out of the bushes and into the Assassin's path.

"Help the pixie!" the prince shouted over his shoulder, and the cry was enough to briefly distract Poniard from his mad charge towards the struggling shape in the muck.

Wheeling with the sharp fluidity that defined his position, Poniard swung the cutlass in a vicious arc towards the advancing prince's neck, but Dullard anticipated the blow, ducking beneath the curve of the blade as his own sword thrust upwards. For a moment, Fodder hesitated, shocked that Dullard had somehow managed to entirely miss the exposed leather torso, but the Rejected Suitor, it seemed, had no intention of landing a blood-spilling blow; his blade followed the line of his opponent's and smacked against the hilt of the cutlass.

Say what you would about Poniard's psychotic tendencies, but there was no denying that, when sober, he was extremely good at what he did. Even as the sword flew from his grasp, he was moving, arching backwards as his fingers lashed out, catching his tumbling weapon and hauling it back into his grasp. With barely a break in stride, he roared and curled his blade back around in a mighty swing towards the man interfering with his mission.

There was something inevitable about the strike. It had power; it had panache; it had a kind of Narrativesque unstoppability that faltered Fodder's stride in anticipation of a second companion in two halves. In any Narrative Quest Fodder could care to name, the Rejected Suitor would have been in pieces.

But Dullard had apparently not read the script. His sword scythed, catching Poniard's blow against the base of the blade. The Assassin staggered. Teeth gritted, Dullard lunged into his instant of confusion, surging forwards as he knocked the cutlass aside with his sword. His hand grasped his opponent's hilt, wresting the cutlass from his grip as he rammed into his right shoulder—hooking one leg under the bewildered killer as he flung his full weight against his body and hurled him to the ground. A moment later, both swords were pressed to the man in dark leather's throat in a steely cross.

"Please, don't move," the prince gasped out almost pleadingly. "I'd really rather this didn't get messy."

"Naahhh!" Poniard, however, appeared to be well past caring about mess. With the bare palm of his hand, he thrust upwards, smacking into the crossed blades and beyond, slamming the heel of his palm into Dullard's chin. Blood splattered, but whom it belonged to was difficult to tell as the prince ricocheted backwards with a squelchy thud into the soft earth. The Assassin flipped with enviable agility to his feet as he roared unintelligibly once more and dived for his blade.

"Oh no you don't, me laddie!"

In the shock of Dullard's fight, Fodder had forgotten his mission to retrieve the beleaguered Squick. But the pixie, it appeared, had no need of a rescuer—the familiar, shimmering needle had already ripped aside the remains of the bolas as the potato-faced little man rose to the air in a furious flurry of pond water. Glittering purple gleamed in his hand.

"I'll give you 'time to die'!" he bellowed. With a hum not unlike that of a rain of falling arrows, he lowered his green-hatted head, raised his dust-filled hand, and charged.

Poniard's hand closed around his cutlass and, teeth gritted with violent hatred, swung the blade in a vicious arc to intercept the pixie's flight path. But this time, Squick was ready for him, his blurry shape buzzing under the blade. Purple exploded, and Poniard the Assassin screamed.

It was a scream with character. It carried within it echoing dollops of frustration, of shock and indignation mixed with none-too-subtle undertones of anger and distress. And underlying it, rippling out of the dusty cloud of pixie magic that engulfed his right arm, came a disconcertingly organic-sounding squelch and the wicked sound of a pixie's cackle.

The dust cleared. For just a moment, as Poniard stood, gripping his elbow and staring down at his hand with horror, Fodder couldn't quite see what he was so upset about. But then his brain kicked in as the truth dawned.

Poniard's right hand was locked in a curled-up fist, the fingers melded together into a solid lump bound by freshly made skin. And that fist, right back to the elbow that supported it, was *back to front.*

Hovering a few feet in the air above his handiwork, Squick gave a wicked grin as he rubbed his chin thoughtfully.

"Not too bad," he mused, struggling and failing to hide his amusement. "For a spur-of-the-moment effort, laddie, I'd say you've got off pretty easy. I left you all the bits you started with—and after trying to kill me, I'd say I'd been generous." His expression darkened abruptly. "But there be plenty more room for redecorating, if you catch me drift. And if they be in the mood to chop you up..." Fodder glanced round to find Dullard, bloodied around the chin and jaw but back on his feet, and Flirt standing close by with sword drawn. "Don't you be thinking I'll be putting you back together again."

Poniard's glare could have ignited the sun. Stumbling backwards, he kept grasping his damaged arm as his eyes swept the glen furiously. "You'll pay for this!" he screeched vilely. "I'm going to get you! I'm going to get you all!"

Shoulders appeared at Flirt's side, his expression sardonic as he struggled to correct his lopsided head arrangement. He snorted at this melodramatic statement. "And *I* was worried about being clichéd!" he declared.

Poniard shot him one last glare of death. With a final bellow of rage, he turned and fled into the undergrowth.

Flirt was staring after him with concern. "Should we go after him?" she exclaimed. "What if he tells the Merry Band where we are?"

Fodder shook his head. "You think they'll let him near The Narrative looking like that? How would they explain his arm being backwards?"

Flirt did not look convinced. "But..."

Fodder sighed. "Flirt, we came looking for Squick because we all need fixing but you. Do you want to run off Assassin-hunting as soon as we've found him? And don't even think about suggesting you go by yourself."

"Maybe I should go with him." With a huff and a stumble, the bound-up Pleasance staggered out of the bushes. "I'd probably be *safer.*"

Flirt ignored the princess, but Dullard hurried over to her side. Although Pleasance's expression remained icy, Fodder couldn't help but notice the barest hint of thaw at the sight of the only one of her kidnappers who hadn't been in favour of her getting her throat cut. Leaving the prince to his charge, he turned instead to the reason they had come.

"Squick, are you all right?" he exclaimed, pulling his helmet off as he did so.

"Oh, I'm fine, laddie!" There was a definite air of satisfaction to the pixie's face as he brushed the last scatterings of purple dust from his fingers, not even glancing over. "Yonder lad was a wee drop more persistent and a dram more sober than he usually is when he tries to do for me, but it ain't nothing I couldn't see to!" His eyes darted to the muddy Dullard, whose dishevelled state was not impressing the princess one bit. "Not that I ain't appreciating your intervention, laddie, but I had matters well in hand. You and your friends had no need to..."

The pixie's gaze had drifted at last to Fodder. His voice tailed away almost as sharply as his eyes widened.

Then he sighed, a deep, echoing sigh of one who knows that trouble has not only come knocking on his doorstep but stolen his milk while it was waiting.

"Oh, *no*," he groaned.

It was not quite the greeting that Fodder had hoped for.

"Hello, Squick," he offered with a pathetic wave. "How are you?"

Squick's eyes darted to Flirt and Shoulders, both wearing tentative smiles of their own. They could smell the tenuousness of the situation as well as he could.

The pixie's stare fixed upon the strange arrangement of Shoulders's neck before darting to Fodder's caved-in head and Dullard's bloodied face. He visibly slumped in the air.

"Better until you lot waltzed in," he growled, his knobbly face wrenched into a hard frown. With a gesture that near enough sent him spinning sideways, he jerked his head in the direction of Shoulders. "And I smell a favour in the offing."

Fodder risked a smile. "Well…"

But one small hand had already darted out. *"Don't."*

Shoulders's unsteady jaw worked furiously. "But—"

"Don't ask me!" Squick's sharp declaration cut across the half-started protest. "It ain't fair! Yon tight-arse Strut has banned me from fixing any of you lads and lasses on pain of up yonder, and it's more than my job's worth if he finds out I ain't obeyed! I feel for you but…" He sighed deeply. "Look," he said, more quietly. "I like you lads, okay? I see more of you Disposables than owt else, and there ain't many parts left in either of you that I ain't patched, woven, or sewn up! But this is getting daft! If I'd've known what keeping my gob shut up on that mountainside would mean, I'd…" He paused a moment, to allow another gusty sigh to slip from his lips. "Well, truth be told, I'd have done the same and be damned for it, but that doesn't mean I'm minded to help you now. You got yourselves into yon mess. You can get yourselves out. Don't go dragging me into your troubles."

With an emphatic *humph*, the pixie crossed his arms and glared down at Fodder with a fierceness that was not entirely convincing. The Disposable stifled a sigh of his own.

"Squick, please." He lowered his voice slightly. "It's been bloody *unbearable*. He hasn't stopped moaning for nearly *two days*. If he doesn't get that head fixed back on soon, he is going to drive us nuts."

The pixie's expression was a sympathetic wince, but it did not soften the stone behind his eyes. "I feel your pain, laddie, true enough," he muttered in return. "But I just can't do it. It'd be *my* head if I did."

"This isn't about what we're doing." Fodder's plea was sincere. "This is about our sanity. Please."

"What are you whispering about?" Shoulders's voice cut in sharply from behind. "You're being rude about me, aren't you?"

Fodder gritted his teeth as his jaw clenched. "Shoulders…"

"Oh, that's *nice*, isn't it?" The interruption was distinctly mordant. "That's lovely. Here I am, two halves of the man I was, sacrificing my head for your precious campaign and what do you do? Bitch about me!"

Fodder fixed his gaze on Squick, I-told-you-sos echoing in his eyes.

"I didn't ask for this, you know! I didn't ask to be dragged along, threatened with dungeons, pushed and pulled around by The Narrative! I didn't ask to have my head cut off again! But do I get so much as a thank you? A word of appreciation? A little bit of sympathy? No! I get insults, behind my back, in my hour of sodding need! What kind of friendship do you call this? I'm suffering here! Does anyone even care?"

Fodder kept staring at Squick. He didn't say a word. He didn't have to.

The pixie sighed the big, gusty sigh of the experienced Shoulders-dealer. "Well, I suppose I could take a look," he conceded as Fodder's heart leapt like a salmon at a waterfall. "But only because you lads stepped in to help me. And because I hate to see people suffer."

He shot a look at Shoulders, who was staring at him with rising glee. Fodder knew how he felt. At last, no more moaning!

"But one thing I want clear, mind!" Fodder snapped back to attention at the pixie's stern tone. "This ain't me joining your merry crusade! I'll help you with this but then we're even, ain't we? You get yourselves into any more calamities, I ain't getting involved! And if you tell anyone I helped you…"

"Our lips are sealed." Fodder couldn't get the words out fast enough. "Squick, you've no idea how grateful—"

"Ah, save yon gratitude for them that wants it." The pixie waved a dismissive hand as he hovered a few inches above Fodder's dented head.

With an analytical glance, Squick pulled out a handful of his trademark dust. "Hold yourself still, laddie."

For a moment, Fodder could only gasp as purple dust ignited in silvery bursts around his head, sinking into his skin and hair, whipping dizzyingly around his face. His head gave an echoing crunch as something substantial shifted; thrown by the jerk, he stumbled as the purple mist cleared. Gently, he lifted his hand to finger where the dent in his skull had been and found only solidity.

He grinned at the hovering pixie. "Squick, you're a genius."

The pixie rolled his eyes. "I'm a professional, laddie, and don't you forget it." He turned to Dullard. "Now you're nice and simple, ain't you, lad? Just a bit of skin and a fractured chin-bone. Stay still."

A puff of dust later and the prince's rips and damage vanished as though they had never been to be replaced by healed skin. Dullard smiled gratefully.

"Thank you very much," he said politely.

"Aye, you're welcome." Squick turned to Shoulders, who was staring at him like a hopeful puppy. "Now you, laddie, you'll be a bit more work. And I'll need some of that paraphernalia out of the way first."

Shoulders moved at once to scrabble at the knots holding his helmet in place. But Dullard, his face freshly repaired, had not moved away but was staring curiously up at the hovering pixie.

"Excuse me," he offered diffidently. "But when you said about our...well, *merry crusade.* Does that mean you've heard about us?"

Squick's green-hatted head nodded emphatically. "Oh aye," he said with feeling and a huff. "I know all about the trouble you're making."

Fodder sighed deeply at the pixie's tone. "We're not trying to make trouble for the sake of it. If you'll let me explain..."

"I don't need an explanation, laddie," Squick cut in sharply. "You know what? I like you, and that's why I'm going to do you a favour and offer up yon advice. What you're doing? It won't work."

"But if you could see—" Fodder started to reply but another huff from the pixie cut him off.

"Lad, you need to listen," Squick retorted firmly. "I know what you're about. You think I'm deaf, dumb, and blind? I ain't heard nothing but you and yours for days. Everyone's talking about yon bold-as-brass

Disposables who've made off with the princess and are out to break with The Narrative, and while I admire the spirit of you, you must be seeing by now that the thing ain't there to be done." He shook his head. "You can change the details, but you can't change the world. You're making waves, but it's nothing up yonder there can't work around. Did you think there ain't been cock-ups before? Lines fluffed, accidents in fights? The Narrative most always finds a way like as it most always has; and when it can't, that's its business, not down to any of you. I've been around a long time, laddie, and I've seen many things and this, it ain't likened to end well for anyone if you ain't real careful. You're a good lad and I respect your guts—hell, I put them in yon belly meself!—but I think you're fighting a battle no bugger round here can ever win. Maybe one no bugger should win, either. And that's the truth of it."

"But we *are* making a difference!" Fodder wished his voice didn't sound so much like a plea, but there wasn't much help for it. "We've changed the story! Bumpkin hasn't got his princess! We've killed off Grim, and we killed off Thud…*twice!* Dullard is on our side instead of being a coward on theirs! Instead of chasing their marvellous Quest, the Merry Band have been forced to chase us."

"But what's changed, really?" Squick's eyebrows were knitted in a pointed frown. "The plot says they chase down a henchman of Sleiss, and they've been chasing you. True, it's for the girl over the jewellery, but the idea was the same, and you've brought the jewellery into it too. Yon Barbarian is back as his own *triplet,* Svenheid! Gort the Dwarf was down to die, and die he did. Prince Tretaptus of Mond has been recast as a lunatic seduced to the dark side, where yon Lord of Sleiss was meant to be. It's like I told you—the details have changed, but the world will stay the same. You can do what you like but The Narrative *adapts.* You can spice the Quest, but you'll never stop it."

Fodder gritted his teeth, the flood of frustration he'd felt at over-hearing his demotion back to henchman returning in a wave. But surely it couldn't be as hopeless as Squick seemed to think; there had to be some way.

"I'm not so sure." The quiet interjection was Dullard's. "I think it's more that we haven't changed the *right* detail yet."

Squick glanced down at the Rejected Suitor quizzically. "I don't know you well, laddie, so I ain't going to scold you," he told him, his voice low but firm. "But you're digging yourself deep into a whole heap of trouble with thinking like that. These ideas of yours are getting *dangerous.*"

"Dangerous for who?" Dullard cocked his head. "I mean, perhaps I misheard, but didn't you say that everyone was talking about us?"

The pixie eyed Dullard with the profound suspicion of one who knew he was being herded but hadn't quite grasped in what direction the predators lay. "Aye."

"So despite the efforts of the Taskmaster and the Courtiers, everyone, or at least a reasonable proportion of everyone, is aware that The Narrative has been defied?"

The potato face scrunched into a ball. "Now wait a minute, laddie."

"Which means they can't merely silence us and drag us off to prison anymore, can they?" Dullard spread his arms wide as he glanced around at his companions. "People would ask questions about where we'd gone. We'll have to be dealt with publicly, and that will give us a chance to explain our case. The idea will be out there."

"I said they're talking about you," Squick intervened sharply. "I didn't say yon folk *agreed* with what you've done. Most of them that's talking think you're barking loonies!"

"But once it's explained, they'll understand!" Dullard was getting excited. "Oh, I know there'll be a few like Poniard who'll take what we suggest the wrong way, but enough people will see the benefits, I'm sure of it! All we need is to find that one final detail that will force the Taskmaster into halting The Narrative and we've…"

His voice trailed away, but Fodder wasn't sure if it was his frantic gestures or the sudden, glacial weight of Squick's stare that had done the job. The moment Poniard's name had slipped out, the pixie's expression of weary tolerance had dropped like a stone. What replaced it wasn't pretty.

"Poniard?" The pixie's voice was dripping with venom. "Are you telling me…that *you* buggers were the ones who put yon pixie-killing ideas in his head?"

The silence was epic. It needed to be to contain such a potent cocktail of fury and whoops.

"I wouldn't say...*put*, per se." Fodder had to admire Dullard's bravery as he dipped a verbal toe into perilous silent waters. "But we did talk to him a few days ago. The discussion was about the possibility of his assisting us in the disruption of The Narrative but unfortunately, he did interpret a couple of our suggestions in a rather...different way. We're terribly sorry that this misunderstanding has caused you trouble but—"

"Misunderstanding?" There was something deeply ominous about the low hum of Squick's wingbeats.

"We didn't tell him to go out and kill you!" Fodder leapt in, desperate to quell the danger, but a cold feeling had lodged in his chest suggesting that it was already too late. "We were talking about something else, and he took it wrong! And it was all from him—you said yourself he'd done this before."

"Oh aye," Squick almost growled. "A few sticks chucked, a few names called by a fool as pissed as moonshine. I knew he hated me, but he never thought to do me any real harm, because he knew the rules and knew it weren't allowed. But you come along with your stupid ideas and put maybes in his head..."

"Squick..."

"And the next thing you know, the bugger's sober as a judge and chasing me down through the woods! Now thanks to you, yon loony will probably run off tattling to Strut that I've helped you, and d'you think he'll be kind, the mood he's in? And all 'cos one nutter listened to you! Didn't I say it? Didn't I say? *Dangerous!*"

"Squick, we're sorry!" Fodder tried again desperately. "We never meant—"

"And that's the most dangerous thing!" The pixie's furious voice echoed in the broken trees. "You don't mean a thing! You're blundering along without a clue for what you're fiddling with! Well, me, laddie, me, I *know* what you're fiddling with! I've *seen* what happens when a Quest goes—"

Fodder had never seen a jaw snap shut so fast. The furious pixie caught himself violently, half-spinning in the air as he cut his own sentence away. He shook himself abruptly.

Dullard too had spotted the hard-to-miss attack of discretion.

"When a Quest goes wrong?" he asked gently. "Is that what you were going to say? Has something like this happened before?"

"Just...never you mind what I meant!" Squick's snapped reply was rich with nervous discomfort as he turned to Shoulders, who was down to his last leather strap. "I'll fix yon miserable bugger's head, but then I want you gone, you hear? I don't want nowt more to do with your nonsense!"

But Dullard was not to be put off. "Because actually, there was something we were going to ask you, and I think it might be related to what you started to say," he declared. In the pit of Fodder's stomach, something uncomfortable was squirming, whispering that the look on Squick's face meant this was not the time to ask this question, not the time at all, and he should really speak up and stop the prince. But at the same time, nagging in his head, there was the need to know.

"We've been hearing a name mentioned, in passing, by the Officious Courtiers, you see." Dullard was persisting in his perilous line of questioning and Fodder couldn't decide if he was glad or sorry. "So we wanted to know—have you ever heard of something called the incident at Quickening?"

The look that crossed Squick's face would stay with Fodder for some time to come. He had never seen the pixie look so *haunted.*

"No," he whispered, his wings frantically beating as he slowly, almost unconsciously moved higher above them. "No... No, I ain't...I *can't...*"

Dullard's expression was wary but he kept pressing. "So you *do* know what it was?"

The pixie was breathing heavily. "Aye, I know. How could I forget? Those *poor...*" He shook himself violently as the haunted fear was swamped abruptly by a sudden fury. "That's it, is it? Taking us back there, ain't you? Why did I...?" He closed his eyes furiously. "*Dangerous!* That's it! I'm washing my hands of every one of you! It ain't safe! Like you I may, but help you I won't! You're not dragging me into yon madness!"

"Wait!" Shoulders's piercing cry broke across the glade—grasping his wobbling head by its final strap, he stumbled forward and dropped to his knees in front of the irate pixie. "What about my head?"

"No more!" Squick gestured sharply, the shake of his head a rapid blur. "No more help! I ain't getting involved! Not when that's where it leads!"

"But that's not fair!" Shoulders screeched. "It wasn't me who wound that loony up; I wasn't even there, and I don't care about their stupid Quickening! You've fixed Fodder's head and he's the one who did this! I'm innocent! Why won't you fix mine?"

"I fix you and you're good to go, ain't you?" was Squick's furious retort. "All good to go out there and make more trouble! But with you with no head, mayhap that'll slow things down! Mayhap that'll stop it!"

"But it *wasn't me!*" Shoulders actually wailed. "They're the stupid bastards. Why am I being punished?"

Squick cocked an eyebrow. "Trust me, laddie," he drawled harshly. "Leaving you in two bits is punishment enough for you *all!*"

"But what happened?" Fodder stepped in desperately in spite of the pixie's rage, for they were so close to knowing, so close to finding out... "What went wrong in that Quest that was so—"

"No!" The exclamation was violent. "No, I ain't talking about *The Chalice of Quickening,* you hear me? Not ever! Just stop yon dangerous playing about and go back to yon homes before it be too late! And *stay away from me!*"

Fodder half-started forwards, but it was already too late. In a blur of frantic purple, Squick rocketed into the trees and was gone.

There was a long, highly unpleasant silence. And then...

"You stupid, useless, big-mouthed, big-nosed git!"

It was only Flirt's dive that felled Shoulders before he could reach Dullard with murder in his eyes. The Disposable gave a furious scream as his hands clawed at the air that separated him from the horrified Rejected Suitor as though to rip it to shreds, but Flirt's arms had clamped down like twin vices, and after an instant or two of furious struggle, the final leather thong parted with a reverberating snap. With a slow and solemn thud, Shoulders's screeching head rolled forwards off his neck and landed with a dull splash in a pool of boggy liquid. Weighed by the helmet tied in place, it sank quickly from sight, leaving only a trail of angry bubbles in its wake.

Dullard stared at the shifting pool with a horrified fascination.

"Ummm...shouldn't we...retrieve him?" he ventured tentatively.

Fodder stared at the curling bubbles thoughtfully. They were still of some considerable size and quantity.

"I'd give him a minute or two to calm down," he suggested. "That is, if you value your eardrums." He stared grimly in the wake of the rapidly departed Squick. "And it's not like anybody around here's going to help you fix them."

He paused a moment, staring at the tumble of bubbles that continued to rise unfailingly towards the surface. Their sheer volume suggested things weren't going to be pretty when their source was retrieved.

They'd hacked off the only person capable of fixing Shoulders's hacked-off head back on, and in doing so had made Shoulders hacked off at Dullard. They'd had answers to this strange, teasing, half-mentioned incident at Quickening dangled tantalisingly in front of them and lost any chance of retrieving them. There was really only one thing left to say. So Fodder said it.

"Bugger."

* * *

Why would this blasted muck not come off?

Keeping himself discreetly away from his subordinate Priests, Strut the Officious Courtier stared down at the black, hardened mass that had solidified around his silken shoe before frantically rubbing it once more against the tree bark. The tight, dark mass failed again to shift, but it did scour away a small line in the surface of the trunk.

He closed his eyes for a moment, breathing deeply as he struggled to fight down the hysteria growing in his chest. He managed to reel it in, but it was a close-run thing.

He was the Taskmaster's taskmaster. His dignity mattered. He had seen them, Primp and the Priests and Trappers who aided him, snickering behind their hands as he'd staggered awkwardly along. He could not afford to lose face now. He had to keep control.

Especially since...

Under his breath, he stifled a groan. They'd been so close. So *close.* How could they have lost them again? And it was growing dark—already the Merry Band were having to make camp, and what if there were no more leads to follow come the morning? What was there to do but keep hunting, keep the Merry Band circling, and try to track those damnable rebels down?

There had to be something more he could do. Something to rein this madness in, something to take back control.

"Been looking for you."

Strut was not accustomed to being startled. Under the circumstances, he restrained the urge to jump a foot in the air with remarkable fortitude as he turned to find, to his extreme discomfort, the dark clothes and furious-looking face of Poniard the Assassin. The Realm's most highly trained killer looked surprisingly battered and he had one arm wrapped intensely around the clenched fist of the other. Strut blinked. There was something very strange about the way that arm was...

He snapped himself back to attention.

"Poniard," he stated flatly. "I don't recall sending for you yet. What are you doing in this forest?"

The oddest look flashed across the Assassin's hooded face. He glanced briefly down at his strange arm. "Forget that!" he snapped. "You need help, right? You've got rebels knocking about, haven't you? Disposables and some bar wench and that stupid poncy prince? And them dragging some princess around?"

Strut's attention was immediately grabbed. "You've seen them?"

"Oh *yes.*" The Assassin hissed the word. "I know where they are— or leastways where they were about four hours back." His dark eyes gleamed. "And I want to help you catch them. I want to cause them pain."

Strut grabbed the man's arm, fighting back a surge of unnatural glee. "Tell me everything you know."

Poniard grimaced. "They took something precious away from me. You promise me I get to hurt them?"

"I promise." Strut felt a wellspring of satisfaction surge through him. "In fact, as soon as you've told me, there's something I was hoping to ask your opinion on. A small matter of *punishment.*"

* * *

Camp that evening was, to put it mildly, excruciating. A protracted dunking in swamp water had not, as Fodder had hoped, dampened down Shoulders's anger about the prospect of a permanent future as two halves of the man he had been—instead, it had congealed his rage into a series of sour, hard-edged observations on his situation that was, in many ways, worse. Fodder, along with Flirt, was accustomed to Shoulders's acidic brand of grouching and, accurate as Squick's prediction that his suffering was the suffering of them all was proving to be, the two denizens of Humble Village were at least used to it.

The problem was that Shoulders's ire was aimed fairly and squarely at Dullard.

It wouldn't have been so bad if the prince had fought back. But Fodder could tell by the look on his face that Dullard was blaming himself for his slip just as much as Shoulders was. His initial, flustered attempts at an apology—offered just after Shoulders's head had been fished out—had been met with a stream of vitriolic rage, and his anxious efforts to re-secure the Disposable's head had been violently rebuffed. Alarmed and repentant, the prince had settled for accepting the abuse in meek, penitent silence: his head bowed, his lip bitten. But this reaction had only made things worse as Shoulders had screamed at him inexplicably about being "a bloody deformed rabbit" and stomped off into the trees as best he could.

Wearily, Fodder had suggested that getting out of the Wild Forest and away from The Narrative might be a good idea. Nestled as it was in foothills on the boundary between the Wild and Mystical Forests—so as to offer both the sinister and wistful options to a discerning Narrative visitor—the artfully constructed Ruined City felt like a good enough place to hide out. He'd hoped, vaguely, that the careful and luckily free-of-any-hint-of-Narrative-presence walk might give Shoulders time to calm down, but by the time they had halted for the evening amongst the mossy, overgrown stone walls and settled down to start a discreet fire, the atmosphere would have blunted a hacksaw.

And that, of course, was when the trouble started.

"But it's all his fault!" Small, skittering creatures whose whole existence had evolved in order to dislodge stones and cause the unwary traveller to turn sharply at the unexpected sound, scattered appropriately at Shoulders's screech of rage. "You want me to pretend it's not? Maybe I should bugger off and hide myself in the trees, would *that* make you happy? Maybe I should sit there milksop and cowed like, like...*rabbit-boy* over there! Maybe I should stroll around full of *honestly* and *goodness me* and *terribly, terribly sorry*! Then everything I do would be right even when it's *stupid!*"

The last word echoed against the crumbling walls and tree trunks that encircled them as Dullard's eyes rose slowly to face his attacker.

"I *am* sorry," he replied, his voice quiet, but there was a hint of tremble edging its way through the undertone. "I really don't know what else you want me to say."

"I don't want you to *say* anything," was the truculent retort. "Your mouth's done *enough* damage for one day."

Dullard's shoulders sagged. Beside him, Fodder saw Pleasance's eyes stray to her fellow Royal's miserable expression, but oddly, he found himself unable to read her porcelain features.

"You know that if I could undo what happened," Dullard ventured forth once more, but the force of Shoulders's stormy rage bashed his tentative ship against the rocks at once.

"Well, you *can't*." The Disposable's voice was mordant. "Not unless you've got time travel locked up in your vaunted vault of hobbies. Watch out, the end of the world is nigh, we've found something the right Royal genius can't fix!"

"Shoulders, come on." It was Flirt's turn to step in. "You're not being fair."

"Fair?" The tone with which the word was expelled suggested to Fodder that, bad as the squall had been, the gale was yet to come. "Yeah, of course! Why waste precious worry on someone you've known since you were an Urchin when you can stand up and defend some stupid Royal pillock you've known for a week? We must be fair to him! Being fair to me doesn't matter, does it? Was it fair for me to get dragged into this mess without even being asked? Is it fair that I'll get punished when I didn't even want to come? Is it fair that I've lost my head when all those to blame around me are keeping theirs? Is it...?"

"Probably not." The crisp intervention sucked the words from Shoulders's lips like a maelstrom as every head in the dell turned in sharp astonishment. From her position against the tree trunk, Princess Pleasance ignored the stares and regarded the beheaded Disposable with regal disdain. "But as you and your companions have gone to great lengths to tell me, shouting about it like a petulant child is hardly going to help."

For a moment, Shoulders could only work his mouth in guppy-like silence, and that moment was enough for Pleasance to pounce once more. "Is it fair that I was dragged into this mess without even being asked?" she echoed sarcastically. "Is it fair that I have had my life and my dreams snatched away? You have an option. Were you to surrender yourself in exchange for your friends, I'm sure Strut would be most understanding."

Shoulders's expression filled with horror. "I wouldn't do that!" he spluttered. "What do you think I am?"

"I think you are an extremely disagreeable and unpleasant man." Pleasance's clipped retort snapped like a bowstring. "And since you will not take the way out you have been offered, I strongly suggest that you stop blaming everyone else for your woes, bite your tongue, and make the best of it. Now if you'll excuse me…Prince Dullard?"

Dullard, who had been staring at Pleasance in open-mouthed astonishment, closed his jaw with a snap and swallowed. "Yes?" he replied uncertainly.

"I have a need to stretch my legs. If you would be so good as to escort me?"

"Umm…yes! Yes, certainly!" Dullard scrambled awkwardly to his feet and pulled her delicately upright. Without so much as a glance in Shoulders's direction, Pleasance turned sharply on her heel and stalked away into the ruins with a bewildered Dullard trailing in her wake.

There was a long moment of silence. Shoulders was still staring absently at the spot where Dullard and Pleasance had been a moment before, and Flirt was regarding him with a thoughtful raised eyebrow. Fodder's brow creased. Maybe…

"You know, mate," he offered gently. "She may have a point."

The instant darkening that washed over his friend's features told Fodder at once that he had misjudged.

"A point?" he intoned furiously. "So you're even siding with the *princess* against…"

"Oh for the love of—!" Flirt cut off her exclamation in favour of taking a deep, calming breath. Her hands extended peacefully out in front of her, she turned to face Shoulders once more.

"Look," she said, far more mildly than Fodder had been expecting. "Shoulders, we're not against you, are we? It's just…you do make it very hard sometimes."

"Oh I'm *so sorry* if I…"

"Shoulders." This exclamation carried a little more force—yet again, the Barmaid took a calming breath before continuing. "Let me finish, will you?" she continued gently. "As I was saying—I'm sorry if I've been grumpy with you lately, and I'm sorry if you feel we've dragged you into this mess against your will. But…" She paused for a moment, apparently choosing her words with some care. Fodder didn't blame her. She was venturing into treacherous waters once more. "You don't make it easy, do you? I've wanted an adventure like this all my life, and Fodder and Dullard are both fulfilling dreams too. But you do have a way of…well, *sucking the joy* out of things. *Please don't yell,*" she added hurriedly, her hands raised in a soothing manner once more as Shoulders's lips parted. "Just listen, please. Nobody here is against you. We are on your side. We're your friends. I only wish you'd listen to us long enough to believe that." She swallowed hard. "So please don't take these things out on us. And Dullard is obviously sorry, isn't he? He can't take back what he said to Squick, so what good is making him suffer for it going to do? Yes, it's a bad situation and we do feel sorry for you. But bickering amongst ourselves isn't going to help, is it?" She risked a slight smile. "Okay. That's what I wanted to say."

Shoulders was regarding the Barmaid with a tight jaw and narrow eyes. Fodder could tell that he was itching to snap and was quite impressed that Flirt's moderate tone had sucked the wind out of those particular sails. He filed the approach away as potentially useful.

"I don't know about sucking the joy from things." When the reply came, it was moody and ill-tempered but not delivered at volume. "I haven't seen much joy about to be sucked."

"Have you been looking?" Flirt offered softly.

Shoulders's jaw hardened. "I didn't ask to be here, you know," he said, though the anger in his tone sounded to Fodder's ears rather more forced than the effortless rage of earlier. "I was happy where I was."

"Were you, though?" Fodder's lips had already parted but again Flirt beat him to the punch. "Whenever you came round to the Archetypal Inn after a fight, it was always Clank and your head, arms up a tree, innards in a ditch. Did you really enjoy that? Because it never seemed like it to me."

This time Shoulders did snap back. "It's better than a dungeon!"

"And maybe if Fodder's right, we can find something better than both." Flirt gave a genuine smile. "And if we don't, at least we will have had a joyful adventure we can mull over in those long, boring hours on the rack."

Silence rolled over the ruins once more. Shoulders's loose head continued to stare.

And then with jerky abruptness, the Disposable lifted his head awkwardly in one hand.

"I want this over," he huffed at his two friends. "One way or the other, I want my bloody life back. Find a way or *I will.*"

It was not the most emphatic storming-off that Fodder had ever seen. Even if he'd suspected that Shoulders's heart was in it, the effect would still have been ruined by the odd, rocking motion of his gait and the fact his head was tucked under his arm.

Fodder glanced at Flirt. She glanced back and risked a smile.

"Well," she said, faux cheerfully. "That went as well as could be expected, didn't it?"

Fodder folded his arms as he leaned back against a convenient tree. "I don't know if it'll make a difference."

Flirt laughed out loud. "If it did and Shoulders stopped moaning, the world would shudder and grind to a halt. I'm not expecting miracles, am I?" She sighed. "I really wish he'd loosen up a bit. He's like a millstone round the neck sometimes." She shook her head. "It's no wonder he can't get himself together In Narrative, is it? All that negativity swirling around is probably killing his willpower stone dead." She pulled a moody face. "It certainly killed any chance we had of getting any more about this Quickening incident out of Squick, didn't it?"

Fodder sighed deeply. "I don't think we were ever onto a winner there. He was already too angry. And we do know a bit more than we did. We know it was a Quest."

"*The Chalice of Quickening.*" Flirt's tone grew thoughtful. "I've never heard of that one."

"It must be old," Fodder agreed. "Very old, by the sound of it. And something happened."

"Insightful, that," Flirt remarked with a sardonic smile. "And we know a bit more, don't we? We know it didn't go to plan, like this one. Something went wrong. Badly wrong."

"He said it wasn't safe." Fodder frowned, rolling the phrases used by the pixie around in his mind. "And he looked very upset about it, almost haunted." He sighed. "I wonder what it means."

"Might be worth knowing," Flirt said pointedly. "For good or for bad. If it's enough to scare the Courtiers and Squick that much, even the threat of it might help us, and if it's something we could use, that's even better, isn't it? We need all the help we can get when it comes to going up against The Narrative."

The words reminded Fodder abruptly of his earlier conversation with Dullard.

"Actually, I meant to say: You remember that chat Dullard kept trying to have with us during the chase?" At Flirt's nod, he pressed on. "Well, I let him finish while we were hiding, and he's come up with a decent theory."

He went on to explain the ideas about Narrative defiance that he and the prince had discussed on the run. As he concluded, Flirt looked thoughtful.

"It makes sense," she agreed. "Mind you..." She chuckled. "It's a good thing you didn't mention this when Shoulders was here. Can you imagine what he'd say when he found out Dullard reckoned he couldn't beat The Narrative because he didn't know his own mind?"

Fodder gave a mock wince. "Not without pain I can't. But he told us to find a way or he will, and since he's already denied he'd ever turn us in, I'd say that means that he'll come around. Eventually."

"You reckon?" Flirt pulled a face.

"Yep." Fodder smiled. "And he didn't defy The Narrative, but he didn't obey it either. And that means that deep, deep down in Shoulders's mind, there might be a tiny bit of hope."

"The trouble is it's surrounded by hulking great heaps of raw stubbornness," Flirt pointed out. "Not to mention the pits of his pride. Even if he did come round to agreeing with us, do you really think he'd be willing to admit it?"

"He doesn't have to admit it to us," Fodder said with a shrug. "He only has to admit it to himself."

"Hmmm..." Flirt did not look convinced. "Maybe. But sorry, Fodder, I reckon he's about as likely to back down as the princess is."

Fodder's mind flashed back to Pleasance's unreadable face as she watched Dullard's humiliation, to the glimpse of open eyes as she was carried through the woods away from The Narrative she claimed to long for, to how she had leapt to the defence of the captor she claimed to loathe not once now, but twice. Even a day ago, he'd have been all in favour of continuing with their gung-ho efforts to see the Quest's love interest bite the Narrative dust, but the look on her face was lingering in his mind as vividly as her defence of Dullard was ringing in his ears. A dead Heroine would certainly thwart the Quest. But what damage could a rogue Heroine do?

It was a massively long shot, the kind that could generally only be pulled off by a Narratively-guided archer. He wasn't even completely sure it was worth taking aim. But just maybe...

"Well," he remarked. "You never know."

* * *

"He had no right to speak to you like that."

Lost in a world of quiet self-deprecation, Dullard's head jerked up sharply at the sound of Pleasance's voice. After her unexpected and probably undeserved leap to his defence at the camp, he had followed her exit wordlessly, encumbered by his guilt.

True to her form of not speaking with him unless forced to, the princess had, until now, made no more effort to begin a conversation than he had. And if he was honest with himself, Dullard had been grateful for that. For once in his life, he was in no mood to talk.

He still couldn't believe he had been so foolish. One rash, unguarded comment, and he had inflicted purgatory upon the one member of their party who was, essentially, blameless. He very well remembered his conversation with Shoulders down by the river only a few days before, of the Disposable's reluctance and bad temper at the turn his life had taken. The prince had, at that moment, quietly resolved to himself that he would find a way to help Shoulders appreciate the benefits of what they were doing. Once that way was found, he had been sure, Shoulders would be much happier in himself and his company. But that hardly seemed likely to happen when he was faced with an indefinitely headless future—a future, in a large part down to Dullard's misspoken words to Squick.

How could he blame Shoulders for being so angry after that?

Dullard probably would have continued his thoughts in much the same vein had Pleasance's quiet, somewhat defensive sentence not snapped him from his reverie.

He stared in surprise at his companion. Princess Pleasance was perhaps two yards in front of him as they wandered aimlessly along beside a row of ornate, half-tumbled, ivy-riddled columns—her shoulders stiffly set, her bound hands clasped in front of her, her eyes staring intensely away into the encroaching gloom of the ruins. She had not even glanced at him as she spoke.

"I beg your pardon?"

It was more surprise than lack of hearing that made Dullard request a reiteration. Pleasance nonetheless obliged.

"He had no right to speak to you like that," she repeated, her words clipped and sharp-edged, her gaze resolutely forwards. "That grubby Disposable has no respect whatsoever for rank."

Dullard quickened his pace, drawing alongside the princess as he glanced down at her pale, pinched expression warily. "I don't think it has much to do with rank," he replied quietly, inwardly wincing at the memory of Shoulders's harsh glare. "I believe it may be more to do with circumstances."

Pleasance gave a surprisingly ladylike snort. "I fail to see that circumstances warranted it either. The man is quite unreasonable."

Dullard sighed. Gratifying as it was that Pleasance finally appeared to be relenting in her previously hard-line hostility towards him, he couldn't escape the guilt of his slip of the tongue long enough to play along with her.

"I did cost him his head," he offered quietly.

"Is it your fault the ridiculous man got it cut off in the first place?" Pleasance retorted sharply, her eyes flashing in his direction before returning once more to their scrutiny of the darkness. "Of course not. And that pixie was never keen to help anyway. That Disposable was blaming you for his own inadequacies, and I don't see why you saw fit to sit there and take it."

"But if I hadn't mentioned Poniard or Quickening..."

"Oh, for goodness' sake!" Pleasance's abrupt halt caught Dullard by surprise—unconsciously, he took a step back as she whirled on the spot to face him, blonde hair swishing, blue eyes ablaze with fierceness as she thrust her bound hands with one wagging finger sharply in front of his face. "Grow a little backbone, will you? How can you call yourself Royalty when you won't even stand up for yourself against a grubby commoner? He is nothing but a nasty ball of unpleasantness and complaints, while *you*..." She paused, gulping in a mouthful of air before plunging resolutely onwards. "Perhaps you are no great looker, perhaps you are awkward and odd and persistently friendly to the point of irritation, but you are ten times the man he is! You're...you're *clever*, and you're quick and...and you can fight! I saw you against Poniard; not even Bold or Valiant could have done as well as you did! Why, from what I could see of it, you even held your own against Bumpkin and Clank—"

He saw the horror fill her eyes, saw her lips slap shut, but it was already far too late. The words were said.

Dullard stared at Pleasance. Pleasance stared back.

"You *were* awake." Dullard's words were a statement of fact. "On the beach and in the woods. You were awake the entire time." He hesitated, mindful of the frozen expression on the porcelain face in front of him, and offered a gentle prompt. "Weren't you?"

Pleasance's lips were quivering as she pressed them tightly together. Her eyes were fixed determinedly over his left shoulder. "I don't know what you're talking about."

The prince smiled gently. "I think you do."

Pleasance's jaw hardened truculently. "I'm sure you have an excellent memory," she returned crisply. "And if you check with it, I think you'll find I've told you several times that I was out cold."

"I'm sorry to contradict you, but you did admit a moment ago that you saw me fight Bumpkin and Clank."

"No, I didn't."

"I think you'll find you did."

Pleasance's glare could have seared the bark from the trees. "Just because I was foolish enough to give you a compliment doesn't mean you have the right to be smug with me. I am your superior in breeding and circumstance! That I consider you marginally better than dirt does not mean—"

"You're trying to change the subject, aren't you?"

"—that you can talk to me like a child! Simply because I happen to possess the compassion to pity a joke of a prince such as yourself—"

"But it's not going to make me forget what I heard, I'm afraid."

"—that I have a sensitivity and consideration for your feelings that you seem to be sorely lacking—"

"So don't you think this denial is a bit futile?"

"—does not mean that you can take advantage of my good nature to bully me! You are nothing more than—"

"You were awake and we both know it."

"—an ill-bred, freakish, unnatural, discourteous, treacherous—"

"I can wait to discuss this as long as you can berate me, you know. And you'll probably feel better once you get it off your chest."

"—disrespectful, smug, obnoxious excuse for Royalty! I can't believe I was so foolish as to breathe your foul name in the same sentence as the likes of Bold and Clank and Valiant and—"

"Bumpkin?"

The torrent of abuse slammed to a halt. Pleasance's mouth worked furiously as she stared at the quietly impassive Dullard, standing with his arms crossed and his expression patient. He met her suddenly vulnerable eyes with his own and softly smiled.

"You *can* tell me," he said quietly. "I'll listen. I'm probably the only one who will."

For a moment, Pleasance stared up at him once more, rooted to the spot like a frightened animal, eyes wide and body trembling.

And then she turned and bolted.

He did not chase her. He did not need to. Instead, he moved quietly through the fading twilight in the direction she had fled, feet crunching softly amongst the leaf litter as he paced the path of her flight—past the ivy-curled columns and into a small, walled garden wild with overgrown flowers and rampant trees that far exceeded the limited space they had to spread. A pond swamped by lily pads lurked half-hidden in the corner. Beside it, a blue-clad figure sat, all but slumped against the tumbled remains of a stone bench, staring down at the round green leaves as though from a thousand miles distant. Her blank stare did not waver as he sat beside her.

"You were awake," he repeated softly.

Her eyes never left the water. But gently, near imperceptibly, the blonde head nodded.

"The whole time too. On the beach and in the forest."

Again, absent and almost unconscious, came the nod.

He was sure he understood now. But she was so close; she had to say it, to admit it to herself.

"So forgive me for asking," he said, his voice hushed and coaxing, "but why didn't you scream for help? Why didn't you run back into The Narrative and leave us to our fate?"

Silence melted over the garden, broken only by gentle gusts of wind against the trees. Shadows cast against the last hints of light began to thicken into darkness.

"Because Bumpkin was there."

It was barely a whisper, half swallowed by the rustling of the leaves overhead. But Dullard heard it as clearly as if it had echoed through the mountains.

Her voice was so different. Stripped of its stridency and verve, Princess Pleasance sounded like a lost and bewildered young girl. Tentative and careful, Dullard laid the very tips of his fingers against the bonds around her wrists and leaned a half inch closer.

"Go on," he prompted.

"If I'd opened my eyes," she said softly, "that would have been the beginning. The romantic first gaze, the echoes of destiny, the feeling of belonging and home and all those other trite phrases The Narrative trots out when a Hero and Heroine meet." Her voice rose slightly as the strength of her emotion kicked in behind it. "And I remember my mother and my cousin and my sister telling me how *wonderful* it was going to be, that first moment of Narrative that fills you up with love and belonging and seals the bond that means this man will be your love In Narrative and beyond it. But as I was lying there on that beach with The Narrative whispering to me to wake and gasp and fall in love, all I could feel was his clammy, horrible hands on my skin and his awful breath against my cheek—it stank! I don't know what he'd been eating but..." She gave a tight, frantic giggle and swallowed hard, clenching her fists into one tight ball as her eyes strayed for a brief, fleeting instant to Dullard's fingers. "The Narrative doesn't mention bad breath and clammy hands; it's gentle touches and wistful stares. There was supposed to be elation, they said. It was supposed to be wonderful and glorious and *right*. It was supposed to wipe away my doubts about him, my first beautiful scene with my love and future husband...I'd waited so long..."

And then slowly, almost painfully, her head lifted, her face turned, and she met his eyes with a gaze so full of fear and hurt it nearly knocked him over.

"But it *felt wrong*," she whispered. "There was nothing there. I was staring through my lashes at the love of my life and there was no joy or anticipation...I was uncomfortable, and I hated it. And The Narrative was pushing and pushing in my head and I knew that all I had to do was open my eyes completely and the elation would come..."

Her voice trailed away as her eyes dropped once more to her bound wrists and Dullard's soft touch against them.

"But," she muttered, partly to herself, "I couldn't do it. Because I realised it wouldn't be *my* elation at all."

"It would be Islaine's." Dullard hadn't meant to speak but the words slipped out of their own accord. To his surprise, Pleasance nodded vigorously as she raised her head once more.

"But I'm the one who'd have to live with it!" she exclaimed, her voice suddenly intense. "I'm the one who'd have to live with *him*. And do you know what? I don't like him. I *don't like Bumpkin*. Ha!" Her body jerked as she flung her head up and stared with a defiant smile at the darkening heavens. "There! I said it!" She gave another wild giggle. "And you know what else? When you stepped up on that beach and belted him one, it was all I could do not to leap up and cheer! I was so relieved! You were a traitor and my captor, and I was happier to see you than I was the man I'm meant to marry! What does that say about the future of my married life?"

Dullard was bright enough to spot a rhetorical question when he heard one. "So you ignored what The Narrative wanted and stayed down?" he probed instead.

"It wanted me to help him!" There was a vaguely manic note to Pleasance's voice now—with the dam of her emotional conflict broken, she seemed to be struggling to keep up with the flood of her own confession. "The Narrative wanted me to leap up and come to his aid. But I knew that I didn't want to help him; I wanted you to win! I knew I shouldn't feel that way but I just couldn't help it. The thought of those clammy hands and slobbery lips…"

The last of the flood waters passed abruptly, taking in their wake Pleasance's intense gabbling. Even as Dullard watched her silhouetted in the gathering darkness, he saw her shrink visibly back as reality stole once more into her mind and dampened down her surge of feelings. Her eyes dropped abruptly from the skies and fell once more towards the lily pond at her feet.

"I don't want to marry Bumpkin." Pleasance's voice, when it came, was subdued once more. "I can admit that. In Narrative or out of it, I don't want him anywhere near me."

Dullard smiled. "Then don't."

Pleasance's head snapped up. Dullard was startled by the sudden fire in her eyes.

"It's all right for you to say that," she retorted with a vengeance. "You and your Disposables! But do you really think the four of you are enough to change the fundamental facts of our way of life? You can trot out trite, pointless phrases if you like, but it won't change anything! Sooner or later, The Narrative will catch up with us, the Taskmaster will thwart you, and I will marry Bumpkin whether I want to or not. So what's the point in fighting it? That pixie was right. All I did on that beach was delay the inevitable. The moment The Narrative catches up with me, I'll be in love with a clammy-fingered, foul-breathed Boy of Destiny, and that'll be the end of it."

But Dullard was already shaking his head. "How can you say that after what you've seen?" he said, his tone soft but intense. "You've seen The Narrative denied; you've seen its wishes ignored."

"And I say again, that's all right for you!" Pleasance snapped back hotly. "But I'm not you! I'm a princess, *the* princess, and things are expected of me! How could I even consider letting my family down the way you have? How could I possibly ignore what The Narrative wants? It goes against everything I was born and raised for; it's an abomination!"

Dullard didn't even stop to think. "And marrying Bumpkin wouldn't be?"

If Pleasance's hands had been free, Dullard was fairly certain that she would have slapped him. He certainly felt her wrists twitch as she dragged her bound hands away from his touch, her expression both fierce and full of horror.

"How dare you?" she hissed. "Maybe I don't like Bumpkin! Maybe the thought of being his wife makes me feel sick to my core! But you have no right to judge me for honouring my obligation to my family! They raised me; they love me. I owe them this!"

Dullard's mind flashed back to the Palace and his life there, to the antiseptic, superficial affection that passed for family feeling, to the acid remarks and cruel banter. He could imagine how they would respond to an admission like this from the daughter they purported to love.

"Why?" he said.

"Why? *Why?* How can you even…" Pleasance glared at him once more, although lingering hints of vulnerability clung to the corners of her eyes. "I can't believe I admitted that to you," she declared coldly.

Dullard cocked his head. "Who else is there that you would admit it to?" he asked carefully. "Your mother? Your father? Your sister?" The three staccato winces were answer enough. "You're only angry because you're scared, you know, and you don't have to be. You aren't alone."

"You have no right," she almost spat.

"Probably not," Dullard conceded. "But believe it or not, I do care about what happens to you. You've admitted to me that you don't think you will be happy with Bumpkin, so how can I, in good conscience, stand by and watch you make yourself miserable? What kind of friend would that make me?"

"Friend!" Pleasance's snort was less ladylike this time around. "You think very highly of yourself!"

"I think very highly of you." Pleasance's mouth snapped shut at Dullard's mild retort. "Which is why I want to help you. Think of it this way…"

He paused, allowing himself to catch his breath and gather his thoughts as darkness finally closed in around them. The princess was a pale shape by burgeoning moonlight.

"You've already defied The Narrative. You may not have meant to, but you did." Pleasance made a half-noise of protest but stayed herself as Dullard moved on. "You found yourself in that moment. You admitted the truth of your own feelings and found the strength there to ignore the commands of The Narrative to rise and meet your destiny. Now, the obligation you feel to your family is commendable and a matter for your own conscience. But if you were to tell your family what you have told me, do you believe that they would be sympathetic? Would they understand and respect your wishes and your honesty?" Her silence was as telling as any reply. "If you don't want to be with Bumpkin, In Narrative or out, the choice, it seems to me, is very much yours. But only you can make it. It's your decision, but it *is* a decision. You do have a choice. You merely need to let yourself make it."

He felt rather than saw her eyes staring at his shadowy form in the darkness. The fire of moments before ebbed away into nothing.

"But what else is there for me to do?" the voice of the lost and vulnerable girl whispered out of the night air. "I'm a princess. I was raised to be a princess, and a princess has to marry the Hero. That's what I was born for. I don't know how to be anything else. If I don't marry Bumpkin, what am I? What's the point of me?"

"I don't know." Dullard chanced his arm, quite literally, as he reached out once more and rested his hand against her elbow. She flinched but did not pull away. "But I'd be happy to help you find out."

He couldn't see her expression, lost in the dark of night. But he could feel her lingering eyes.

"It's dark," she said suddenly. "We ought to go back to the fire."

"If that's what you want." Carefully, Dullard pulled himself upright and extended his hands towards her. "Here, let me help you."

Gently, he eased her to her feet and guided her as best he could through the maze of flowerbeds and hanging branches until they emerged together into the moon-washed street and its shadowy ivied columns. Pleasance's pale, half-visible face tilted towards him. Her expression was unreadable.

"Thank you," she said softly.

"You're welcome," he replied.

And then, without another word, they moved off into the darkened ruins towards the glow of the camp.

* * *

Shoulders was pacing.

To be more accurate, his body was pacing, up and down, turning clumsily but firmly as it strode a heavy-footed path between two crumbling wall lines. His head, resting crookedly in the gap between two weather-worn stones, was watching his body pace with a hypnotic intensity. He could feel the rage inside his mind bubbling, the irritation and the frustration, but one word was pounding like his heartbeat and echoing in his veins.

Enough. Enough. Enough.

He'd had *enough*.

It was all very well for them, for Fodder and Flirt and that *bloody big-mouthed bastard* Dullard, with their hopes and dreams and aspirations. He'd never hoped, he rarely dreamed, and he'd certainly never aspired in his entire life. They wanted this mess. *He didn't.*

He wanted it *over.*

Over, over, over, over…

Over to *what?*

The quiet thought invaded and somehow, in spite of the angry shouting that roared in the rest of his head, it echoed far more profoundly. And as it poked at him, some distant, half-drowned-out corner of his brain had to concede it had a point—where would *over* take him? To a dungeon? To be made a messy example of? Or right back to the everyday grind of life in muddy gutters as Clank sent his head flying off into the undergrowth without a moment's respect for his feelings...

Violently, he forced the thought away, clenching his jaw as he dragged his body out of the jerking, badly controlled stumble the distraction had driven him into. He resisted a sudden urge to summon his body back over to slap himself across the face.

Never mind the details. He wanted it over. Just...over.

But details matter, pressed the whisper. *You want it over. But not in a bloody dungeon or speared up on a castle gate!* Which meant...which meant...

Shoulders felt his teeth grind as his jaw rubbed against the stony resistance of the wall.

Which meant the only way out he had was *their* way.

Fodder and Flirt had been his friends for his entire life. Conceding to help them shouldn't have felt like a wrench, but after all they'd bloody well put him through, they didn't bloody deserve it! And he didn't even want to think about *rabbity bloody* Dullard...

But over was *over.* And to make that happen, there needed to be a plan.

Kill the princess In Narrative. Even in his manic state, the thought was enough to bring a smile to Shoulders's face. Pleasance had been a noisy, irritating thorn in his side for what felt like an eternity and picturing that moment, the look on that pale, haughty face as her precious Quest fell down around her ears... And of course, bloody Dullard was forever trying to persuade them to let her off, and seeing his reaction to her reaction could only be a bonus.

Kill the princess. Slice her, dice her, find a way.

And it had to *matter.* It couldn't be a death that a picky Narrative could miraculously reverse. Head away from shoulders, body lost or beyond repair or...

A distant thought chimed in the back of his head. Flirt, Fodder, and Dullard, gathered at that stupid cave after they'd bothered to wander back to find him and the princess, blathering on about what they'd heard Strut say about how important it was that...

His body froze. He felt the grin that spread across his cheeks. Oh yes. Oh yes, that was absolutely *perfect.*

It took only a moment to summon grasping hands to lift his head before he sent himself staggering awkwardly back in the direction of the campfire.

He'd said he'd find a way and he'd found one. Let them object to this!

* * *

"Well, we don't have a better plan, do we?"

There was a frankness to Flirt's expression that didn't fill Fodder with great hope. He sighed.

The conversation between the Disposable and the Barmaid had not gone quite how Fodder had hoped. When he'd suggested that Pleasance did seem to be winding back her resistance in the face of Dullard's kindly assault, Flirt had been frankly incredulous and dismissed his suggestion of joining the campaign to recruit her out of hand. And when Fodder had hinted gently that it might be beneficial to hunt down a plan that didn't involve wiping her out, Flirt's latest retort had offered no encouragement either.

"It was just a thought," he offered wearily. "I can't believe you haven't noticed it too. She's weakening; I'm sure she is."

Flirt's snort carried with it the strong suggestion that she didn't agree. "You couldn't weaken Princess Pleasance with a twenty-foot battering ram. Fodder, I'm sorry, but I think it's in your head. Our best option is still to kill her off."

Fodder sighed again. "I know you're probably right. But I thought it might be worthwhile to try and find some way to get our point across that doesn't involve butchering the princess."

A pale shape at the edge of his vision killed his sentence hurriedly. For, standing in the shadows at the perimeter of their camp, Princess Pleasance was staring at him.

Fodder couldn't help but notice that there was an odd cast to her pale features as she and Dullard stepped back into the circle of firelight. Her eyes had fixed upon him and for once, he could see an unexpected turbulence beneath the blue depths. A step behind, Dullard was watching her carefully, his eyes thoughtful and his expression cautious. It was the face of a man carrying a tower of delicate ornaments down an uneven staircase.

Something had happened. That much was—

"Did I hear you correctly?" The clipped, terse tone of the princess's voice quelled the maelstrom in her eyes. Her blue gaze, fixed on Fodder, became unnervingly intense as echoes of firelight danced over her face. Dullard looked at her sharply.

Fodder blinked. "Ummm, sorry?" he offered.

"You." The word was almost a slap. "You said you wanted to find a way out of this without getting me killed."

Fodder could feel Flirt's accusing gaze against the side of his head. "I was only considering options," he hedged.

But Pleasance's expression was suddenly ardent, her features tight, and her eyes were those of a woman groping for a treacherous lifeline.

"Then that's easy!" she proclaimed. "Take me back home!" Her eyes bored into him. "Take me home right now, and you have my word that nothing bad will befall you. I'll put in a good word for you, all of you! I'll talk to Strut, tell him to let you go back to your old roles with no recriminations! In fact, I'll get you better roles, guaranteed speaking parts in the minutiae! You can go back to doing what you do best, Dullard can take up a new sideline in villainy for this Quest, and everything will be exactly as it's supposed to be! I'll make it happen! Take me home!"

Dullard was staring at Pleasance with a strange mix of horror and disappointment. "Pleasance…" he half-started, but the princess wheeled on him instantly, one long-nailed finger thrust under his nose.

"My choice!" she screeched. "You said that, you said it! This is *my choice*! I want it so none of this ever happened! I want to go home!"

"But…"

But Pleasance had already turned away from him, wheeling back on Fodder with a wild, nearly pleading expression on her face.

"It wouldn't be difficult!" she exclaimed desperately. "We aren't far from Maw the Dragon's cave here; it's only in those mountains! You said yourself the importance they've put on that scene when you came back this morning; I heard you! Let…" She seemed to choke for a moment but steeled her shoulders and forced herself to carry on. "Let Bumpkin save me from him as he's supposed to save me! I'll make sure you don't get

punished. I'll tell them I won't come back if they don't let you go free!"
Her eyes darted rapidly to Dullard but dragged themselves hurriedly
away before he could catch her eye. "It'd be so easy if you'd—"

"She's right there."

The abrupt voice cut off Pleasance's rambling sentence cold.
Grasping his head awkwardly but with care at shoulder height, Shoulders stepped out of the shadows. He was grinning.

Fodder wasn't sure he liked the look on his friend's face. Surely he
wasn't saying...

"You want to give up?" For the sake of friendship, Fodder managed
to make it a question rather than a statement. "You want to take her
offer?"

Shoulders's violent snort was as telling as Flirt's had been.

"'Course not!" he retorted disdainfully. "You think I'm stupid,
mate? Even if she's not lying through her teeth—she can draw whatever
promises she likes from Strut, but I'm not thick enough to believe for a
second the bugger would keep them once he's got her back. No." He
rocked his head sideways in an awkward, manual approximation of a
shake. "Much as I hate to say it, and I do hate to say it, I've been thinking
and I think you're right: the only way out of this mess is your way. And
that means going back to the plan." His smile was nearly predatory as
Pleasance shrank back. "We want her killed off, nice and easy,
absolutely no returning, right? Well, she's given you the answer."
Shoulders's eyes gleamed by the light of the flickering fire. "The same
answer I came up with just now! Because I vote that tomorrow morning
we head up into these mountains and wait for The Narrative to show up.
And when it does, we feed her to the Dragon."

* * *

"No, no, no! Get your filthy hands off me, you monster! Do you think
I'm going to sit here nice and docile while you appalling, maggoty
excuses for human beings drag me off to feed me to a slavering beast?
Let me go! I won't take it, I won't...*mmph!*"

With a dexterity surprising in one whose head was resting on a tree
stump three yards away, Shoulders's hands finally succeeded in
securing the previously abandoned gag around Princess Pleasance's

mouth. Pleasance, her golden locks dishevelled and her blue eyes wild, glared at him with the force of a cloudburst but Shoulders's shoulders gave a shrug as his body sauntered quite cheerily back to where his head was waiting. His lips were whistling.

"This is going to be a thing of beauty," he muttered blithely as he lifted his head and cradled it within his arms, wandering past the watching Fodder with an actual smile touching his lips. "All the kicking and the screaming and the insults—it'll be worth it to see those big, chomping jaws come roaring down and *snap!*" He tilted his head wistfully off towards the grey skies overhead. "No more princess! The Narrative will have to call it a day and this whole sorry mess will be over...."

Pleasance's shoulders slumped noticeably. The defiance in her eyes melted into something much more akin to fear.

There it was again. The same unpleasant jab that had stabbed at Fodder the night before as he'd watched Shoulders stampede over Dullard's reticent protests and his own misgivings with Flirt's support and the strength of his own manic fervour. The same sharp pinprick that had nicked him again as he'd permitted Shoulders to restore the hysterical Pleasance's gag when she had refused to calm down following the reiteration of the plan at breakfast. This was not something he'd expected to feel after days of insults and pain from that walking irritation they'd kidnapped—what felt like Quests ago—but the feeling was indisputably there and making itself felt.

Guilt.

He felt guilty. He felt bad.

He was frank enough to admit that a part of it was the loss of the long shot, but he was also honest enough to acknowledge some human feeling for the princess had started to waft in as well. His eyes drifted involuntarily to Dullard. The Rejected Suitor was extinguishing the fire with silent care. Indeed, he had hardly spoken a word since breakfast, when—despite admitting that yes, he knew the Most Savage Mountains well, and yes, he could guide them to the Perilous Pass that led to the Dragon's lair—he had braved Shoulders' fervour once more and expressed his misgivings about the new plan. But his attempt to articulate what he viewed as the injustice of the situation had fallen on

Shoulders's spectacularly deaf ears.

"Oh, don't be so wet!" the headless Disposable had exclaimed with a dismissive wave of his hand. "It's not like it'll kill her, is it?"

Dullard's expression was probably best described as an elongated wince. "But being eaten by a dragon—it can't be easy to put yourself back together after that. Is it even possible?"

"Of course it is." Shoulders half chuckled. He'd been unnaturally cheerful ever since his master plan had been reluctantly approved. "Haven't you ever wondered why we have the same cow for dinner every week? One of the Duty Pixies pulls it back together and replaces the bits we've digested. Simple."

"I'm sorry, I've never really had much to do with the livestock. But a person..."

Shoulders had pulled a face that had told Fodder exactly where his mind had drifted to. It was a place that Fodder had spent several Quests trying to remove from his own.

"Oh, it's been done," Shoulders had replied grimly. "To me, as it happens. Three or four Quests back, I was eaten by the ravaging Swamp Monster during an ambush gone wrong." He glanced up at Fodder. "Remember, mate?"

Fodder had winced. "I try not to. Do you have any idea how unpleasant it is to sit there and wait for someone you know to be reconstituted from a pile of Swamp Monster marsh dung?"

Shoulders's glare had been incredulous. "Not as bad as sitting there *being* the pile of bloody swamp dung!"

Fodder had raised an eyebrow. "You told me you didn't feel a thing between the swallow and being woken by Squick after the rebuild. You said it was like floating!"

"Yeah, but there was the swallow first!" The tone of Shoulders's voice had almost been one of relish. "You don't know how it feels to see that great gob descending on you, to feel the tingly crunch of those huge jaws as they munch away on your poor, helpless body, the rough, sloppy feel of that massive tongue as you get pulled to pieces and shoved towards the vile infinity of the *throat*..."

At which point, Princess Pleasance had erupted into hysterics and the conversation had been over.

Fodder had not missed the look of both concern and reproach that had graced Dullard's ungainly features, and the genuine fear in the eyes of the princess was not helping. Killing off the princess In Narrative had been their aim and their goal for nearly as long as they'd had one. So why did the idea of feeding her to a dragon suddenly make him feel so uncomfortable?

"I really don't think this is the right thing to do, you know."

Fodder started sharply back into the present. Lost in his thoughts, he hadn't heard Dullard's approach. He glanced up to find the prince stood by his side, his pack slung over one shoulder, wearing the same uncertain look as he stared absently over at the tree against which Princess Pleasance was slumped.

Fodder looked away, trying to avoid following his gaze to the place where guilt was brewing.

"Shoulders is right," he managed, hoping he sounded more convinced than he felt. "We've got to get this wound up, and killing the princess In Narrative is still our strongest option. And seeing her eaten is hardly something The Narrative can fix up, is it?"

But Dullard was shaking his head. "I'm sorry but I have some serious reservations. Quite aside from the obvious distress the idea is causing Pleasance, I met Maw the Dragon while I was exploring these mountains following some rich geological seams. And whilst he is a pleasant chap, as enormous, fire-breathing monstrosities go, he's not—how to put this kindly?—he's not the brightest person I've ever met. Stomping, roaring, and burning things are his forte, and philosophical questions about the meaning of our life and standing up for our independence are likely to go rather over his head. He has his routine and he's comfortable with it. I'm just not sure he'll be willing or even able to defy The Narrative for us."

Fodder pulled a face. "He'll get the idea of being able to win, though, won't he? Actually getting to eat the princess instead of being thwarted?"

Dullard shrugged. "I honestly don't know. But I'm not convinced."

Fodder sighed. "The trouble is we don't have a better plan right now. We have to try something, and this is our best shot."

"But is it?" Dullard's voice was suddenly impassioned. "Because ever since we spoke to your friend Squick—"

"I'm not sure he's my friend anymore."

Dullard winced but ignored the interjection. "—I've had this nagging feeling that we're missing something important. What he said about The Narrative finding ways to compensate for whatever we do…" He shook his head. "By going to the Dragon, we're obeying The Narrative. We're taking the princess exactly where the story needs her to go. The Narrative will have fewer things to try and compensate for if something goes wrong—indeed, it'll be right where it needs to be to get back on track. We both heard them say how important that scene is and if it were to go against us, everything we've done will have been for nothing. Do you really think that's a good idea?"

It was a point. The nagging stab of guilt was joined by the persistent prod of concern.

"It's the best plan we've got," Fodder repeated, painfully aware of the doubt creeping into his voice. "What else are we supposed to do?"

Dullard took a deep, dramatic breath inwards. "Sit down and reason with Pleasance," he said.

Fodder blinked, trying to ignore the additional jab of the long shot. "Ummm," he managed, glancing at the gagged and sagging princess warily. "Dullard…"

"I know, I know!" The prince extended his hands carefully before him. "But before we came back to the fire last night, I honestly believe I was getting somewhere with her. She doesn't want to play the part and live the life that's been laid out for her, and she admitted that, but she's too afraid to back away because she can't imagine an alternative." He sighed. "Poor girl. I know you'll find this hard to believe, but if you get past the outer shell she throws at the world, I very much like her, and I really do think that if we take the Dragon—indeed, the whole idea of killing her—off the table, we may well be able to persuade her to join us. Consider what she could achieve as the princess if she set out to subvert The Narrative from within! She could reject Bumpkin, and what could they do? Force the marriage? She could refuse to ride to his rescue and leave him to his fate. She has a power to influence The Narrative that we lack, if we can persuade her to use it, for her own sake as much as ours. And I think we can. Because deep down, I get the feeling she wants to be persuaded."

Fodder stared thoughtfully at the prince before letting his eyes drift back to the slumped bundle of blonde hair.

"You really believe that?" he ventured. "It's crossed my mind, but, Dullard, it's one hell of a long shot."

Dullard nodded firmly. "I really do. We aren't being fair on her. Let's at least give her a chance before throwing her into the Dragon's den."

Fodder pursed his lips as he allowed the combination of stab, jab, and prod to ease him in this new direction. "If you're sure," he said, "then maybe we should—"

"Hey, Fodder!" Fodder jumped at Flirt's call as the Barmaid hurried over to where he and Dullard were lurking. Her expression was thoughtful, and one hand was resting on her sword hilt.

"I was thinking," she exclaimed, casting a quizzical look at Dullard's slight-but-distinct expression of disappointment at the interruption. She elected not to ask, however, and instead ploughed on. "It's all very well for us to head up and talk to the Dragon, but what about The Narrative?"

Fodder frowned. "We should be fine as long as they don't know which way we went. They're probably still messing around hunting for us in the forest."

"But we need them to know, don't we?" Flirt's expression was pointed. "It's well and good to say we'll get the princess eaten In Narrative, but what's the use if there's no Narrative for it to happen in?"

Dullard pulled a face. "She has a point," he offered quietly. "If you want this to work, we will have to find some way of letting The Narrative know where we're going."

"Hang on, that's stupid." Shoulders's interruption was typically blunt as he staggered over to join them, holding up his head. "No, it's worse, it's suicidal! You seriously think we should just let The Narrative know our plans? These are the Most Savage Mountains! You can't simply saunter up any route you'd like; it's the Perilous Pass or nothing! And they'll be on us before we're halfway there!"

"Shoulders is right." The Disposable seemed torn as to whether to glare or look smug at the prospect of Dullard agreeing with him. "If we alert The Narrative, the Merry Band will be hot on our heels almost at once. They'll be using the Perilous Pass as well, and it's too long and too narrow for us to clear on foot before they reach us on horseback. That's not a place I'd like to be caught in The Narrative. The potential for natural intervention via a landslip or an avalanche is massive."

"But we have to get to the Dragon before they do, or we won't be able to talk it into eating the princess!" Shoulders gestured to the pouch at Fodder's waist. "Can't we use the Ring of Anthiphion to jump there ahead of them?"

Fodder frowned wearily. "I've already explained it's only a piece of costume jewellery outside of The Narrative. We'd have to take it into The Narrative to use it." He shook his head. "If The Narrative is ready for it, we're buggered. I think we should keep the Ring for last resort."

"We need a delay." Dullard was tapping one finger against his nose. In spite of his reluctance, the prince couldn't resist an intellectual challenge. "We need to find a way to alert them as to our direction but leave ourselves enough leeway to arrive before them. Perhaps a physical barrier of some description."

"Mysterious powers," Flirt pointed out grimly. "They can blast or fly over pretty much anything we can put in their way, can't they?" The Barmaid paused, staring absently for a moment at her sword hilt. "What if I stay behind?" she offered suddenly. "I mean, I could distract them, couldn't I? Lead them on a merry dance for a bit and draw them the right way when you've had enough time."

"*No.*" Fodder surprised even himself with the force of the retort, but he couldn't help himself, unable to resist the glacial cold that had gripped his insides the moment he'd grasped what Flirt was saying. The memory of her dash into the forest, his fear for her, gripped him anew. "This isn't some Narrative plot demanding a noble sacrifice for the sake of the mission," he declared. "Flirt, there's no way that I'm leaving you standing poignantly behind to hold off the enemy hordes single-handed. And don't deny it because we both know that's what you meant. We've been through this. We're sticking together. No one gets left behind for some greater sodding good."

Flirt pursed her lips, regarding Fodder and his fierce expression for some moments. As the cold anger drained away, Fodder began to feel a slight prickle of discomfort under her scrutiny. But he made sure to hold his truculent ground. The cause was one thing, but not if it meant sacrificing his friends.

"Okay," she remarked at length. "No noble sacrifices. But what else can we do?"

"Tracks." Dullard's inexplicable explanation drew three pairs of curious eyes. "Tracks!" he repeated more insistently, waving his hands around as though the gesture would explain everything. "We can leave tracks for The Narrative to follow that lead towards the Perilous Pass. That should give us something of a head start until they find them." He paused, his eyes involuntarily darting in Pleasance's direction. "Or we could lay false tracks in that direction, sending them fruitlessly to the Dragon to waste that important scene, while we find another plan that doesn't involve—"

"But we'll never know when they're coming, will we?" Flirt pointed out, cutting off the rest of Dullard's deferent sentence. A sudden expression of alarm slipped over her features. "And besides—what about the tracks we've already left? We haven't exactly been covering up after ourselves, have we?"

There was a long moment of silence, laced with overtones of *uh-oh*. Tracks!

Fodder swore to himself in the privacy of his own mind. Of course they'd left tracks; there would be battle marks around Cackle's home and footprints in the dusty earth all the way up to the Ruined City and, lulled by the security of knowing that the aerial surveillance arm of his enemies had no desire whatsoever to actually find them, it hadn't even occurred to him to cover them up until now. But they were using Trackers, and if Poniard had gone running to Strut, they'd have a place to start. What if the Merry Band were to find them? What if they'd found them already?

"Well, I suppose it will save us backtracking to lay fresh ones," Dullard offered up with a distinctly uneasy attempt at a smile. Fodder didn't miss the guilt or the reluctance on his face as he helped them to plot the consumption of the princess in spite of himself. "A few decent scuff marks on a trail to the Perilous Pass, and we'll be well on our way."

"And what if they're well on their way already?" Shoulders

exploded. "You said yourself, we're buggered if they catch us in that pass!"

Dullard's sigh was epic. Slowly, deliberately, he pulled his spare grappling hook free of his pack and stared at it almost resentfully. He shot a glance in Pleasance's direction that was outright apologetic. "Actually," he said with reluctance, "the Perilous Pass takes a long and winding course, and as the crow flies, the Dragon isn't far from here. So if we absolutely must go to his lair, there is one quicker way."

* * *

"You *can't* be serious."

Shoulders's burst of cheer surged away like air from a punctured bladder. And as he stared up at Dullard's prospective quicker way, Fodder could see why.

Stretching upward was not so much a rock face as a wall. A three-hundred-foot wall. A three-hundred-foot wall of solid granite. A three-hundred-foot wall of solid granite with a vast overhang near the top.

The suggestion of going over mountains as the crow flew had been taken up without much thought. They'd deliberately left a set of scuffed and pointed tracks up to the narrow neck that led towards the Perilous Pass on the off chance of potential surveillance, before following carefully in Dullard's wake as he led them over unyielding and trackless rock to a mountain trail he remembered. The prince had repeatedly assured them that he knew this section of the Most Savage Mountains well and that there would only be one "slightly dicey climb" between them and the Dragon's den. "Slightly dicey" had suggested to Fodder a few loose rocks and a bit of a scramble. It had not offered up this image of a sheer colossus in stone.

Flirt too was shaking her head. "Dullard," she started uncertainly, "are you *sure* about this?"

"Absolutely!" Fodder wasn't sure whether it was a good sign or not that the prince was beaming like the rising sun as he stared fondly up at the wall of rock. "I've done it myself with relative alacrity. I'd have ascended quicker, but I stopped along the way to study the wonderful geology it has. This face has some truly fascinating diorite intrusions running through it." With a grunt, he pulled on his second climbing boot and set to work briskly tying the laces. "Once we've cleared this face, the mountain routes are relatively easy heading up to Maw's cavern. The Perilous Pass will take the rest of the day and probably half of tomorrow too, even with The Narrative's aid. If we get this right, I believe we can reach Maw tonight, a full half-day ahead of them."

"If we get this right?" There was well-founded scepticism in Flirt's tone. "Dullard, it's the only plan we've got, but you're the only one who's ever climbed before. We've only got one set of equipment. Princess Pleasance *is tied up*. Do you really think this is realistic?"

Dullard patted his tied boot and rose to his feet, carefully uncoiling his rope as he examined his grappling hook and an alarming selection of leather harnesses with an absent expression. "Perfectly. I'll take point, and I'll set up a rope for you as I climb. Then I'll stop at selected safe locations and come back to help you. As for Pleasance—well, I've carried heavier packs in my time." He smiled reassuringly over at the gagged princess, whose expression of unrestricted alarm wavered only a touch into irritation at being referred to as luggage. "Honestly, with some basic instruction, I think it'll be much more straightforward than you expect it to be."

"Straightforward." It was the tone. It was the flat tone carrying a sprinkle of shimmering anger that whispered the volcano was willing to jump from gently smoking to full-scale devastation in the very near future. Fodder took a gentle step back from Shoulders and spotted Flirt doing the same.

Dullard was still smiling. Bugger. "Well, yes," he offered to Shoulders with a disconcerting obliviousness to the impending explosion. "I really don't think this will be as difficult as you seem to think. Good climbing is nothing more than careful co-ordination."

"Co-ordination?" Smoke was billowing from the summit of Shoulders's rage. "And how the bloody hell do you expect me to be co-ordinated when I'm using one arm to *carry my own head*???"

There was a long, dangerous pause. Fodder saw Dullard bite his lip, clearly pondering a placatory response. But it was too late.

"You didn't think about that, did you? You didn't give one bloody thought to the predicament that is entirely your fault when you concocted this genius scheme! What did you expect me to do with it?

Stick it in my pack maybe? Tuck it between my knees?"

Dullard's lips twisted. "Well, I'd be more than happy to fix it back in place for you like before. I have offered several times."

"You think I want your help?" Shoulders lifted his head up to emphasise the point. "No, I'm not going to grovel for your humble assistance! I'll find a way to fix my head back on myself and I will climb up there without any help from you!"

Fodder felt it was time to intervene. "Shoulders, mate, you know you're not a good climber. Even when your head was attached…"

"I'll manage!" The snapped retort cut away the rest of the sentence. "Now, if you'll excuse me, I'm off to prove that it doesn't take a smug Royal genius to keep my head on my shoulders!"

Flirt glanced at Fodder as they watched the Disposable storm away to where the packs were resting. "We'll be pulling him up bodily, won't we?" she said with prudent softness.

Fodder could only nod. "Yep."

Flirt shook her head. "You get set up for the climb. I'm going to head back and scout for the Merry Band. I think I'd like to know we've got plenty of time, wouldn't you?"

Fodder ignored the chilly prod offered by his insides. "No sacrifices," he replied bluntly. "I mean it, Flirt."

"I'll be careful, won't I?" Flirt regarded him sternly. "Besides…" She flicked her stare in the direction of Shoulders's volcanic expression. "It's got to be safer than here."

* * *

As she slipped back down the barely visible goat track towards the mouth of the Perilous Pass, Flirt had been ready to find many things: a gang of recruited Woodsmen industriously tracing their trail, The Narrative hovering over the Merry Band as they pounded boldly towards the pass, or the complete silence that suggested that no one from amongst their pursuers had yet picked up on their carelessness. One thing she most certainly hadn't expected, however, was to find an AFC meandering casually along the line of their carefully laid false trail as, with artful stretching sweeps of his leathery wings, he obliterated it from view.

Under normal circumstances, Flirt would have been buoyed to once again see such solidarity from a group who had previously protested they wanted nothing to do with the cause. But on this occasion...

"Stop it!" She didn't raise her voice. She didn't have to. She'd already seen the AFC's ears twitch in her direction. "Don't rub the tracks out! We left them on purpose, didn't we?"

The AFC halted sharply. His wings fanned out and with a single pump of them, he launched himself abruptly into the air. Keeping his face thrust towards the sky above, he circled carefully for a moment before descending in a lazy spiral to land with a thud upon the rocky crag close to Flirt's head. His winged back was turned firmly towards her.

"Strange things I'm hearing on the wind today," he exclaimed with the typical toothy lisp that an excess of ivory inflicted on the Assorted Freakish Creatures in most of their forms. "'Cos there I was, minding my own business, stretching my sore wings out, when I could've sworn I heard a voice. Can't have been, though, daft things it was saying. Must be the wind playing tricks, I reckon."

"It's a windy day, isn't it?" Flirt agreed as the playful air brushed at her face and set her dark curls dancing. "But this breeze wasn't being daft. We left the tracks because we want The Narrative to go up the pass and—"

"Don't need to be listening for things like that," the AFC cut in sharply. "Ain't my place to hear it. Look, I've had sore wings for a while, yeah? Sorry, but I already stretched 'em all the way up that hill." Flirt felt her heart sink. But how could she be angry with someone who'd thought they were helping them out?

The answer was that she couldn't, of course. But maybe they could do better than tracks.

"Well, maybe your wings are feeling better now?" she offered up nonchalantly. "And maybe, if you felt like it, you could give me—*the wind* a bit of a start before flying off to Primp and Strut and telling them you saw us heading up Perilous Pass at—"

"Ain't lying." The firm declaration cut across Flirt's casual suggestion sharply. "Looking at interesting trees and pretty birds and giving your wings a stretch, that's one thing. Giving a good mate a fair chance

to make something of himself when he ain't had a shot at it before, yeah, we'll do that too and maybe go along with letting his mates try for it into the bargain. But we ain't taking sides. We have orders, right? Orders we have to obey that say if we *see* any of you, we fly as fast as we can to report it. And I ain't saying I've seen what I ain't either. We're doing what we're told to the letter, okay?"

"Okay." Flirt managed to keep the disappointment from her tone, but it was a close-run thing. The irritation was, she could understand his point. Dullard was a good friend of the AFCs, and they didn't want to see him get punished. But they'd already stated they weren't about to help outright for a cause they didn't much care for. The AFCs' game of playing it by the book had done Flirt and her friends plenty of favours already. It wasn't fair to expect more from them.

So she'd have to take a risk. No sacrifices, Fodder had said. But he hadn't said anything about near misses, had he?

"This wing stretching," she inquired. "Did anyone with sore wings happen to be hanging around between Cackle's dell and the Ruined City too?"

"No point," was the offhand response. "Our mate Primp was in that bit of the Wild Forest first thing this morning with Strut and that nutter Assassin, looking at the ground and pointing. Then Strut grabbed Cackle the Crone and Primp got Fang and Gibber to carry him up into the mountains to see Maw the Dragon. We're on call for a possible fight in the Ruined City in the next couple of hours."

Bugger. Damn Poniard, she knew they shouldn't have let him run off! Thanks to him, their pursuers were closer behind than Flirt had hoped. But they had to be sure the Merry Band picked up their trail to the Perilous Pass. If they found the real trail and caught them pinned halfway up that epic rock face, they might as well chop their own limbs off and hand themselves over because it'd be easier than what the Merry Band and their mysterious powers would inflict on four helpless targets.

No choice, by the looks of it. She had to go down and relay the obliterated tracks.

"Okay." Flirt took a deep breath. "Now your wings are feeling better, what say you go for a little air patrol, scouting around for maybe half an hour or so? And in half an hour or so, if you happen to come back this way and spot a set of footprints heading up towards the Perilous Pass, well, that'd be the sort of thing a sudden attack of initiative might encourage you to report seeing, don't you reckon?"

The AFC cocked his head thoughtfully. "I ain't known for my initiative," he admitted. "Like I said, I'm to the letter and we ain't been told to find no tracks. But I reckon I might have the right sort of attack of it if you give me half an hour for a little air patrol."

Flirt smiled in relief. "Then I reckon you've listened to the wind for long enough, don't you?"

"Yeah, reckon you're right. Time old Frenzy got moving again." The AFC, or at least the back of the AFC's scaly head, offered a rather backwards nod. With a jerk, his wings burst out once more and he flung himself sharply skywards.

"Thanks, Frenzy," Flirt added quietly. She couldn't be sure he'd heard but she liked to think he had.

So. She had half an hour to get back down to the Ruined City and lay the fake tracks back up to the mouth of Perilous Pass, whilst hoping that the Merry Band were far enough away not to catch her in the act. It was going to be a close-run thing.

Well, you'd better get to it, hadn't you?

The dusty road that connected the lower regions of the rocky Perilous Pass to the Ruined City was rimmed along its sides by a ragged jumble of mossy boulders and scrubby trees, the kind of random scenery often used to fill in gaps between important landmarks of the Quest. Flirt briefly considered attempting to trot backwards down the incline in order to save time on track laying but since this would involve turning her back on the potential location of her enemy, not to mention the fact she would still have to come back up anyway, it seemed a bit daft and instead she ducked into the scrubby borders of the road and made her way down as rapidly as she dared from there. There was no point in leaving downwards tracks to confuse the matter.

Somewhere ahead, The Narrative was waiting. The Merry Band were approaching and more than ready to pounce. It would take only one mistake, one step out of line and she would be facing the challenge of a lifetime yet again. She could feel the pounding of her heartbeat as the adrenaline surged.

She grinned. Now *this* was more like it.

Shoulders, she knew, thought she was reckless. But it wasn't recklessness exactly. It was an urge, a need, a desperation to prove to herself and to the rest of the world that she was worth so much more than they liked to believe. Her designated role in life had never been a challenging one. Where was the skill in waving a bosom that wasn't even hers, in serving pints of ale, giggling as they slapped her backside, simpering as they called her darling and moved in for the lips? It was so hard to move past the label of her birth, for even when she had flourished a sword, defeated a Warrior Woman, and slain a Barbarian, what had they called her? Still, after that, what was she?

She wasn't even prepared to think the bloody word. It had haunted her for her entire life, labelled her and dragged her down. And there were days that she had wondered—was this all she would ever be? Was this all she could ever be? She had always felt down in the depths of her heart that she could do more if she were given the chance to prove it, but some corner had always nagged, whispered that word and said, *You're fooling yourself, girl; you're assuming you'd be better because you know you'll never have the chance to try.* But she had the chance and she knew she could get past it. It was about belief, about finding yourself, Fodder and Dullard had decided, and she liked that. She liked the person she'd been in The Narrative, she liked that being her had felt so right, because she could be sure, for herself, that there really was more to her. And any opportunity, any chance at all to show the world what she had found, that she was more than just some bloody W-word, had to be taken without hesitation. And if that was reckless, so be it.

No sacrifices, Fodder had said. But this wasn't a sacrifice, and she had no intention of being the lamb. She had always believed those brave lone stands by heroic, tragic companions of the Hero as they fought madly, boldly, and ultimately stupidly until the overwhelming odds got around to overwhelming them, to be a bit daft. Where was the skill in losing? Dying for your friends was one thing but living to keep helping them was probably more useful. The challenge was in the winning. The likelihood of losing only made it more fun.

She would be careful. Of course she would. But if things went wrong, she'd be ready for it.

A large pile of mossy boulders loomed ahead as the track curved around a sharp bend in preparation for its descent towards the edge of the Ruined City. Haloed in the sky beyond, there was a very familiar glow.

Grabbing the lichen-covered bark of a small tree, Flirt pulled herself to a hurried halt. She dropped down onto the green-stained heap of boulders and crept forwards, flat and facedown towards the crest of the pile. A hollow gap that opened a void between two oddly shaped rocks almost sent her a cropper but she adjusted her route carefully and, keeping her head low, she peered between the cracks of two mossy stones and down into the plateau below.

The Ruined City unfolded beneath her, crooked, lancing spires and worn stonework wrapped in the descriptive embrace of The Narrative. A quick shift of position was enough to tell Flirt what she suspected—there, on the carefully situated viewing crag a little further along the mountainside, the Merry Band were gazing down upon the city with appropriate levels of wonder and awe. She was careful to keep low, although she was sure that, with the artfully constructed wonderment below, a patch of mountainside wouldn't be of much interest to them. A moment later, she saw Magus flick his robed arm and The Narrative view congealed and narrowed as the Merry Band dropped off the crag and down behind the limited visual expanse of the walls on the city's far side.

She didn't have much time.

The Ruined City was a decent-sized area, but all it would take was one lucky line of sight through the tumbling walls and cracked towers to catch her scampering up the open, hundred-yard stretch of dusty track below to put her in a very challenging situation. Perhaps she could have left it, could have started the tracks from where she was standing, round the corner and safely out of sight. They would take longer for the Merry Band to find that way, give them more leeway to get up Dullard's monstrous dicey climb. But they would also be suspicious. Even the densest Narrative character would wonder why the tracks had appeared out of nowhere partway up a slope. They would become sceptical, wary of traps and trickery, and that was the last thing she and her friends needed. They wanted a confident Merry Band, convinced of the stupidity of their enemy in not concealing their trail as they boldly rode them down. They didn't want them stopping to think that there might be more going on. That might lead to sweeps and searches and deep, deep heaps of doo-doo.

No doubt the fact that there was only one set of footprints was going to make them suspicious enough. But she didn't have time anymore to do anything about that. She could only hope that, buoyed on by finally having some direction, they were feeling a bit overconfident.

The Narrative was dim and distant. It was now or never.

As rapidly as she dared, Flirt flung herself over the crest of the boulder heap, rolling in a bruising, silver-mailed ball down the far side. A tree was nicely positioned to break her tumble with a painful smack, but Flirt had no time to dwell on the squeals of protest from her beleaguered ribs. Dragging herself back to her feet, she careened down the scrubby, uneven stretch of mountainside, trying to ignore the skidding and sliding of her feet, the bursts of pain as her cart-wheeling arms caught branches and boulders with a passing whack, and the alarming speed with which she lost control over her direction. Ahead, boulders and scrub gave away abruptly to green grass and meadow flowers— apparently thrown by this uncalled-for change of surface, her feet decided this would be a good time to give up the ghost and suddenly she was falling, rolling head over heels down the lessening slope as she fought down the urge to give a W-word-like squeal.

As the slope flattened out, she caught a glimpse of stonework. A moment later, a weathered cherub was pressed against her face.

Her momentum was too great to be halted by a mere gate column, however. Her body *thwacked* against the gate carvings and bounced with an undignified crash out into the middle of the road.

For a moment, there was only a whole world full of ouch. Eyes closed as she lay flat on her back in the dusty gateway, Flirt ran a brief inventory of herself in search of some part that wasn't aching and found an alarming lack of positive responses. But she was down. That was the important thing. So all she had to do was start a trail of footprints from the meadow and get back up the hill before any of the Merry Band saw her.

Easy!

Flirt opened her eyes. From the jagged, pitted edge of the gate tower, the wide eyes and open mouth of Swipe the Thief stared down at her.

Ah.

Her brain kicked in before her battered body was able to follow suit.

"Your character's been sent scouting ahead, has he?" she said hoarsely.

On his high perch, irritatingly out of reach even if she'd been upright, Swipe's eyes had switched from wide to narrow. From his crouched position, his hands were closing on his dagger hilts.

"That's about the size of it," he said casually. "Just waiting here for them, I was, and look what rolled in."

"And you'll be summoning The Narrative right about now?"

The narrow eyes were joined by the slight edge of a smirk. Swipe always had been a smug bastard. *"Oh,* yes."

"So I probably ought to run for it?"

Swipe's smirk grew definition. "You're welcome to try, girl. More fun for me that way. You ready?"

"No!"

"Never mind." The smirk blossomed into fully-fledged smirkdom. It was a vast smirk, an epic smirk, a king amongst smirks. "Ahem." He rather pointedly cleared his throat. "ELDER! OVER..."

Light...

"...here!"

Certain that his companions would have heard his echo-strengthened cry, Slynder could not quite believe his luck. To accidentally stumble upon the mail-clad female guard like this! As she scrambled desperately upright from the tumble he had witnessed moments before, the thief was already moving, his daggers in his hands with lightning speed as he flung two blades in rapid succession at his quarry. But the woman was surprisingly nimble, the first blade thudding into the dusty road where her head had lain moments before, the second glancing with a clatter off the shoulder of her mail as she turned and bolted for cover behind the worn stones of the opposite tower…

Gone…

Flirt knew she had seconds. Grasping her sword, she yanked it from the scabbard as she tore through the cracked and ruined walls of the gatehouse, scrambling over tumbled stone as she fought to get further away before…

Glimpse…

…Slynder saw a flash of silver mail and dark hair as he vaulted the wall in one easy leap, caught a glimpse of her pale face as she flung herself around the corner and out through the narrow doorway that…

Lost…

The gatehouse opened into a courtyard, an alarmingly *wide* courtyard covered in cracked slabs of stone. Flirt didn't dare pause as she rushed across the width of it towards the tattered remains of what looked like a stable block and the tumbled and distinctly blocked-up pile of rubble that had once been the arch leading in. Oh blimey, she was going to have to vault that mess and Swipe wasn't that far…

Behind…

As the courtyard opened out ahead of him, Slynder had already palmed a dagger, his arm swinging round as he hurled it at the fleeing woman, trying to fight the discomfort he felt at attacking a female, even though she was a known enemy. But the woman had already dived aside, the dagger clattering against the broken stone arch as she leapt onto the crumbled remains and staggered her way awkwardly over the top of them.

"Don't do me any favours!" she bellowed inexplicably over her shoulder.

Slynder was already pounding across the paving slabs, his nimble feet carrying him with fleet rapidity as he closed upon her ruthlessly.

"Give it up, girl!" he called out breathlessly. "Surrender and you won't be hurt!"

"Bugger that!" With an impulsive leap, the woman flung herself forwards over the blocks of hefty stone, rolling in the dust beyond as she dragged herself to her feet and vanished into the street...

Ahead...

Well, at least he hadn't called her the W-word. Though "girl" wasn't much of an improvement....

A street opened out before her, narrow and lined with the broken remains of small, battered buildings. She could see slender alleys arching off between damaged walls and a winding maze of passages had to be a better option than open ground right now. Because she needed to do something more than simply be chased. She had to take him out whilst the rest of the Merry Band were still too far away to interfere, she had to give herself time to make it back up to the road to the pass before she was trapped and outnumbered...

Sight...

...Slynder pulled out of his elegant diving roll and came instantly to his feet, his eyes fixing on the woman as she sprinted up the street towards a narrow gap in the buildings. Once again, his blades whipped into his hands as he sent his largest dagger screaming through the air towards his quarry, forcing the woman to hurl herself aside and away from the gap she had targeted. As she tumbled on the broken paving, the woman jammed one foot against a cracked stone and turned herself sharply, diving forwards into the open mouth of one of the buildings beside...

Hidden...

Flirt scrabbled to her feet, clambering over the remains of a stone oven as she vaulted the interior walls and hurtled towards the slender doorway she had spotted nestled in the far corner. A nice, crooked alley, lots of twists and turns—that surely wouldn't be too much to ask...

Glimpse...

...Slynder flung himself through the doorway in time to catch a fleeting glimpse of mail and dark hair as the woman darted through a slender doorway...

Lost...

Flirt plunged down the three steps into the narrow and, bloody hell, very straight alley beyond but she could see at once that she stood no chance of making the end of it before Swipe's pursuit made it chancy. Instead, she grasped the shoulder-height edge of the nearest wall and dragged herself up and over, praying The Narrative wouldn't surge around the corner and catch her in this undignified...

Chance...

...and saw the woman's mail-clad backside as she hurled herself over a relatively low wall nearby. Slynder rushed forwards, hands outstretched as he fumbled to grab her ankles, but one ruthless, mule-like kick from the woman's foot sent him reeling backwards as she vanished beyond...

Lost...

The narrow stream that gurgled through the overgrown garden was unexpected, but it did add some interest to her landing. Flirt plunged headfirst into the shallow water with a breath-choking splash, fumbling desperately to bring her shocked and sodden body to order as she pulled herself to her knees in the tumbling water. Above, the threatening glow of The Narrative gleamed as scrambling hands sounded against the wall, an acrobatic man preparing to vault it, and she knew she would have one shot at this, one moment of surprise. Grasping the wall with one hand to steady herself in the torrent, her hand tightened around her sword hilt as she brought it sweeping up and...

Pain...

"Ah!"

The pain was as agonising as it was unexpected. Slynder twisted in the air, grasping at his stricken thigh as he slammed down against the stony edge of a torrent of rushing water. He saw her then, crouched in the water but already half on her feet as she dragged the sword blade she had skewered him with so efficiently from its sheath in his flesh and started to wheel for a second blow. But Slynder had managed to turn, his painful leg doused in water as he dragged his long knife from his belt, made determined by the knowledge that even should she swing the blow, he would still have time and proximity enough to bury the blade between her eyes...

"Bugger!" With a furious glare, the woman leaped away from his supine form, pulling out of the attack as she turned and bolted. Slynder dropped his knife as he rolled on his face in the overgrown undergrowth of what looked like it had once been an ornamental garden, his hand dragging free instead another of his innumerable supply of throwing daggers as he pulled himself up onto his elbows and hurled it after his attacker with all of his strength. But it was too late—the dagger bounced harmlessly against a limbless stone statue as the woman dodged efficiently from his path and threw herself out of the rotten remains of the gateway and into the street beyond...

Passes...

Perhaps she should have gone ahead and finished him. But an injured man would slow The Narrative more than a dead one, and Swipe was quick; betting her speed against The Narrative's in a game of blade quick-draw would have been too risky. She couldn't afford to get

Narratively killed.

Staggering into the broad avenue beyond, Flirt hesitated for a necessary second to try and get her bearings. Even from the far side of the city, she knew the rest of the Merry Band, with the advantage of fast horses, were probably barely a minute or two away and that was without any mysterious powers. She had to orientate herself, get back to the gate where she'd started and up the hill, whilst making sure they saw her only briefly. The jig was up in terms of a low profile and there was no point in not using that to her advantage, however dangerous it might turn out to be...

Wait a second.

The Narrative was still with Swipe. She could see it glowing beyond the garden wall, probably driving him against physical probability to get to his feet and limp bravely on after her, driven by adrenaline and willpower. And though she was no longer in The Narrative's sightline, as Swipe himself had proved, you could be heard by The Narrative without being swallowed by it....

It would be on her quickly. Flirt hurriedly took in her surroundings, that shattered spire, the collapsed dome—she'd seen them when she'd looked down from above and yes, that meant the gate she needed was somewhere over *there*.

The Narrative was glowing. Swipe was on the lurching move.

"Quick, lads!" she roared at the top of her voice, and was pleased to note the resonance her voice acquired as The Narrative tugged at its edges. "Take the princess and run! I checked and the perilous pass is clear! We have to get up and over it before they catch us up!"

And now you're chasing all of us, Flirt thought to herself as she bolted down the avenue away from The Narrative's approaching gleam. *At least as far as you're concerned!*

She permitted herself a Swipesque smirk. She felt she'd earned it.

That was, as long as she got away.

She had nearly reached the end of the avenue, the building with the vast collapsed dome filling her path when The Narrative suddenly blinked out behind her and she could see its glow away to her distant right instead, further from her but making rapid progress in her direction as it shifted its attention to the approaching and more mobile horse-backed members of the Merry Band. Damn, she didn't have much time. They'd be on Swipe in seconds, and the moment he told them what he'd heard...

An alley opened to her right, the way she needed to go—but was The Narrative on the street beyond? She'd have to risk it. Darting down, she hurried along the narrow passage, noting to her relief the lack of glow ahead, but she could see The Narrative closing off to one side, getting closer and closer.

She stumbled to the end of the alley and glanced out. Hang on, this was the street she'd just come from, wasn't it? Yes, there was the tumbled arch and the courtyard beyond and past that, to her left, the dead end of the city walls blocking any exit. On the right, the street continued past the house she had escaped through to join a wider avenue of columns beyond; and along that road, a vivid glow was rapidly advancing.

Uh-oh. Time to run.

She couldn't wait. She didn't dare. She needed all the head start she could get. From a standing start, Flirt hurtled out across the road, legs pumping as she closed rapidly on the archway's rubble remains, trying to ignore the tug at the corner of her eye as the glow of The Narrative cast itself like an inverted shadow against the far side of the street, creeping nearer and nearer as the Merry Band approached...

With every last scrap of strength remaining to her, Flirt flung herself up the rubble and hurled her body into a heap on the courtyard beyond. In the space where her ankles had been less than a second before, Narrative light gleamed.

Flirt did the sensible thing. She bolted.

It was the work of seconds to run the length of the courtyard once more, to scramble back through the watchtower and out under the beautifully carved gateway where her troubles had begun. She permitted herself a second to make a rude gesture at the cherub she had face-planted against and then, laying some very definite tracks, she hurled herself up the trail.

How long would she have before she was above the level of the masonry? How long before some hawklike pair of eyes would pick her fleeing figure out? Forty yards to the corner, thirty-five, thirty, bloody hell, her legs were killing her, twenty yards, fifteen, ten, just ten and…

Light…

"There!" It was Slynder himself who had cried out, for even as he had leaned against the tree-trunk-like support of Svenheid to point in the direction of the pass he had heard spoken of, a dark-haired figure in silver could be seen hurtling up the slope towards the corner.

"Run, lads! Keep running! They're coming!" Buoyed by the echoes of the mountains, the woman's voice carried even from so far away as she gestured frantically to some companions unseen beyond the twisting corner of the trail. "Get to the pass!"

Zahora had already taken aim at the distant figure, her bow arching up; but it was too late, for the woman in mail was too far ahead and a moment later she rounded the corner and was…

Gone…

Scrambling over, Flirt flung herself behind the concealment of the mossy boulders. The hollow she remembered opened out beneath her and, sucking in her breath, she squeezed herself into the cramped void below, ducking her head as she crouched in an uncomfortable heap. She knew she'd never make the pass ahead of the Merry Band—that would be a heroic sacrifice too far. And though there would be only one set of footprints to the corner and none beyond, would the Merry Band really be looking? Of course not! They were in hot pursuit of a seen enemy and knew their destination. Who needed tracks?

Her heart was pounding. Her lungs were burning. Her veins were fizzing.

Bloody hell. That had been fun!

It hadn't felt it at the time, maybe. But now…

She'd challenged The Narrative alone, and she'd won. She'd tricked them and they'd fallen for it hook, line, and sinker. Let anyone call her the W-word now!

She hadn't exactly intended to do anything so dramatic when she'd started out. But that only made it sweeter.

There. Hadn't she told Fodder she'd be fine? Who needed noble sacrifices when you had skill and brains? Noble sacrifices were the easy way out!

The sound of hoofbeats silenced her moment of self-congratulation. Vivid light stole around the edges of her concealment as she heard a pack of horses thunder past at a distinctly not track-hunting speed.

Flirt was prudent enough to wait until the last traces of hooves had vanished up the slope ahead. Dragging herself free of her cramped hidey-hole, she started back up the trail towards Dullard's goat track. She traced the tracks of the Merry Band as she walked and, as she'd hoped, they vanished up into the Perilous Pass. In the not-too-faraway distance, she could hear the echo of their hooves against the mountains.

They were going a bit fast...

Oh blimey.

Flirt was quick to find the goat track and return to Dullard's epic wall of rock. In its shadow, Shoulders fiddled sulkily with something white. Dullard was strapping some kind of harness around the very alarmed-looking princess. But it was Fodder who fixed on her at once, abandoning the ropes he had been untangling and hurrying over to her side.

"You took your time!" he exclaimed, and his eyes betrayed hints of his earlier concern. Flirt had noticed how seriously Fodder was starting to take his new responsibilities, both as their accidental leader and their friend, and she couldn't help but feel sorry for him. He had a lot on his plate at the moment. "We saw the glow of The Narrative go by on the horizon and—"

"Yeah, they found the tracks." Flirt saw no need to elaborate. Fodder didn't need to worry himself any more than he already was. "They've headed up the pass."

"We thought as much." Fodder squinted at her carefully. "You were gone awhile, you know, and when we saw The Narrative..." He pulled a face. "I was starting to think you'd done something...*stupid*."

Flirt considered this, considered the conversation with Frenzy, her fall, the chase-battle with Swipe, and her flight back up the hill, and came to a conclusion.

"No," she said easily. "Nothing stupid at all. So, how about we get a move on before the Merry Band beat us to Maw?"

* * *

Shoulders wasn't as heavy as one might have expected. That was a bonus.

The Disposable hadn't been happy when Dullard had taken the lead on the hauling, but the prince had concluded that dangling on a rope hundreds of feet up on a rock face didn't leave him much time to be picky. It was a tricky business—the knotted scarf with which Shoulders had secured his head was loose and looked close to giving way altogether. But Dullard made no further overtures of help, knowing they would be rebuffed, and he was braced and accepted the repeated haranguing his involvement drew at every rest location on the climb. He considered it a small price to pay under the circumstances.

Pleasance, too, proved less of a burden than he'd feared. Retreating back into quiet, she simply hunkered down when tied securely to his back, her face buried in his shoulder and her small hands digging into his ribs. Her flood of blonde curls proved an occasional hazard to his eyesight, but it was nothing he couldn't deal with.

She was scared, though. He could feel her shaking against his back. Whether it was the height of the climb or the prospect of what lay at the end of it, he couldn't be sure, but all the same, he offered reassuring words at every juncture that he could spare breath. But although the gag had been removed, she made no response and simply clung on to him.

He needed to speak to her again. Fodder hadn't been unresponsive to his suggestion of talking her round. If he could persuade her to confront what he knew that she was feeling...

A brush of hair against his ear and a muffled squeak told him Pleasance had looked down, reminding him he probably ought to be concentrating more thoroughly on the job in hand. After all, there were only a few more yards of overhang to go before he could secure the line at the head of the face and settle down on the craggy summit to help the others. Dangling by his fingernails from a three-hundred-foot drop probably wasn't a good time to get philosophical.

Gritting his teeth, he dug in, securing his footing as best he could when gravity was against him and hauling himself hand-over-hand up the last few tricky holds, before bending lithely and sliding himself up onto the craggy jut that marked the pinnacle of the sheer wall. The debris-strewn ledge was wide enough to allow safe movement; carefully, Dullard bent and secured the end of the rope to a metal peg driven into a solid crack in the sturdy stone. And then, he gently but firmly released the buckles of the harness holding Pleasance in place on his back.

"We're up," he told her quietly. "You can let go now."

She didn't move. Little fingers dug, if anything, more tightly into his ribs as her nose pressed down against his neck.

Tentatively, Dullard flexed his shoulders. Oddly pleasant as the sensation of her pressed against him was, she would be somewhat of a hindrance if he needed to abseil down to assist his friends.

"We're at the top," he repeated a touch more firmly. "Honestly, it's not like the ledges on the way up. This is it. The end of the climb."

Pleasance had not enjoyed the ledges. She had whimpered and groaned every time he had unhitched her on those yard-wide, slippery juts, in order to free himself for the necessary Shoulders-hauling. She had almost seemed relieved when the time came to cling to his back once more, although the task of unpeeling her from the rock face had been challenging to say the least.

But still, there was no response. The whimpering and snuffling had stopped but the little hands clung on. Ignoring the odd sort of feeling that was swirling in the base of his stomach, Dullard reached down and gently but firmly began to unpeel one delicate finger at a time from his torso.

"Come on," he said more firmly still. "It's fine, you're perfectly safe, but I do need you to let go. Can you please do that for me?"

The unpeeled fingers appeared to waver for an uncertain instant. And abruptly, her warm weight on his back was gone and he turned in time to see Pleasance stagger, red-faced and wide-eyed to a nearby rocky outcrop, where she slumped in a saggy heap of velvet and limp, messy curls and buried her face in her hands.

The others were waiting for his signal, but Pleasance was upset, and there was no part of him that could allow that to lie. Softly, he padded over to join her, depositing himself tentatively beside her on the outcrop. He raised one hand, hovering it for an uncertain moment before allowing it to drop down gently onto her shoulder.

"Are you all right?" he asked quietly.

Pleasance's face appeared sharply from her palms, still red, still blotchy, but her eyes were narrowed dangerously.

"Am I all right?" she repeated with a hiss. "I've been dragged up a sheer cliff like luggage, left clinging to rocky ledges that a mouse would struggle to balance on, so that a headless psychopath can feed me to a dragon! What part of that, do tell me, do you think I might not be all right with?"

But Dullard could see the trembling in her fingers, could hear the tentative edge to her rage, and he chose not to rise to the bait.

"I understand that," he said simply. "But there's nothing I can do about that in this moment. I do want to help you but…"

"You want to help, you want to help!" Blue eyes burned at his face. "You say that time and time again, but you never do anything about it! You want to help me? Fine! Don't tie me back up! Leave me here, turn your back, and let me go! Let me go *home!*"

He met her gaze, ignoring the fire, pushing on past it to where he knew the real Pleasance lay.

"Back to Bumpkin?" he said softly.

Her eyes tore away as she buried her face back in her hands. He sighed, reaching down as he fumbled in his pack for a moment and pulled out his flask. "Here," he said softly. "Have some water."

The flask was snatched unceremoniously from his hands. Pleasance took several dramatic swigs before she tossed the bottle back into his lap and thrust her wrists towards him with a flourish.

"Go on then!" she exclaimed, her tone defiant but unable to hide the tremulous edge to her voice. "Bind me up and toss me to a slavering beast, why don't you? If this is what you do when you want to help someone, I dread to think what you'd do to people you dislike!"

Dullard sighed again, wholeheartedly. Much as he longed to broach the subject of an alliance with her, the others were waiting and he hardly had time for the long task of persuasion and barrier-piercing that he suspected lay ahead of him. "Pleasance, I do want to help you. But…"

A particularly powerful gust of wind slammed into him, nearly knocking him sideways into Pleasance's outstretched hands; the princess herself jerked backwards with a small screech as she battered at the sudden wildness the wind had mustered in her skirt and hair. And then, he heard a distant clamour that filled him with alarm.

"No, *no, no*…AAAAARRRRRGGGHHHHHHH!!!!!!"

"Shoulders!"

"Dullard! *Dullard!"*

The barrage of cries echoed up from below and jerked him from Pleasance at once. Abandoning the dishevelled princess, he rushed to the edge of the overhang, then peered over hurriedly as his eyes sought out the ledge where he'd last left his friends.

"What?" he cried out. "What's happened?"

He could see their upturned faces, Flirt and Fodder, staring at him with horror as they clung half to the rock and half to the flailing arms of their companion. Beside them was Shoulders's down-turned neck.

There was no sign whatsoever of either his head or the scarf that had held it.

Oh no.

He caught a glimpse of fluttering, dirty white below them. At once, he grabbed his pack, snatched out his telescope, rushed back to the cliff edge, and peered over again, focusing quickly on the whitish splash.

It was Shoulders's scarf. Caught upon a slender, struggling outcrop of twig, it jerked and twisted in the wind, weighed down by Shoulders's helmeted head as it bounced unceremoniously around in the air like a ball on a string in a child's playpen. Even from his distant vantage point, Dullard could hear his long, thin, keening wail of horror as his head swung back and forth, loosening visibly within the clutch of his helmet at every bounce and jiggle.

Dullard sighed yet again. Oh, lord. Well, he couldn't say he hadn't offered a more secure alternative.…

A part of him was tempted. He was honest enough to admit that. That corner that had sniped at Bold that afternoon and allowed Dullard brief moments of uncharitable thought about others was making it known in no uncertain terms that after days of snaps and insults,

Shoulders didn't really deserve to have his help. But, as ever, Dullard's fundamental Dullard-ness overrode his brief moment of doubt—turning sharply, he snatched up his harness, clipped himself back to the secured rope, then turned and braced himself at the edge of the drop once more.

And he saw Pleasance, her hair a tangle, her dress whipping in the wind as she stared at him wide-eyed.

He hadn't tied her back up.

He met her eyes, held her gaze just an instant.

"Please," he said softly, pleadingly, almost desperately. "For your own sake as well as mine, Pleasance, please. *Stay here.*"

And then he loosened the clip and hurled himself over the edge.

The abseil down to the ledge where he'd left the others took barely any time at all.

"Keep his body calm!" he called out to Flirt and Fodder as they huddled together against the rock, each grasping one of Shoulders's arms as firmly as they dared. "I'll fetch his head!"

He saw Fodder nod, heard Flirt call out something, but her words were snatched away on the wind as he plunged downwards once more, sailing on as fast as he dared in the gusty winds of the face. Below, he could see the jerking, jiggling scarf, stretched taut by the weight of the helmet it was tied to, and Shoulders's head, his mouth working wildly as he dangled from his headgear by only the width of his ears. Dullard shook his head. It was a long plunge down and he had no idea whether or not a detached head was capable of healing the kind of damage it was likely to suffer if it were to make a splashy impact on the rocks far below. He suspected not. And whilst, as that uncharacteristic corner of his mind pointed out, the silence would be golden, it would hardly be fair on poor Shoulders to be left in such a state when there was no hope whatsoever of repair.

He had to move quickly.

"Ahhh! Ah! Ahhhhhhhhh! Ahhh!"

The keening cries grew louder as he approached. Bracing himself against the rock, Dullard began a careful traverse towards the outcrop of twigs where the head dangled.

"Hold on!" he called out quickly. "I'll be there in a minute!"

Shoulders's watery eyes snapped in his direction. "You!" he wailed. "I don't want any help from you!"

"Then you won't get any help at all!" The stern riposte surprised even Dullard himself. "For goodness' sake, don't be so ridiculous! I'm here to help you!"

Shoulders's unshaven chin hardened as his head whirled in a dizzying circle. "I don't need..." he gasped out, "your kind...of help!"

And that was it. The limit. As much as he could take.

Prince Dullard was a nice person. He prided himself on that fact. He liked to help people. But after days of insults, of princesses who failed to see what was right in front of them, and of repeated, constant apologies for a simple slip of the tongue, to be derided for abseiling in such a way to try and prevent an unpleasant head-splashing incident was really too much to bear.

And so he stopped. He wrapped his arms around the rope, leaned back with his feet against the rock, and fixed Shoulders's spinning head with the firmest glare he could muster.

"Very well," he said coolly. "Rescue yourself."

He saw Shoulders's mouth drop open as his face travelled in a wide, windblown arc.

"What?" he managed.

"Rescue yourself," Dullard repeated loftily. "I fail to see why I should waste my time helping someone who clearly doesn't want to be helped."

Shoulders's head was slipping slowly sideways as his scarf began to lose purchase on the inside of his helmet. "But..." he gasped. *"But..."*

Dullard sighed at the bereft look on Shoulders's face, trying and failing to fight the pity seeping in to swamp the newly dominant part of his mind.

"Look here," he said, a little more kindly. "This whole thing is getting silly. There's only so many times I can apologise, and I'm sorry, but it's really not fair for you to keep punishing me for this. I accept it was my fault and I want to do everything in my power to make up for that mistake. But you won't let me." He shook his head at the frantic expression on Shoulders's face. "Your constant sniping is making a terrible atmosphere. How are we supposed to hold firm against The

Narrative if we can't even get along between ourselves?"

Shoulders was making whimpering sounds as his spinning, slightly green-tinged expression grew more and more lopsided.

Dullard smiled at him. "So what do you say to a truce? I'll help you out with fixing your head and whatever else you need, and in return, you stop deriding me. Do we have a deal?"

"Deal!" Shoulders's voice was a good two octaves higher than normal. "Absolutely! Deal! When we reach my hand, we'll shake on it! Now heeeeeeeeelp!"

One swing was all it took. Dullard caught Shoulders's head easily as he yanked the scarf free and dropped back to the line of the route they had earlier climbed. Jiggling carefully for a moment, he slung the scarf into a rough sling and, balancing Shoulders's head in its cradle against his chest, he began the gradual ascent back up.

"I didn't know you had that in you." Shoulders's voice was muffled by the sling, but Dullard could understand him well enough as he dragged himself back up the rock face.

"Had what?" he asked curiously.

"That." Shoulders gestured emphatically downwards with his eyebrows. "You're not as rabbity as I thought you were."

Dullard allowed that inexplicable statement to pass. "I'm sorry I left you dangling like that," he confessed. "But you've got to admit, refusing my help in that situation was frankly ridiculous."

"All right, all right." Shoulders pulled a face. "I was being daft. But it's just…"

"You needed someone to blame?"

Shoulders's eyebrows rose sharply at this statement. "I suppose," he conceded grudgingly. "But it *was* your fault."

"And I've admitted that. But carrying this business on any further will only make things unpleasant." Dullard pulled a face of his own. "Now, I feel a bit mean saying this to a captive audience but I have noticed that you do seem to feel the need to blame others for the problems in your life."

Shoulders half growled. "That's because my problems are other people's faults!"

"I admit that may be true," Dullard conceded, grunting as he negotiated a tricky traverse. "But has it occurred to you that if you spent a little less time blaming the world and a little more time getting on and trying to solve those problems, things might actually be better resolved and you more contented as a result?"

There was no response.

So Dullard kept climbing.

Out of nowhere came the muffled voice once more.

"When we get to the top," Shoulders said, rather grudgingly, "will you help me fix my head up like you did before?"

Dullard nodded, his eyes fixed to the rock face. "Of course I will."

"Okay." And then, softly and very reluctantly he added, "Thanks."

Dullard knew better than to smile. "You're welcome," was his solemn reply.

Fodder and Flirt were much relieved to see their friend's head retrieved, and Dullard volunteered to secure Shoulders's uncoordinated body to his back and carry him and the disconnected head the rest of the way. Shoulders, to Dullard's surprise but also relief, had raised no argument.

That problem, it seemed, had passed. But was a new one waiting at the top?

Had Pleasance stayed?

His anxiety was not helped by Shoulders and his choice of conversation.

"This'll all be over soon," his muffled voice insisted as Dullard started his way up the tricky overhang. "Soon as we feed that princess to the Dragon, we'll have The Narrative right where we want it. Fodder can make his grand speeches and I can get my head fixed back on and everything is going to be fine."

Dullard gritted his teeth. "Can you please keep quiet?" he asked as politely as he could. "Your jaw is jerking and it's affecting my balance."

Shoulders's mouth snapped shut. Dullard stifled his sigh of relief as he hauled himself over the difficult jut once more, his eyes searching desperately as he pulled himself and his passenger onto the summit.

But his heart sank through his boots as he found nothing waiting for him.

Princess Pleasance was gone.

* * *

Perhaps he should have stayed.

Dullard bit his lip. No. This was the best way.

After all, Shoulders's head had been fixed, albeit hurriedly, back into place and both Flirt and Fodder were competent enough climbers to cope without his help. His presence assisting their climb had always been more for Shoulders's benefit than for theirs.

It was Pleasance who needed him now.

And if there was one thing she didn't need, it was Shoulders's special brand of charm. So, in spite of the Disposable's hearty protests, Dullard had managed to persuade his distinctly antsy companion to stay and watch over the last leg of Flirt and Fodder's climb with his newly secured head whilst the prince himself rushed off into the fading light of late afternoon in search of the vanished princess.

He couldn't deny it had hurt when he'd topped the cliff and found her gone, the pain not helped by a barrage of fresh insults from Shoulders on the discovery that his prized source of dragon food was missing. But he'd really thought that he was starting to get through to her, that she was beginning to understand that the way she'd been taught from birth to accept was not the only way, and for her to run off just when she was so close to escaping a life he now knew she would despise...

He would try one last time. But if she was so determined not to be herself, what could he do?

He moved hurriedly along the gravel goat trail, grasping the strap of his pack anxiously in one hand. He had to find her. He had to. How could he let her go back to a life that would make her so unhappy?

He'd never forgive himself. Not without trying one more time.

She couldn't have gone far. It was difficult terrain, especially for someone in such regal attire, and he hadn't been gone for a ridiculous amount of time, so surely, surely, she had to be close by...

He rounded a large heap of rock, and there she was.

She did not leap to her feet and start to flee from him as he'd half expected. Instead, she remained where she was, slumped in a trembling heap of velvet with her back against a hefty rock, her face tear-stained and her eyes defeated. She stared at him almost blankly when he moved with care towards her, his feet gentle, his tread nervous, approaching as he might a frightened deer. When she neither balked nor fled from him, he lowered himself to a careful crouch and, sure at last that she would not bolt, he dropped to a sit at her feet.

And then he waited.

"I couldn't do it."

She didn't look at him as she said the words, gazing off instead into the darkening sky of early twilight.

"I wanted to." Her voice was distant, faraway, along with her eyes. "I wanted to run all the way until I found The Narrative and was safe back where I belonged, and there was my chance, my only chance and what happened?" Her laugh was bitter. "I got this far and found I couldn't do it."

Her eyes drifted back down towards his face, raking over his features slowly, carefully, the barricades flung high for so long within them seeming to tremble as much as she did. "I should hate you," she said, barely audible. "You've ruined everything I ever wanted."

He nodded gently in acknowledgment. "I know."

"I wish I'd never met you."

Dullard raised an eyebrow. "We've known each other since we were children," he pointed out. "You and your sister used to pelt me with iced buns from your balcony whenever I sat and read in the gardens."

Pleasance's eyes narrowed slightly, the distance fading as the spark of irritation drew her back to earth. "You know what I mean," she informed him with rather more pointedness. "We were acquainted but..." She sighed. "We didn't really *know* each other."

Dullard shrugged. "In all honesty, Pleasance—who at the Palace does?"

Her shoulders slumped. "This was so much easier when it was three common ruffians dragging me across the countryside," she muttered, her eyes focused on the hem of her dress as she toyed with threads of the badly frayed material. "I could hate them easily. They treated me like luggage, and I knew I was better than they were. But *you*..." Her eyes snapped up. "From the moment you let your friends stick a sack over my head, you've been there, trying to understand me, trying to get under my skin, being considerate and generous and...nice! *Why*? Why did you do that? I'm a prisoner, a means to an end; you didn't need to get to know me. Why bother?"

Dullard gave a gentle smile. "Because I thought you were worth bothering *with*."

Pleasance snorted. "What, the bratty little girl who pelted a gawky adolescent with iced buns because her sister thought it would be funny?"

Dullard gave a lopsided shrug. "But it wasn't your idea."

"That didn't stop me doing it."

"Because it was expected of you." Dullard leaned forwards, resting his elbows against his knees as he crossed his lanky legs. "That's the difference, Pleasance. Most of the people of the Palace enjoy that life, want that superiority to make themselves happy. But everything you've done has been to please the expectations of others."

Pleasance stared at him. "Are you serious?" she exclaimed with incredulity.

"Perfectly." Dullard did not break her gaze. "You said it yourself when we talked in the ruins. You feel the responsibility to please your family, even at the expense of your own happiness. And that's why you are worth bothering with." He smiled at her. "Because unlike most people at the Palace, you care about the feelings of others. And you do it even knowing they don't care a jot for yours."

For a moment, she simply stared at him, her face marked by the tracks of her tears, her eyes red and her hair wild. She blinked.

"You really believe that, don't you?" she murmured.

Dullard nodded. "I really do. You don't always care in quite the right directions, but at least the emotion is there. And you are worth a great deal more than trying to please such an ungrateful bunch as our family."

He'd half-expected a sharp rebuke, but to his pleasant surprise, she did not rise to it, instead allowing her gaze to drift thoughtfully downwards once more. Her voice, when it came, was barely a whisper.

"Some people would call that weak, you know," she said blankly. "Princess Pleasance the easily led, caring more about what others think of her than what she thinks for herself."

Dullard risked a smile. "Not weak," he ventured. "It can be a way to hide, to escape responsibility for your own life. But it can also be your greatest strength, if you let it. It's your choice."

Her reluctant smile was oddly wry. "It's my choice. You've said that before."

"It's good advice."

She actually chuckled. "You're persistent, I'll give you that."

Dullard cocked his head. "Is it working?"

The chuckle died away. There was a long and echoing silence.

Her eyes lifted slowly and he caught their gaze, coaxing them up further, holding them there. A whole world seemed to open up within them.

"A choice," she said at length.

"Yours alone." His gaze did not waver. "If you want to go right now, I won't stop you."

Her brow creased. "What about your great mission? Don't you need to kill me?"

"We'll find another way. For you and for us."

She frowned, her porcelain skin furrowed, and he could see the thoughts churning, hardening behind her eyes. "All right," she said at last, slowly, carefully, as though reaching one hand into a blazing fireball and waiting for the burn. "My choice is to make a deal with you."

He nodded. "What do you propose?"

Her hand tightened to a fist around the hem of her dress as the words spilled out from her lips. "You let me stay of my own accord. No more ropes, no more gags, no more being tossed around like a sack of potatoes. You keep me away from dog-breath Bumpkin and any magical, loving connection with him that means we end up married."

Dullard fought to conceal the rush of euphoria that swamped him. "And in return?" he managed calmly.

Her jaw hardened as she swallowed firmly. "No Narrative death for Islaine. No stabbings, no beheadings, no drowning, and absolutely, completely, and utterly *no feeding me to dragons*. Even the thought of it..." A shudder racked her body. "You said I could choose and I choose not to be eaten! You have to absolutely promise me I won't get digested, because if I wake up in a pile of reconstituted dragon dung, I will personally lead the hunt to track you down and throw you in the deepest, dankest dungeon in existence for the rest of your miserable lives!"

She took a deep breath as she slowed her rapidly accelerating speech down once more. "Well?" she said, her voice somehow managing to be both firm and tremulous at the same time. "Do we have a deal?"

Dullard bit his lip. If it was merely up to him, he'd have bitten her hand off, and he suspected Fodder would be willing after their earlier exchange. Flirt might be tricky, though, and as for Shoulders...

But he would try. Whatever it took, he would try. It was too good of a chance to be allowed to pass by.

"That sounds very fair, but I can't promise anything yet," he admitted cautiously. "I mean, you've met Shoulders, after all." Pleasance pulled a face as he continued. "But you do have my word that I will do everything in my power to do as you ask."

Her head nod was slightly frantic. "Then you have my word that when I'm off the Dragon's menu, I'll do whatever I can to help you." Releasing her fist-like grasp of her dress, she extended her right hand. "A deal?"

He took her hand, warm and delicate and gentle, and shook it firmly. "A deal." He scrunched his considerable nose. "Now all I have to do is persuade the others."

Dullard wasn't sure whether to be pleased or fearful at the almost desperate hope that flashed behind Pleasance's eyes. Her voice was a bizarre, impossible cocktail of wryness, sincerity, and sarcasm.

"Good luck with that," she said.

He risked a smile. "Well..." he said as he pulled himself to his feet, reaching down to offer her a hand. "I've always liked a challenge."

Her skin was soft against his palm as she daintily placed her hand into his and allowed him to pull her up from her seat against the rock.

"I haven't," she said frankly, and there was a strange relief to her posture, as though the tense barriers she'd been holding in place had finally fallen away. Her smile, for the first time since he'd known her, was warm. "But I could be converted."

He was staring at her pale face, unable to keep himself from smiling at the sudden openness there, which was why he saw the exact instant when her expression changed, when her eyes widened, when her jaw dropped, when she half-staggered back as a truly eardrum-shattering scream burst from her lips. A massive shadow stole away the last of the evening light that had gleamed against her skin. He managed to half-turn, his fingers groping for his sword hilt, but it was too late.

He caught one brief glimpse of crimson, scaly skin and a truly epic set of claws before the giant foot slammed into him. He felt Pleasance slap against his pack and most definitely heard her deafening screech fill his ears as the vicelike grip tightened, yanked, and dragged their feet from the ground. A moment later, there was nothing but beating wings and sky as they wheeled violently through the rushing, battering air, rocky mountains retreating beneath them for an instant before hurtling back with terrifying clarity as they plunged sickeningly downwards towards the gaping mouth of a huge black cave.

Darkness swamped them, leaving nothing but the breathless echoed remains of Pleasance's drawn-out scream. The grasp that had snatched them from their feet released abruptly and in a flurry of limbs and velvet, prince and princess clattered to the ground with a thud. A moment later, a gust of wind half-knocked Dullard sideways as the giant shape breezed overhead once more and vanished into the twilight of the cave's opening.

Dullard felt the ground shift beneath him as he pulled himself up on the uneven, cluttered cave floor. A hand grasped his arm. By the light of the distant entrance, he caught a shadowed glimpse of Pleasance's face. She stared down at the surface on which they'd landed, her lip curling in a mixture of astonishment and disgust. But Dullard knew enough to know what he'd find without even needing to follow her gaze.

For what good was a dragon's lair if it wasn't carpeted with bones?

Dull white glinted as far as the eye could see, a bumpy, brutal blanket of beautifully fashioned remains in the finest traditions of monsters' caves everywhere. The bony fingers curled in lingering agony around the broken spear were a nice touch, the half-munched ribcage well crafted. But the pièce de résistance was most definitely the human skull locked in the crushed, battered remains of a knight's helmet, its skeletal jaw still agape with a final cry of horror. The chaps down at the Artisans Quarter really had excelled themselves with these…

Almost too well, to judge by the look on Pleasance's face.

"They aren't *real*," he exclaimed hurriedly as she started to recoil, her lips parted for what he suspected would be another in her fine line of epic vocal gymnastics. "The Artisans make them—I've seen the workshop!"

Pleasance hesitated, the sharp draw of breath she had inhaled in preparation for further screaming deflating like a punctured bagpipe.

"Oh," she said. For a moment, her velvety chest heaved as she hurriedly gathered her composure, her eyes darting up to the rocky crack through which they had been carried. "What happened?" she managed. "What was that thing?"

"Maw." Unsteadily, Dullard pulled himself up to his feet, crunching regretfully on several nicely shaped femurs as he bent to help Pleasance. "That was Maw the Dragon."

He felt her tremble as her arm wrapped abruptly around his, her head burying itself against his shoulder with surprising fervour.

"Why did he bring us here?" she asked tremulously. "Is he going to...eat us?"

Dullard shook his head, his mind racing. "He doesn't really eat people," he muttered absently. "That's just for the Quests. But he must have some reason for catching us, and initiative is not his forte. I think we need to get out of here."

Pleasance raised no argument as he started to lead her awkwardly but firmly up the bone-scattered slope towards the gaping mouth of the cave.

"Where did he go?" she asked breathlessly. "Why did he leave us here?"

Dullard shook his head as he placed one hand delicately against her warm, slender waist and lifted her over a sizable knot of questing knights.

"I don't know," he replied, his eyes darting briefly with alarm to the flutter of bats overhead before turning back to the matter in hand. "But I have no wish to stay and find out."

"*You* have no wish?" Pleasance grimaced as she stomped one dainty foot down amongst the remains of a noble warhorse while they ascended rapidly through the last, tattered remains of the fake killing field towards the vast exit. "You aren't the one that a bitter Disposable and his friends want to jam down that thing's ill-smelling gul*leeeeeeet!*"

Inevitably, it was the dress. Even as Dullard turned, he caught a brief glimpse of velvet skirts wrapped around the substantial jut of an equine ribcage before two delicate hands clamped onto his doublet and dragged him down with a bruising crash into the bed of bones.

Dullard had seen such falls before. In Narrative, they generally fell between Hero and Heroine, a graceful plunge to the ground that ended with the would-be couple staring into each other's eyes for a profound instant before leaping back into the fray against whatever danger, battle, or peril had caused them to tumble in the first place. And whilst he would never have even dreamed of presuming himself worthy of being party to any aspect of that scenario, he had to admit that the prosaic reality he got was jarring.

Pleasance's elbows plunged into his stomach, driving the wind from his lungs. And then they shared in the glorious mutual profoundness of cracking heads.

The world swam. Black sparkles danced before Dullard's eyes, circling and mingling with the bats swirling around the ceiling to create a strange, dullish haze from which it was difficult to pick reality from hallucination. Somewhere far away, he could hear Pleasance groaning, could see a dizzy glimpse of blonde curls as she tumbled off his chest. Her voice was an echo, trembling in his skull. He thought he heard her call his name, felt a distant grasp against his arms; then he was shaken. Somehow, he felt himself push up on his elbows, the world a swirling rainbow of silvery sparks as an indistinct shape of blue and gold yanked him to his feet. He could feel curls tickling against his ear. He stumbled forwards, slumped, his weight half-held by another, and suddenly the shadows thinned into twilight, into the fading orange of the sun as his vision began at last to clear and his hearing to return.

It was not well timed.

Pleasance's ear-piercing screech nearly shattered his skull. Something vast and crimson swooped down to fill his clearing eyesight completely. The downdraft of huge wings all but knocked him to his knees as a massive, scaly, red-horned head curled down towards him, lantern-like yellow eyes gleaming as the enormous, toothy maw parted to reveal row upon row of curving teeth and a truly horrendous case of halitosis. Within the grasp of his claws, directly overhead, something was squirming.

Hovering for an impossible instant, Maw the Dragon cocked his head and eyeballed them.

And then, his claws flexed, parted, and released their burden. Dullard had time to catch a brief glimpse of Shoulders clinging frantically to his head, Flirt's wide eyes and mad curls, and Fodder's alarmed face plunging lower and lower and far too close.

Dullard didn't even have time to brace himself before the full weight of the Disposable slammed onto his head and hurled him into blackness.

* * *

The scream came from nowhere.

But Erik knew it instantly, instinctively, as it tore at his blood and dragged at his soul, that cry so achingly familiar, as distinctive as the first day he'd heard it, high in that distant mountain pass. Even as his companions reined in, their eyes raking the horizon in the fading light, Erik was already moving, spurring on his horse as he clattered with reckless abandon up the rocky path in front of him.

"It's the princess!" he heard himself cry out. "Princess Islaine needs us!"

He heard Elder's bellow, heard the hoofbeats of his companions as they spurred their mounts rapidly in pursuit. After so many futile days, random wanderings, near encounters, and rogue tracks, at last he knew for sure that his Islaine was nearby and this time, no power on earth would prevent him from riding to her rescue.

He was certain of it.

Blood boiling, Erik surged on in the direction of the plaintive cry...

* * *

Princess Pleasance had a scream that could shatter mountains and ruin a glassmaker's living. It was certainly enough to get Fodder's attention.

He'd barely had his feet on the top of the crag, breathing hard and groping for horizontality as Flirt coiled up their rope, when the earth-cracking scream had almost knocked him back over the edge. Shoulders, who had been only a couple of sentences into his tirade about her disappearance, was startled into silence by the scream, but it took only a brief exchange of glances for the friends to roughly grab their things and belt in the direction of the sound. Frantically, they'd scoured the rocks and crags in front of them for any sign of Pleasance's blue velvet or Dullard's lanky frame, which was why it came as something of a surprise when a giant scarlet shadow swooped out of the twilight and snatched them from their feet.

The next few moments had been a confusing, sickening trip through mid-air, gusty winds whistling through his hair and battering his body as he jerked and bounced along with his captor's awkward flying gait. Fodder could hear Shoulders's long, keening wail off somewhere to his left but he couldn't catch a glimpse of him as they sailed awkwardly along, unable to turn in the firm grasp of the long, curved claws. He scrabbled desperately anyway, a bone-shattering tumble most likely preferable to whatever was about to happen, but the claws were much stronger than he was and the act was futile. And so it also came as something of a surprise when his captor swooped suddenly low and, with little ceremony, flung him down for a very uncomfortable landing.

It proved even less comfortable for Prince Dullard.

Fodder caught one glimpse of the prince's pale, slightly woozy, and distinctly resigned face before he slammed into him and they crashed in a tumble of limbs to the ground. For a moment, he was too winded to move, slumped on top of his unfortunate human cushion as he gasped air into his lungs, but then an indignant screech stung his ears and two small-but-potent hands battered violently against his side.

"Get off him! Get off him, you Disposable oaf, look what you've *done*!"

"Ow! Hey!" Fodder, still winded and confused, could only make a token effort to stave off the attack. "Stop hitting me!"

"Oi!" A rather firmer pair of hands came to his rescue as Flirt, her expression grim, darted in and caught the princess by the wrists, dragging her back from her assault. "That's enough!"

"But look what he did!" Pleasance screeched and wriggled in Flirt's grasp, her eyes suddenly wild and her face strangely frightened. "Look! *Look!*"

Crawling awkwardly back from his bony cushion, Fodder looked.

And indeed, beneath him lay Dullard, his body motionless, his face still, and his skin pale. His eyes were closed. A long, nasty-looking cut was dribbling blood from his temple.

Fodder winced. "Oh blimey," he muttered as he clattered awkwardly on his knees to the prince's side. Gently but firmly, he tapped one hand against the unconscious man's cheek. "Dullard? Dullard, mate, can you hear me?"

"Of course he can't hear you!" Pleasance's voice was frantic. "You've knocked him out cold, you stupid, you idiotic—" She paused, breathing hard and fast as she struggled against Flirt's unyielding grip. "And...and..." Her voice shot up by a wild octave. "I...I need him awake! He understood and...and we had a *deal!* I need him awake and you...*you*...!"

"Ummm...Fodder?" Shoulders's voice sounded oddly shrill.

"Deal?" Flirt ignored his call, her eyes fixed suspiciously on the princess. "What deal?"

"Can this wait until later?" Carefully, Fodder reached down, trying to arrange the prostrate Dullard into a suitable position for transport. "Only I think we should get out of here before—"

"*Fodder!*" Shoulders's screech cut away the rest of his sentence. A shadow stole the last of the sunlight away as the earth shuddered under a very heavy impact. A wash of putrid breath festered in the air.

Fodder didn't need to turn. He could feel the looming presence over his shoulder. But nevertheless, he did turn.

Two vast, lantern-like eyes scrutinised him from a mere few feet's distance. Scarlet scales, cast in orange relief by the last hints of the sun, traced the contours of a long, tooth-lined snout with flared nostrils and a sharp, bony face crowned by a pair of delicate, crested, horny ears. A length of scaly, snaking neck fell sinuously away behind it to connect to epic leathery wings that sprouted from the shoulders of a vast barrel of a body balanced on four heavily clawed and well-muscled limbs. An elongated, ridged tail thrashed at the growing shadows, rounding off in a ball of hefty, mace-like spikes.

Maw the Dragon stretched open the maw that had named him, his breath suitably foul and rich with hints of warmth that whispered of potential fire. His yellow eyes narrowed as his neck lowered and he squinted at the motionless, terrified Fodder for what seemed like an eternity. Visions of being roasted alive, of spending a repair-less, floating eternity in limbo as a pile of ashes flashed through Fodder's mind as he stared down the barrel of one of the land's most lethal killing machines. The Dragon cocked his head and slowly drew back his snout to reveal his plethora of teeth. A giant tongue thrashed and...

"'Ullo," he said.

Fodder blinked. "Pardon?"

"'Ullo!" Maw repeated. With a heavy thud the Dragon dropped to an ungainly sit, his hind section thumping down as one clawed hand swung out and with an unceremonious swipe, swept the wide-eyed Shoulders, the incredulous Flirt, and the wriggling Pleasance down into a rough heap at Fodder's side. Casually, the Dragon settled down, the bulk of his vast body curling round as he efficiently blocked the exit to the cave mouth in which they crouched.

They were trapped.

But yet, the Dragon, such as he could, appeared to be...smiling?

"I found you!" he rumbled cheerfully, vast head rearing over them almost proudly. "They said to me, they said find you, and I found you!" He darted close, foul breath causing the four unfortunate conscious humans to wince and gag. "I said to 'em, I said, I dunno 'bout that, mate, you two-leggy things, you all look the same as eggs to me! But they said to me, they said, there's a couple of yellow-topped things and some dark things and a brown thing and all I had to do, they said, they said all I had to do was find you and keep you and I did it!" He gave a tooth-filled beam as his vast tail thumped, crushing a pile of artful bones to a whitish pulp. "I like it when I do things right!"

Fodder's mind flashed back to his conversation with Dullard, when the prince had delicately pointed out that Maw the Dragon was not the brightest spark in the lightning storm. Dullard, as ever, had been on the generous side.

Shoulders, who was grasping his lopsided head as he steadied it awkwardly, managed to stagger to his feet, squinting up at the Dragon with less fear and more anger.

"You were sent to find us?" he managed breathlessly.

"Yup!" The Dragon gave a cheery nod. "The little man with the book, him that comes up here and tells me who's gonna be slaying me in the big, shiny light today—he told me, he did, he told me to grab you and bring you here and keep you 'til the light comes. Then, he said, then I stomp on you and the kid with the big sword—Boy of Destiny, right?— well, he zaps me with specticel—spextax—speccolour...*big, bright* magic, takes the fuzzy yellow one off into the morning and hey ho!" It was less a grin and more a display of several rows of teeth. "It'll be fun!"

At the mention of stomping, Shoulders had gone rather green and Flirt had gone distinctly red. But to Fodder's surprise, it was Pleasance who had turned deathly pale, staring at the Dragon with something close to despair in her eyes. The glance she cast briefly at the unconscious Dullard was both accusing and desperate.

She said they had a deal...

Fodder stared down at the heap of prince before him. He'd been so insistent about trying to talk Princess Pleasance round instead of throwing her to the Dragon. Had he tried? Had he succeeded?

"The morning?" Flirt's alarmed exclamation interrupted Fodder's thoughts. "When will they be here?"

Maw cocked his head. "Dunno proper," he said. "They said to me, they said it ain't gonna be morning, though." He grinned gruesomely. "'Cos they said to me, they said I'd be stomping by moonlight!"

Oh blimey, they're closer than they should be. Fodder grimaced. The Narrative wasn't above cheating time and distance, apparently. They were going to have to act quickly if they were to...

"Yeah, but didn't they tell you?" This time it was Shoulders's voice that interrupted his thinking—he glanced up to see a highly thoughtful gleam in his friend's eyes as he tilted his chin up so that he could address the Dragon eye to giant eye. "The plans have *changed.*"

The Dragon squinted down at the Disposable uncertainly. "Little man with the book ain't been by," he said with slow, deliberate care. "He comes by if it's gonna be diff'rent."

"He's very busy at the moment, isn't he?" Flirt chimed in, picking up on Shoulders's plan at once. "He asked us to pass it on!"

Confusion was writ large across the Dragon's scaly face. "He did?" he rumbled.

"Of course!" Shoulders tilted his head back and forth with a finger in his best approximation of a nod. "That's why he was so keen that you pick us up! So we'd have time to tell you about it."

From beside Fodder came a low and profound groan. Glancing down, he saw Dullard's lanky limbs starting to twitch.

About time! Now hurry up!

He was sure that he knew where Flirt and Shoulders were about to take this. And it was logical. It was clever. It was their plan, for goodness' sake. But the look of despairing defeat on Pleasance's face, the desperation with which she had stared down at the unconscious Dullard had made him think again about taking aim for the long shot. To convert the princess would be far more precious than simply bumping her off, but he couldn't interfere, he couldn't sabotage what was currently their best option if he didn't know for sure…

Dullard, wake up.…

Maw, it appeared, was no great thinker, and the slow, pondering look he fixed upon the pair before him implied he was struggling to re-jiggle his universe to comprehend the idea of someone else providing instructions. Dullard had been right when he'd suggested that the Dragon would probably not be won over by the intellectual merits of the cause. He probably wouldn't even know what *intellectual merits* meant.

"He asked you to tell me?" he repeated uncertainly.

Fodder caught the glance that Shoulders and Flirt exchanged. They knew as well as he did that this was going to be a long conversation.

"That's right," Shoulders reiterated carefully. "And he wants you to listen carefully to what we are about to say because things are going to run differently. First up, you are under no circumstances whatsoever to stomp on any of us here." He waved his free hand for emphasis around their cluster. "Okay?"

The Dragon frowned distinctly. "No stomping?"

"No stomping."

"But the little man said there was stomping."

"Well, now there's no stomping." Shoulders tried and failed to keep the edge of irritation from his voice. "Absolutely no stomping of any of us."

"No stomping at all?" There was a plaintive note to Maw's voice. "I *like* stomping."

A familiar manic gleam manifested in Shoulders's eyes. "Well, if you're desperate to stomp," he offered gleefully, "there will be this chap in armour..."

"Oi!" Flirt interrupted him sharply, clearly noting the Dragon's expression of utter bewilderment. "You'll confuse him, won't you? Keep to the important parts!"

Shoulders gave an angry huff but let the idea of Clank-stomping die a dignified death all the same. "Fine," he grouched. "No stomping at all."

The Dragon looked a bit downcast at that. "I like stomping," he repeated mournfully.

"Well, never mind." Shoulders grinned at him. "Because there'll be something better. There'll be chomping."

"Chomping?" Maw's vast ears pricked, although to Fodder's surprise, there was no great amount of enthusiasm in the exclamation. "Who'm I chomping?"

Shoulders beamed a great beatific smile and pointed cheerfully at the slumped form of Pleasance. "That yellow-haired princess," he said.

And these words were enough to send Pleasance surging back into life. Ripping her stare away from the still-twitching Dullard, she jerked, gasped, and began writhing furiously in Flirt's grasp once more.

"No!" she screeched. "No! Don't listen to them! They're lying to you, they—mmph!"

Deftly but firmly, Flirt slapped one hand over Pleasance's mouth and managed a wan smile in the Dragon's direction as she struggled with her prisoner.

"Don't mind her!" she declared. "She's just a bit...ow!...over-excited!"

Dullard's eyelids were flickering, his groans strengthening as his brow creased. Fodder leaned over him.

"Dullard, mate, can you hear me?" he whispered urgently. "Because the princess said you'd made a deal and if you don't wake up soon, she's going to be dragon food. Okay?"

A distinct grimace crossed Dullard's face as he batted one wild hand in Fodder's direction.

"Naaaargh," he managed to ramble. "Naarrr...naar... Noooo..."

But the Dragon was frowning too. "Eat...the princess?" he said blankly. "But...but that ain't...right."

"Yes, it is!" Shoulders was working his manual nod again. "You wait until the big shiny light comes along and then chomp! You bite down on the princess, you chew, and you swallow. Simple!"

Maw's expression, however, suggested that the prospect of princess-chomping was anything but a simple one. His giant head was shaking slowly back and forth as he clambered with sudden awkwardness to his feet. "But that ain't how it goes..." he reiterated with heavy hesitancy. "I think...I think you've got that wrong 'cos...I always try and eat her, right? But then there's the big epic battle and the magic and the Boy of Destiny kid with his big sword and I get slain." He stomped a massive foot bullishly. *"That's* how it goes!"

Shoulders looked a tad less certain at the introduction of stomping to proceedings but nevertheless, he ploughed on. "Well, today, it's going differently. Today you get to win." He shrugged, almost dislodging his own head in the process. "Congratulations."

Maw was, as far as was possible, pouting, a most disturbing expression on a giant scaly face. "That don't seem right," he said again. "I think I need the little man with the book."

"Forget the man with the book!" Shoulders's retort was rather less patient. "He asked us to tell you this!" He took a deep breath. "You said you like it when you do things right, didn't you? Well, imagine what the little man with the book is going to say when the big, shiny light comes and he finds you've ignored what he asked us to tell you to do! Do you think he'll be happy?"

Maw's expression was so bewildered that Fodder started to feel sorry for him. He clearly lacked the necessary brainpower to process this and forcing it upon him didn't seem quite fair.

"I don't wanna get in trouble," he rumbled sorrowfully.

Flirt, who was attempting to marshal the thrashing Pleasance, cast a look at Fodder that was laced with guilt. Clearly, she was feeling it too. Converting someone of their own free will was one thing but tricking someone not bright enough to understand was quite another.

"So do what we're telling you." Shoulders, however, remained unafflicted. "And everything will be fine."

"Okay." The word was slow and ponderous and sent Pleasance into a fresh round of struggling. "Try again. You want me to eat her?"

"Yep." Shoulders affected a nod.

"When the big shiny light comes?"

"Yep."

Maw frowned. "And you ain't gonna fight me?"

"Nope, we want you to do it." Shoulders sounded chirpy. "Aside from anything else, she's a pain."

Pleasance gave a muffled screech of indignation but the Dragon ignored this interjection as he battled with the unfamiliar concept. "So, no fighting at all?" he managed.

"Nope."

"No calling me names?"

Shoulders gave another awkward shrug. "What for?"

"No zapping me with spectacle-er magic?"

"Haven't got any, mate." This wasn't strictly true once The Narrative came into play, but Fodder had no plans to intervene and confuse matters further.

Maw was clearly still struggling. "And you ain't gonna set one of them Boy of Destiny kids loose on me with a big sword so I can be slain real easy, like?"

Shoulders laughed. "Do any of us look like Boys of Destiny to you?"

Maw ignored that remark too. "So you want me to eat her?" he stated ponderously.

"That's it." Shoulders spread his hands. "I mean, isn't that what you're here for?"

The Dragon gave a vast, huffy, and distinctly malodorous sigh. "But I ain't supposed to, you know, do it! I'm supposed to be…gawd, what's the word, you know, when you're gonna do something and someone jumps in and stops you? Goes *thhhhh.*"

Shoulders frowned slightly. "Thwarted?"

"That's it!" The Dragon stabbed an emphatic claw perilously close to Shoulders's wobbly head. "Thwarted! I'm supposed to get thwarted at the last moment!"

Shoulders smiled up at him. "But this time, you won't be thwarted. You can eat her. You win. We surrender."

"But just eating her? No stomping, no fighting, no zapping, no swords?" With a thud that shook the very rocks, the Dragon collapsed back to the ground, resting his forelegs under his vast chin as his bewildered yellow eyes gazed into the darkness.

"I'm getting a headache," he muttered mournfully.

"You're getting a headache?" Shoulders murmured under his breath.

"I suspect mine is better." Fodder jumped sharply at the unexpected voice—distracted by the exchange, he hadn't seen Dullard's eyes open as the prince pulled himself awkwardly up onto his elbows on the bone-strewn ground. His bleary eyes blinked as he drank in the scene around him: Fodder's anxious face, Pleasance thrashing in Flirt's firm grasp, and Shoulders engaged in earnest conversation with a confused dragon. A look of alarm crept over his features.

"Fodder," he said softly. "Is Shoulders trying to persuade Maw to eat Pleasance?"

A nod was all the response that was needed. Dullard's eyes widened. "We have to stop him!" he exclaimed, wincing as he touched his fingers to the blood that stained his temple before forcing himself to his knees. "Pleasance will help us, she's agreed! But only if we keep her away from Bumpkin and don't feed her to a dragon!"

"But I don't *like* eating you two-leggy things!" The Dragon's sudden exclamation was approaching petulant. "It's no fun. And just eating her, I mean, raw?"

"You can cook her if you like." Shoulders was battling on as he gestured to the Dragon's vast maw. "Fire-breathing and all..."

"But eating two-leggy things is blooming messy!" Maw's huff half-knocked Shoulders from his feet and set his head rocking. "And then there's the fuss with that pixie picking around in me dung, trying to find a few good bits to use to put 'em back together! And...and...it ain't even like people are tasty! I mean, look at her!" He gestured to Pleasance, who stared at her potential chomper with outright horror. "I mean, she's skin and bones, ain't she? No meat on her! And that hair stuff'll get tangled in me teeth for weeks and as for the blue stuff she's wrapped in...gawd!" He sighed unpleasantly as he turned and began to trot around in circles on the rock nearby. "You ain't got no idea how hard that is to pass! I hate eating two-leggy things! They gimme the gips, they really do..."

Shoulders was gritting his teeth. "Yeah, but the little man with the book says…"

"Shoulders!" The Disposable jumped as the rather wobbly but uncharacteristically determined-looking Prince Dullard strode abruptly in front of him. "Could you please stop it now?"

Shoulders pulled a face at him. "You what?"

Dullard squared his shoulders awkwardly. "You need to stop," he repeated more firmly. "I'm sorry, but you can't feed Pleasance to that dragon."

Shoulders folded his arms, his expression alarmingly truculent. "I bloody *can*," he told the prince stubbornly. "And I'm bloody going to. Aside from the fact that her getting chomped is the only thing standing between me and a life in prison, I've been looking forward to it!"

Dullard frowned but allowed that comment to pass. "But really, it isn't necessary," he emphasised firmly, glancing at Pleasance, who Fodder noticed was staring at the prince with something resembling gratitude. The expression was so out of place on her face that it required a double take. "Pleasance has agreed to help us of her own free will. But only if we treat her with respect and *don't* feed her to any dragons."

Shoulders gave a violent snort. "Oh yeah, right! And you believe her? You know, there's thinking well of people, Dullard, and there's being a gullible sap."

"I'm not going to let you do it!" The force of the exclamation surprised everyone, most noticeably Dullard himself—but nonetheless, he squared his jaw and laid a hand pointedly against his sword hilt. "Look here," he insisted. "If you keep pressing this, I'll feel very guilty about giving you a thrashing and chopping off your limbs and I'll be happy to apologise for it in whatever manner you see fit. But that isn't going to stop me from doing it."

It was the most mild-mannered threat that Fodder had ever come across. But the fact it was a threat from Dullard, who, regardless of anything else, was more than capable of carrying it out, seemed to have shocked Shoulders into silence.

"Blimey," he muttered. "Who's spiked your mead today?"

Dullard was doing his best to look stern. It wasn't working but he persisted anyway.

"Flirt, could you please let Pleasance go?" he said awkwardly.

Flirt pulled a face. "She'll run off again, won't she?"

"Not if we agree to this." Dullard glanced over his shoulder to where Maw the Dragon had wandered away into the nearby shadows out of earshot, scratching at his head and looking bewildered. "As long as we don't go through with that plan, she'll help us. And her help could do more damage than being eaten by a dragon ever will."

Flirt sighed, glancing down at Pleasance, who had stopped thrashing in her grasp. "All right," she conceded, and let go.

Pleasance staggered free. It took a moment for her to regain her composure after her long battle, straightening her stained and tattered dress and raking a pointless finger through her maelstrom of hair. She squared her shoulders.

"It's the truth," she said, her voice thin but firm. "You have my word that I will do whatever I can to help you as long as I have your oaths that you will not abuse me, tie me up again, kill me off In Narrative by any means but particularly via a dragon, and that you will under no circumstances whatsoever allow me to be forced into love with that dreadful oik Bumpkin!" She swallowed hard. "Are we agreed?"

Dullard nodded at once. "Of course. You've had my agreement already."

Pleasance flashed him such a genuine smile that the last, lingering corner of Fodder's doubts faded away. The long shot was quivering in the gold.

"You've got my word too," he said. "Welcome aboard."

Flirt's nose was crinkled with doubt but at Fodder's acquiescence, she gave a defeated sigh. "I suppose you've got mine too, haven't you?" She glanced over to where Shoulders was waiting, head lopsided and arms crossed. "Shoulders?"

The Disposable glanced from one face to another, his expression incredulous.

"You're all stupid," he proclaimed without preamble. "And you'd better remember I said that when she has us hanging in the torture chambers of the Grim Fortress. But since I'm outnumbered, I've got no choice, have I? I'll agree and I'll keep to it as long as she does."

Pleasance gave an awkward nod. "Very well. Now…" she breathed out. "To get to the point, The Narrative is almost here and we're being held prisoner by a moronic dragon you keep trying to persuade to eat me. What are we going to do?"

Shoulders gestured to where Maw had wandered off to. "He's not looking," he whispered. "We could run for it."

Dullard was already shaking his head. "He's quick, and he can see in the dark better than we can. We need more time than just bolting will give us. I have an idea. Maw?" Raising his voice, he turned to the pacing Dragon, who glanced up and trotted his way back to where the five companions were waiting. Dullard smiled at him.

"Maw, do you remember me?" he asked gently.

"Ummm." Maw gazed avidly down at the prince for a moment. "Hang on, mate, you lot all look the same to me."

"I came up here a while ago, to look at the rocks?" Dullard prompted genially. "My uncle Primp introduced us? He gives you your instructions."

"The little man with the book!" The joyous exclamation nearly knocked Dullard to his knees. "That's it! You know the little man with the book!"

"Indeed I do." Dullard smiled at him. "Well, he asked me to tell you that he does need to talk to you about what you have to do but he can't come up here to do it. He's waiting for you down in the valley, on the edge of the forest, and he needs you to fly down there straightaway to see him. Can you do that?"

Maw gave his toothy grin. "The little man with the book!" he repeated with such sincere relief that Fodder's guilt returned in a rush. "Yeah, I need the little man with the book! They've been saying this stuff and making my head hurt and..."

"Uncle Primp will make it all clear." Dullard's tone was soothing but insistent. "But only if you meet him at the edge of the forest immediately."

There was something about the light. Fodder could sense it changing, feel the night air weaving, deepening, carrying a too-familiar sensation on the breeze, and one look at the set of Dullard's shoulders was enough to show he felt it too.

"The Narrative," he heard Pleasance breathe. And she sounded as scared as he felt.

"Yeah, the little man! I'll go see the little man! Thanks!"

With a down-blast that set their hair whipping and their eyes stinging, Maw the Dragon launched himself into the night air and vanished abruptly into the darkness as the air thickened noticeably behind him. The night horizon grew distinctly more vivid.

Dullard turned to his companions, rubbing his hands together as he relaxed his shoulders with a sigh.

"Well," he said breathily. "Now that we've dealt with that, may I suggest that we run?"

The sharpening darkness was pushing against the air, tightening it, wrapping it up as it surged against the mountains. In the distance, Fodder could hear the clatter of hooves against stone.

"Good plan," he said.

"Yep, all for it." Flirt nodded.

"Me too!" Shoulders agreed.

"I'm certainly in favour," conceded Pleasance.

And then, as one, they bolted.

But as the darkness deepened, strengthened, and whipped around them, they knew it was already too…

Glimpse…

"I see something!" Slynder's sharp eyes, more accustomed to darkness than daylight, had picked something out of the gloom. "Figures, people, there are people running…"

Lost…

"Cheating!" The exclamation burst furiously from Pleasance's lips as she stumbled awkwardly on the loose rock and skidding gravel of the rocky slope that had proved their temporary salvation. "It's night— there's no way he should have been able to see."

Fodder didn't give much of a hoot about the unfairness of the situation. All he knew was the brief duck below the horizon would not protect them for long against the Narrative reach of good night vision.

Not being so blessed himself, he could only squint ahead, struggling and staggering on the uneven, sloping ground, breathing hard as he risked a glance at his night-washed companions—Shoulders, his head joggling awkwardly and his eyes wild; Flirt, her face pale but determined and her sword half-drawn; Pleasance, teetering and scrabbling as she fought a battle as much with her own skirts as the footing; and Dullard, anxious and helpful all at once as he dithered alongside their new recruit, apparently torn as to whether he should be helping her or respecting her independence.

"Head right!" the prince called out suddenly, his voice a breathless gasp. "We'll be trapped at the ravine if we don't!"

That was reason enough for Fodder. Veering away from the downwards slope, he scrambled along the line of the scree, keeping his head as low as he dared with the horizon's darkness gleaming vividly. A rock took a nice gouge out of the side of his foot—clamping his teeth together to avoid a giveaway screech, Fodder staggered on. Flirt nudged at his shoulder to keep him on track as they staggered down into a rocky crevice. Fodder heard Shoulders give a nasty *oof* as he met the solid, craggy wall of the slit in a rolling ricochet, and a gasp from Pleasance suggested she had only narrowly avoided a clichéd ankle-buckling. Groping now in shadows, their pace slowed by necessity, they grabbed and stumbled their way onwards into deeper darkness. Fodder ignored the pain when his hands scratched against the jagged rock, his skin bruised from unseen impacts, but the crevice was opening up, a rocky plateau sloping towards a moon-washed, glimmering tarn, and if they could get a few more yards...

But the darkness thickened, the moon brightened, and the plateau was washed in gleaming night. The Narrative!

"They came this way; I am certain of it! Stay alert! We must find them!"

Thud's Narratively-enhanced voice echoed from the mouth of the crevice beyond. Teeth gritted, Fodder froze, with his companions, in an awkward, cramped huddle, not daring to talk, hardly daring to breathe. To their right, Fodder spotted a deeper patch of shadows nestled behind an outcrop of rock—reaching out, he found a chain-mailed arm, presumably Flirt or Shoulders, and gave a none-too-subtle yank.

Carefully, he reached out his fingers, groping for the concealment of the rock wall, pulling whomever he happened to be holding along with him; and to judge by the mass of dark shapes beyond, the grasp had been passed on. A few more feet, and they would be safely out of sight.

Fodder reached out his foot.

There was nothing underneath it.

The Disposable just had time to note that perhaps the reason for the depth of these shadows was that they were in fact a socking great hole in the rock face before he dropped like a stone to the muffled gasps and shrieks of the companions he dragged after him. There was a moment of stomach-churning, blind falling before the illusive surface finally found his foot and jolted him into a rather deeper darkness.

After narrowly escaping from ravaging wolves, the
princess and Erik find themselves trapped in a cave
where the dragon attacks them — Erik's powers burst
into life and he defeats it, before they escape
together on Erik's horse, which found him instinctively. It is then that Eldrigon arrives and reveals
his destiny — he is in fact Erikhelion, the last
descendant of Avikhelion and Elder's own other
daughter, the Seeress Mydrella, who was murdered by
Craxis when she prophesised his downfall. Young Erik
is the only one who can use the Ring against Craxis
and has inherited the magic of Eldrigon's line. Elder
promises he will understand more when they seek the
guidance of his ancestor in a place of special magic.

"Who d'you reckon they are?"

There was a foot in Fodder's face. Given the pointy nature of the shoe he could feel attached to it, he was fairly certain it wasn't his own. Neither was the bony elbow digging heavily into his side, nor the chain-mailed behind that was squashed against his kneecaps. Heavy planks pressed against his back beneath his warm, fleshy blanket of body parts. His own body parts, fortuitously still attached, ached loudly but felt, at least, to be in usable nick. However, in the heavy blackness that had enveloped him, there was little else that he could tell.

"Dunno. You reckon we should have left them there?"

"Nah, couldn't do that. They were blocking the track."

The voices were gruff, nearby, but muffled by the weight of what-ever—or to judge by the heat and squishiness, *whoever*—had been piled into this cramped, confined space around him. Echoing in the dark, he could hear the clank and squeal of iron wheels, the rattle of a chain, and the steady plod of footsteps.

"D'you reckon they might be those ones that his nibs was talking about?"

"Which ones?"

"You know! The ones he was moaning about. The troublemakers."

"Could be, could be. But I ain't much bothered by what goes on up there. We'll take 'em to his nibs and he can sort 'em out."

As Fodder made a discreet effort to shift his pinned-down body, his ears pricked up. Trapped as he was, he certainly felt like a prisoner, but the casual, unconcerned nature of the conversation implied his captors viewed their task less as prisoner transport and more as a moderate inconvenience. But given the choice, he didn't feel much inclined to move from this unconcerned guard to the mysterious *his nibs* who felt them worthy of a moan.

The darkness was waning. It was gradual, barely perceivable, but light was leeching onto the edges of the shadows, picking out distinctions of shape, colour, texture that had moments before been invisible. Fodder could see now that the limp foot prodding at his nose belonged to Princess Pleasance, that the bony elbow was attached to the curled-up form of Dullard, and the chain-mailed backside pressing none-too-delicately against his kneecaps was Flirt's. Shoulders's head was bouncing loosely by his feet.

None of them were moving. Either they had decided discretion was the better part of valour or they had yet to rouse from their fall. Given that Pleasance's nose was perilously close to Shoulders's armpit, it was probably for the best that it be the latter.

Did he dare try to speak? Should he risk trying to rouse them? He certainly wasn't going any-bloody-where until the heavy buggers woke, and he felt a definite urge to be moving. He risked a great deal in a moan-provoking prod at Shoulders's head with his toes but it simply jolted slightly.

Fodder sighed. Shoulders definitely wasn't awake. If he'd done that to a conscious Shoulders, discretion or not, everyone within a five-mile radius would have heard about it.

Abandoning any hope of movement for the time being, Fodder focused instead on working out where the bloody hell he was. In the dim but growing light, thankfully natural and not Narrative, he could see the wooden planks that made up this strange, slant-sided box into which they had been unceremoniously piled. Through the gap between Pleasance's knee and Dullard's wrist, he caught glimpses of the shadowy contours of a rocky ceiling moving by at a slow but steady pace, presumably walking speed to judge by the ongoing, steady tromp of heavy-duty boots. He caught a glimpse of two sets of thick, knobbly, hairy hands grasping the wood a couple of feet above his head but he could see no hint of any faces.

Who were these people? Where were they? And where were they taking them?

"Hate this place." The first voice, presumably the owner of one knobbly set of hands, piped up grouchily. "Too much bloody light—it kills my night eyes cold."

"Glad we don't come here much," the other agreed. "Still can't believe his nibs, he volunteers for it here when he ain't up top. He *likes* the light. Why does he need it all?"

"Wuss, isn't he?" was the uncompromising retort. "Hates the dark, hates the tunnels—if he had his way, he'd be up there on top all the bloody time. Dunno what's wrong with him. Born funny in the head, I reckon."

"Least it saves any of us having to do it," his companion pointed out. "Going up there, pratting about in the light and that open air? No thanks!"

Tunnels. A bell rang in Fodder's head. True, he had never had much to do with them except as a reluctant participant in the occasional Final Battle, but they lived underground, didn't they, down in tunnels, and didn't they moan like champions about coming out to fight in the light?

Dwarves.

Underground tracks. Mining carts. Could the voices he was hearing be dwarves?

But how could that be right? The Dwarf Mines were miles from here, on the far side of the Turbulent Inlet.

The ceiling was stretching up and up as the tunnel opened out into a vast cavern, a huge crack in the roof allowing the flood of pale morning light that washed the cave below with a whisper of day. The two presumed dwarves pushing the cart along made noises of painful displeasure, lifting a knobbly hand apiece to guard their squinting eyes as they emerged into the relative brightness. In the distance, Fodder could hear the gentle splash of waves against a rocky shore.

Where were they?

And then Shoulders groaned.

It was a full, proper Shoulders groan, loud and pointed and replete with despair and irritation and the unfairness of the world, and the sound raised a twitch from Dullard's elbow and a sigh of princessly weariness from Pleasance's lips. A pair of heavily bearded faces peered thoughtfully over the top of the cart at the sound. Dwarves. They were! But how? What were they doing so far from home?

"'Allo," one of them muttered. "I think our sleeping beauties are coming round."

"Better dump them," said his friend. "Heave!"

Fodder didn't even have time to brace himself. With startling abruptness, the cart heaved sideways and in a painful, thudding flurry of limbs and skulls, he and his companions crashed in a heap onto a rocky, unforgiving floor. Even as Fodder gasped, the breath driven from his lungs by the impact of Dullard's shoulder in his chest, he saw Shoulders's head spinning in a wild circle nearby, giving out bewildered gasps of horror.

"Some of them are still down," a gruff voice noted clinically. "Best to rouse them, I reckon."

Heavy boots padded away as Fodder floundered to free himself, catching glimpses of rock and beards and distant sky through the flailing of many disorientated limbs.

The footsteps returned.

Pleasance's voice, shrill and anxious, cut sharply into the air. "Don't you da—" she started.

And then there was wet.

Fodder only gasped in shock as the icy cold, salty water splattered his skin and armour and doused him thoroughly. Pleasance, however, was less discreet.

"…rrrrreeeeeeeee!!!!!"

Pleasance's screams, always a work of art, were agonising enough in the open. But this scream, replete with anguish and fury and indignant rage, was amplified with terrible shrillness by the rock walls, reverberating like a ricocheting weapon as it dominated every inch of free air and ripped against the ears. His eardrums shrieking in sympathy, Fodder managed to haul the floundering, dampened, and bewildered-looking Dullard off his midriff. He bolted half-upright just in time to avoid being kicked in the jaw as the dripping princess swung her legs around, grabbed her skirts in a ball, and staggered, hair soaked and eyes wild, to her feet. Her eyes fixed upon the suddenly frozen, bearded dwarf in whose hands was clasped a large wooden bucket.

"Why, you little...!" she shrieked. "How *dare* you? What's left of this dress is velvet! And as for my hair..." She grasped a dripping lock and waved it accusingly. "When I get my hands on you..."

"Oh, bloody hell!" One look at her fierce expression was enough to convince the dwarf that he was in trouble. Dropping the bucket, he backed hurriedly away, but his flight was not quick enough to escape the strides of the furious, sodden princess, whose fingers lashed out, digging into his beard as she hauled him onto the tips of his toes by its roots.

"I'm going to tear your beard out hair by hair, you obnoxious—"

"Pleasance!" Dullard's voice rang across the cavern as he rocketed to his feet. "Pleasance, don't! Put him down!"

"But my hair!" The princess's eyes were almost glowing with anger. "And the disrespect! Doesn't he know who I *am*?"

"I doubt he cares." Dullard was speaking very carefully now, one arm outstretched in a placatory manner. "Pleasance, please. Look around you. And put him down."

Pleasance looked. And so did Fodder.

Everywhere were carts, carts half-laden with boxes, bales and barrels, sacks and bundles of wood and cloth that filled the cavern—no, the coastal cave—from side to side. And surrounding them, loading them, pushing them, and grasping an alarming array of crowbars, tools, and pickaxes, were wall-to-wall dwarves.

Each one was staring at the newcomers. Each one was tightening his grip on the nearest blunt object.

Pleasance stared for a moment, her grip not loosening; meanwhile her face, a moment before locked in a fierce rage, began to slip to a more moderate expression. Her fingers released the beard, dropping the dwarf back to his feet. He quickly scrambled away from her, his hands held protectively around the long drape of his facial hair, stroking it. She took a deep, calming breath.

"Very well," she said, her voice quiet, her words directed towards the dwarf, although Fodder did not miss the pointed way that they darted towards Dullard as she spoke. "But I am not happy."

"No bloody kidding," Fodder heard Flirt mutter under her breath.

But in an act of what Fodder considered to be outstanding bravery, Dullard did not let the matter go. "I understand that," he replied gently. "But one bad turn should not beget another. I think you owe that poor gentleman an apology."

The turn of Pleasance's head was a slow, dangerous motion, not unlike a cobra swinging round to strike. Her eyes narrowed.

"I owe him?" she exclaimed, her voice low and threatening as she shook her dripping head. "Have you seen my hair?"

"Well, you did say only yesterday that you felt it needed a good wash." There was no doubt in Fodder's mind—Prince Dullard was feeling suicidal. It had to be the double knock to the head. "And I'm sure he didn't mean any harm." He smiled kindly. "I'm certain you'll both feel better for it."

For a moment, Fodder thought that the tightness of Pleasance's features was a prelude to a strike. But then, her lips forced themselves into a mordant smile and she turned to face the beard-stroking dwarf, who was still staring at her as though she was a circling dragon.

"I'm so *dreadfully* sorry," she declared lavishly. "I don't know *what* came over me."

It was possibly the least sincere apology in the whole history of apology-dom. But it seemed to do the trick. The atmosphere in the room relaxed noticeably as the dwarves returned to their tasks. Only the beard-stroker and a couple of pickaxe-holding companions remained.

"You lot, you stay put, okay?" he said shakily, waving his non-beard-holding hand at them nervously. "We've called his nibs to deal with you!" With a hefty *humph*, he pulled himself up onto a nearby box and grabbed a pickaxe from a passing companion. His eyebrows knitted, he glared at them.

Slowly, warily, Flirt and Fodder also came to their feet, Shoulders scooping up his head as he joined them. Dullard rested his hands gently onto the taut Pleasance's shoulders and drew her back to his side.

"Are you all right?" he asked softly.

Her smile was brittle. "I'm soaked, lost, publicly humiliated, and have probably made the most ridiculous mistake of my life by agreeing to go along with you. Take a *guess.*"

"I am sorry." Dullard's expression was contrite. "And please don't feel you've made a mistake. Honestly, you haven't."

"We'll see," she huffed, although the fierceness of her expression had slipped around the edges. "But if you ever embarrass me like that again, I'll break off that nose of yours and make you *swallow* it."

"Of course." Dullard took this threat of cannibalistic violence in his stride. "But it was necessary. The dwarves are one of my uncle Primp's responsibilities and he's told me a little about them. If you hadn't apologised, they might have attacked us. Dwarves are very big on good manners."

Shoulders glared round at the clusters of bearded figures, brushing water droplets absently from his helmet as he rested his head on his hands. "Must be about the only thing they're *big* on."

Flirt's hand slapped around like a hurricane to wallop across Shoulders's half-hefted mouth and gag him. "Oi!" she hissed. "Don't say things like that! We don't want to hack them off, do we?"

"Actually, dwarves have no particular sensibility to height-based humour," Dullard offered. "To them, we are the freaks of nature. You can make as many short jokes as you like as long as you are prepared to face a barrage of tall jokes in return."

Flirt raised an eyebrow but did not comment. Reluctantly, however, she did release Shoulders's mouth. The Disposable lifted his head to give her a pointed look before swinging around the room to take a look.

"Where the bloody hell are we?" he exclaimed, shaking his dampened fingers by his nose and sniffing unpleasantly. "I smell salt. Is this seawater?"

"Looks like it, doesn't it?" Flirt gestured to the nearby opening in the vast crack in the cavern, where waves wandered gently in from a rolling sea to lap against a stone quay carved out of the edge of the rock. The tracks in the cave appeared to stem from there, piles of boxes resting on the water's edge before they were flung into nearby carts, then pushed away down a dizzying array of openings. In the distance, a sail was slipping out of view beyond the cliff wall. "I wonder what this place is?"

Fodder was shaking his head. "I thought the dwarves lived on the other side of the Turbulent Inlet at the moment. And unless we've been out much longer than I thought, we can't have been taken over there."

"Oh, the dwarves have mines and tunnels all over the Realm," Dullard corrected him brightly. "I've come across them often in my caving—they are excellent places to trace rock strata. I always assumed they were for emergencies—one never knows in a Quest where and when one may need an unexpected dwarf. But I've never entered any of the tunnels when they were in use before." He frowned thoughtfully. "It would appear to be some manner of logistics operation."

"And using words the rest of us understand?" Shoulders retorted acidly.

Dullard regarded him for a moment. "They move things around," he clarified, not unkindly. "By the looks of it, supplies. My guess is they take in goods via the sea and distribute them throughout the area using the underground."

Fodder frowned. "I thought that's what carts were for. That's how we get ours at Humble Village."

"That's the most practical way on flat farmland, I'm sure," Dullard agreed. "But can you imagine trying to take a cart into the Wild Forest or the Most Savage Mountains?"

He had a point. And the operation seemed to be a pretty well-oiled affair—already the boxes, bales, and barrels, presumably left by the departing vessel, were disappearing rapidly, as an assortment of bearded figures deposited them into mining carts and vanished down the honeycomb of tunnels. Dwarf numbers were already lessening.

"They don't seem to be paying us much attention, do they?" Flirt eyed the emptying room critically. "Other than Pleasance's beard-stroking friend and his mates, none of them seem to care less." She lowered her voice as her hand strayed to her sword hilt. "I reckon we could be out of here in ten seconds flat if we wanted. And it might be a good idea before this *nibs* of theirs arrives, mightn't it?"

But Dullard was shaking his head. "I really don't think violence is wise. Not unless we want fifty angry dwarves on our tail for the rest of our journey." He glanced over his shoulder at the cluster of guards. "Why don't you let me talk to them first?"

Shoulders's eyes darted to the bearded gang of pickaxe holders with their brows frowning and their eyes grim. "Yeah, good luck," he muttered. "Especially after Her Highness's little performance." He cocked a pointed eyebrow in Pleasance's direction. "You'd almost think she *wanted* us to get duffed up."

Pleasance's features flared up violently. "Now listen, you headless cretin…"

"Hey!" Fodder intervened hurriedly, even before Dullard, so keen was he to prevent the inevitable row from gathering pace. "Shoulders, if Pleasance was going to turn us in, she could have done it at Maw's cave with one scream. And, Pleasance, don't let him wind you up, okay? He's being himself; he can't help it." He took a breath as two pairs of eyes glared but fortunately did not rise further. "Dullard, give talking a go. But if it doesn't work, Flirt, hand on your sword, okay?"

Neither the prince nor the Barmaid looked entirely contented by this decision but both nodded. Dullard turned towards the dwarves wearing his usual friendly smile.

"Hello there!" he greeted. "I wonder if I might have a word?"

Pleasance's victim was still stroking his poor beard in a vaguely protective fashion as he squinted irritably at the approaching prince. "If you want," he replied uncertainly. "But hands off the beard!"

Dullard raised his hands in a soothing manner. "I wouldn't dream of it," he said reassuringly. "I was wondering—would it be all right if we go now?"

The dwarf blinked, and he wasn't alone. "Pardon me?"

"I was wondering if we could go." Dullard made a vague gesture towards the opening of the cavern. "We very much appreciate you picking us up after our fall and bringing us here, but we do need to be on our way."

The dwarves were staring, nonplussed, at the prince. So were Fodder and his friends. Whatever manner of persuasion he had anticipated—a discussion on their cause, perhaps, or a plea for mercy—he hadn't expected that Dullard was just going to *ask*.

"Well, not really." The bewildered dwarf had even released his beard.

Dullard raised an eyebrow. "Oh dear. Why not?"

The dwarf floundered. "Because I reckon, well, because you're our prisoners?"

The prince pulled a face. "Oh goodness me, whatever for?"

This was not a question the dwarf was prepared to deal with. "Ummm..."

One of his friends stepped in to rescue him. "We were told, I reckon. We had to keep an eye out. For troublemakers."

"Troublemakers?" Dullard frowned. "What troublemakers?"

It was the second dwarf's turn to be confused. "The troublemakers!" he repeated more fervently. "The ones his nibs has moaned about. The ones on the surface."

"Oh dear." Dullard tapped one finger thoughtfully against his lips. "I hadn't heard about this. Whatever have these troublemakers been up to?"

The second dwarf glanced around at his suddenly panic-eyed friends for aid. None was forthcoming. "Ummm...making trouble!" he declared.

Fodder bit back a smile as Dullard's logic finally slipped around at the back door and came knocking.

They don't know what's been happening.

"How terribly unfortunate." Dullard shook his head. "I didn't know a thing about this. Did any of you?"

He glanced over his shoulder at his companions, who shook their heads in hurriedly orchestrated denial. Dullard turned back to the dwarves.

"It's news to us," he reiterated. "We were escorting the princess to her confrontation with the Dragon when we fell foul of one of your air vents." He gestured to Pleasance, who graced the dwarf with a rapidly regal smile. "And our poor friend there was even decapitated by the fall. Landed on his sword, you know." Shoulders gave an unconvincing grin as he hefted his head. "So I'm sure you understand why we really have to get going. There are preparations we have to make, heads to get repaired, princesses to dry off, and not much time to do it. Strut would be terribly angry if we missed our cue because of you." He bit his lip. "I dread to think what he'd have to say."

There was a long pause. Several squint-eyed gazes of alarm were exchanged from above trembling beards. A flurry of anxious whispers followed.

"What do you reckon?"

"Do they look like troublemakers?"

"What do troublemakers look like, anyhow?"

"Dunno. Never seen one."

"He said that's the princess, that is! Princesses ain't troublemakers!"

"But what if they are and we let 'em go?"

"What if they ain't and we *don't?*"

"I don't care if they are or they ain't. All I care about is, if we don't leave for the Mystical Forest caves in half an hour, we'll be late for card night!"

This statement earned a thoughtful pause. Apparently this was a point worthy of deeper consideration.

"I like card night," one gruff voice offered plaintively. "I've been looking forward to it."

"Well, you mustn't!" was the harsh retort. "Dwarves hate elves, right? It's the rules, it's nature, it's the way it's meant to be! Any time we spend in the company of those lanky, underfed, beardless ponces should be a test of our endurance!"

The plaintive voice piped in. "But we play cards with them twice a month and then get pissed on mead. Last time, you and Windblossom had your arms around each other and started singing the song about gremlins."

"Yeah, that's as may be!" the second dwarf retorted. "But I didn't enjoy it, did I?"

There was another thoughtful pause. This one was slightly more cynical.

"We're off the point, I reckon," a bearded voice of sanity intervened. "What are we going to do with them?"

"We could wait for his nibs."

"He could be ruddy ages yet. If he's off on one of his wanders *out there...*"

There was a collective shudder.

"If I may?" Dullard intervened delicately. Bearded faces glanced hopefully in his direction. "How about we be on our way, and if your friend wants a word with us, all he has to do is catch up with us back at

Maw the Dragon's cave for the obligatory slaying, which I'm sure isn't far away." He beamed ingratiatingly. "I wouldn't want you to miss your important grudge match with the elves. It would be awful if they took your absence as a win by forfeit when you would so clearly thrash them thoroughly in a fair bout."

"Yeah." The elf-hating gremlin-singer nodded curtly. "Wouldn't put it past the stringy, cheating, long-haired bastards."

"And they're bringing the mead," another voice injected. "Cackle's good stuff, Moonbright said."

There was a smacking of lips and some appreciative nodding. The mention of the good stuff seemed to be swaying the doubters.

"All right then." The beard-stroker stepped in. "If you absolutely insist you ain't troublemakers, we'll take your word for it. But don't think we won't be checking up!"

"Absolutely." Dullard's face was razor straight. "So, if you could point us back in the direction of Maw's cavern?"

Relieved of the duty of guarding them and the threat of curtailed drinking time, the dwarves were suddenly pure helpfulness.

"That's the tunnel you need," one of the dwarves replied, with a helpful gesture of the pickaxe. "It'll take you right back the way you came. An hour or so down the way and you'll be right next to it."

"Thank you so much." Dullard smiled cheerfully as he turned, scooping his pack from the tumbled pile of their belongings next to the mining cart and gesturing to his companions. "Shall we?"

Fodder didn't need telling twice. With the most ingratiating smile he could muster, he grabbed his pack and, with his companions, fell quickly in behind the casually strolling prince.

"Do we want to be going back this way?" Flirt murmured through her smile in a hiss of breath. "We barely escaped last time, didn't we?"

"We only need to get out of sight." Dullard's lips barely moved behind his fake cheer. "You have the rest of my climbing gear in your pack, I assume?" Fodder nodded and the prince's cheer gained sincerity. "Good. That means with one air vent or natural cave system, we can leave wherever we choose."

The tunnel was closing fast. The guard dwarves' attention had wandered, apparently already focused on their night out on the piss with their traditional enemy, and only a few others remained, loading carts with the last of the goods for distribution. Just a few more feet to the tunnel mouth and they would be...

"Hey! Hey! That's them! The *troublemakers!* That's the one who killed me!"

Bollocks.

"The troublemakers? Why, you lying buggers!"

"That's rude, that is!"

"Can't be having rude. Let's get 'em!"

"Take out their kneecaps! Stop 'em! Stop 'em quick!"

"Leg it!" Fodder didn't need Shoulders's screech to pick a course of action. He had already bolted for the tunnel's mouth hot on his friend's heels as dwarves everywhere bolted to attention. It wasn't lost yet, if they could get out of sight and find a place to hide.

"Oof!" Fodder barely managed to stop in time, bouncing painfully off the corner of the mining cart that heaved suddenly into view in the tunnel mouth and slapping with a smack against the floor. Shoulders was less lucky.

Fodder caught one quick glimpse of his fellow Disposable's legs waving frantically in the air as his body somersaulted upside down over the cart's rim, his head snatched out of the air by one of the bewildered-looking dwarves pushing it. But when a pickaxe missed Fodder's own, better-attached skull by inches, it rather distracted his attention.

"Hey! Get off him!" A sword blade flashed across Fodder's field of vision as he staggered to his feet—with a bellow of pain, the attacking dwarf staggered back, clutching his fingers.

"Oi!" he bawled furiously. "That's my *dealing* hand!"

Flirt's hand grabbed Fodder's shoulder, pushing him forwards as he groped for his own sword.

"Wait, wait!" Dullard's anxious voice cut into the blossoming melee. "Everyone, please calm down and I'm sure that we can..."

But the dwarves, it appeared, were no longer in any mood to listen. A short, angry figure charged at the prince from behind, his pickaxe swinging wildly.

"Look out!" Dullard had not even drawn his sword, but Pleasance had seen the danger. Grabbing the prince's arm, she hauled him wildly backwards out of the path of the down-swinging axe. The blade skimmed the back of the stumbling prince's hose before burying itself emphatically into his calf.

"Ah!" Dullard dropped instantly, off balance and in shock as the dwarf yanked his blade free, anxious for a second strike. But he had not counted on the intervention of one irate princess and a pointed, hard-swung shoe approaching at groin height. A further strike quickly became the least of his worries.

"Bloody stop staring and run!" Flirt's grab on Fodder's arm was insistent. "We'll come back for them later, won't we?"

Dwarves were circling them now, far more than Fodder had thought remained, hefting crowbars and tools in a threatening manner. Fodder leapt quickly to avoid the swing of the iron bar, planting his foot on a barrel as he hurled himself out of the way. Flirt's grip vanished as she turned, swinging her sword in a series of wild arcs to drive back their attackers, but she would have done better to watch where she was going—her heel caught on a low box and she went flying backwards. Dwarves pounced onto her in seconds, pinning her struggling form to the ground with surprisingly strong knobbly hands. Even as Fodder paused, torn between going to her aid and his own flight, he saw Pleasance, despite a spirited resistance involving the pickaxe of the dwarf she'd felled, also being dragged down beside the wounded Dullard and the separated Shoulders.

And the pause was a mistake. Dwarves were closing fast from all directions—he turned, desperate to flee, but a bearded figure launched himself out of a nearby mining cart, crowbar held high. Fodder just had time to reflect that today was really not going his way when the bar descended on his skull with a crunch and yet again, everything went dark.

* * *

"Oi! Wakey, wakey, tall-arse!"

Something was prodding with irritating insistency against his shoulder. It felt like a pickaxe.

That couldn't be good.

Blinking and reluctant, Fodder pried his eyelids apart. His head was pounding, although the insistent itch implied it would not be long before this non-Narrative damage would pass. The stone floor against which his face was pressed offered little in the way of soothing, although the fact that he could see it in the glowing light of the huge, fiercely burning lantern that was hanging from the ceiling was a reassurance. He looked up slowly. Iron bars, the bars of a cage, glinted in the light.

The pickaxe poker, Pleasance's beard-stroking friend from earlier, squinted into the cage at him with satisfaction.

"Copped you a good'un, I reckon," he said with irritating cheer. "Spark out, you were. Teach you and your troublemaking mates for lying, won't it?" He sniffed irritably. "You can wait here for his nibs but I'm off. Card night, isn't it?"

As Fodder pulled himself painfully to his knees, he saw the dwarf turn and trot off towards a narrow exit. A moment later, he vanished down a tunnel and was gone.

"Fodder?"

Something marginally softer poked at his shoulder. He turned.

From the neighbouring cage, Flirt smiled at him wanly. Her wrists and cheek looked bruised from her tussle with the pack of dwarves.

"All right, are you?" she asked quietly.

"My head hurts. But I'm okay," he replied wearily. "You?"

"Battered, aren't I?" Flirt shrugged. "But still in one piece."

"Lucky you," came a mordant voice from beyond Flirt. "And at least you didn't have any bloody dwarves sticking fingers up your nose."

Flirt rolled her eyes with resignation. "Yes, Shoulders. We know."

"I'm really so terribly sorry." Another familiar voice, apparently yet another cage distant, intervened weakly. "I should never have tried to deceive them. I knew how they felt about bad manners, but it did seem the only way to leave without violence…"

"Dullard, it's fine." Fodder stepped in to halt the apologetic ramble. "It was a bloody good idea and it nearly worked." He chuckled grimly. "I had no idea you were such a fine quality liar."

"I did." Pleasance's voice had an odd note beneath it. "He conned me right into your trap back at the Palace, after all."

"I prefer to think of it as *acting*." Dullard's voice sounded distinctly uncomfortable. "I learned a great deal when Doom let me join his amateur dramatics society—he really is quite the thespian. And it's a skill I only use when I really have to..."

His sentence broke off with an audible wince. Pleasance's voice tutted fiercely beyond it. "You mean like pretending that leg of yours isn't bothering you at all?"

Fodder had forgotten that Dullard too had been injured in the scuffle. "Your leg! How bad is it?"

"A bit sore," came the understated reply, undermined by the incredulous snort of the princess. "I've bandaged it up and it should be fine in a day or two, but until then, walking may prove challenging." There was a gentle clang against distant bars. "Not that walking is an option at the moment."

"It scuppers our escape plans, though, doesn't it?" Flirt pointed out with a grim shake of the bars. "We can hardly make a run for it if one of us can't run."

"What escape plans?" Shoulders snorted incredulously. "They've dragged us down who knows how many tunnels and dumped us here—if you know the way back, you're doing better than me! And these cages are locked tight, remember?"

Fodder sighed. "Did you try picking the locks?"

Flirt returned his sigh. "We established a while back, didn't we, that none of us know how to pick locks."

"Even Dullard?"

Dullard peered along the row of cages, his brow creased. "I'm afraid it's not something I've ever had call to do." His voice brightened a tad. "I'd be happy to have a go at it, though, if you'd like me to. I've always found the mechanics behind locks to be a fascinating subject and I have been meaning to look into it for some time. In fact, I've wondered for a while if it might be possible to manufacture a lock that is immune to any picking possibilities. I'm sure with the right manipulation of the pins and latches..."

"Which would be of great use here," Shoulders drawled, interrupting the academic flow, "in a world where every lock is there for the bloody Hero to pick. Get to the point, will you? Can you get us out?"

"I can have a go." Dullard's reply was slightly subdued at the interruption of his pondering. "I'd need an implement of some kind, long and thin, to try and manipulate the bolt. Does anyone have anything?"

There was a profound silence that spoke volumes on the lack of thin, long objects.

"Hang on," Shoulders intruded suddenly. "What about her? Miss Princess, keeping silent, she's bound to have a hair pin or something! But no, she's sat there quiet as a mouse because it's to her good if we don't..."

"A hair pin?" Pleasance cut in harshly. "Do you think if I had a hair pin, my hair would look like this?"

"So we've got nothing. Great." Fodder rested his aching forehead against his hands. "Magnificent even. So what the hell do we do now?"

"An apology'd be a start."

Fodder jumped at the unexpected voice. His head whipped round to find the small, inevitably bearded figure standing cross-armed in the tunnel entrance. Although his expression was stern, his eyes were drifting nervously towards the rocky ceiling and his face...

His face was familiar, if rather more mundane than the last time Fodder had seen it, artfully strained in death and etched in vivid Narrative light.

"Gruffly." He said the name almost instinctively. "You're Gruffly, aren't you? You're Gort the Dwarf from the Merry Band."

"I *was*," came the pointed retort. "Until that git friend of yours slaughtered me."

"Oi, hang on!" Shoulders's voice was indignant. "That was your precious bloody Narrative, not me! I didn't get a say in it!"

"You can't blame Shoulders!" Flirt also intervened fervently. "The Narrative wanted you dead—it tried to get me to do it too! Your death was in the instructions, wasn't it?"

"Yeah, yeah, yeah, I know all that!" As Gruffly entered the room, his eyes continued to dart towards the rock around them. In the back of Fodder's mind, something was prodding at him about the dwarf's behaviour, a memory, a familiar voice—but why? What had it said?

"I know I was due to die!" The dwarf sounded anxious beneath his irritation. "But it was supposed to be a heroic moment, a rescue, a noble act of self-sacrifice, my life for the Hero's! I wasn't supposed to be blundering like a clumsy oaf into some nutter's sword swing because the whole plot was so messed-up that nothing worked like it should! And that was down to you!" A hairy finger jabbed accusingly at the air. "Do you know how hard it is to get respect as a dwarf up there on the surface? Not even the Taskmaster gives much of a damn! You know what I reckon? I reckon they killed me off because I'm *short*. You never see them tall, skinny elves getting sacrificed, do you, oh no! It's always the little bloke! Easy to overlook, that's the trouble! And it doesn't help when my one moment of Narrative glory gets ruined by the likes of you!"

The voice at the back of Fodder's mind was prodding at him as insistently as any pickaxe. But for the moment he chose to work with what he had. "But it wasn't us who set you up to die," he pointed out in his best reasonable tone. "That was down to the Taskmaster and..."

Gruffly's harsh snort was enough to stifle the rest of that sentence. "Don't even try it. I know your game; I'm not like those insular idiots out there. I've been playing around up top! If you think you can turn me against The Narrative, then you're even thicker than you look!" His eyes darted once more towards the roof of the cave. "Narrative calls are the only relief I *get*."

Gruffly. Did you know he's scared of enclosed spaces?

Donk's voice. That was it. How long ago did it feel that he had heard his fellow Disposable mutter those words in the Archetypal Inn as Bard had sallied forth with the *story so far*? Fodder hadn't thought twice about what was said at the time. But now...

A *claustrophobic* dwarf. That had promise. And it certainly explained his twitchiness and the anxious note underlying his tirade. This was a dwarf on edge and their best chance, for conversion or escape, was probably to keep him there.

And if the comments he'd heard earlier were anything to go by...

"You're 'his nibs,' aren't you?" Fodder said.

Gruffly's bearded face darkened. "Still call me that, do they?" he growled. "Charming, that is! No respect, that's what I get round here!"

"I don't know," Fodder offered mildly, very much aware from his experience with Shoulders and Dullard that when someone is determined to rail against the world, the thing most inclined to keep them railing is moderate reason. "They seem to regard you as something of a leader. They didn't seem to want to act without your opinion."

"Ha!" Gruffly's exclamation was explosive. "They wouldn't have thought twice about me if it wasn't surface business! They can't cope with surface business! You want to know how much they respect me? How about this?" He gritted his teeth. "I told 'em that you were dangerous troublemakers and I needed a group to guard you while I went to the surface to get help. And you know what they did?"

"Nothing good?" Fodder provoked with faux sincerity.

"Less than nothing! They *buggered off!*" Gruffly waved his fists at the lantern in impotent rage as a rant that Fodder suspected had been held against his heart for a long, long time finally spilled out into the open. "To their precious card night! Every one of 'em gone and left me here to watch you by myself! I told 'em how important it was, but would they listen? Not to his bloody *nibs*, no, the fresh-air-loving wuss! They wouldn't even go for help on the way! Because saving our way of life is so much less important than getting pissed over a game of blackjack with a species we're supposed to hate!" He took a deep, angry breath, apparently too far along to care who his audience were. "Dwarves and elves hate each other. That's always the way In Narrative so it has to be the truth in life, it's nature, it's a matter of bloody course! I get that! And they know it too, in their own thick-headed way, but does it stop 'em when there's mead and blackjack on the line? Does it buggery! And so I'll have to wait right up until tomorrow morning for 'em to reel back in singing that bloody song about gremlins before I can send for Strut to deal with you!"

Filing that revelation carefully under "useful to know", Fodder exchanged a quick glance with Flirt. Her eyebrow was cocked thoughtfully and her lips pursed.

"I hate to say it, don't I?" she said mildly. "But it sounds like you're right. They don't respect you much, do they?"

"Course they bloody don't!" It was a bit like dealing with a short, bearded Shoulders. "It's obvious!"

"So, why do you stay here?" Fodder asked with rather less mock-curiosity. "Why don't you leave and go and live in the sun?"

The look Gruffly fixed him with was as long and pointed as a broadsword. "Because I'm a dwarf, dopey. How stupid are you? *Dwarves live underground.*"

"Most dwarves do," Dullard injected into the conversation. "But most dwarves aren't Principals. They don't know any differently."

"Principals are a breed apart." There was a certain pointedness to Pleasance's tone—Fodder heard Shoulders huff loudly in response. "We are the lynchpins upon which a Quest swings. Our needs should be respected, our service rewarded. Our lives beyond The Narrative should not be dictated by Narrative rules."

"In other words," Fodder picked up the thread, "if we get our way, Narrative rules will stay in The Narrative. Your fellow dwarves can bugger off to play blackjack with the elves without feeling they have to justify not hating them. Principals won't be expected to marry whatever goon they end up having to snog in the Quest regardless of their own feelings. We won't get treated like dirt just because we end up lying in ditches. And you..." He smiled slightly. "You can enjoy the sunshine without feeling like it's wrong."

Gruffly stared at them. His hairy jaw snapped shut.

"You're mad," he said, his words unpromising but his tone uncertain. "They'd never allow it."

"Why not?" Flirt's tone was gentle. "The rules have already changed, haven't they? Who's to say we can't change them some more?"

Gruffly's expression was incredulous. "The Taskmaster?"

There was a brief silence. Surprisingly, it was the hitherto uninvolved Shoulders who stepped into it.

"Look, mate," he declared. "I know how you feel, okay? I get no respect In Narrative or out of it..." He shifted his hands to turn his head in order to fix Flirt and Fodder with a quick glare. "I only want a quiet life and it sounds to me like that's what you want too. But I don't reckon you'll get it around here with the pickaxe prats, do you?" He shrugged his headless shoulders. "If you dislike this life so much, what've you got to lose?"

"My freedom?" Gruffly was fiddling with the lower reaches of his beard. "They'll lock me up!"

Shoulders twisted his head to rake the room. "And that's worse than this?"

"Imagine if we succeeded." Dullard quickly picked up the flow. "Imagine that fresh air. There must be some place, I'm sure, where you'd like to make a home out there."

A vaguely wistful glint crept into Gruffly's eyes. "Well..." he said absently. "There is this one spot, along the cliffs, on the edge of the Most Savage Mountains. Such a sweet little deserted village, so quiet, so much sky..."

For a moment, the dwarf was lost in airy contemplation. But with a sharp jerk, he shook himself.

"It's a dream!" he snapped. "A stupid, pointless pipe dream! What about my other dreams? What about my missus? We were planning to have kids!"

Fodder blinked at this unexpected revelation. "You're married?"

Gruffly glared at him. "Course I'm married! All dwarves are married! We get married as soon as we come of age! The missus heads off to the Deep Mines to stay out of the way and the mister joins the cart runs! If I buggered off to live on the surface, they'd never let me down to see her!"

There was a dangerous hint in the narrowing of Flirt's eyes as she gripped the bars of her cage. "You wouldn't take her with you?"

Gruffly's incredulous glare was getting very familiar. "How could I do that? The missuses ain't even allowed into the Shallow Tunnels, let alone on the surface."

Pleasance's voice contained an equally threatening note to Flirt's. "And why exactly not?"

Gruffly blinked. "Because you don't see female dwarves. The Narrative has always made that clear. So if you don't see 'em, they can't be seen. But we do kind of need 'em, you know, for continuing the species? So they live in the Deep Mines out of the way."

Pleasance's tone could have powdered diamond. "How *charming*."

Flirt's was little milder. "I think that's another thing we'd put a stop to, isn't it? If your missus wants to come up, I'd say she can."

Gruffly creased his nose. "I don't know if she'd like it."

"At least she'd have a choice, wouldn't she?" Flirt's tone was acidic.

Gruffly sighed gruffly. "This is daft," he muttered almost to himself. "Why would you people want to help me out? Why would you care?"

"We care about everyone." Dullard was the only one present who could have pulled such a statement off. "We're trying to make the world a better place so that people can have a chance to obtain their dreams rather than living the life forced upon them by circumstance. We help you and in turn, you can help us to help others."

The dwarf frowned. "Help how? My part's done. I don't know anything useful. What good would I be to you people anyway?"

"You mean apart from opening these cages and letting us go?" Shoulders drawled mordantly. Flirt's fingers smacked his arm through the bars and he grunted indignantly and glared at her. She ignored him.

"We need to get attention," Fodder explained. "And the only way we know to get it is by interfering with The Narrative. You've lived with the Merry Band; you know how it works. You could make a splash with them."

Gruffly looked bewildered. "But I couldn't get near 'em. They stay In Narrative virtually the whole Quest. And my character's dead."

"Exactly!" Flirt exclaimed. "And imagine if a dead character appeared in one piece back into the story without explanation. That'd get some attention, wouldn't it?"

A look of sudden and worrying alarm flashed across Gruffly's features. "Betray the Merry Band? Betray my friends?"

"It wouldn't be a betrayal," Fodder intervened quickly. "Not really, not in the long run. It'd be for the good of everyone..."

"Betray my companions?" There was something strange behind the dwarf's wide eyes. "Betray my Quest-mates, my companions-in-arms? Betray those I consider closer than my own brothers and sisters? Closer than my kin?"

"I thought you didn't even like your kin," Shoulders pointed out with his usual sensitivity. "And you said you didn't get any respect up there. Why would you care?"

"But they are my *companions!*" The oddness behind Gruffly's eyes was swimming into his voice. "You cannot understand!"

"I've come up against good friends too." Fodder attempted to draw the dwarf back down to reason once more. "But I think they'll understand why I did it when all's said and done..."

"Understand?" Gruffly's voice was anguished. "How could anyone understand such a foul betrayal? I fought with them, I died for them, and you would have me cast that aside like it was *nothing?*"

"Fodder…" Dullard's distant voice contained a distinct note of warning. "Fodder, don't push him. We have to let him calm down…"

But Fodder, bewildered by this strange turn of attitude, could not let the dwarf's last statement pass.

"But…" he said gently. "Gruffly, that was In Narrative. It wasn't real."

"NO!" The desperate roar echoed through the small chamber with painful power. "No, *no*, NO!" His hands clapped to the sides of his head and his face screwed up in agony, Gruffly the Dwarf swung around and fled in a clatter of steps into the dark tunnel. A moment later, only the echo of his denial remained.

Shoulders gave a loud sigh. "That went well," he said.

Dullard's sigh was softer. "It was going well. Until the Merry Band were brought into the matter."

Flirt was shaking her head. "Why did he react like that? He was listening fine, wasn't he, until they came up. And then it was like talking to a different person."

"In effect, we were." Dullard grunted as he shifted his bad leg. "Didn't you see the look in his eyes, hear the change in his voice? That wasn't Gruffly at the end. It was Gort."

"But Gort's a character," Shoulders exclaimed. "And a dead one at that."

"But he's also a part of Gruffly and he always will be." Dullard's voice was saddened. "Have you ever heard of character-planting?"

Fodder's mind flashed back to the Treacherous Gorge, to the weird sensation of being swamped by thoughts and feelings not his own. He shuddered.

"It happened to me once," he admitted. "I got past it, but it wasn't fun. For a few minutes, it was like I stopped being myself."

"Exactly." Dullard sounded concerned. "I've always been lucky— my characters have never been especially strong-minded or lengthy in appearance and I've always found it relatively easy to shrug them off once my limited Narrative time was done. But I never used to feel quite myself for a few days after—I always had to start a project or a hobby to remind myself who I was. But to be in the Merry Band…" He released a puff of breath. "To be immersed in the will of The Narrative, in one's character day in and day out for hours, days, Quests at a time—it's easy to see where the lines might get blurred. And such characters must be prepared in advance, in detail, and with precision so that one can slip easily into their skin at once and stay there convincingly for a whole Quest—I can't imagine anyone can ever quite be free of those thoughts, of that life when it's over. And traits from a character, and perhaps their loyalties too, will always remain. Narrative brides marry Narrative grooms, regardless of how they felt about each other before, because the Narrative love lingers. And companions stick together."

"He's right." There was a wan note to Pleasance's voice. "I've seen a lot of family come back after leading a Quest. They're never quite the same."

"So Gruffly won't help us because the Gort left in him won't betray his friends?" Flirt asked. "In spite of what he wants for himself?"

Through several sets of bars, Fodder saw Dullard's nod. "I believe so."

Fodder closed his eyes. "So what do we do next?"

The words darted into the cold air of the cavern, dancing from wall to wall until they were finally swallowed by silence. But no one broke their passage to reply.

* * *

Hours passed. How many were impossible to count in the daylight-denied world of their prison. They had talked a bit. They had slept a bit. And now...

With a weary and entirely swallowed-by-circumstance sigh, Fodder leaned back against the bars of his cage and closed his eyes. In truth, he longed to close his ears but, given that was a physical impossibility, he had to settle for the next sense in line and pray the raucous argument that had erupted between Shoulders and Pleasance would pass before the force of it ruptured his eardrums.

"No bloody way!"

"If you would stop your selfish whining for one moment and listen to reason—"

"Reason? *Reason*? What's reasonable about telling me I should *cut off my own arm*?"

"I merely suggested that—"

"That I cut off my arm! That's what you sodding suggested!"

Pleasance's voice was brittle. "All I said was that with your arm detached, it would fit through the bars of the cage—"

"Detached! Oh, I like that, detached! Like it wouldn't hurt! And like I can just screw it back on again!"

Pleasance ignored the interruption. "And you could use your fingers to pull across to the pile of our packs and weapons on the far side of the room and find something there that might help free us."

"Which is all very well and very clever." Shoulders's retort had a mordant, sing-song quality to it. "But why does the arm have to be mine? Hmm? Why not hack off your own dainty fingers for the job?"

Pleasance gave an unladylike snort. "I hardly think so!"

"Yeah? Why not, huh?" Shoulders's pitch was more than a touch irate. "Why's it okay to chop off the arm of a Disposable but not the pretty forearms of a Principal?"

Pleasance sniffed. "I believe you'll find the answer to that in our respective titles!"

"Ha!" Shoulders stabbed a finger from the end of the arm in dispute into the air. "You see? And she calls *me* selfish! She doesn't respect us or believe in anything we're doing! She hasn't changed at all!"

"I've hardly heard you filling the air with ringing endorsements of your precious cause!" Pleasance's retort was barbed. "And since when have I pretended to believe any of it? I told you when I made my deal— a deal, if you recall, that involved not doing me any harm—I'm doing this to get away from Bumpkin! I don't care what you're doing and why as long as you keep me away from my appalling *true love* and I don't deny that!" She *humphed* loudly. "Because unlike some, I am not a hypocritical weasel who only believes when it suits him and is unwilling to sacrifice a small limb from an already mangled body to..."

"Small limb?"

Dullard's voice, soft and soothing, intervened. "Now really, this is getting out of hand. Perhaps if you both..."

"Shut up!" The voices of Pleasance and Shoulders mingled in perfect unison.

"Oi!" Unlike Dullard, Flirt made no effort to be civil. "Knock it off, the pair of you! It's pointless arguing anyway, isn't it?"

"Pointless?" Pleasance retorted shrilly. "At least I'm trying to help! That ratty Disposable does nothing but undermine me at every turn! My plan is perfectly—"

"Impossible." Flirt's firm declaration shut down the remainder of Pleasance's sentence. "Because like you said, our weapons are over there, aren't they? So what the bloody hell do we cut off Shoulders's arm *with?*"

There was a partly smug and partly embarrassed silence. Fodder took a moment to drink in the glorious respite for his ears. He suspected it wouldn't last long.

He was right.

"So that's the end of your oh-so-perfect plan." Shoulders's voice was dripping with smugness. "Unless you plan to hack my arm off with your boyfriend there's nose…"

"Boyfriend?" Pleasance's indignant shriek almost shook the walls. "How *dare…*"

Against the white noise of renewed yelling, Fodder sank deeper into his sensory withdrawal. His finger rested for a moment against the pouch at his waist where the Ring of Anthiphion still lingered—although the dwarves searching them had stripped them of anything with a blade, they hadn't bothered to remove what to their eyes was probably a fairly gaudy piece of costume jewellery—and drank in that brief reassurance that, even if The Narrative were to show up with them behind bars, he'd have some way to try and fight back. Even without the element of surprise, maybe he could do something. After all, what was a pointless, shiny piece of decoration now was the most powerful magical object in the world once The Narrative got hold of it….

Tap tap tap.

For a moment, lost in contemplation and the sonic flood of his rowing companions, Fodder barely registered the prod against his shoulder. It took a second prod to rouse him.

Tap tap tap.

Fodder blinked his eyes open foggily. Did Flirt want a quiet word? It was hardly likely he'd be able to hear much of what she said but…

His eyes opened. And they reminded him of something. Flirt, who sat in the cage in front of him, was leaning against the bars with a weary air, staring at the unfolding argument beyond. Her back was to him.

And Fodder's back was to his bars. Not the bars to Flirt's cage, but the bars that faced the tunnel exit...

Fodder wheeled. A nervous, bearded face peered back at him from beyond the iron.

"Gruffly!" he exclaimed.

To his blessed relief, the cry was enough to stall out the slanging match going on in the neighbouring cages. As he heard his companions scramble to attention, Fodder peered into the face of the uncomfortable-looking dwarf in the desperate hunt for hope.

And there was something, just something about the look in his eyes...

"I don't know if I can trust you lot, you know." It wasn't the most auspicious beginning, but Fodder wasn't arguing. "I really don't. And I don't want to help you either. But the thought of staying down here forever..." His eyes drifted to the rock walls as a shudder ran through his body. "So I'm thinking like this. I let you go, you let me go, okay?"

Fodder frowned. "I'm fine with the letting-us-go part. But what do you mean 'let you go'?"

Gruffly took a shaky breath. He appeared to be struggling with himself. "I mean, you don't ask me to help any more, got it? I get you out and take you to the surface and then you go your way and I go mine—I go to my village and stay there. There's a boat I use to fish moored near there—you can have it. In return, you don't tell anyone I'm there and you don't come anywhere near me again. That way, if you win your little fight, I get to stay, maybe ask the missus up and start a family. And if you don't..." He swallowed hard. "Well, they'll have to find me, won't they? And since my grandpa died, no one else knows about the village. No one else cares. My family's never been big on being underground. That place has been our secret getaway for generations." He glared fiercely. "And I want it to stay that way, okay?"

"Of course." Fodder was quick to reassure, although a part of him did chafe slightly at the lost opportunity. "That's fine by us, no problem at all. We'll stay away from you."

Gruffly gave a torrid sigh and shook his head as though banishing demons from it. "I can't believe I'm doing this," he muttered half to himself. "The chance to be *outside...*" He shivered as his eyes darted desperately up to Fodder's face. "But you have to understand—I'm doing what I have to, for my own sake, but I don't like it. You don't...you can't know what it is to be part of a Merry Band. The bond that forms." He shook his head. "I can't betray them, whether I want to or not. Merry Bands, they're special, aren't they, and that feeling stays forever, even when The Narrative's gone. There was this one Band, way back when, they got so close that when their Quest was done and dusted, they all left their families and set up house together out here, in the middle of nowhere! My village, that's what it is, that's where it came from—they lived there! They were so close, they couldn't bear to be with anyone but each other!" He sighed wistfully. "Maybe that's what's so special about the Place of the Quickening."

Quickening.

Fodder's brain kicked into high gear. That word again, the mysterious Quest from long ago that had everyone so frightened.

"Place of the Quickening?" he intervened, trying to subdue the urgency that crept into his voice. "Where's that?"

Gruffly stared at him as though he was stupid. "My *village*," he stressed pointedly. "That's what it's *called.*"

"Strange name." *Stay focused, stay calm; we need these answers.* "Why's it called that?"

"How should I know?" Fodder's hope for answers fizzled and died at Gruffly's curt and irritable response. "My grandpa said he got the name and the backstory off a pixie, Quests back. That's as much as I know about it." Hairy eyebrows knitted together. "Do you want out of here or shall we keep prattling on about history?"

"Out." Shoulders's voice chimed in from behind. "Definitely out."

Without another word, the edgy dwarf reached down and dragged a huge set of keys from his belt. It clanged as he twisted one in the lock on Fodder's cage and hurried on to Flirt's.

Fodder pushed on the bars. They swung away easily. Stretching his cramped muscles, he crawled out on his hands and knees and staggered painfully to his feet.

It didn't take long to free the rest of his companions and soon they were pulling on their packs and rearming themselves. Dullard's limp remained pronounced but, with unexpected consideration, Pleasance fell in beside him and offered her arm and shoulder in support. Gruffly watched them all, his expression one of intense discomfort.

"You said there was a boat?" Fodder asked the dwarf as he strapped his sword into place. "Near this Place of the Quickening?"

"All yours, if you want it," Gruffly repeated tersely as he moved towards the tunnel exit, grasping the huge lantern he'd lowered from the roof like a talisman against the darkness ahead.

"I think we will, thanks." Ignoring the pointed look he received from Flirt, Fodder fell into step behind the dwarf and his guiding light. A finger poked into his back.

"Forgotten, have you?" Flirt hissed in his ear. "Don't you remember the chat we had right before that waterfall appeared? None of us know how to sail, do we?"

"I don't care about the boat," Fodder murmured beneath his breath. "But I do care about getting a good look at anywhere called the Place of the Quickening, don't you?"

There was a moment of silence. Fodder felt rather than saw Flirt's nod.

"Okay," she whispered. "But what do you think we'll find there?"

"No idea." Fodder stared into the dark tunnel at the glowing light that was guiding them slowly but surely towards the surface. "But I'm looking forward to finding out."

* * *

Dawn's pure light stained the surface of the Vast Ocean as it rippled away in gentle crests towards a distant arch of horizon. Sunrise broke free of the lapping waves, illuminating strips of cloud that punctured the pinkish sky like a halo of streaking arrows. The tinted light chased away the shadows of lingering night from the craggy and savagely jagged mountains that towered around them, raking at the brightening sky like razor jaws waiting to consume the world. Only the narrow, cliff-top ledge along which they travelled was free of their harsh, spiky reach, washed in the sun's first gleam as the mountains sought and failed to swallow the first hints of a beautiful, clear, calm day. It was a sunrise any

Narrative would have been proud to lovingly describe.

Fodder was more than a little relieved it hadn't yet had the chance.

He had to admit, he'd been nervous. When they had reached the top of the winding tunnel that led back to the surface, Gruffly had insisted on going ahead to check the way was clear, and he had been gone long enough to give Fodder's nerves plenty of time to frazzle. Indeed, he had been right on the verge of calling the whole deal off as a bad one and heading off to find their own way out when the dwarf had returned, apologetic that he had been distracted by the spectacular sunrise now spreading to their left. The way was clear.

Progress was, unfortunately, slow. Dullard had used the delay to reclaim his climbing gear and fix Shoulders's head-securing helmet contraption back in place, so he at least was reasonably fit to travel. But it was the prince himself who was holding matters up. The terrain was difficult, rocky, and unstable underfoot, and his leg wound was a serious one—ligaments, muscle, and bone had all been damaged in the dwarf's wild swing at him and healing was taking time. His mobility was increasing by the hour, but he was still unable to place his full weight upon his leg and Pleasance's unexpected help was the only thing holding him upright on the slanted, unsteady ledge. And to judge by the princess's look of irritation and weary resignation, she was starting to regret her gesture. Fodder couldn't help but wonder how long it would be before her fortitude abandoned her and poor Dullard was pitched off the cliff edge and into the lapping sea.

But strangely, despite the princess's ill temper, it was Gruffly who was most impatient at the delay. He chafed and griped at Dullard's slow pace, insisting he had to go faster, that they had no time to waste. Fodder could only assume that the dwarf wanted to get far away from the tunnels and any chance of discovery as quickly as possible so as to be rid of them faster. In spite of his clear relief at the sight of open sky, he seemed almost more anxious than he had done in the tunnels.

And Fodder was not the only one who'd noticed. At midmorning, as they paused by a small trickle of water to wet their respective whistles and rest Dullard's leg and Pleasance's beleaguered shoulder, Shoulders came bundling awkwardly over to where Flirt and Fodder were sharing a canteen, his expression one of highly familiar distrust.

"I don't like this," he muttered without preamble, wiping at the dampness around his neck that indicated he had managed a messy attempt to drink.

Flirt glanced over to him, her expression of resignation mirroring Fodder's feelings. "You don't like anything much, do you?" she offered without rancour but with definite pointedness. "Anything in particular made off with your goat this time?"

"Him!" Shoulders attempted to jerk his head but the result was more of a slipping lurch. Pushing himself back into line, he settled for a jerk of the thumb instead. "Gruffly! I don't trust him!"

Fodder glanced over to where the impatient dwarf was standing on the rocky route ahead, fingering his water bottle and shuffling his feet, his eyes darting often to the ever-higher sun. "I'm not sure I do much," he admitted quietly. "But I don't think he means us any harm. He just wants us out of his beard so he can enjoy the sky alone."

Shoulders's jaw hardened. "There's more to it, I know it!" he hissed under his breath. "What about the time he was gone at the tunnel entrance, hmmm? How do we know he wasn't setting us up? How do we know we aren't walking right into a trap?"

Flirt sighed. "If it was a trap, we'd be prisoners already, wouldn't we? If he'd found the Merry Band close enough to the tunnel, they'd have jumped us there and then! And he didn't have time to go looking for them, did he? He was gone awhile but not that long!"

"But he was gone that long before!" Shoulders was apparently not going to let this one go. "We were in those cells for hours alone! He could have easily gone for help!"

It was Fodder's turn to sigh. "Then why let us out? Why not keep us safely locked up and let The Narrative pick us up from prison!"

"Because he can't hand us over In Narrative!" Clearly Shoulders had been thinking his paranoia through carefully. It was a bad habit he had. "He's dead! And they can't exactly recruit one of his brainless, hungover mates to do it! He goes out, grabs the first passer-by he finds, and tells them to tell the Merry Band to meet him somewhere distinctive—say this village he keeps banging on about? He leads us there, The Narrative pounces, and we're buggered!"

Fodder slowly shook his head. "But he didn't want us to come to the village. I suggested that, remember? Because we wanted to know about Quickening?"

"And he suggested that boat!" Shoulders stabbed a finger into the air in front of Fodder's chest. "And I bet he's running to a timetable, moaning about how slow we are! I'm telling you, it's a trap!"

Flirt's expression was long-suffering. "Shoulders, you said the same thing about Cringe at the Grim Fortress, didn't you?"

Shoulders's eyes were narrow. "Exactly! Look how that turned out! And I bet I know who else is in on it. Her."

His narrowed glare swung awkwardly in the direction of Pleasance, who was uncomfortably helping poor Dullard to replace the dressings on his injured leg.

Fodder could feel impatience overwhelming his brief tolerance of his friend's suspicions. "Shoulders..."

"See how keen she is to keep Dullard moving?" Shoulders's features were truculent. "Since when has she shown a whit of concern for anyone when it hasn't been to help herself? Why would she help him if not to make sure he ends up in the trap too?" He growled angrily. "Arm-chopping, stuck-up bitch..."

Flirt's eyes had rolled high up to rake the jagged mountaintops above. "I'm no fan of the princess, am I?" she said firmly. "But, Shoulders, that's stupid." With a swig, she finished the last of the canteen of water and turned to fill it anew. "She's on our side and so is Gruffly, near enough. So please, get over it, will you?"

Shoulders glared. "But..."

"*Shoulders.*" Fodder stepped in, resting one hand on his friend's shoulder. "I understand you're worried, okay? And we'll keep our eyes open. But we need to get a look at that village and we need Gruffly to take us there. So for now, can we keep going?"

His fellow Disposable glared at him. "It's a mistake."

Fodder nodded. "You may be right. But we need to make it. So come on, yeah?" He patted his shoulder gently. "Let's keep going."

Shoulders glared at him for a moment more. But then, with a clink of chain mail, he turned and stumbled off down the uneven ledge. A moment later, the rest of his companions followed.

They walked, awkwardly, slowly, and with difficulty for hours more. The sun rose and rose until it blazed high above their heads on the clear-skied day, burning clouds away into nothing but the subdued blue of non-Narrative sky. The mountains darted higher, as savage as their name implied, a near-impenetrable wall of artfully worked rocky harshness that looked all but impassable. Dullard, however, was eyeing them with a thoughtful look.

"You know, I think I've been here before," he exclaimed as they rounded a corner to open up a fresh expanse of rocky coastline. A huge crack had carved its way through the cliff not far ahead, spreading from sea to mountainside like a vivid scar. "That mountain up there looks terribly familiar and so does that coast about a mile away. I'm sure I emerged accidentally near here on one of my caving expeditions. There's a valley not far ahead. It looked to me like it's probably used for occasional Narrative mountain access."

"Whoop-de-do." Shoulders's drawl was somewhat less than enthusiastic. "Does it help us in any way?"

Dullard's expression was slightly bewildered. "Well, I suppose not, but I thought you might be interested."

Shoulders smiled mordantly. His mood had remained foul ever since the dismissal of his paranoia. "We're not."

Gruffly, however, had been paying deeper attention. "You know the area?" he said, unmistakable alarm creasing the edges of his tone.

Dullard smiled. "Not the over-ground part, not really. I stuck my head out of a cave, sat on a beach and ate my lunch, and headed back underground. I didn't look around."

"So you don't know where my village is." There was a strange note of relief to Gruffly's voice.

Dullard shook his head. "I didn't see a village, no."

"Good." The dwarf breathed out heavily. "See that crack in the cliff up ahead?"

"Bit hard to miss," Shoulders grouched uncharitably. Flirt's elbow plunged into his ribs as she came alongside him.

Luckily, Gruffly didn't react to the rudeness. "Well, in the bottom of it there's a trail that leads down to the beach. My boat's moored up in an inlet on the side of the bay." His smile was nearly sincere. "So here, I reckon, we part ways."

"Part ways?" Fodder exchanged a brief expression of alarm with Flirt. "We aren't going to see your village?"

Gruffly's face was instantly wary. "No," he said with rather more force than was necessary. "I told you, the boat is down there. The village *isn't*. You go your way, I go mine."

Ignoring Shoulders's cynical huff, Flirt stepped in. "But after everything you told us about it, it'd be a shame not to see it for ourselves, wouldn't it? Don't worry, we aren't planning to move in with you. We only want to take a quick look around."

Gruffly's bearded jaw began to tremble. "Why'd you want to come to my village?" he snapped suddenly. "You said the boat, you wanted the boat, and the bloody boat's down there! It's *my* village! What's it got to do with you?"

Dullard offered up his most placatory tone. "My friends are merely curious..."

"Well, don't be curious!" Veins were standing out on the dwarf's knobbly brow. "It's none of your damned business! It's my place, it's private! I want to be left alone!"

Fodder tried again. "We just..."

"I don't care what you just!" The dwarf erupted, his face reddening by the second. "Take the boat or be damned, I don't care anymore! But *leave me alone!*"

With a scrape of his heavy boots, Gruffly wheeled sharply and stormed away towards the crack he had referenced. Huffing with anger, he vanished over the edge.

"Gruffly!" Fodder rushed forwards, but by the time he reached the edge of the crack, he could already hear the scrabbling of boots—as he peered over the edge, he saw the angled stony ledge that led down to the crevice's uneven, sloping bottom. The bearded shape of Gruffly vanished beyond a rising twist in the rock.

"Gruffly!" Fodder called out again, his voice echoing loudly in the open tunnel of the crack, but he knew it was useless. The dwarf had been moving at speed, partly he suspected because of the cave-like surrounding he had entered, but mostly out of a need to get away from them. A guided tour of the mysterious Place of the Quickening seemed unlikely.

"Great." Shoulders's droll voice stepped on the heels of Fodder's sigh. "Because that wasn't suspicious *at all.*"

"He went up, didn't he?" Flirt was peering into the crack at Fodder's side. "He said this village of his was overlooking the sea and near his boat, so it's got to be around here somewhere. I say we follow him up and take a look anyway."

"Why are you so bothered about this ridiculous village anyway?" Pleasance crossed her arms disdainfully, having lowered Dullard to rest on a convenient rock. "It's another peasant hovel. What does it matter?" She pursed her lips, her eyes examining the vicious mountains with a lack of admiration. "Let's take this boat of his and get out of this godforsaken place."

Shoulders reeled to face her. "Oh, you *would* say that, wouldn't you?" he exclaimed, jabbing one finger triumphantly into the air. "Because you'd love us to walk into your little trap, wouldn't you? Admit it! You and he cooked this up together, didn't you? So what is waiting for us down at that boat? The Merry Band? A battalion of Palace Guard? What are you setting us up for?"

Pleasance's expression was one of genuine affront. "Excuse me?"

"No, I won't!" Shoulders exclaimed wildly. "You've been plotting with Gruffly! This is one big trap!"

Pleasance's tone was dripping with ire. "Plotting when?" she drawled acidly. "Because when since the moment we crossed paths with that dwarf have I ever been out of your sight to hatch a secret plot?"

Shoulders's mouth opened. It paused. It closed with a perturbed snap.

"Precisely." Pleasance's voice had the air of a slamming portcullis. "I haven't." She shook her head, messy ringlets bouncing with disdain. "When are you going to get it through your thick, detached skull that I am nominally at least on your side? You really are the most ridiculous man I've ever met."

"If you're done?" Flirt intervened before both sides could hit full flow once more in their mutual ire. "We need to get going, don't we?"

"That may be a problem." Dullard was peering over into the crevice from his rock perch with decided uncertainty. "I don't think I can make it down that ledge yet. It isn't wide enough for support and my leg isn't quite strong enough to hold me. I'm afraid if you're going in either direction down there, you'll have to go without me."

Fodder's brow creased. "Are you sure you couldn't do it? Maybe with help..."

"I think it would be more sensible not to risk it." Dullard tilted his head. "My leg is much improved. I think perhaps an hour or so more healing will be enough. But for now—I'd rather not." He smiled. "It's no great issue if we are considering coming back this way. I'll wait here for your return."

"Are we returning, though?" Flirt queried. "We never had much real intention of taking the boat, did we?"

"Yeah, but the Most Savage Mountains are mostly impassable," Fodder pointed out. "We'd need to take the valley, the boat, or even those caves Dullard mentioned to get anywhere anyway, and that means down to that beach. We'll be coming back." He turned to Dullard. "Will you be all right here on your own?"

"Excuse me?" Pleasance interjected before Dullard could reply. "Will this village of yours contain a suite of luxury bathing facilities or a change of good quality gown?"

Fodder and Flirt exchanged a glance. "I doubt it," Flirt said sceptically.

"Then I have no interest in it whatsoever." Sweeping the remains of her skirts around, Pleasance dropped to a dainty sit beside Dullard. "And so he won't be alone. I'll stay here with him."

"As you like." Fodder saw no reason to argue. "Come on then, Shoulders."

The Disposable stared at him grouchily. "What makes you think I'm coming?"

Fodder sighed wearily. "You want to stay here with the princess?"

Shoulders's expression was answer enough to that question. He did not elaborate, however. "You said we're still going down to that beach, didn't you?" he groused instead. "After all my warnings that it's a trap?"

Fodder was in no mood to beat about the bush. "Yep."

Shoulders huffed as he folded his arms. "Well, there's no bloody way I'm going anywhere near that place unless I know it's safe. So you and Flirt can bugger off and prat around in some stupid village if you like. But I'm going to find a vantage point and check that bloody beach is *safe.*"

Privately, Fodder felt a shameful hint of relief. If Shoulders wanted to waste time sating his paranoia, let him. It would certainly make the search for the village easier.

"If you want," he conceded. "Just don't fall off a cliff. We'll meet back here in a couple of hours, okay? Coming, Flirt?"

"Try and stop me." The Barmaid was already edging her way down the ledge. With a nod to Dullard, Fodder turned and followed her.

The crack was difficult to manoeuvre into and difficult to ascend, but Flirt and Fodder persisted. There was no sign of Gruffly—the arguing of the others had put pay to any hope of following the dwarf to his hideaway, but after a quarter-hour or so of clambering, the Disposable and the Barmaid emerged from the head of the crack onto a small, windy plateau strewn with hardy-looking wildflowers. Sharp-ridged mountains towered around like sentinels, clouds tangling around their peaks like carded wool, born to be lovingly described from a safe distance.

Flirt's narrowed eyes told Fodder her thoughts mirrored his. "This place has had Narrative time, hasn't it?" she said quietly. "It's too describable not to have."

Fodder nodded. "I reckon so. I think that's a pass up there. It's probably a way over to that valley Dullard mentioned."

Flirt squinted up at the narrow saddle between two towering peaks that Fodder was referring to. "Hang about, though," she said thoughtfully. "That pass doesn't look very passable, does it?"

Fodder looked harder. And indeed, he could see Flirt's point—the obligatory gash in the rock between the two mountains looked, on further inspection, to be piled high with a tumble of heavy-looking boulders.

Fodder frowned. "Landslide?" he said thoughtfully. "A Narrative peril, maybe, that they barely escaped with their lives?"

Flirt was shaking her head. "But they'd clear it afterwards, wouldn't they? It'd take Higgle a few seconds to shift that lot away. Why cut off a perfectly good area of land from Narrative use?"

"Maybe they didn't see a need," Fodder offered, though his brain was prodding at him for his lack of imagination. He could see its point. "Like you said, Higgle could clear it in seconds. Maybe they'll fix it when they need it."

"Or maybe they don't want anyone wandering in here unsupervised." Flirt said what Fodder's brain had been proclaiming behind his caution. "Maybe there's something here they don't want anyone to see."

The words came easily: "Place of the Quickening?"

Flirt nodded grimly. "Place of the Quickening. Let's find this village, shall we? It's time for some answers."

As they started forwards along the coastal edge of the plateau, Fodder began to scan the horizon for any sign of habitation. Ahead, the ground sloped away, presumably into the much-discussed valley—indeed, Fodder could see the faint remains of what looked to have once been a trail leading from the direction of the blocked pass towards a gap in the landscape near the coastal cliffs, marked by a large, scrubby tussock of grass. It seemed they had been right about the area seeing Narrative use.

"Hang about." Flirt caught Fodder's arm, her eyes suddenly narrowed. "That's a roof, isn't it?"

Fodder followed her gaze, scanning the cluster of scrubby grass by the plateau's edge that she was apparently referring to. It took him a moment to realise that the dried-out, mossy, overgrown mass he was seeing was not a tussock but ragged thatch. The faint trail he'd noticed vanished over the plateau's edge nearby.

"Blimey," he muttered. "Well spotted."

Flirt took the compliment with a nod. "Let's take a look, shall we? And watch out for Gruffly. I don't think he'll welcome us following him to his precious sanctuary, will he?"

They hurried forwards and as they approached, the horizon sank to show the ragged roof ahead more clearly. It had obviously not seen attention in Quests; hardy mountain flowers, moss, and scrubby grass adhered to a wall of wind-and-saltwater-battered wattle and daub. As Fodder and Flirt crested the edge of the plateau and looked down, they found a little hollow huddled charmingly. It clung to the plateau's sheer edge like a swallow's nest to roof timbers before plunging beyond its rocky border down to the mouth of a winding valley and the crashing waves of the shore. And at the hollow's centre, scattered gently within a circle of tough wildflowers and clumps of outcropping rock, lay a cluster of round thatched huts, their roof-crowns running wild and the higher reaches of their white walls wind-flecked and flaking. But lower down, the vegetation was carefully trimmed back from the paths, the lower walls cleaned and repaired, tidy pots piled by doorsteps and wooden doors neatly scrubbed, the iron padlock on the highest one's lock showing only minimal hints of rust. The stone circle of the well in the village centre was tidy, the mortar neat, and the wooden cover showing signs of repair, sealed by a new-looking iron clasp. It was as though the whole village had been restored and cared for after Quests of neglect by someone somewhat limited in reach.

Fodder and Flirt exchanged a glance. There was no need for words when they had so clearly found what they were looking for.

"Stupid place for a village," was Flirt's only comment as they followed the faint remains of the trail and made their way down into the exposed, windswept hollow and the silent ring of huts that huddled within it. "Clinging to a cliff like this, they'd be exposed to the weather, wouldn't they? No place to grow food or graze animals that isn't a decent hike away, and that well'd have to be a couple of miles deep to hit the water table here, wouldn't it?"

Fodder frowned. The ever-practical Flirt had a good point. "Maybe they got fed by dwarf logistics?" he suggested. "Maybe there's a tunnel nearby?"

Flirt pulled a face. "Why would Gruffly have dragged us all the way along that cliff path if we could simply pop out at...oh." She paused and gave a rueful smile. "Claustrophobic dwarf, stupid question." She glanced around. "I don't see any tunnels, though, do you?"

"They'd be well-hidden." Even as he replied, Fodder had noticed something else. "But it mightn't always have been so cut off. What's left of that trail heads straight over the edge, by the look of it." He pointed to where the shallow road vanished without pausing over the sheer drop not far ahead. "Unless they rode off into thin air, I reckon there used to be a bit more hillside here, perhaps even a way down to the valley, until someone got rid of it."

"You mean Higgle, don't you?" Flirt's eyes were raking the huts, an odd look wrinkling her features. "Who else would it be? And closing the pass on one side and the trail from the valley on the other; without Gruffly's secret cliff path, no one would even be able to get up here at all, would they?"

"Gruffly." Fodder hesitated. "Hang about. Where is he?"

Flirt also paused, her eyes searching the hollow ahead. But apart from the hum of the coastal breeze and the slight creak of the thatch as the wind caught against it, there was no hint they were anything but alone. Despite the dwarf's head-start, there was no sign of him.

The first creeping hint of nervousness poked at Fodder as his earlier dismissal of Shoulders's suspicions jumped into his mind.

"He was so keen to get here," he muttered almost to himself. "And this place is sealed off. Where else would he have gone?"

Flirt too betrayed a hint of worry in her tone. "Maybe he went for a wander?" she offered uncertainly. "Or maybe he realised we were planning to follow him and went another way to throw us off?" She sighed. "To be honest, Fodder, I don't care why he's not here, do I? I'm just grateful. Let's get a look at this place, find what we're searching for, and get out before he gets back."

"You know what we're searching for?" Fodder couldn't help but grin. "You're doing better than me then."

Flirt shared the grin. "Well, a diary listing the terrible events of the incident at Quickening would be nice, wouldn't it? But otherwise, I hope we'll know it when we see it. Still..." She shook her head. "There's something off about this place, isn't there?"

It was true. As Fodder glanced around at the cluster of daub huts with their wild thatch, he knew something was wrong, out of place, but quite what it was lay beyond his grasp.

"You check over there and I'll do this side," he replied. "And keep your eyes open."

"Don't I always?" Flirt flashed him a smile and stuck her head inside the open door of the nearest hut, hand on her sword hilt. With a returning nod, Fodder moved the other way.

And it was a village. True, the thatch had gone to wrack and ruin, and clearly, other than the care taken by Gruffly, no one had much troubled the place for a large number of Quests. But it was just a village.

Each hut was much the same—a small, round home with daub walls and two small windows, a central hearth pit lined with stones, the rotten remains of a straw pallet and blankets laid on a bunk, a few old chests filled with pots and scraps of clothes, random knickknacks and plates and cups and a lantern hung from the rafters. It looked the perfect state of ancient domesticity. Fodder examined a few cups and knickknacks but there was nothing that appeared out of the ordinary, nothing that wouldn't seem right at home in any cottage throughout the land.

Except...

Flirt was right. Something was *off.*

It was nothing definable. But as a village-dweller of long standing, Fodder knew this place didn't feel like any village he'd ever lived in. It didn't feel comfortable. It didn't feel...

But the elusive word to pin the feeling down escaped him. One thing that hadn't escaped him, though, was Gruffly's suggestion that a pack of Principals had come here to live the quiet life together. Unless the Principals of ancient Quests were a different breed to their descendants, he found it hard to picture Noblemen, Knights, and warriors of great standing giving up their cosy life in the Magnificent City to sleep on a straw pallet and cook on a smoky hearth on a cliff outcrop in the absolute middle of nowhere.

One hut alone varied from the pattern, its furnishings shifted, the straw pallet topped with fresher-looking blankets and piles of black-ened pots by the door. Clearly, this hut was where Gruffly and his ancestors had spent time camping out. But the dwarf was not there.

He skirted his side of the village, hut by hut, and—with that one exception—in each he found the same, uniform arrangement. Had these people made no attempt to make their homes their own? Had they no imagination at all? It felt less like a village and more like...

A prison.

Just before the final hut, that of the remote first roof they'd seen that lay high up in the hollow's corner, Fodder paused. Could that be it? Could it be these people had been hidden away, trapped, locked in this remote village to punish them for some misdemeanour or keep them from talking about what they'd seen? Was this how Officious Courtiers of the past had dealt with a Merry Band who'd disobeyed the instructions or seen them disobeyed? Had they dumped them in a distant village cut off by Higgle's powers to moulder in silence and out of trouble? Was that why no one had ever heard of *The Chalice of Quickening?*

It seemed unlikely. But it was possible.

"That's it!"

Flirt's abrupt exclamation from somewhere over his shoulder made him start. As he turned in surprise, he saw her dropping down the wooden cover of the well with a triumphant smile on her face. She glanced around and, spotting him staring, hurried up the slight rise to join him.

"Got it, haven't I?" she declared without preamble. "This place, why it feels so off? I'll tell you why. Because no one's ever *lived* here." She crossed her arms. "This place is for show, isn't it? This isn't a village, mate. It's a set."

Fodder blinked as the air rushed out of his inflating prison theory. "What makes you say that?"

"Piss-pots." Of all the answers Fodder had expected, this was not high on the list. "Other than in Gruffly's hut, there's not one decent piss-pot in this whole place, no latrine pits dug anywhere about. If they were living here, where the hell did they piss and crap without stinking the whole village out?"

"Off the edge?" Fodder offered with distinct bewilderment.

Flirt raised a pointed eyebrow. "That'd be half-practical for you maybe, mate, but not for me unless I wanted to go to a very undignified death at the first big gust of wind! Trust me. No one's done their business in this village."

"That still doesn't mean..." Fodder ventured, but Flirt cut him off.

"What about the hearths?" she pressed on persistently. "They're neat and tidy enough but there's not a hint of a scorch on the pit or the stones and no sign that those cauldrons or pots have ever seen flame. In an exposed spot like this, you wouldn't have no fire and no hot food or drink, would you? There's no hint of smoke blackening the thatch either, is there? And where round here would they even get firewood?" She took a breath and plunged on. "And the doors and doorframes— there's no sign of wear on the locks or the hinges. No one's ever drunk from those cups or eaten off those plates. The wattle and daub that made those walls is awful stuff, slapped together, and it'd never keep out the wind for long. There's not even any water in the well—it's barely ten foot deep cut into solid rock and dry as a bloody bone! It was seeing Gruffly's camp that made me see it, didn't it? That's been lived in. And you should know, yourself—you've lived in Humble Village, a working, lived-in village, all your life and I'm telling you what you know inside, aren't I? I don't care how long ago they say it was; those signs don't go away, do they? I'd bet anything you want to wager that no one's ever lived in this place. And that's why it's wrong." She met his eyes. "There's no signs of *life*."

And she was right. Fodder thought through the huts he'd visited, the things he'd seen, and though they showed signs enough of age, only one had revealed a hint of actual use. It wasn't a place to live. It was someone's idea of what a place to live should look like.

He couldn't help it. He sighed.

Flirt frowned at once. "What?"

Fodder shrugged. "Nothing much. Only I had this happy little theory brewing that we'd stumbled on the secret prison of a pack of previous anarchists, but if no one lived here, that's blown it right out of the water. We're back to square one."

Flirt pondered. "Good theory, but you're right: it doesn't work now, does it? Sorry."

Fodder pulled a face. "But if you're right, why bother? Why would anyone create a whole fake village with rumours of a Merry Band pact in its past and go to the trouble of cutting it off if nobody was really living there?"

It was Flirt's turn to sigh. "Not a clue. But I can't help what I can see, can I?" She thought for a moment. "You know, it could work, couldn't it? Maybe this place was a ruse? They sent out this story that they'd gone off together to hide the fact they'd locked them up as anarchists. After all, keeping them from spreading the word would have been key, wouldn't it? And then they made a village you can see at a distance but cut it off so no one gets close enough to see they aren't actually there?"

"It could be." Something didn't quite fit right in Fodder's mind, but it did as a working theory.

Flirt did not look entirely convinced either. "So much for this place having answers," she said wryly. "Should have known it wouldn't be that simple, shouldn't we? Are we done poking around?"

"That's the only hut I haven't done." Fodder gestured to the highest hut, but something made him pause. He stared for a moment at the loneliest hut in the village, stared at the fact that, unlike every other hut, its door was sealed by a sturdy and only slightly rusted padlock, stared at the fact that it alone of the huts was completely lacking in windows. Perhaps the rest of the village hadn't been a prison...

Flirt had also hesitated. "You see what I see?"

Fodder nodded. "I see a hut no one wants people poking around in. Why else would they lock the door?"

"No windows either, are there? No prying eyes. And it's bigger than all the others too." Flirt squinted thoughtfully. "I don't know about you, but that makes me very interested to get in."

Stepping forward the last few yards, Fodder rattled the padlock. "Interested or not, we're no more able to pick locks than we were this morning."

"Sod the locks." With two quick strides, Flirt was at his side. Narrowing her eyes, she stared not at the door with its heavy wood and thick frame but at the wall beside it.

And then, she pivoted on one leg and struck.

The first blow of her booted foot left a dent. The second left a crack. By the time the fifth battered in, a distinct hole was forming.

Pausing and shaking her drilling leg, Flirt grinned. "I told you, this wattle and daub? It's terrible."

Gallantly, Fodder stepped in to help and after several minutes of hacking and kicking, a sizable hole had formed in the wall. Sunlight flooded into the gap for the first time in what Fodder suspected was some while. Against the ground, something glinted.

And Flirt stared. "What the hell is that?"

There was no furniture here. There was no fake hearth, no fake bed, no fake knickknacks. Fodder could see no effort had even been made to smooth the floor—natural bumps of rock and tussocks of wildflowers coated the expanse of natural ground concealed within the hut's embrace, and all of them glistened like diamond in the sudden light.

For almost the entire expanse of floor inside this locked-up, hidden hut was coated in flowing, undulating, smoothed-out crystal.

And there was something...something compelling, something revolting, something hypnotic about that strange, glittering expanse. It followed the lay of the land like a viscous coating, covering every flower petal, every rock, every blade of scrubby grass to a precise depth, as though it had been measured and placed by an unseen Artisan of astounding skill. But the sculpture of crystal earth was not perfect by any means, for across its smooth surface, great chunks had been hewn out as if by a careless hand, leaving shattered fields of shards lying in heaps like giant pieces of broken glass, a jigsaw with tight-fitted pieces torn ruthlessly out. Rough edges and cracked corners glinted accusingly in the newfound light. A single broken flower lay snapped from its companions amongst the nearest patch of debris, along with a small cluster of odd, reddish-brown chunks heaped together on the edge of the dead, light-deprived grass beyond the crystal's apparent protection.

"It looks like ice." The words slipped from Fodder's lips unbidden. "Like water that froze in an instant."

Flirt was shaking her head. "It can't be ice," she whispered. "It's not cold enough, is it? And it would have dripped under the flowers, not covered them."

"What is it?" Fodder spoke the words swimming relentlessly in his own mind.

"I reckon it's our answer, isn't it?" Flirt replied. "The trouble is, I don't think we know what the question is."

"It could just be old magic." Fodder spoke slowly, painfully as the crystal glinted up at him. "The leftovers of a Narrative spell."

"Can't be. It would have vanished as soon as The Narrative did, wouldn't it? We need a closer look." Cautiously, the Barmaid leaned forward through their clumsy hole. With delicate care, she reached down towards the shattered pieces nearby.

"Careful." Why had he said it? Fodder had no idea. But there was something about that crystal that felt disturbing, that felt wrong on a deep, fundamental level. It was beautiful, but yet it hurt to look at it, hurt him right down to his soul. This stuff, whatever it was, was dangerous.

"It's fine." Gently, Flirt caught hold of a few nearby chunks, lifting them one by one and passing them to Fodder. Together they stepped away from the strange sight inside the hut and stared at what she had retrieved.

One shard was a simple piece of crystal, smooth on top and bottom but sharp and cracked along its side where it had apparently been pulled out by force. There were signs of scratched tool cuts against the crystal surface.

Fodder hefted it. "Someone broke this up, took pieces of it away. Why?"

Flirt was holding the crystal-coated flower. "It's perfect," she whispered, twisting it carefully in her grasp. "It had to be there before they built the hut, didn't it? But it looks like it flowered yesterday." She touched her fingers gently to the bottom where the snapped-off stalk touched the apparent surface. She frowned. "It doesn't feel any different. It feels crystal right through to me."

But Fodder wasn't listening. He was staring instead at the strange, reddish-brownish-whiteish piece that Flirt had retrieved with horrible, stomach-churning recognition.

Blood. Bone. Sinew. Muscle. He'd been a Disposable too long not to recognise body parts when he saw them, even ones cut into a slice of crystal. He wasn't sure if it was human—it was a small shard and there wasn't enough left to guess—but there was no doubt that this had once been something alive.

But it was crystal. He ran his fingers across the profile of the slice, the surface that should have felt tacky and lumpy and vile and yet it was crystal through and through, crystal blood, crystal bone, crystal sinew and muscle as though it had been carved that way by some sick artist's hand. How could something alive change so utterly to become a piece of crystal to be shattered?

Had it simply been a piece of butchered meat in the wrong place? Or had some living thing been awake and aware when this had happened?

Flirt was also staring at his shard with no little hint of revulsion. "Is that...?" she started.

Bang!

The shard jumped from Fodder's hand at the shocking sound,

tumbling to strike the stones at his feet. It shattered into pieces on the rock.

As he turned, he found Flirt had already swivelled round, hand grasping her sword hilt. Her eyes widened.

"The well lid," she hissed. "I closed it, didn't I? But now..."

Fodder followed her gaze. The well lid was pushed back open.

"The wind?" he whispered without much conviction. Flirt's glare was enough to quell such a thought.

"Come on," she replied under her breath, hand still grasping her sword as she shoved the crystal flower in her belt pouch. "Let's take a look."

They moved closer, the gaping maw of the shallow well newly exposed for all to see. With Fodder a step behind, Flirt took the lead, creeping forward with her sword half drawn as she peered slowly over the stony rim.

"I don't see..." she started.

Hands. The shove against Fodder's back was rough and violent, sending him staggering forwards into Flirt's unbalanced form. Carried by their shared momentum, the pair pitched forwards with a joint screech headfirst into the dark well—a brief plunge, a rush of air, a painful smack against the neck. He could feel Flirt's body pressed upside down against his in the tight quarters as they both squirmed and struggled to right themselves.

Fodder glanced up.

And there, glaring down out of the ring of light and sky above, the bearded face of Gruffly stared down with rage glowing in his eyes.

"I told you!" he screamed into the echoing pit. "This place is *mine!*"

And then with a shuddering smack, the well lid was slammed shut above them.

* * *

It was a trap. A trap. He was sure of it.

Shoulders pulled an irritable face as he hauled himself over the latest outcropping of rock that blocked his path on the route of the crack in the cliff down towards the much-mentioned beach and boat. He was absolutely certain there would be no trace of the latter. For why would there be? That sodding dwarf had clearly set the whole bloody trip up to betray them, so why bother with a boat at all? There would be a pack of guards lurking at the bottom to ambush them or else the vivid glow of The Narrative waiting to pounce. He was so sure of what he would find and he could picture it in his head so perfectly: the betrayal by that dwarf, the princess laughing as they were dragged away and she fell into the arms of her one true love, while declaring what gullible mugs they were…

And nobody else would believe him!

True, he hardly expected it of Dullard, with his rabbity, wet smile and his air of naïve optimism—even if the bloody princess handed him over to the guards and watched, cackling as he was hung, drawn, and quartered in front of her, his head would probably keep babbling on about how it was all a misunderstanding and she didn't really mean it. Oh, she had that drip eating out of her hand and no mistake!

But as for Flirt and Fodder—Shoulders had known them both his whole life. They were supposed to be his friends. But no, ever since this whole stupid business had started and puffed up their heads like a pair of bellows, they hadn't been prepared to listen to a word he bloody said! Oh, they listened to Dullard, with his plummy voice and posh ideas, a man they'd known for a few days, but would they even give five minutes to someone they'd played with as Urchins? No!

What did he get? *Don't fall off the bloody cliff, Shoulders! Don't get smashed up satisfying your para-bloody-noia!* It's what they were thinking, he knew it! And what would they care if he did? They'd probably be relieved that he was…

His foot skidded on a patch of lichen, interrupting his mental rant as he scrabbled to regain his balance. For a moment, his toes teetered dangerously at the lip of the crevice, but a solid grasp on a jut of rock steadied him and he pulled himself back to his feet with a gasp. Carefully, and with an air of resolution, he righted his head.

This was just…*just*…

It hadn't been so bad when they'd had a decent plan. Kill the princess, now that was a plan—not only would it have kept them out of prison, but it came with a whole heap of job satisfaction. But suddenly there's Dullard bleating on about how she's changed and she's on their side and Flirt and Fodder lapping it up when she'd said it herself, to their faces, that she was in this for no one but herself. She would betray them, he was sure of it. The moment it suited the stuck-up cow, she wouldn't even hesitate...

And of course, because the princess was suddenly on their side—hah!—that meant their precious and only plan was shot to buggery.

The end had been in sight. One chomp of that thick Dragon's jaws and...

But that was gone. And where did they go from here?

So much for getting this over with. So much for getting his head back!

And he hadn't asked for any of it! It wasn't fair!

Well, he wasn't giving up, that was for sure. The old plan held as far as he was concerned. If he got the chance to knock the princess off In Narrative, he, at least, was going to bloody well take it! And he was not going to be fooled by suspicious dwarves into walking straight into traps!

Ahead, the cliff edge flattened into a rocky headland, circled by flocks of crying gulls. He could hear the lap of waves on sand.

Huh. So there was a beach. The short-arse git hadn't lied about everything.

Well. Time to see what kind of trap they'd laid. Would there be an army of fellow Disposables huddled on the sands? Would they have hauled the Dragon down from the other side of the mountains to stomp on them? Would there be AFCs circling, the Merry Band proclaiming? Just what had they got in store for them ahead, for he was not being paranoid and he knew he was right and there would definitely not be...

Shoulders pulled himself over the crest of the final jut of rock and stared.

An expanse of empty golden sand swept across the valley's mouth before him, rippling, grassy dunes and gentle, rolling waves spilling against a shore that stretched over to the rocky edge on the far side of the bay. A small boat, moored to an outcrop of rock by a sturdy rope, rocked easily at the touch of the sea as it danced cheerfully a few yards out from the shore. There was no sign of anybody, any ambush or trap or even footprints in the sand to show that human beings had been near the place in Quests.

Shoulders's shoulders dropped like stones. He sighed.

"Oh bollocks," he muttered, slamming his hands down on the rock. He stared over the edge into a small hollow shaped into the rocky face beyond in despondent irritation.

And came face-to-face with the Priest.

It was hard to tell who was the more surprised. The Priest's mouth dropped open as he stared up out of his hidey-hole, wrapped in his robes against the sea breeze. A half-eaten apple hovering in a pale hand an inch below his lips, he jerked his gaze away from the crack in the rocky pathway which Shoulders and his friends had been expected to blindly walk down. His free hand hung frozen in shock beside what looked like a coloured length of rope that wound down into a tiny gap in the rock below. His fingers twitched.

And Shoulders stared. Stared down at this minion of the Task-master and of Strut, who had no business lurking in a hollow in the middle of nowhere, at this man who could only be here for one reason and one reason alone. Jubilation and raw terror flooded Shoulders's body in equal measure.

"I was *right?*" he gasped.

The Priest started. His lips parted as his hand jerked towards the rope.

Shoulders didn't know what the rope was for. He didn't know if anyone else would be in earshot of his cries. But he knew one thing...

I am not getting caught!!!

Fuelled by a combination of adrenaline, fear, and the thought of his friends' faces when they found out he was right, Shoulders launched himself over the crest of the rock and flung his full weight down on the unfortunate cleric beneath. The man tried to screech, so Shoulders shoved the apple the man was holding deep into his mouth, muffling the cry into a choke, as the Disposable struggled to pin his wriggly victim down. Fortunately the man was a young Priest, soft and unused to activity, not one of the stately, portly figures expected of Priests in later maturity. His arms and legs were weak and doughy and thin as incense sticks. Shoulders, on the other hand, was no Donk, but Quests of combat had honed him to a certain fitness, and even with his head gyrating back and forth and blurring his vision, it was no real contest. Yanking the Priest's scrabbling fingers out of his nose, Shoulders pinned the man's flailing limbs and grabbed him roughly by the hair. Three quick blows of his head against the rock saw him motionless.

For a moment, Shoulders could only sit, breathing deeply, his head wobbling slightly as he stared down at the man he had beaten unconscious. The apple was still clamped within the Priest's jaws as blood leaked down the rock against which his head was resting. But the head wound wasn't too bad. The man wouldn't be out for long.

So now what?

He could take the man to the others, try to find out what the trap was and prove who the traitors in their midst were once and for all. But the climb down had been tricky enough for a loose-headed man and the climb up would doubtless be worse and probably impossible for a loose-headed man carrying an unconscious Priest on his back. Besides, what were the chances he'd be alone? The rocks were probably crawling with watchers—it was likely only sheer luck Shoulders had got this far unseen. That made trying to get information from the Priest when he woke unworkable too, for who knew who was within earshot waiting to pounce?

He was probably already surrounded. They might even be closing in as he pondered. Perhaps the others had already been captured, he was here alone, they were all doomed, so doomed, and he'd said it, he'd tried to warn them but would they bloody listen...

Through his apple, the Priest groaned. His limbs twitched.

"Bugger!" Muttering under his breath, Shoulders abandoned his panic to deal with more immediate concerns—after a further bash of the man's head against the rock for good measure, the Disposable set to work ripping a few lengths off the Priest's tumble of robes. He gagged the man, apple still in place, and bound his hands and feet as tightly as he could with the cloth. It probably wouldn't keep him confined for long—the sharp rock would make a cutting escape fairly easy. But hold on—hadn't there been a rope?

He turned. And yes, a piece of coloured rope, sealed at the end with a lump of red wax, was poking out of a small crack in the stone nearby, resting against the edge of the hole as its waxy end prevented it from slipping down. It vanished into the hole below, into the darkness that…

But hang about. Shoulders's eyes narrowed. Perhaps it was the sunlight above playing tricks, but the darkness of the hole didn't look all that dark.

Carefully, one hand steadying his head, Shoulders lowered himself to peer into the crack. The rope tumbled away below and from what should have been darkness trickled up the unmistakable flicker of torchlight.

"Where are they?"

Shoulders started violently at the sudden echo of the voice carried from beneath. From within the hole below, there was a hint of movement, shadows that blocked the light. And he knew that voice too well…

Strut.

And if Strut was here, the Merry Band soon would be.

They had been stuffed. Gruffly *had* sent word and turned them over in those lost hours in the cages. It was the only explanation.

He had been right. He had been so utterly and completely right in every way that his brain, more used to his paranoia being ruthlessly dismissed, struggled to comprehend it. But the satisfaction of that feeling was fast being rampaged over by the sheer, unbridled fear. And for once in his life, he couldn't panic. He had to find out what was going on. Gripping the rock heavily, he lowered his head closer to the hole and listened.

"We have been waiting in this miserable dwarf tunnel for too long." Strut's voice was cold and clinical as ever, but a hint of frustration was creeping across the edges of his tone. "Gruffly assured me that he would deliver them to this beach by midday, but there is no sign of them. We cannot keep the Merry Band running around inside these tunnels for much longer—The Narrative is growing dull! But yet the signal bells do not ring!" Shoulders heard a gentle ting as the rope before him swayed as though knocked from below. "They do not come!"

"Would you like me to send out scouts, sir?" Although Shoulders did not know this voice, he recognised the tone as one of Strut's army of priestly minions. "We could check the area for signs of them…"

"We cannot risk being seen. There is too much at stake." Strut took a heavy breath. "At worst, we can see them from here ourselves once they reach the sands. And Penitence will stay out of sight and keep a good watch on the path and the cliffs. If he sees them coming, he will signal. I trust him."

Given that Penitence was currently trussed-up with an apple jammed in his mouth, having been caught on the hop by a clumsy Disposable, Shoulders felt that Strut's trust was a little misplaced. But it also loosened a tiny corner in the knot that was gripping his stomach. There were no other guards or watchers. The man he'd beaten up was it.

There was a pause. It smelled of a pending question, and a moment later, Strut's companion posed it. "If you'll forgive me, sir—we are putting much faith in Gruffly in this matter. Can we be certain it is not misplaced? When he came to me last night, sir, and I suggested this plan to him, I was not entirely sure he wanted to go through with it. At times, he could barely speak."

"He is of the Merry Band." There was something deep in Strut's tone. "At heart, that is all that matters. He cannot betray his companions-in-arms, even if he wanted to."

"If you say so, sir." The Priest did not sound convinced. "Would you like me to check on the Merry Band, sir?"

"Please do, Pious." Footsteps faded away down what Shoulders presumed was the tunnel below.

Okay. So. The Merry Band were underground and waiting to pounce at a tinkle of a set of bells on a rope. Gruffly had set them up but cocked it up at the last minute with his hissy fit. But the moment any of them went near that beach...

He had to warn the others. Fast.

As he started to rise, his head gave an ungainly lurch. Shoulders paused a moment, tugging at a leather thong as he tightened his odd contraption once more to secure his head. He would need it for the climb and...

"Sir!" The anxious cry from below caught his attention. Abandoning his adjustments, Shoulders dropped back to his listening post. A moment later, Strut's voice, thick with unpleasantness, echoed from beneath.

"What..." he drawled icily, "are *you* doing here?"

From below came the anxious whistle of frightened breathing as the voice of Pious the Priest cut in. "We found him in one of the abandoned tunnels, sir, the steep one leading down from that old village. He hasn't said a word, though."

Slow, dangerous footfalls sounded. "I ask again," Strut's voice echoed dangerously. "What are you doing here? Why are you not out there leading the traitors to their doom?"

"I—I—I—" The stammer was barely a word, but it was enough to make Shoulders grimace with fury. Gruffly.

Strut's voice was a sudden glacial roar. "Answer me!"

"I *couldn't!*"

The cry was desperate and in the silence that followed, it ricocheted around hidden caves before fading into nothing. And then, Strut's voice carved into the quiet like a heated blade.

"What?"

"I…" Gruffly stammered again. "I tried! I really, really tried! But I couldn't do it! What they offered, I want it, I want it so much but I couldn't—I couldn't betray—" His voice choked. "So I just left, I left 'em! I did what I could! Please!"

"And what," Strut's voice was liquid menace, "could they possibly offer that would make you throw away the loyalty you owe to your Realm, to your Taskmaster, and to the true and steadfast companions you made in the Merry Band you rode with?"

"I want to be outside!" The response was a keening wail. "I want to live in the sun and watch the clouds, not stare at rock and be called 'his nibs' and laughed at and made fun of! I want to live in my village and be by myself! What's wrong with that, hmm? Why's it so bad for me to want that?"

There was an icy silence. Strut's voice, when it came, was dripping with a vile mixture of condescension and disdain.

"Because it's *wrong*," he all but hissed. His tone became richer as more familiar patronisation flooded through it, speaking as though lecturing a naughty child. "You are a *dwarf* and dwarves live *underground*. Everything the Taskmaster has ever taught us in the Quests tells us that. To do anything else, to want anything else, is frankly perverse. And you know that. You of all people know that. You who have felt The

Narrative flowing in your veins, you know who you should be. You know where your loyalties lie. Would Gort want to live on the surface?"

"I'm not Gort." Gruffly's voice was barely a whisper.

"Yes, you are." Strut's was stern. "In the ways that matter, you are. Gort is the better part of you, the part the Taskmaster made. Gort is all you should want to be. Gort, who would lay down his very life to save his dear, *dear* companions..."

From deep below, there came a painful whimper.

"Now..." Strut's voice was like the sound of a circling cobra. "Where did you leave them?"

"I..."

"Where are they?"

"I—I left them."

"Where did you leave them? Or would you see your companions left to circle in darkness forever, their destinies thwarted, their futures ruined? Would you?"

"The crevice!" The word was expelled almost against Gruffly's will. "Halfway up the cliff! I left them at the crack and went to my village! But..."

Shoulders felt as though he heard the hairy lips clamp shut. But it was too late.

"But what?" came Strut's harsh, beguiling reply. "Come now, your dear friends need you."

"No." The word was so small it was half swallowed. But Strut pounced upon the emotional rift it opened.

"So you would abandon them? Your dearest friends and comrades-in-arms? Poor young Erik, his destiny never to be fulfilled? Elder, never to see his charge take his true place in the world and avenge his family? Svenheid, never to catch the murderer of his brothers? Zahora, Slynder, Sir Roderick, are they to be left to suffer at your hands because you cannot bear to do your duty? You die for them only to let them down after?" His voice dropped from throbbing beration to soft insistence. "Listen, can you hear their voices echoing nearby? They yearn for what you were about to say."

None of those people exist, you idiot! They're made up! The words shot through Shoulders's head unbidden. But although that fact was clear to him, it seemed that Gruffly was struggling with it. And a moment later, he cracked.

"I cannot betray my companions," he whispered, his voice, as it had by the cages, altered subtly by echoes of Gort. "So I must tell you. Two of them followed me up to my village. I concealed myself at their approach and stayed out of sight in the hidden tunnel mouth while they wandered at will in my private place. But after they desecrated one of the huts, I could stand no more. I tricked them to the well, pushed them, and locked them inside. I was so angry at their invasion, I thought to give them over but when I entered the tunnels…" His voice faltered. "I hate being underground!" he wailed suddenly, his voice dropping its rich edge. "It was so horrible! I could remember why I…why I was going to let 'em go! And then he came along and found me and brought me to you…"

The dwarf's voice broke down. There was a distant sound of sobbing.

"You have done the right thing." Strut's tone was the most conde-scending thing Shoulders had ever heard. "Your companions will be grateful, and you can do them one last service." A sniffle from the dwarf did not sound a promising reply. "Be Gort a final time. Go out, find the other two traitors and the princess, and lead them to the village too. I will dispatch your noble companions and they will take the traitors off your hands. If you do that, I will make sure that the Taskmaster overlooks this heinous lapse in judgement. Will you do that, for your companions' sake?"

Gruffly's voice, when it came, had slipped back into character. "I will."

"Well done. Now go." Strut's tone hardened. "Pious, find the Merry Band and guide The Narrative this way by means of the signs we discussed. It is time to go outside."

Shit. As Shoulders scrambled to his feet, he knew they were in trouble. Dullard and the bloody princess were sitting openly by the crevice, unaware of the danger so close by, and with Dullard's leg they had no chance of a quick getaway. And if what Gruffly said about Flirt and Fodder was true…

Oh, hell's teeth. It was all down to him.

He had to save them all.

Bollocks.

From below, he heard the scrunch of footsteps on the sand, followed by a clink of pebbles. He looked down.

At the seaward entrance to the crack in the cliff about ten feet below, a pale and trembling Gruffly the dwarf was making his way upwards.

Shoulders firmed his jaw. "No, you don't, sunshine," he muttered under his breath. A large, convenient rock teetering on the brink of the crevice caught his eye; resting his shoulder against it for leverage, he set it rocking and, steadying his head to aim with one hand, he forced his weight against it and sent it hurtling downwards.

The shot was a beauty. It caught Gruffly full on the crown of his skull and dropped him like a stone. His body rolled into a gap between two boulders, where he rocked to a halt out of view from all but the watcher above. He lay in a heap and was still.

He wouldn't be out for long. But it was start enough.

Shoulders glanced at Penitence the Priest. Two shocked eyes stared at him over the apple gag.

For the sake of completeness, Shoulders reached out and bashed his head against the rock one more time. There was no point in taking chances.

From the hole in the rock, a new, brighter, more vivid shaft of light drifted upwards.

"Sod it!" Abandoning his two victims, Shoulders turned and bolted away up the cliff as, behind him, the sands glowed with the power of Narrative light.

The Merry Band was on its way.

* * *

"Well, I'm hardly an expert." With her nose wrinkled in a firm expression of martyrdom, Princess Pleasance carefully rebound the rough bandage wrapped around Prince Dullard's calf. She climbed awkwardly back up from the dusty ground onto the rock that afforded her only seating arrangement, wiping her hands as best she could against the ruins of her dress. Oh, for a decent washbasin… "But it certainly looks less repulsive than it did earlier."

"It certainly feels better." Dullard flashed his odd smile at her as he ran his long fingers over the restored bandage cautiously. "I doubt I'll be running any races for a day or so, but I think it might hold my weight at least."

Pleasance gazed at her hands. They felt worse after their encounter with her beleaguered dress than they had before. A good washbasin, perhaps some of that gorgeous scented soap that made her skin feel so soft and delicious, a fluffy, warm towel touched with a dab of perfume to dry herself with...

"Does that mean you won't have to cling to my shoulders like a fleshy cloak anymore?" she replied, her eyes slipping down to her fingernails—or rather what was left of them. It hurt to look, it really did...

"Hopefully." She could feel Dullard's gaze staring over at her, although she did not raise her eyes to meet it.

"Good," she returned archly, examining the ripped remains of her index nail absently. "To say it was becoming tiresome is an understatement worthy of you."

"I very much appreciate it." He was staring again. She could feel it. And while she knew that even in her current state, she was easily the most attractive thing to look at in the immediate vicinity, she did wish he'd turn his goggle eyes somewhere else. There was something about that gaze of his that burrowed, and burrowing made her uncomfortable. "I know you didn't have to."

"Of course I didn't have to," she retorted, picking carefully at the remains of her little finger's nail to try and free the wedge of dirt that had lodged there. "And I shouldn't have had to either, if any of those bloody peasants had any manners."

He was still staring, for goodness' sake! "What do you mean?"

Pleasance pouted. "I mean I found it charming the way that they left the smallest and least sartorially well-equipped member of the group to help you along. Did even one of them offer to relieve me or even to help along that miserable excuse for a path? No!" She huffed loudly as she extracted the filth and flicked it disdainfully off towards the ocean. "They merely left me to it! The selfish pack of..."

"I think they may have had other things on their minds." Always he made excuses for them. Dullard and his rose-tinted view of just about everything!

"Oh yes, I'm sure they did!" Pleasance took a deep breath of salty air. "With the two of them busily obsessing over some random peasant hovel when we should be fleeing for our lives—I mean, what are they after, housekeeping tips? And as for the other one..." She took another deep breath, this time to fuel her anger. "When is he going to get it through that solid skull of his that I am not some kind of...*plant?* Fine, I admit, you can keep your lofty ideals as far as I'm concerned. But that doesn't mean I'm going to leap back into The Narrative and turn you all over at the first chance I get!"

"I know that." Dullard's voice was soothing. "He'll realise it too soon enough. He simply needs time."

"I don't know about that." Pleasance stared at her wrecked nails and soiled hands furiously. "Does he think I'd be in this state if I didn't have to be? I mean, look at me! My hair's a nest, my dress is rags, my skin is filthy, my nails are ruined! In the last couple of days alone, I've been hauled up a cliff, grabbed by a Dragon, almost fed to it by that bloody Disposable, chased, fallen down a hole, knocked out, piled in a cart like rubbish, soaked, attacked by dwarves, locked up, and forced along a cliff dragging you like a dead weight! I miss my bath and my bed, my dresses, my hairbrush, my Servants! I miss warm food and cold drinks! I miss being treated with honour and respect because I certainly don't get it from those three. Honestly, I don't think I'd even be here if it wasn't for..."

You.

She nearly said it. The word teetered dangerously on her lips for an instant before her brain caught up with her mouth and swallowed the word down before it could escape. She improvised hurriedly.

"Bumpkin!" she expelled. "If it wasn't for him...if I didn't have to marry him."

"Of course not." Those damned eyes, they burned like embers against her. "But I'm sure it'll be worth it in the end."

Where had that come from? When had she developed an actual respect for the man who'd got her back into this mess by hauling her out of her home? When had she started to...

I can tolerate him now. I think—I think I'm almost starting to...like him.

Oh lord.

That won't do. Stop it.

"It'd better be," she retorted brusquely. "For being stuck with the terrible trio with only you to turn to for a vaguely intelligible conversation."

He gave a tiny chuckle. "Thank you."

"It wasn't a compliment," she returned at once. "It merely means you are marginally better company than a shrew of a Barmaid, a dull Disposable, and his headless friend who thinks I'm going to betray him any second!"

"That's something, I suppose." The feel of his eyes dimmed. Pleasance risked a glance up to find him gazing absently out to sea. His brow creased. "I wonder what's become of...*Shoulders!*"

Pleasance started at his exclamation just as her eyes too found the scrambling, wobbly-headed form of the wretched Disposable who refused to trust her hauling himself up the rocks with wild eyes and flushed cheeks. He was breathing violently, the remains of his surcoat rippling near his sliced neck, the air circulating by any means it could. Dullard was already on his feet; she rose too, following his limping form as he hurried to the edge of the crack to meet him.

"Shoulders!" Dullard exclaimed again. "What's wrong?"

And in spite of the fact he was gasping with abject exhaustion, in spite of the anxiety that was written large on his features, for an instant, a flash of smug triumph crossed that unsteady head.

"Told!" he rasped breathlessly, jabbing one finger at Dullard's chest as he doubled over and leaned against his knees with his free hand. "You! *So!*"

Dullard's face creased with confusion. "What...?"

And then the sky glowed. A shaft of vivid light burst free of the overhanging twists and turns of the crevice perhaps a hundred yards below, yearning for a moment towards the unending heavens before being swallowed again by the concealment of the sunken cliff path. Only a few leaked flashes marked its progress up.

"Oh dear," Dullard whispered.

Pleasance felt her stomach drop like a stone. *Oh no, please, not Bumpkin, not that chance for true love's first gaze...*

With Shoulders still struggling to speak due to the perils of headless heavy breathing, Dullard took up the slack. "It was a trap? Gruffly betrayed us?"

Shoulders tried to nod, made a heinous mess of it, and settled for sticking up his thumb. "Strut! Tunnels! Waiting!" he managed to expel. "Beach!" He jabbed his finger in the direction that Flirt and Fodder had earlier taken. "Trapped! Warn! Run!"

Dullard was shaking his head. "I can't run, let alone up there—I can barely hobble. We'll hide. You'll have to find them and bring them back to us!"

Shoulders's expression spoke more eloquently than any words what he thought of that plan. Below, the flashes of light were edging closer.

Dullard bit his lip. "All right. Find the others, hide, and meet us down at the beach."

Shoulders's face grew, if possible, even more incredulous. "The bloody beach?" he managed as he started to get his breath back. "Why there? *They're* there!"

"And so is a boat, a tunnel and cave, and a valley full of places to hide. It's our best chance." Dullard's face was insistent. "Please, Shoulders."

"Oh, whatever." Shoulders turned, his hands on his hips as he uncrumpled his body to stare at the approaching darts of light with a combination of horror and resignation. "Get out of sight—they know we were here. And don't let her get you caught!"

Pleasance managed an indignant gasp, but the Disposable had already turned, plunging back over the side of the crack towards the rising path.

"Good luck!" Dullard called anxiously after him and received a dismissive hand wave in response. A moment later he had vanished.

Pleasance wasted no time in grabbing Dullard's arm and hauling him backwards. "Hide!" she hissed.

A cleft in the cliff face provided shelter enough—they grabbed Dullard's pack, which Pleasance lugged as Dullard hobbled awkwardly inside. They ducked behind a boulder and huddled together. They were barely in time.

Vivid light flooded the mouth of the cleft. The sky above glowed a brighter blue.

"I see no one!" Harridan's voice echoed with Narrative power. "There are places of concealment I can search..."

"There is no time!" Magus's voice was more vibrant, echoing from the crack below as he called up. "If it truly was the man of Sleiss Erik saw trapped in his vision, this may be our only chance to find the princess! Come!"

Footsteps pounded against the rocky path. A moment later, the light flickered and was gone.

Pressed shoulder to shoulder in the shadows, Pleasance saw Dullard's brow crease. "They could have left Harridan behind," he muttered thoughtfully. "It was foolish not to do a proper search really."

"Well, I for one am glad they didn't." Pleasance pulled herself awkwardly back to her feet, untangling her skirts as she leaned towards the entrance to the cleft. "A stupid enemy is a bonus, not something to be criticised."

"Enemy?" Dullard took Pleasance's proffered hand as he too came to his feet. "I wouldn't put it that strongly."

"Well, they'll do until a real one comes along." Pleasance was in no mood for pedantry. "Come on, let's get out of here while we have the chance."

A quick peek out of the entrance told Pleasance that in the wider confines of the higher parts of the crack, The Narrative's light was continuing to rise. Grabbing Dullard firmly by the arm, she hurried to the entrance of the crevice.

To call it pleasant would have been akin to suggesting that Shoulders was a chirpy, rainbow-loving optimist. The confines were narrow and dark, the rock slimy and coated with lichen and moss, and the floor was an uneven tumble of rocks and boulders. It didn't take long for Dullard to struggle, and their progress was painfully slow as they descended. Fortunately, the drop was not a huge distance and at last they reached a corner up which the normal light flooded with the sound of gentle waves and circling gulls beyond. Pleasance was not ashamed to breathe a large sigh of relief.

"Do you think anyone will be there?" she whispered as they approached the final bend, stepping around a strange, hairy mass lying in the shadow of two boulders to reach the corner.

"Possibly." Dullard's face was bathed in sweat, his lips pursed painfully as he struggled with his injured leg. "They can't have taken horses up here, so someone may be watching them. We'll be fine as long as it's not someone with the power to summon The Narrative to their point of view."

Carefully, the prince grabbed the edge of the rock, Pleasance catching his shoulder. Moving as one, they peered around the bend.

Golden sand rolled away, and a boat rocked easily in the swell of waves. A cluster of horses were gathered near its mooring rope, tethered to the anchor by their reins. And sitting, casual as you like in the sand beside them, picking irritably at his fingernails with his knife blade and massaging a bandaged thigh with a look of discontent...

Two heads retracted hurriedly. Two pairs of eyes met with resignation.

"Swipe." Pleasance pulled a face. "Naturally, it would be a Principal, wouldn't it? Why on earth would they leave him here and not take him up with them?"

"The same reason we didn't go up, I suspect." Dullard worked his painful leg awkwardly. "It looks like he's been hurt In Narrative. Perhaps without horses, he couldn't make it on foot with his leg damaged and they didn't want to be slowed down." He frowned slightly. "I wonder how that could have happened."

"Who cares?" Pleasance dismissed his ponderings impatiently. "If he sees us, he can bring The Narrative, and that's all we need with you in this state. What matters is getting rid of him so we can escape. And on that matter..." An idea had swirled into her head, a bold idea, a wild idea, but possibly their only chance to get out of this without invoking The Narrative. She took a deep breath. *"I'll* deal with this."

Dullard's eyebrows shot up. "You?"

Pleasance felt a flare of indignation. "You think I can't?"

"No! It's just..." Dullard floundered, and Pleasance leapt on the weakness like a cat.

"You don't trust me?" she exclaimed.

"No, of course not!" Dullard gave a gusty sigh as he saw Pleasance's face. "I mean, yes, I trust you, it's just…" He gave a wan smile. "If you have an idea, do it. But please be *careful.*"

He looked so concerned for an instant that Pleasance almost felt sorry for him. Almost. Definitely almost.

"I will," she reassured, forgoing her usual barb. "He'll think I've escaped. It'll be fine."

"Don't let him call The Narrative," Dullard added once more.

Pleasance's returning look told him more eloquently than words that she had not lost the power to remember things she'd herself said less than a minute before. "Stay out of sight," she admonished. "Whatever happens."

Distressed. That's what she was going for here. Distressed and put-upon but determined not to look absurd. She could do that. After all, hadn't she lived it for the first days of her captivity?

Carefully, she selected a rock of suitable size and weight and, grasping it firmly in one hand behind her back, she moved out into the open.

She had reached the sand before Swipe spotted her, so preoccupied was he with taking a knife to his dirty fingernails, the unkempt oaf. His mouth dropped open in a pleasingly gobsmacked manner.

"Princess!" he gasped before breaking off to yelp as he drove the tip of his knife into his fingertip. He hurled the knife onto the sand and pulled himself to his feet with an agility that defied his bandages. "You're here!"

"And you're observant!" The sarcasm was coated in a heady enough mixture of wobbling terror and angry distress that Pleasance got away with it. Awkwardly, she mirrored a limp with one hand clasped against her thigh so as to act injured rather than appearing that she was hiding a large rock in said hand with intentions to brain her would-be rescuer. There was no point in taking chances.

"I'm sorry!" she declared, her voice dropping to a trembling sob as she limped her battered way towards the Thief. He made no move to advance towards her, an act she found deeply unchivalrous. The leg was surely Narrative damage, nothing more than an itch outside of it—why did he not rush to her aid? "I'm sorry, but I've been through so much, and it's been so *horrible* and now finally to have escaped their brutal clutches and find an ally close at hand..."

She dissolved into artful sobs as her limp slipped to an uneven sway. And still he didn't move closer. Foul knave! Was she to stagger the whole way herself?

At last, the Thief got the message. He hurried forwards.

Pleasance tightened her grip on her rock as she faked a rolling half-faint, reeling on her feet. *Just a little closer...*

"I'll call The Narrative!" Pleasance's head snapped up at Swipe's enthusiastic exclamation. "You'll be safe in seconds if I—"

"No!" The keening screech brought Swipe's advance to a halt, but frankly Pleasance could live with it if it meant he wasn't calling in the cavalry. Bewilderment crossed his face.

"What?" he managed. "Why?"

"Why? *Why?*" The brief interlude gave Pleasance enough time for a change of tack. "What kind of a brute are you? After all I've been through, all I've endured to reach the arms of my true love in The Narrative, you would have me enter it looking like *this?*"

Swipe blinked. "What?" he repeated.

"Like *this!*" Moving ever closer, Pleasance made a dramatic sweep of her body with her free arm. "My hair, my dress, my nails! Look at the state of me! I would sooner suffer a thousand Narrative deaths than have my big moment of love and rescue ruined by the fact I looked like a scarecrow's sister!" She drew a melodramatic breath as she advanced, five more steps, four, three...

"No, no, no!" she exclaimed. "Before we let The Narrative anywhere near me, I will need a washbasin, some scented soap, a good shampoo, a hairbrush and comb, a decent nail file, a new dress, new shoes..." She came to a halt beside him, glaring up at his shocked-looking face. "I mean, look at this shoe!" She pulled her dress back to reveal the battered object in question. "Well, go on, look!"

His expression holding at one of abject bewilderment, Swipe leaned reluctantly forwards. And his expression remained equally bemused right up until the moment when Pleasance's rock descended on his head with a crunch several times in sharp succession.

It was a perfect knockout. Features frozen at bewildered, he dropped to a crumpled heap at her feet.

Pleasance beamed, hefting her rock in one hand and pulling her foot out from under the supine figure of the Thief.

"So gullible," she muttered to herself as she turned on her heel.

And came face-to-face with Strut.

He stood perhaps eight yards distant, the sound of his approach swallowed by the sand that trailed his footfalls back to a curtain of vines that no doubt concealed a tunnel mouth hidden behind in the rock. And his face—she had known Strut all her life, respected him, done everything she could to get into his good graces so as to ensure her own success when the perfect moment came. She had seen him smile thinly and frown sternly, but the range of his expressions had always been limited to a certain degree of cool control and firm authority overwritten by a superior air that many a Royal had yearned to master.

She had never seen him look jubilant. She had never seen him look relieved. And she suspected she never would again, for even as she stared, that uncharacteristic face full of joy was draining away to reveal one so stark as to be painful. Swipe's expression had been confused but Strut was deep in shock. His hands, a moment before outstretched towards her, began to tremble.

"No," he whispered.

Pleasance's grip on her rock tightened as she stared at the man who until very recently had guided her entire world. "Strut," she said briskly, trying to conceal the coldness in her stomach as she raised her chin imperiously. There was no point in playing again, or trying to front it out. He'd seen what she'd done and heard what she'd said. Her act was not going to fool him.

Strut *knew.*

It was an odd feeling. For until this moment, as far as the world knew, she was the innocent victim, dragged in against her will and longing for freedom and her Narrative destiny. There had been a kind of a way out, an escape back to her old life, a chance to retreat if it had been needed.

But now Strut knew. That chance was gone.

His eyes were desperate pools of horror as what he had witnessed began to sink in. The mask of control that had always filtered his feelings had apparently been shattered by the seeing of it.

"What are you doing?" he whispered, his voice pleading for an explanation that wouldn't destroy his duty and shake his world to pieces. "Why did you do that?"

Pleasance held firm despite the rolling in her stomach as her own horror sunk into her heart. *This isn't a game anymore. I can't go back...*

"He was in my way," she declared coolly.

"How?" His voice was almost a moan. "How could he be in your way? He was your ally. He was of the Merry Band; he could call them for you! He would have taken you to The Narrative and to your true love."

"And therein lies the problem." Pleasance was quite proud of how she managed to hold on to her air of defiance. "I don't want to go."

Strut staggered as though struck, but somehow he clung to a lifeline of hope a moment longer. "If this is about how you look..."

"It isn't." Her two brusque words crushed his final fragile hope into dust. "This is about me."

Strut's expression was fraught with utter betrayal. Rage was seeping over the shock in his eyes. "What have they done to you?" he hissed. "Have they played with your mind, rallied you to their 'noble cause'?" He spat the word. "They would destroy our world!"

Pleasance chose to ignore the final statement—she had no desire to get into a debate on the merits of a cause she didn't really believe in. "I'm not trying to be noble," she stated instead. "As it happens, I'm being selfish. It just so happens their...nobility, as you call it, and my selfishness coincide."

Strut was shaking his head, cold fury rising over the shocked emotions of moments before. "I know you," he exclaimed icily, advancing a couple of steps across the golden sand. "To be a princess, the Heroine— that was your dream, Pleasance, all you wanted from life. What manner of abomination could persuade you to abandon that?"

Pleasance shrugged, but her grip on her rock tightened at his approach. "I wanted that life, I admit. I still do in a way. However, I don't want what comes afterwards. Happy ever after with an oaf like Bumpkin? I don't think so!"

Strut was eyeing her with the air of a mantis stalking its prey. "But the Quest will change him, Pleasance." Cold rage was slipping into beguiling honey. "You know that. It will make him better, as it does all who accept the gifts it has to offer. Once you have Islaine in your heart, you will understand. She will guide you, be the better part of you. Everything will be well again."

Pleasance shook her head as he closed on her once more. She longed to step back but did not dare show the weakness. The rock dug into her grasping palm.

It was another lifeline, she knew, a last chance to step away, abandon this foolishness, and take up her destiny. She thought of her family and what they expected of her, of her life, of all she would be leaving behind if she committed beyond hope to this ridiculous band of rebels and their wild ideas. She thought of the disrespect with which they had treated her, the lack of trust and the disdain. Why would she want that when she could have Islaine, her perfect princess, everything that she had ever aspired to be, finally on the verge of touching her mind?

Because Islaine belonged to Bumpkin's Erik. And that could never be her.

Dullard's voice, soft, persuasive, urging her to know her own mind, to think for herself. And yes, she wanted the beautiful life, the respect, the luxury, the glory that awaited her if she simply took Strut's hand, returned to The Narrative, and let her character guide her. Her life would be as she'd always dreamed.

But it wouldn't be her living it.

"I don't want Islaine in my heart," she replied, praying the tremble in her voice was her own imagination. "I want myself. That's well enough for me. But I don't think that will be enough for anyone else."

The honey was gone in an instant, swamped by glowing rage. Strut's features contracted.

"You stupid little girl!" His scream of anger took her completely by surprise—the step back was unavoidable. "You know nothing; you have no idea! You think you somehow matter? That you are more important than what you must become?" Spittle sprayed from his lips. "All that matters is Islaine! And be it in your mind or somebody else's, she will live! I will find a way! You are not *irreplaceable*, Pleasance!"

"What?" Pride swamped over Pleasance's defiant fear in an instant. "Don't be ridiculous! You think you can recast when The Narrative has seen me over and over again? I am Islaine, whether you like it or not, and she is mine to do with as I please!"

"I thought you did not want her!" Strut snapped. "I thought she was not worthy of your precious heart!"

"That does not mean *you* can have her!" Pleasance tossed her head in true princess style, as she'd been taught from childhood. "Whether I embrace her or discard her is up to me! It is my choice and no one else's! And you cannot take that away from me!"

"Oh, we'll see." Coldness had once more damped the fires of Strut's blast of anger as he towered over Pleasance's form. "We'll see, won't we? When The Narrative catches up with you, we'll find out who you are! And when you see the only weapon your wonderful new allies have falter as if it were nothing, when you are standing and facing a fate worse than dungeons and disgrace, worse than anything ever dreamt of in the Realm before, then, oh, *then* you will be sorry!"

She swung the rock with all her might, desperate to drive him back, but he caught her hand, snatching the rock away, kicking her ankles and knocking her backwards onto the sand. His eyes gleamed madly as he raised the rock to strike...

And glazed abruptly as the hilt of a sword descended into the side of his temple with a violent crunch. He folded neatly to the sand beside Swipe and lay still.

Dullard stared down at the Taskmaster's taskmaster, his face a cocktail of shock, pain, and exhaustion. He was grasping his leg tenderly.

The sight of him gave Pleasance the chance to think about something other than what had just happened. "I told you to stay out of sight!" she snapped.

"He didn't see me," was the breathless response. "But if we don't move, The Narrative might! Come on!"

And there it was, that taste in the air, that hint of light. Dullard was right: The Narrative was coming, and Pleasance didn't consider herself in any state to face it. She vaulted to her feet.

"Come here!" she exclaimed, grabbing Dullard's arm and looping it over her shoulder. He made no protest and, as quickly as they were able, the prince and princess bolted in search of cover.

* * *

How long had they been stuck in that miserable well? Fodder wasn't sure. He only knew it was not a good place to be.

He'd been fairly sure of that from the beginning. But it hadn't been too bad for a while, once he and Flirt had sorted themselves out and managed to squirm, with much careful limb placement and numerous awkward apologies, into an upright position. As Flirt had stated earlier, the well wasn't excessively deep and there was plenty of scope for using the bone-dry walls for balance. Flirt had clambered onto his shoulders and set about using the tip of his sword—refusing, as ever, to use her own blade for anything that didn't involve wholesale slaughter of their enemies—to dislodge the catch holding them inside. And it had been going quite promisingly right up until the moment footsteps had sounded outside and the unmistakable dulcet tones of a member of the trapping community had sounded from above, informing them gruffly that he had been press-ganged as a bounty hunter to hand them over to the Merry Band and they were to sit tight and shut up until they arrived.

And to drown out their protests, he'd started singing. Badly.

They were not nice ditties. The one about the wayward monk had a pleasant enough tune but by the time they reached the fifth verse about the hay-barn adventures of the tinker's daughter, Fodder was starting to feel queasy and Flirt had turned purple. The word *wench* had not yet slipped into the lyrics but, given the man's repertoire, it seemed only a matter of time; and once that moment was reached, Fodder feared no force on earth would stop Flirt from leaping back onto his shoulders and stabbing her sword into the wooden cover in the hope of a lucky strike.

And perhaps he should let her. It didn't seem likely they'd find any other way out of there before the inevitable vivid glow washed over the deserted village and left them in deep unpleasantness of a whole new kind. As a precaution, though, he had already slipped the Ring of Anthiphion onto one finger. If nothing else, perhaps he and Flirt would have time to vanish before anyone from the top of the well had time to shoot…

Bawdy lyrics cut into the air, loud and oppressive. A knight errant had dropped by to keep the tinker's daughter amused.

Flirt's voice leaked menace. "If I get the chance," she breathed, "I'll break that man like a bloody *twig.*"

"As he dumped all his armour upon a rough bench!" *Oh no, not a good lyric, not good, not good.* "He bellowed, 'Come hither, my fine lusty'—oof!"

"You value your life, mate?" For quite possibly the first time in his entire life, Fodder felt his heart leap at the sound of a too-familiar voice. "Don't sing that!"

"Shoulders!" With little respect for his dignity, Flirt grabbed Fodder by the head as she scrambled up his body and hauled herself onto his shoulders. "Shoulders, down here!"

"I know that!" was the breathless response. "I heard Gruffly tell Strut he dumped you down here, given that this was a *big trap* and *I was right* and everything! I followed the singing right to you! Hold on, I'll get the catch!"

There would be smug. Fodder knew this instinctively as he heard his old friend scrabbling to free the well catch. But to be honest, if it got him out of this well and away before The Narrative arrived, a bit of Shoulders's smugness was a small price to pay. He'd earned a bit of being right.

The well lid rocketed back. Shoulders's loose-headed silhouette stared down at them as he chucked the bucket and rope into the minimal depths for them to pull themselves up with. Above him, the air was thickening noticeably.

"Hurry up!" he beckoned, sounding frantic. "They were right on my tail even before I had to slow down to sneak up on matey-boy and his dodgy singing!"

Flirt was already halfway out of the hole as Fodder grabbed the rope to follow her. Both his friends caught his arms and hauled him out bodily.

The horizon on the plateau above was glowing with Narrative threat. Rich voices echoed with its power.

"Hide!" Grabbing her two friends by the arm, Flirt plunged all three of them into the open doorway of the nearest hut. As they dropped into a huddle, flattening themselves beneath the window, the world without went bright.

"Mongrel's blood!" Clank's curse vibrated with Narrative feeling. "They cannot have escaped us again!"

"Search the village," Magus snapped in response. "This man is warm; he has not long been murdered—they cannot have got out of this place without passing into our sight. They are here…somewhere."

"What do we do?" Shoulders's voice was barely a breath as his chest continued to heave from his exertions.

Fodder stared down at his finger, his knuckles clenching. He swallowed hard.

"The only thing we can do," he whispered back. "Go into Narrative and use the Ring to jump away."

Shoulders's expression offered a plethora of silent protest but Flirt's, while nervous, also contained a wordless, if eloquent, declaration that they didn't have any better ideas. The three stared at each other. Shoulders sighed.

Fodder had no choice but to take this as an assertion. He rose to a crouch with his companions to either side of him.

"Keep hold of me," he hissed as a shadow moved with deep intent towards their hut. "I'll jump to Dullard and Pleasance and—"

"They're heading to the beach." Shoulders pulled a face at Fodder's incredulous look. "Rabbit-boy's idea. Don't look at me."

"Fine, the beach." The shadow was looming now, big and bulky. There was only one Merry Bander who could pack that kind of outline. "Ready?"

Flirt nodded. Shoulders glared.

Fodder braced himself as he crept forward towards the bright light streaming through the doorway. Three, two…

One…

"Here!" But the cry had barely left Svenheid's lips before a sweep of a beautifully fashioned sword drove him stumbling backwards. Erik saw Elder start, saw his lips begin to move in a rapid incantation as the man of Sleiss and his two companions gripped each other in the doorway, the man himself already raising the finger upon which impudently glistened the most renowned magical artefact in history. But where was the foul prince who had stolen his love away? And where, oh where was his beloved Islaine?

"They are three again!" Over the rising maelstrom of his fury, Erik heard Sir Roderick's hiss. "I beheaded one of their number but their complement is restored! They must have met an ally in the forest!"

"We'll be off then!" the man of Sleiss proclaimed, stumbling with his allies out of the hut as around him, Zahora, Svenheid, and Sir Roderick circled, weapons drawn. "Bye!"

The Ring flashed red, a stunning crimson glow. The air began to ripple.

"*Khelai tiarh!*" With a roar towards the heavens, Elder crashed his hands together, the power of his magic rippling like a shockwave through the air. With a dying flare, the red light died abruptly.

"Fodder!" The woman gave an inexplicable screech. "Now would be a good time!"

But the man of Sleiss was staring down at the Ring, his eyes filled with bewilderment. Madly, he shook the hand on which it rested, tapping the gem as though such motion would spur it back to life.

"It's not working!" he exclaimed.

His new companion, dressed in armour that ranged strangely at the neck and a helmet dangling with strips of leather, was reeling as though drunk, his eyes wide.

"Shit!" he whispered painfully.

It was the woman who acted. Grabbing her two associates by their respective collars, she hauled them backwards away from the closing ring of warriors, ushering them towards the solid rock wall to delay what was only inevitable.

"Where is the princess?" Elder's eyes were glowing with magic. "Tell us where to find her and we will grant you the blessing of a quick death!"

"Sod off!" the woman retorted crudely, waving her sword blade in threatening circles.

"Yeah!" There was a sudden solidifying of the strangely dressed man's jaw as an odd gleam slipped into his eyes. "We'll never tell you she and the prince were heading down to the beach!"

"Shoulders!" The woman gave another inexplicable screech as the soldier's eyes widened with horror.

"I didn't mean to say that!" he gibbered, jamming one fist against his mouth. "I didn't mean to, I didn't want to, it made me!"

Erik's heart leapt. For he knew, deep in his veins and bones, that the strange soldier had not been lying. Islaine was close!

And Elder knew it too. His eyes glinted.

"Thank you for that," he declared, his brow knitted as he held the spell he had mastered to contain the power of the Ring. "That is all we needed." He nodded to the three warriors. "Take them."

Zahora's twin swords sliced at the air lazily as she advanced. Svenheid gripped his axe as a grin teased his bearded features. Sir Roderick's expression was grim and businesslike as he hefted his broadsword and approached.

The small rock-face that dropped from the plateau above loomed behind them as their back met stone. They were trapped.

Sir Roderick's voice was cold. "Now is the time you will pay for your infamy, traitors!"

"The way down!" The screech slipped out of the throat of the strangely armoured man as though squeezing out some blockage. "I heard...I heard them say... Ack!" With a shuddering whimper, the staggering man wheeled, beating his fists in wild futility against the solid stone. "Find it, find it...leave me alone, I need to...I need..." His fingernails scratched at the rock as though to cling to it, as though some unseen force sought to rip him away. "It has to be...it has to..."

Erik gaped at the wild-eyed lunatic. It seemed the madness of Prince Tretaptus was rubbing off on his subordinates.

"Oi!" The man of Sleiss started up from his futile Ring-waving. "I am nobody's bloody subordinate!"

But the woman was watching the wild flailing of their other companion and suddenly, her eyes widened. Her face hardening, she turned back to her advancing enemies.

"That's the way it is, is it?" she almost spat. "Three of you against one woman?"

The man of Sleiss looked over with a hint of indignation. "Oi, what am I?"

The woman glared at him. "Back off. Now."

"But..."

"Back off fodder!" the woman repeated with inexplicable addition. "Look after shoulders!" She glared at him pointedly. "He needs help, doesn't he?"

And in spite of his earlier exclamation of independence, the man did as he was bidden, dropping back to join his madly groping companion. Bizarrely, he too began to run his hands along the stone walls as though caressing them in his fear.

And so the woman stood alone, her beautiful sword grasped between her fingers. "Come on then," she exclaimed. "Three against one, isn't it, like I said! What are you afraid of? Two big boys against one little girl? I can see why harridan over there might be worried, given how the last time we fought, I duffed her up—I mean, she wouldn't want to go in without backup, I get that, but you two?"

Zahora's expression had turned dark at the woman's insult but it went to purest black at this slight upon her bravery. "You think I could not take you, some common she-wolf scum who thinks that armour and a stolen blade make her a warrior? You were lucky before!"

"Want to see if my luck's holding?" The woman's eyes glinted. "Or are you going to let the boys do the rough stuff for you?"

Zahora's jaw steeled like iron. "Step away!" she roared at the bewildered-looking Svenheid and Sir Roderick. "She is mine! She has impugned my honour!"

Sir Roderick was shaking his helmeted head. "Zahora, I think this is not wise!" he exclaimed. "It is a game! She is playing on your rage!"

"I know it." Zahora's voice was a hiss, her dual swords clattering blade on blade as she rubbed them together in anticipation. "But I am ready nonetheless! And she will pay for it!"

But Erik could not afford to wait on Zahora's pride. "The princess is so close! We have no time for this!"

Elder could only stare in horror as the boy turned and bolted back in the direction of the beach where they had left their horses. But he could not pursue, not without risking the lifting of his spell and losing the Ring and its thieves...

"Sir Roderick!" he commanded instead and, with a grimace, the knight abandoned the standoff and hurried in pursuit of the boy.

Zahora was advancing on her hated enemy, her expression fierce. "You will pay for your impudence!" she exclaimed angrily. "The time has come!"

The woman's expression was equally determined. "Looking forward to—"

"Hey, flirt?" The diffident interruption came from the man of Sleiss. "You know the time? And what you were spending to buy it? No need. We've just found a nice piece of art for you to spend it on instead. So if you're done with the agreed lack of noble sacrifice..."

With a flash of outright annoyance, the woman swung round to glare at her rock-groping companion. "Can't you give me..."

The moment of distraction looked fatal. With a roar, Zahora charged.

But the woman was faster—with a lunge, she slapped the warrior woman's swords away and turned on her heel, rushing frantically over to where her two companions were huddled. As the man of Sleiss grabbed his babbling companion and yanked him aside, she burst upon them; swinging her sword in an insane arc, she sliced into the very rock face itself. The sound of tearing canvas rent the air—even as Elder stared, he saw the impossible sight of the cliff face peeling away to reveal a small, neat, dwarfish tunnel, much like the ones they'd earlier utilised to cross the mountains. A painting! The entrance had been concealed beneath an ancient painting!

And the man of Sleiss did not hesitate. Side by side with his companions, he dived into the rip and was...

Gone...

"Run!" Fodder didn't need Flirt's shriek to think of that—with Shoulders stumbling alongside, he plunged into the dark tunnel as the voices of the Merry Band echoed, bewildered, in their wake.

"After them! She cannot escape me, she..."

"No!"

"But, Elder, the Ring!"

"And my revenge! She owes me a battle, a fair fight."

"The princess matters more! We must make haste to the beach!"

"We can't let them get away!"

"We must! Don't you understand that?"

The argument faded as they stumbled into blackness blindly, staggering as the tunnel began to slope away in front of them with alarming steepness. But the lack of light, or at least more vivid darkness, could only be good. It meant The Narrative, already split between its characters, had hesitated.

"I can't see!" Shoulders gasped from nearby.

"So they can't see us, can they?" Flirt snapped. "Keep going!"

A bruising impact against his right shoulder told Fodder the passage had turned. He changed direction to compensate and bounced off Shoulders.

"Ow!" was the indignant response to this. "Slow down!"

"You want them to catch us, do you?" Flirt retorted from somewhere ahead.

"We don't know where we're going!"

"Down seems a good bet right now, doesn't it?"

"There are Priests in here! Strut's in here!" Shoulders's rasp was reproachful. "I saw them when I found out this was here! They're using these tunnels to hide!"

"Then why were you so keen to bring us down here?"

"Because I was half-drugged on The Narrative and it was better than back there!"

Fodder heard thudding footsteps somewhere behind, a grunt and wallop as their pursuer discovered the awkward corner. There was no thickening darkness, no brighter black to show The Narrative ran with him, but Fodder's heart dropped nonetheless. If it was a Merry Bander, as they knew to their cost, The Narrative could switch to join him in an instant.

"They've split up more!" he hissed. "Shut up and run!"

The tunnel continued to drop and they carried on with their awkward scurry in the darkness. Bizarrely, it felt as though rails had been carved into this precipitous slope—either the landscape had suffered a dramatic change since the tunnel had been dug or the dwarves who had pushed carts in this direction had got very fit indeed.

And at that moment, somewhere not far ahead, a hint of light flickered.

Fodder's eyes widened. Unpleasant as stumbling at speed on a slippery slope in solid darkness was, light would be worse. If the following Merry Bander had enough light to see them by...

A shadow loomed to their right. On pure instinct, Fodder groped out, grabbing whatever part of his companions he first found and hauling them both sideways. Rusting metal and soft, rotten wood touched his grasp—it felt like a mine cart had tipped on its side, possibly when the landscape was altered long ago, and had lain mouldering ever since. But for this second, it would do. Dragging his companions with him, Fodder leapt behind it.

Below, the light was growing brighter. A white-robed figure, tonsure glowing beneath the lantern he carried, peered around the corner.

"Hello?" he declared.

"Who's that?" Thud's boom echoed from alarmingly close behind. As Fodder, Flirt, and Shoulders ducked deeper into the shadows of their cover, they saw his bulky frame illuminated by the lantern as he puffed to a halt just below them. "Where are they?"

"It's Pious." The Priest's face was bewildered. "Thud, where are who?"

"The bloody Disposables! They ran into this old tunnel!" Thud was breathing heavily—without the free conditioning The Narrative provided, it seemed his fitness was not what it could be. "They came this way! You must have seen them!"

Pious shook his head as he gestured right, down the tunnel from which he had emerged. "I was minding the bells while Strut went to speak with Swipe. No one passed me."

Thud's head whipped left. "It's this way then, they must have! Come on! And bring that bloody light!"

With a strange, staccato mix of heavy Barbarian and light priestly footsteps, the odd pair disappeared down another, broader tunnel that Fodder hadn't even noticed. The light faded round a bend and dimmed.

"Other way?" Flirt whispered.

Fodder nodded before remembering this was imprudent. "Yep," he settled for instead.

The tunnel did not travel far. Around only a couple of bends and past a strange arrangement of bells dangling on a rope through a hole in the rock ceiling, a thick curtain of vines concealed the tunnel exit. Sand had spilled into the rocky entrance and gulls cried beyond.

Shoulders was eyeing the bells thoughtfully as Flirt sneaked towards the vine curtain to take a careful peek outside.

"Fodder," he said shakily. "I'm sorry about up top. Saying about the beach..."

Fodder forced a smile. *It wasn't his fault, not really. It's that bloody Narrative...*

"It's all right, mate," he replied as reassuringly as he could. "It wasn't your fault. And if you hadn't come and known about that tunnel, me and Flirt would really have been buggered."

"Yeah, you would." Shoulders crossed his arms. "I told you it was a bloody trap."

"I know, I know." Fodder conceded the point. "If we get out of this without getting dragged back into Narrative, you've got the smug rights, feel free."

"I will." The response was emphatic, but in the dim green light creeping through the vines Flirt held, Fodder saw Shoulders glance at the dangling bells again. "But The Narrative—the whole Merry Band didn't follow us, so they'll be racing down that crack, right?"

"I guess so." Fodder shrugged.

Shoulders grinned. "So, I think I might have—"

"You sure they didn't slip past you?"

The echoing voice of Thud cut off whatever it was Shoulders had been about to say. Lantern light gleamed in the tunnel behind.

"Bollocks!" Caution was abandoned. Catching Shoulders's arm, Fodder charged up behind Flirt and thrust all three of them out onto the sandy beach.

And there, hobbling along beside the distinctly bashed-up-looking forms of Swipe and Strut...

"Dullard! Pleasance!" Flirt's yell got their instant attention. Both pairs of eyes widened.

"Narrative!" Dullard bellowed in response as he gestured to the crack. And indeed, the spurts of light from the path in the cliff crevice were closing rapidly towards the final bend.

Flirt and Fodder sprinted across the short gap to where the pair had staggered to a halt.

"That cave!" Flirt exclaimed. "The one you knew! How far is it?"

"The far side of the beach!" Dullard was shaking his head. "But I can't run. Even if you carry me, we'll never make it in time to get out of sight!"

"What about the horses?" Pleasance declared. There was a strange, distracted look in her eyes. "We could ride!"

It was Dullard who shook his head. "If The Narrative catches us on horseback, we'll be thrown."

Pleasance glared. "If we leave them here, they'll ride us down anyway! We may as well!"

Dullard grimaced as he shifted his leg. "I suppose that's a point. And we established the boat isn't much use..." Suddenly, he started. "Wait. Where's Shoulders?"

Fodder reeled round but only two sets of footprints had stained the sand from the vines to the cluster of horses. The third, uneven set had darted up the mouth of the crack straight towards The Narrative's jaws.

Flirt started forwards, her eyes wide. "What the hell is he...?"

But in that moment, Shoulders appeared, running at full tilt with a manic-looking grin on his face. "Grab a horse!" he shouted. "Let's ride!"

Flirt was shaking her head. "There isn't time! The Narrative..."

Shoulders beamed blithely as he stumbled over, grabbing the reins of Clank's enormous warhorse and hauling himself up with distinct satisfaction. "...is about to be very distracted! Trust me! There's time!"

Flirt's expression was incredulous, Dullard's politely sceptical, and Pleasance's outright indignant. But what choice did they have?

Avoiding Erik's magical horse for prudence's sake, Fodder hauled himself onto Harridan's black mare and dug his heels in. The horse bolted.

The ride across the sands was both exhilarating and terrifying—Fodder could almost feel the tickle of The Narrative against his neck but somehow, the far side of the sands was looming and still the landscape had not burst with vivid light, either from Thud emerging from the tunnels or the Merry Band breaking onto the beach. As they reached the cliffs opposite, abandoned the horses, and bolted towards the cover of the cave that Dullard pointed out, Fodder risked a glance back.

The glow of The Narrative shimmered in the mouth of the crevice, unmoving, as though frozen. Following his gaze, Shoulders grinned even wider.

"Serves them right," he muttered merrily. "Him too, the little snitch."

Fodder shook his head in disbelief. "Shoulders, what did you do?"

Smug, as permitted in the earlier discussion, rolled from his friend in waves as they ducked into the concealment of the cave and safety. "Well…"

* * *

"We are nearly there!" Young and agile, Erik scrambled ahead of his companions over the difficult terrain. He had caught a hint of Sir Roderick struggling to pursue him in his armour, had heard his cries to hold a moment and was sure that the others would not be far behind, eager to catch up with him. But it mattered not, for he could not wait—all that mattered was Islaine, was finding his princess and making her safe from the evil clutches of Tretaptus and his foul minions who had so abused her.

The final corner before the sands where Slynder waited with their horses loomed. Just a few yards more and…

"Bloody hell! What hit me?"

Erik froze. And Erik stared.

It couldn't be. It couldn't be, it couldn't…

No, it was impossible. Halheid had perhaps had a wellspring of brothers to take his place but this, it could not happen, it could not happen again but...

Sitting propped in the very centre of the path, his gaze filled with a strangely absent air as he staggered to his feet and rubbed his crown tenderly, Gort the very dead and extremely buried dwarf reeled in a circle, saw Erik, and froze. His eyes widened.

"Ummm..." he said. "Hello..."

"Gort?" The word slipped from Erik's lips unbidden. "How can this be?"

"It can't?" The dwarf blinked unsteadily. "I'm...dead?"

"Yes, you are." Erik could not seem to gather his thoughts. "You are dead."

"I am dead." The dwarf repeated this slowly. "Ummm...yes!" He straightened abruptly, raising his hands and shaking them in a tremulous fashion. His voice deepened noticeably. "I am indeed your dead companion! For I am the ghost of Gort, summoned from beyond the grave to inspire you on your quest!" He shook his hands fiercely, swaying on the spot in a slow, languorous undulation. "Woooooooooo!"

Erik stared. Erik blinked.

"Eldeeerrr!" he screeched...

* * *

"So, what do you think?"

Dullard glanced up at Fodder's question before returning his intent gaze to the crystal flower held delicately between his fingers. He turned it slowly, allowing the light of the morning sun to glint off its glassy surface like silent music as he traced its contours with his eyes.

"Fascinating," he whispered reverently. "It's beautiful."

"But do you have any idea how it happened?" Fodder tried to keep the anxiety out of his voice. The prince was their unofficial expert on just about everything, and if he didn't have an answer...

"None whatsoever." The hope shrivelled in Fodder's heart. "I've never seen anything like it."

"It's not natural then, is it?" Flirt posed the question from where she was stretching out her bruised knee nearby. Their underground travels of the last day had left them all rather more battered than when they had gone in, but they had not been followed into the caves and that, more than anything else, was what mattered.

Dullard sighed as he traced his finger along the lines of the flower. "I don't think so. But if it's Narrative born, it shouldn't stay like this." He shook his head. "It's such a pity I didn't get a look at this hut of yours. It sounds intriguing." He frowned thoughtfully. "The Merry Band would surely have moved on by now. Perhaps..."

"We are not going back!" There was a shrill note to Pleasance's voice as she chimed in from beside the trickling brook by which they had come to rest. She pointedly dabbed at a bloodstained elbow. "If you think you're getting me back in there, think again!"

This was a sentiment that Fodder could relate to. When they had first shooed away the horses and ducked out of sight into the narrow crack in the rock, which Dullard had indicated offered a passage right through the Most Savage Mountains, he had been relieved to be safely out of sight. And when the prince had assured them that the route he recalled was relatively easy and, even with his weakened leg, he would be able to lead them down it, Fodder had—naively, as it turned out—expected a tunnel much like the dwarf ones. But, as with the "slightly dicey" climb, Dullard's idea of easy and the rest of the universe's had failed to coincide.

There had been climbs. There had been drops. There had been crawls through tunnels so narrow they had squeezed the breath from their lungs and the marrow from their bones. There had been perilous swims through icy underground rivers and even a submerged tunnel to negotiate that had involved such blackness of water and screaming of lungs that Fodder shuddered away from the memory. Even the torchlit beauty of the stalactite-filled chamber in which they had snatched a respite of sleep hadn't punctured the horrors. By the time they had emerged, blinking and battered, from the hole carved by this brook as it surged free of underground, and found themselves unexpectedly in the following morning, Fodder had reached the point where he gave serious consideration to kneeling and kissing the grass.

"I think Pleasance is right," he said moderately, attempting to conceal the driving ulterior motive of never going anywhere near those bloody caves again. "Going back won't change anything. We need to make a new plan."

"Like what?" With a huff, Shoulders deposited himself on the grass nearby, finishing the final adjustments to his loosened head-holding contraption after the wobbly clamber. He'd yet to use much of his smug allocation but it hung in the air, waiting to pounce like an AFC in the bushes. "We can't kill the princess anymore because you've made your bloody deal with her, stabbing us straight through the foot in the process." He ignored Pleasance's glare and ploughed on. "And we can't even use magic anymore because the Ring's buggered up."

Fodder sighed as he reached down to the pouch where the Ring had been stowed after its failure to fire in the village. "I still don't understand that," he muttered in frustration. "This thing is supposed to be the greatest magical object of all time, the unstoppable force, the thing that, in the wrong hands..."

"Like yours," Flirt intervened with a slight grin.

Fodder returned it wanly. "Like mine," he conceded wryly. "It should be able to destroy the world—why else are they so keen to keep it away from the Dark Lord? If my zapping us away can be stopped by Magus muttering a few weird words, why does it matter so much in the Quest?"

"It can't." Dullard's voice was distant—he continued to turn the flower between his fingers absently—but Fodder's head snapped towards him.

"What do you mean, it can't?" he exclaimed.

Dullard glanced up in surprise. "The Ring of Anthiphion can't be stopped by normal magic," he said, as though such a thing was self-evident. "That's been clearly established in the Quest."

Fodder blinked. "But it was, I told you."

The prince placed the flower carefully in his lap and directed Fodder his full attention. "Then somebody is cheating," he said bluntly.

Bells rang in Fodder's head. Dullard was right; no one should have been able to stop the Ring with ordinary magic when it was the most powerful object in The Narrative. So how, how had Magus managed to block his escape? They had clearly been ready for him, worked a way around the surprise he had pulled in the confrontation near the waterfall. They had been prepared for him to leap his friends into nothing, and Magus and his muttering had put a stop to it.

But he shouldn't have been able to. Would the Ring have worked if he'd tried something other than vanishing into thin air? There was no safe way to know. But to stop him, The Narrative had broken its own rules. The gloves were clearly off. But the question was, how did he work his way back around the cheating and remind them of how it was supposed to be? How could he get use of the Ring back?

"They were ready for us." Flirt echoed Fodder's whirling thoughts. "So what now?"

Fodder glanced up at Pleasance, seated a little way away from the rest of them as she worked on her blood-caked elbow. "Well, there's the princess."

Pleasance's head shot up. "What exactly do you mean by that?"

Dullard's expression was equally perturbed. "Fodder, we had an agreement..."

"I'm not going to break it." Fodder lifted his hands calmly, ignoring the disappointed look on Shoulders's face. "But, Pleasance, how would you feel about being an inside agent?"

An odd, unreadable cocktail of varying emotions flittered over the princess's face in quick succession. "Inside agent?" she said with a distinct lack of enthusiasm.

"Yeah, you know." Fodder tried to smile encouragingly, but Pleasance's expression remained profoundly uninspired. "Like what Shoulders did with Gruffly, but you'll be there on purpose. Go back and pretend to have escaped and mess up The Narrative from within. Knee Bumpkin in the goolies and tell him he smells. Cut Magus's beard while he's asleep and pour treacle into Clank's armour. Mess them around and make them look stupid. Do you think you could do it?"

Pleasance's face was white, her expression immobile. Her lips parted.

"No."

Shoulders's inevitable flare-up was too rapid for Fodder to cut it off. "And why not, eh? Maybe you haven't turned us in yet and you weren't in on the last trap..."

"Oh thank you, a fine concession!" Pleasance snapped.

"...but I bet you would if it served you!" Shoulders's volume swelled over Pleasance's retort. "You're playing both sides, aren't you? You say you're with us, but you haven't committed, have you? You haven't stuck up two fingers and told your old pals to get stuffed!"

Pleasance's expression tightened. "As it happens, I have. Albeit less crudely."

Shoulders glared. "Oh yeah? When?"

There was such an odd look in Pleasance's eyes, a strange mixture of defiance, resolve, and pain. "On the beach. And that is why I cannot do as you ask. Because aside from the fact that rejoining The Narrative would see me risk making a loving connection for eternity with a squalid oaf, Strut *knows* I've defected. He saw me knock out Swipe and he called me on it. He threatened me! If Dullard hadn't hit him, he would likely have dragged me off by the hair, so no! I don't think I can be an inside agent, do you?"

There was a moment of uncomfortable silence. In the privacy of his mind, Fodder swore loudly. Yet another plan was officially up the swanny.

Shoulders looked slightly awkward, but he bullishly pressed on. Being right once had clearly tightened his resolve. "We've only got your word for that..."

"And mine." A rare hint of steel clanged in Dullard's tone. "I heard the end of what was said. It wasn't friendly. And no, it wasn't purely for my benefit because neither of them saw me coming."

Shoulders fell silent. His expression was irritated but, to Fodder's relief, he did not press the point.

"Doesn't help us decide, though, does it?" Flirt offered wearily. "What the bloody hell do we do?"

There was a long silence that no one tried to fill. There was only the wind in the trees around them and the distant howl of a wolf that...

Wait. A wolf?

"What was that?" Fodder wasn't the only one who had caught the sound; Pleasance came sharply to her feet, gripping at her battered dress as though poised for immediate flight.

"It sounded like a wolf." In contrast to the sudden concern on the faces of his four companions, Dullard remained calm and seated, returning to his examination of the crystal flower. "As I recall, the pack used for Narrative duty is kept somewhere in this area."

"The Narrative pack?" Now Shoulders had stumbled to his feet as well. "As in the wild-eyed, ravaging horde of furry fiends that are trained from birth to rip innocent travellers to tiny shreds and scare the bloody hell out of the Merry Band?"

"That's right." Dullard hadn't moved. Flirt, on the other hand, joined Fodder in rising as a fresh howl echoed through the air.

"That sounded closer, didn't it?" The Barmaid's face was pale. "Are they headed this way?"

"They probably have our scent." The academic absence in Dullard's voice was growing irritating. "We are upwind of them."

"Then, if you'll forgive me for interrupting your study..." Pleasance's tone was acerbic. "Would it not be an idea for you to put that damnable flower away and get up so we can run?"

The howls were growing in number, swelling into a cacophony that rolled out of the trees like a burst of wailing thunder. It sounded like the kind of sound that falling lightning *ought* to make. And it was not just howls—barking and snarling slipped out of the rising mass of noise and the distant-but-closing rustle of foliage.

Dullard blinked as though waking. He stared at the crystal flower for an agonisingly long moment more before creasing his brow and abruptly pushing the flower into the pouch at his waist.

"Yes, of course!" Shaking his head, the prince finally scrambled back onto his feet. "I'm sorry, I..."

"Apologise later!" Flirt's hand was on her sword hilt as the roll of noise tumbled closer, closer, howls and snarls and snaps that tore at the air like jagged fingernails, reaching for them. There was no doubt whatsoever left that the wolves were heading their way. "Run now!"

It would have been sensible, Fodder reflected in hindsight, to have headed back into the caves. But at the time, the fresh memory of the horrors within and the fear of being trapped with his legs sticking out of a tiny passage while wolves chewed his toes off led him to bolt after Shoulders into the trees. And it took only seconds to realise that this was likely to be a mistake, for the valley ahead—a narrow, tree-lined curl that wound like a green serpent into the heart of the Most Savage Mountains—was sealed at its head by an enormous, unnaturally symmetrical monster of a mountain, a steep-sided spire whose tip was shrouded by a distinctly arranged-looking spiral of slowly rotating clouds. On the "dicey climb" scale, Fodder suspected even Dullard would pause a moment and suck at his teeth before setting off, and to try and scramble a route up such a monster would be no easy feat with time and no pressure on their side. So how were they supposed to manage it with a pack of vicious wolves snapping at their heels?

It was a good question. Fodder wished he had time to think of an answer. But for the moment, only one thought was making itself known in his mind.

Run.

Run, run, run, run, run, run…

His heart pounded like the beat to the chorus of howls churning in his wake. His feet smashed down upon the uneven ground, one step, two step, one step, two step, catching on briars, bouncing off stones, skidding on leaves, but somehow he stayed upright, stayed running, the primal fear of the rip of sharp teeth, the crunch of strong jaws, an unrepaired oblivion of digestion driving him forwards by the strength of sheer adrenaline. To his right, Flirt was dancing through the trees with irritating skill, her hand lingering around her elegant sword hilt, her face flushed and her curls streaming as she glanced repeatedly back into the thrashing undergrowth that howled like a hurricane behind them. To his left, Shoulders was making a damned good showing for a man in two pieces, one hand steadying his head as the other arm pumped out his momentum. Pleasance was struggling more, her skirts and heeled shoes tangling her progress, but her lips were taut and her eyes determined as she bounced with breathless screams of rage from tree to bramble and back again. And Dullard…

Was falling behind.

Oh no.

The prince was doing his best; anyone could see that. But his leg, though mostly healed, remained fragile and the trek through the caves had hardly been restful for him. His face was an uncharacteristic grimace as he struggled, limping, on but it was clear he would not be able to run much farther.

Behind him, the bushes were thrashing. Howls rent the air and the eardrums, so close, too close behind. Flashes of grey fur stained the greenery.

Terror rolled through Fodder's heart in waves: the crunch, the chew, the floating black that any Disposable knew was the fate of the eaten. But he couldn't simply leave him...

"Dullard!" Fodder started to slow but the prince's face solidified at once with determination.

"Don't wait for me!" he gasped out, waving one hand in dismissal as he grasped his leg with the other. "Keep going!"

Fodder struggled to catch enough breath to reply as golden eyes flashed in the bushes, mere yards away. "But..."

"Go!" It was an order. But Fodder was no longer accustomed to obeying Royalty.

"Sod off!" He darted back in spite of the prince's attempt to look harsh, grabbing his loose arm and throwing it over his shoulder. "Now come on!"

The cacophony of wolfish noise was deafening. And there, to the left, a sleek grey body with jagged teeth zigzagged in the undergrowth alongside them and there, to the right, a one-eyed wolf, battle-scarred and hard-muzzled, darted ahead. Fodder could almost feel the pant of their breath as his own squealed from his lungs; he could feel the heat of their bodies, the burn of their eyes...

"Ah!" And Dullard was down. Fodder staggered, pulled off balance by his fall, and barely had time to see a grey shape launch at his fallen friend before a flying blur hurled itself out of the bushes, clawed feet thudding into his chest as he was flung onto his back and smashed with a painful cry against the ground. Sky and leaves and the edge of swirling cloud flashed for an instant across his vision before all that lay before him was wolf, golden eyes ablaze, teeth glinting and a huge, dribbling maw gaping wide as a shuddering tongue...

...raked the length of his face. And again. And again.

Fodder paused. Had that wolf just *licked* him?

He glanced up at the large beast sitting on his stomach. Despite its grizzled, one-eyed appearance, without the howling and thrashing of undergrowth, it suddenly seemed distinctly unthreatening. Its pose was more that of a playful dog than a savage beast, its tail wagging, and the fact it hadn't ripped said face off and eaten it was more than anything an indication that perhaps it didn't mean any harm. And other than nearly drowning him in affectionate saliva, it didn't seem to have done him any harm either.

He heard Dullard chuckle somewhere nearby. "Dullard?" he called out tentatively.

The prince's voice also sounded very much as though he was intact. "I'm fine. I think they were playing with us, weren't you? Yes, good boy! Down off my friend now!"

The weight of the giant wolf lifted as the alpha male that had pounced him bounded gracefully off his chest. Fodder pulled himself, bewildered, to his knees, and found himself in the midst of a small sea of furry grey, of panting wolves that nudged at him playfully and licked him with a distinct joie de vivre. A few yards away, Dullard's head peeked out of a similar cluster, smiling as he rubbed their heads and patted them.

"They're harmless." Fodder spoke the words half unconsciously, dredged from the depths of his surprise.

"I don't know why we thought otherwise." Dullard rubbed the ears of the wolf currently licking his face, who reacted as though he had made his century. "After all, the AFCs aren't ravaging monsters when The Narrative leaves them. Why should the wolves be?"

Fodder had to admit he had a point, in hindsight at least. But when a howling pack of face-eating brutes was charging through the forest towards one, it hadn't felt the time to hang around a second to check if they were friendly. And besides…

"Why did they chase us if they didn't want to tear us to shreds?" As Fodder rose to his feet, a swell of grey bodies bumped against his legs. He waded carefully in Dullard's direction.

"Practice probably. They would need to be taught to chase into The Narrative but it would take care of the brutality when they got there." With a final ear rub to his wolfish new best friend, Dullard accepted Fodder's hand and clambered awkwardly upright. "Bless them, they're really quite sweet."

Fodder couldn't help but agree. Once you got past the look of them as animals that would gulp you down as soon as look at you, they were…

"Oi!" A pack of wolfish ears pricked up at the sudden cry from somewhere down the valley. A whistle rent the air. "Where've you gone, you daft pack of beggars? You're supposed to be chasing me, not running off into nowhere! Get back here!"

Fodder was half-braced to leap into hiding at the voice of what he could only assume was a wolf trainer. But as it turned out, there was no need—after a final, affectionate butt of their kneecaps, the wolves turned and, tails wagging like happy puppies, they streamed off into the trees down the valley. A moment later the howls of the chase flared in a whole new direction.

"Are you two all right?" Fodder and Dullard both turned at the sound of Flirt's voice. The Barmaid was standing poised in the trees ahead, her sword drawn and her expression incredulous. "I came back, didn't I, as soon as I saw you were gone. I was going to help but..." She shook her head slowly. "You didn't seem to need it."

Fodder shrugged. "Looks like not. I think we wandered into a wolf training exercise by mistake."

Dullard was staring over his shoulder in the direction of the howls. "We don't know how many other men are back there," he added thoughtfully. "This valley is quite narrow—I doubt we'd be able to sneak back down without either the wolves or the trainers picking us up. We may need to find somewhere to keep our heads down."

"Speaking of that." Flirt sheathed her sword as she summoned the two men with a flick of her finger—Fodder offered his arm to Dullard, but the prince shook his head and persevered with his limp. "Before we noticed you'd gone, me, Shoulders, and the princess, well, we got to the foot of that monster of a mountain, didn't we? And we found something unexpected."

Vaguely intrigued, Fodder and Dullard followed Flirt up to the head of the valley where Shoulders and Pleasance were waiting. As the trees thinned into scrub and to stony debris ahead, the mountain loomed, its painfully steep, spire-like profile screaming out in contrast to the genuine crags of the mountains surrounding it. The slow rotation of the cloudy spiral above bore no reflection to the clouds or wind direction of the area around it. This was a Narrative location if ever Fodder had seen one.

But why maintain something like this in the middle of nowhere? And what good was it when it was clearly impossible to reach the...

Fodder paused in his musing. For as he stepped out of the last of the trees, he realised that the profile of the monster mountain in front of him was not quite as perfect as he had believed. Wrapped around it in an ascending spiral, something was indented into the rock.

Fodder blinked. "Is that a staircase?"

And it was at that moment that the man in the toga fell out of the sky.

* * *

Fodder had seen many a good plummet in his time. As an experienced Disposable, he'd watched assorted colleagues being flung through the air by force of magic and, of course, there had been that bloody stupid jump from the Grim Fortress that made his stomach churn at the thought. Generally, a good fling or a plummet invoked a classic look of horror and a high-pitched, unmanly scream of rage or terror—role dependent, obviously—ending in occasional undignified dangling from tree limbs, rocks, or rooftops as appropriate. But never, either In Narrative or outside of it, had he ever seen anyone look so happy about it.

Perhaps they should have left him there. They'd had ample opportunity to leave as the plummeter swung gently back and forth, dangling in the branches of the trees from the remains of the strange arrangement clamped to his back and gazing, with an odd kind of bliss, into the middle distance. But the cry of wolves in the valley below indicated that whatever exercise was in place was moving about in their vicinity. There was no way of knowing whether the wolf trainers had enough command of their charges to make for a threatening chase if they were seen. They needed another way to go, and the only safe route was the staircase up the mountain. And given this man appeared to be part of whatever lay at the top...

"Mate, hold still, yeah?" A branch thwacked across Fodder's nose— he grimaced but ignored it and pressed on up the tree, Flirt making irritatingly superior progress up its neighbour as they closed on the slowly swinging man above. He'd had little choice about the climb—

Dullard's leg was fragile after the chase, Shoulders was no climber even in one piece, and one look at Pleasance killed any prospect of even asking. But he would have felt better about it if he had more of a notion that the man he was scrambling to rescue actually wanted to get down.

He could nearly reach the tangled mess of silk and willow and rope from which the man was dangling. Ignoring the bark grazing his elbow and the stump of a branch digging in his thigh, he paused a moment. Fair warning and all...

"Mate, my friend and I are going to cut you down." Still no response, just a vague twitch of one eyebrow and a dreamy smile. "It's a bit of a drop, though, so it'll sting a bit. But you'll be right as rain soon after."

"I will not fall." The voice that rippled from the man's lips was as dreamy as the smile, faraway and blithe. "For I am *flying*."

Oookay... Gritting his teeth against his own misgivings as much as the battering he was taking from the tree, Fodder awkwardly pulled his short sword from its sheath. Nodding to Flirt, who was already working away at the far side with the sword she had borrowed from Shoulders, he reached up and set about freeing the last of the ropes.

And the strange man hadn't stopped smiling blissfully and staring into space when the wreckage parted and he plummeted once more.

By the time Fodder reached the ground again, Dullard and Shoulders had helped the strange man to his feet. Other than his vacant expression of mild bewilderment and a hint of bruising on his leg, he appeared unharmed by the tumble.

And on closer inspection, most notably from Pleasance and Flirt, who were eyeing him with a certain interest, their dreamy friend was quite a fine specimen. His hair was blond and wavy, his eyes a bright blue, and his face, with his high cheekbones and perfect nose, showed signs that it had—not too many Quests back at least—been irritatingly good-looking. He was more weathered now, although his body was well-toned beneath his wind-battered half-toga. He did, however, have what looked very much like the remains of two small golden wings strapped to his ankles with heavy bindings.

"Are you all right?" Dullard waved his fingers gently in front of the vacant features. "Are you stunned? Would you like a drink of water or a sit down?"

Miraculously, the man blinked, his eyes focused, and he stared, first at Dullard's fingers, then at Dullard, and finally at the other four each in turn, his eyes widening with realisation.

"Have I cometh this day upon the humble earth?" The man's voice rolled like an oration. "Art thou of our mortal flock?"

Shoulders pulled an incredulous face. "You what?"

The man's face filled with concern. "Be not afraid, gentle mortals!" he exclaimed, raising his hands, palm out as though in soothing invitation. "I fear my glory must intimidate thee, but be not startled, for I am a kindly God! I will not visit my wrath upon thee for looking on me thus!"

God? Fodder blinked. Had that man just called himself...

"A God?" Flirt beat him to it. "So..." She looked the man up and down, drinking in the battered toga, the piecemeal golden wings, and the ageing face. "You're a God, are you?"

"Indeed I am so." The man or God or whatever smiled beatifically. "I have thus been known sometimes as Hermiol or as Brontiane or as Erithos. All hath been given to me and..." His brow creased. "In truth, I knoweth not which art my true name, for every one felt true in the glory of the light and the power of eternity. But through them all, I have and shall ever be The Messenger."

The glory of the light. Fodder had not missed the phrase and one glance at Dullard told him the prince had not either. Narrative names; this man, The Messenger, was reeling off his Narrative characters, the names of Gods of previous Quests. But why would he use those fleeting names to identify himself instead of the one he was born with?

Gods. Fodder had to admit he'd never considered how they lived or where they came from. They appeared in Quests as required: visitations, whispered voices, a push in the right direction, a thwarting in the wrong one, but in a strange way they seemed almost constructs of Narrative magic rather than actual people. He knew vaguely that there was a family that bred the required divinities, but he'd never considered how they lived without the glory of the light, as The Messenger had called it. True, most families and clans of the Realm lived the lives of the characters out of Narrative as well as within it, but the Gods...

To live a God's life was one thing. But to believe it to be true?

"Thou art bewildered, I see it is thus." The so-called Messenger's smile was ever so slightly condescending. "And of course, thou art mortals—thy tiny minds must struggle to grasp a being as divine as I. Do not be overawed by my glory—I will not harmeth thee. Those who cometh to worship me art ever welcomed."

There was a long pause. It resounded with cynicism.

"So you say you are a God, a glorious being of power and divinity." Pleasance's voice, when it came, rippled with scepticism—clearly the idea of having someone look down on her was not sitting well. "So, why did we mere mortals have to rescue you?"

The God blinked. "My child, what meanest thou?"

"She meanest that thou was stuck up that tree," Shoulders intervened bluntly. "And Fodder and Flirt had to get you down. If you're so bleeding divine, why didn't you float down on a cloud of bloody glory?"

For the first time, a hint of doubt spread across the strange would-be God's face. His brow wrinkled and his eyes were bewildered.

"I knoweth my divinity." The words came somewhat anxiously. "I have felt the power floweth in my very bones; I have known all and seen all. I can *fly!*"

"So you've said, haven't you?" Flirt drawled. The Messenger ignored her.

"But…" His voice trailed away for a moment. "But without the glory of the light, I am…*less*, somehow." He shook his head. "The power is not at my call and it is thus for us all. But I remember." His jaw firmed suddenly. "I knoweth I can fly. And if I can fly again, perhaps it will returneth. Perhaps the glory of the light will findeth me again."

His voice trailed away. He stared towards the sky.

Pleasance was staring at the man in mute horror. Her eyes flicked to Dullard.

"Is he planted?" she whispered. "Has The Narrative done this? Has it actually made him believe?"

Dullard sighed, exchanging a look with Fodder that spoke volumes before he responded. "He's had the memories of a God inside his head," he replied in a hushed tone. "Three times, by the sound of it. A character of such power must be nearly overwhelming. He seems to have forgotten ever being anything else."

Fodder felt a sickening surge of horror. Planting. He still remembered the vile invasiveness of what had befallen him in the Traversable Gorge, not even realising what was happening until Cringe had pointed it out. To turn someone into something else for your own whim and leave them bereft when it was gone...

He stared at The Messenger with sudden sympathy. "So that's what the contraption was about?" he asked more kindly. "You were trying to fly?"

The Messenger's face developed a sudden sheen of enthusiasm that was vaguely Dullard-like. "It is so! Long have I turned my vast intellect to the problem of mastering flight so as to summoneth the power once more! I believed this device and another I holdeth like it were the answer and for some time, I was in flight..."

Fodder didn't like to mention it had been closer to falling more slowly. Dullard, however, was tapping his chin with one finger, his expression alarmingly thoughtful.

"The theory is sound enough," he said. "I believe the device was simply a bit front-heavy. Perhaps with a tail to counterbalance the rear, I certainly believe gliding for some distance would be achievable..."

Pleasance's sharp slap against his wrist halted the flow. "Don't encourage his planted delusions of grandeur!" she hissed.

"Why not? We have to encourage yours." Fodder was deeply grateful that the princess was too focused on berating Dullard to catch Shoulders's barbed whisper.

Instead, she ploughed on, oblivious. "He thinks if he can fly, he's a God, Dullard! If you help him, you'll make it worse!"

But it was already too late. The Messenger was staring at Dullard with sudden glee. "Truly, my divine presence hath inspired thy mortal mind to greatness! I will reward thee! Thou and thy companions will thus joineth me on the Mountain of the Gods to solve this tangled problem! Come!"

Catching Dullard's arm in an iron grip, he made a beeline for the nearby stairs. Shoulders baulked.

"You want us to trek all the bloody way up there? Are you nuts?"

"I would raiseth thee upon a divine wind or raft of cloud, but as I told thee, such gifts hath deserted me." There was a tetchy edge to The

Messenger's tone. "Wouldst thou reject a God's hospitality?"

Fodder glanced up the enormous mountain and the equally vast spiral of stairs. He glanced back to the woods, filled with the howls of the wolves and the calls of their trainers. Did they have a choice?

Besides, from the looks of it, The Messenger and his family needed serious help. Maybe they could offer some.

"Of course not." Shoulders and Pleasance gave Fodder equally dirty looks. But nonetheless, they reluctantly joined him as he, Flirt, and Dullard trailed after The Messenger and began their ascent of the Mountain of the Gods.

This was going to be interesting.

* * *

The stairway wasn't as bad as it looked. The steps were even and smooth and spaced so that a comfortable gait was possible; they were wide enough for four persons to walk abreast if necessary and lined by a chest-high stone wall that kept the vast height from filling the brain with terror in the way an open drop would have managed with ease. The only issue was the sheer bloody number of them.

At first Fodder had merely concentrated on the climb. But, as the sweat gathered on his brow, as the pain congealed in his joints and the wind cut at his lungs, he forced his brain into pondering what lay before them. And since the sweat and the pain and the wind only got worse as more steps passed, he decided the best way to push them to the back of his mind was to give his ponderings a voice.

Unfortunately…

"You want to help him?"

The slightly breathless incredulity in Shoulders's voice was not encouraging. But Fodder pressed on, his eyes drifting a few steps ahead to where The Messenger was gesticulating with fervent enthusiasm in the limping Dullard's direction. A step behind, a sceptical-looking Pleasance had removed her impractical shoes and was carrying them under one arm as she wrestled her ragged skirts up the stairway.

"Look at what the Taskmaster's done to him," Fodder emphasised, trying to ignore the throbbing pain in his knees and hips as he plodded on and on methodically upwards. "If we could make him realise that, we'll not only be helping him back to himself, we'll be gaining an ally. How angry would you be if you discovered someone had messed with your head like that?"

"Yeah but, mate, you're forgetting the most important thing." Shoulders could not look round—the lines securing his head made eyes-front a necessity—but Fodder could see the expression on his profile. "He's a raving nutjob."

Fodder sighed. "Shoulders..."

"He thinks he's a God, mate." Shoulders's eyes darted in his friend's direction. "What makes you think anything a mere mortal has to say will penetrate that brain?"

Fodder shook his head. "We have to try, though."

"And I think you'll fail," was Shoulders's blunt response. Unexpectedly, he sighed. "Look, I overheard Gruffly talking to Strut. And from what I heard, it didn't matter what the squealing little toerag did or didn't want for himself in the end, because all Strut had to do was trip the right triggers and Gort popped up to go along with him. I don't think this planting lark is something you can just talk somebody out of."

"Cringe talked me out of it," Fodder pointed out. "And Dullard talked round Pleasance."

"Yeah, but you'd been planted for what, ten minutes? And the princess never really got started." Shoulders huffed. "Besides, if I thought I was a God of infinite power and someone rocked up to tell me I was actually only some oik in a toga, I'd be more pissed off at him than some Taskmaster I couldn't see. People don't like having their comfy illusions shattered."

"He's got a point, hasn't he?"

Fodder sighed as he glanced back over his shoulder to the figure a few steps behind them. He'd been hoping Flirt would be on his side.

"No one likes to hear they're delusional, do they?" Flirt was red-faced from the climb, but her features were set. "It's in their nature. People shoot the messenger, don't they?"

Shoulders's eyes glinted up the steps ahead. "Does that mean I can—"

"*No.*" On this at least, Flirt and Fodder were unified. A gust of cold wind whipped across their faces, driving the breath away and stalling the conversation for a moment. Fodder used the respite to massage his screaming knees as Shoulders caught his arm for balance. Flirt rested her hands against both their backs as they huddled together for a moment. Above, they heard Pleasance squeak as her skirts and hair swirled in a tangle of harsh wind.

"Be not afeared, gentle mortals!" The voice of The Messenger rippled over as the gust died down. "Thou art near thy reward! The Home of the Gods and my holy kindred lie close before thee!"

For the first time in a while, Fodder glanced up. And there, bizarrely close above their heads and looking almost solid enough to touch, the great spiral of cloud continued its silent circuit of the mountaintop. Just below its slow embrace, the steep rising of smooth rock above came abruptly to a halt. A circle of carved marble columns, joined by flowing arches, rose from the rocky base to line the edge above their heads.

"At last!" Pleasance's relieved exclamation beat Shoulders's "About bloody time!" by only an instant. Both princess and Disposable made an immediate beeline up the remains of the stairs—towards the marble gateway with its decorated golden gates that sloped downwards above a marble stair, visible in a small cleft in the rock about twenty yards in front of them. The Messenger was already striding his way before them, with Dullard limping along a few steps to his rear.

Flirt stepped up to stand beside the motionless Fodder. "You coming?" she asked quietly.

Fodder looked at her for a long moment. "You really think we should leave him like this?" he asked instead of replying. "Stuck in a dream world, believing he's something he can't be and waiting for his few minutes in the glory of the light?"

Flirt sighed. "I didn't say that, did I? But there's ways and means, Fodder, and after Gruffly we need to tread more carefully, don't we? Do you think The Messenger's ready for the real world? And do you think he'd appreciate being chucked into it headfirst?"

Fodder gazed at the swirl of cloud overhead for a moment. "Then what do you think we should do?"

"I say we see what we find up there." Flirt's expression was familiarly practical. "And if they're all like him. And if they are..." She shrugged. "Then we persuade the God and let the man come round in his own time. Besides..." Her smile was tight. "If we get what we want, at some point we'll have to talk a godlike being round to our way of thinking, won't we? Look on this as good practice."

She had a point. Fodder had to admit parts of his mind shied away from the prospect of what might lie at the end of this journey, of persuading the Taskmaster, the overseer of their whole universe, that their opinion mattered too. And Flirt was right; this was the closest thing they were likely to get to a practice run.

He nodded. "Then let's get to it."

Fodder had a feeling that, on a Narrative day, the elegant golden gates before them would have parted with a gentle swish and a trumpet of heavenly music. But thankfully The Narrative was nowhere to be found and instead, as Flirt and Fodder approached, they found the prosaic reality of The Messenger, a grimace on his face, jamming his arm through the curling gold lattice of the bars to try and free the sticking catch.

"By my own divinity!" he swore irritably. "Why doth this cursed lock never open upon command?"

"Would you like me to try?" Dullard offered politely but received a snappish look for his trouble.

"Thou standeth before the gates to the realm of the Gods," was the edgy retort. "Only one divine may part the way!"

"Only if one divine has some oil on him," Shoulders muttered under his breath.

Luckily, The Messenger did not hear him, his face contorting as he worked his fingers through the gap to try and pry loose the lock. His eyes widened.

"My brethren!" he cried out abruptly. "Dear Child! Canst thou aid me? The Portal of Divinity art sticking again!"

"Hold and I will aid thee!" The voice that replied was possibly the strangest that Fodder had ever heard, and, given that he had in his time spoken to toothy AFCs, a bewildered Dragon, and Preen the Officious Courtier, this was some achievement. Though it was clearly a man's voice, a voice of natural depth and baritone register, it had been pushed up as many octaves as vocal cords would permit, emerging as a rather desperate squeak. A figure was trotting down the marble steps now and, again, accounting for Preen and indeed Bard, he was the strangest of sights to behold. Six feet tall and wrapped in layers of pudgy plumpness, the man nevertheless wore a white tunic that was an alarming, verging on embarrassing, number of sizes too small for him, seams straining at its edges as it battled to contain the squashed lumpiness within. His face was childlike, containing traces of what must have been an angelic childhood cuteness, but adolescence had passed through some time before and left its mark with a vengeance—old acne scars stained his cheeks and his golden ringlet curls hung in greasy clumps around his ears. His simple smile left oddly proportioned dimples in his flabby cheeks.

"I will aid thee, brother." Fodder winced at the strain on his high-pitched voice as he spoke. The Messenger, however, clearly saw nothing odd in the man's appearance as he stepped back and allowed him to tackle the lock. After a few moments of much more naturally pitched grunting as chubby fingers gave battle, the catch freed with a clunk. Emitting a screech that yearned for the blessed release of oil, the gate opened.

"Come!" With a superior sweep of the hand, The Messenger ushered them inside to where the strange newcomer was standing, smiling at them blandly. "My brother, these mortals cometh at the call of providence to aid me in my quest to regain what lieth within the glory of the light once more. This one"—here he caught Dullard's shoulder and jerked the unbalanced prince inelegantly sideways—"hath the inspiration to assist me. But these others, his bosom friends, art at liberty. Willst thou taketh them to meet our brethren whilst we work?"

"Of course." The bulging figure nodded his head. "Go to it."

The Messenger beamed. And then, his hand wrapped firmly around Dullard's shoulder, he turned and started hauling the limping prince away up the steps.

"Wait!" There was a hint of alarm in Pleasance's voice. "Where are you taking him?" Her eyes darted to Fodder and his companions. "We shouldn't split up!" she appealed. "We know nothing about this place! We should stay together!"

"It's fine!" Dullard flashed a brief smile back down the steps as he was all but manhandled upwards. "I'll find you when I'm done! Stay with Fodder!"

"Be not afeared!" The Messenger's vaguely patronising tone drifted down from above. "Despite his great youth, The Child is a divinity, just as I am. Be not fooled by his infant face; he will care for thee well!"

"The Child?" Flirt stared at the towering man with his bulk and his pockmarks, a man who had clearly left childhood behind quite some time before. She blinked.

"That is correct." The so-called Child's squeaky voice cracked. "I am the youngest of the Gods, left forever youthful so to express innocence into a harsh and blighted world!"

Slowly, deliberately, Shoulders raked his eyes from the sandals that barely straddled two toes, up over the alarmingly restricted tunic and the acne scars that rippled over the remains of his dimples, to the mop of greasy ringlets. His expression was molten cynicism.

"Long time, no glory of the light, huh?" he drawled.

The Child's face creased. "It hath been some time," he admitted. "But thus I wait and all will be well when the light returneth to us."

Fodder's mind reeled. How many Quests had it been since he'd heard of the Gods getting involved? Three? Maybe four? There had been a couple in *The Vile Rose* but he didn't remember a child God showing up. How long had this strange man been clinging desperately to a youth that was well past saving?

"Come!" The Child beamed. "You shall be honoured by the presence of my sacred brethren!"

He set out up the marble steps, an anxious-looking Pleasance and a cynical-looking Shoulders following reluctantly behind. Fodder hung back a step and tapped Flirt's arm.

"Still think they don't need help?" he whispered.

Flirt cast a look after the figure of The Child. Her eyes were unreadable. "Ways and means," she simply replied. "Tread carefully, Fodder; we've been scalded too often. You should test the water first, shouldn't you?"

Fodder didn't reply. But he gritted his teeth and with Flirt, headed up the steps towards the summit.

Beneath the rooflike dome of the swirling cloud, the summit of the Mountain of the Gods was a strange place. It was scattered with a series of odd-looking dwellings, a variety of marble mock-temples, a bower twisted out of a cluster of brown-leafed trees, a feasting hall, and a smooth tower teetering on the brink of the drop, into which Fodder caught a glimpse of Dullard being hustled—presumably the home of The Messenger. And in the centre of them all, on the highest clump of rock, a rounded dome balanced on soaring marble columns over a floor that sank into the ground itself. From within, a painfully off-key ballad was being played on a stringed instrument that sounded in dire need of tuning. So indeed did the male voice that accompanied it.

The Child beamed. "Ah, the sweet song of The Muse!" he exclaimed. "Come forth and hear it better in our gathering hall! Few are blessed to share in his heavenly talent!"

"Heavenly talent!" Shoulders snorted under his breath. "I've taken more pleasure listening to weasels get strangled!"

Pleasance's smile, a sudden mask over her anxious glances in the direction of The Messenger's tower, was barbed. "Didn't it bother you to hear your relatives in pain?"

"Children." Flirt's firm intervention prevented the inevitable wrangling as Shoulders's lips parted. "Not now, okay?"

"But..." Shoulders attempted a rebuttal, but Flirt's expression shot him down in flames.

"Not now," she repeated more firmly. "You can have your bitch fight with the princess later, can't you?"

Shoulders huffed, glaring at Pleasance. "Don't think I won't."

"Well, we can look forward to that, can't we?" Flirt was apparently in no mood for this. "But for now, shut up, the pair of you."

It was Pleasance's turn to huff, a far more ladylike effort than Shoulders's snort. But to Fodder's relief, the verbal exchange seemed to be over.

The marble dome opened out before them as they followed The Child over its threshold. Within, the circular marble floor dropped in wide steps down to a central circle where, crudely painted upon the surface, was what looked like an old Quest map of a land arrangement long abandoned. Scattered across its surface were a series of small clay figures, inexpertly moulded and gripping tiny stick weapons or wands in their hands. And spread out on the steps around them were the men and women Fodder could only assume were the Gods of the Quests.

And what a collection they were. Nearest to the new arrivals, an enormously fat man with a bushy beard and wine-stained tunic lay snoring in a heap of his own dribble as he cuddled an empty bottle to his chest like a precious baby. A bit further down, a wiry, dark-haired man dressed in a patchwork jacket was trying, with a distinct lack of success, to master a tricky shuffle of a pack of cards. Beyond him, two near-identical women, both scantily clad, one in deep, clinging magenta satin and the other in heavy black velvet, sat together practising come-hither swirling motions with their arms. In the far corner, a plump, harried-looking woman with a voluptuous bosom and wilting flowers tangled in her hair was trying, without much success, to re-pot a withering begonia. The source of the painful music lay to their left—a wistful-looking young man with frizzy hair, strumming tunelessly on a lyre. And finally, seated to either side of the painted map, an old man in a long robe sat stroking his enormously overgrown white hair and beard while his companion, a burly figure dressed in scanty armour and a leather kilt, placed one of the clay figures with a firm plonk onto the island.

"Thus I call the mortal hero, Sir Kyrtin!" he boomed. "He shall slayeth the beast of the rampant caves and bring harmony once more to the shores of this tortured island!"

The old man nodded thoughtfully. "A nice move, Warlord," he conceded. "But the people of that island are warlike. If they fight not the beast, will they not fight their neighbours?"

The Warlord smiled smugly. "Is that not my art? Am I not the Lord of War?"

The four newcomers stared blankly down at the strange scene before them. It was Pleasance who asked the question.

"What on earth are they doing?" she declared incredulously.

"What in *heaven*, meanest thou?" There was a bit of a smug edge to The Child's reply. "The Warlord and The Father playeth with the fate of mortals. The Muse, with his endless artistic talents, fashioned the likeness of the world and the mortals that tread upon it, and their moves create chaos or harmony on the mortal coil, as they chooseth." His pudgy face stilled for an instant. "True, it doth not feel as it once did to play this game. The power at one's fingers is...lacking. It is almost as though the mortals do not obey our commands...."

"I should think they don't," Pleasance murmured archly. "Sir Kyrtin was Bold, my brother-in-law, and I haven't seen him heading off to slay any cave beasts on islands lately. He's too busy swaggering and plucking his eyebrows."

The Child stared around the circular chamber artlessly. "My brethren are all of great talent," he stated with appalling sincerity. "We know these talents are within us. The Muse is the master of art and music." He gestured to the pallid young man battling with his lyre, who gave them a dreamy smile before returning to his off-key ballad. "In the power of the light, his art shines as though to step into very life and his music can swell a heart or break it clean in two!"

"It's breaking my bloody ears," Shoulders muttered, but Flirt kicked him into silence before any further caustic commentary could follow.

"The Mother is mistress of fertility and nature and plants, and flowers blossom wherever her feet should fall!" The Child swept on, gesturing to the large-bosomed lady garlanded with dying flowers, who was staring at her half-bald begonia with the slightest hint of despair. "And then there are the sisters; the Siren is the dark lady of the heavens, a powerful seductress who will enchant or destroy you with a single look from her dark eyes!" The woman in black velvet, her eyes heavily smudged with eyeliner, looked up from her arm gestures with a tart little smile. "While her counterpart, The Amour, seeks only to love all men and spread the joy of love throughout the world!" The blonde lady in magenta winked as she motioned with a beckoning finger and wiggled her eyebrows suggestively.

Shoulders was watching The Amour with a certain degree of interest. Fodder could see the appeal—there was a lot of flesh and not much satin to suggest the pleasures that lay within—but now was not the time. He smacked Shoulders on the arm.

His friend shot him a sideways glare. "Will you people stop bloody beating me up?" he hissed. "I was *just looking.*"

"And of course, here is The Merrymaker!" At the sound of his name, the prostrate, dribbling mound of blubber near their feet snorted, his eyes opening as he blinked and gazed up at them with bloodshot eyes.

"Tha's right!" he roared abruptly, his words slurring like a snake with hiccups. "I am The Merrymaker, the maker of merry stuff! I can eat…whateva I wants to eat, like…an' I don't get fat!" He slapped his enormous paunch, which wobbled alarmingly. "I can drink all night an' day an' all them other bits too…an' I don't get the teeny weeniest bit pissed!" He clenched his fingers in a pinching gesture with one hand as he rolled onto his side, waving the empty bottle with the other. "I never sleep! I never rest! I never…"

What else he never they were not to learn, for at that moment, The Merrymaker's eyes glazed and he dropped like a pole-axed bull to the marble floor. A moment later, he began to snore once more.

The Child's smile had a slight edge to it after that interlude, an edge that gave Fodder a spark of hope—could he see, somewhere inside, how absurd this situation was? But whether or not it was so, he ploughed on.

"And at last we have The Trickster, feared by mortal men for his wiles and lures!" The wiry figure in the patchwork jacket glanced up, his face lighting up at the sight of the four visitors.

"Mortals!" he exclaimed, scrambling to his feet and gathering his scattered cards as he darted up the steps to stand before them. His crooked smile arched across his face.

"I can offer many things, sweet mortals!" he exclaimed, his eyes rolling in a slightly concerning manner as he limbered on the spot before darting up to grab Fodder's shoulder and thrust his face in front of his eyes. "I can offer power and glory forever!" He capered, limbs flailing, to grab Shoulders and peer around from behind him. "I can offer the eternal love of every desirable woman who ever lived!" He hurled himself towards Flirt, but even divinity could see when something was a bad idea, and he stopped short of actually laying hands on her when he caught a look at her glare. He cupped his own cheeks with open palms instead. "Men too! Any man you want can be yours! And any riches!" Again, good sense prevailed when he reached Pleasance, who was still cradling her heeled shoes in a pointed fashion in her hands. Instead, he circled around her, hands raised over his head in a lingering reach. "Any dresses, any silks, any furs, any wealth and luxury your heart may desire! All can be yours if you can best me at a game that has flummoxed and confounded the greatest mortal minds of the ages! A game so fierce and fervent, so impossible, so inconceivable that none has ever bested me in this great and deadly joust of wits!"

He leapt in front of them once more, dropping to the stone step below as he laid three of his cards onto the marble. He grinned and flashed the centremost one to reveal a picture of a queen in a golden crown and a blue dress. He slapped it down again.

"Find the lady!" he exclaimed.

Shoulders blinked. "Is he having a ruddy laugh?"

Fodder was thinking much the same thing. But he simply watched, pained, as The Trickster shuffled the three cards in a circle with a maddened smile upon his face. He waved his hands frantically in an effort to mask his movements before halting his progress with a flourish.

"So, sweet mortals!" he exclaimed. "But be aware—if you lose, you must be my slave for all the days of your brief, mortal existence, doing my bidding forevermore! So! Who will face my challenge and risk everything for great reward?"

Flirt's expression was profoundly unimpressed. She folded her arms. "It's on the right," she said dryly.

Fodder watched as The Trickster peeled up the corner of the card to the right. He caught a glimpse of blue and gold. The card slapped down again.

The Trickster's smile was manic now. "Wrong! You lose!"

Flirt's face did not change. "No, I didn't, did I?"

The Trickster pouted. "Yes! You lost!"

Flirt did not budge. "Show us the card then," she drawled.

The Trickster shook his head wildly. "There is no need! That is not the card!"

Flirt raised an eyebrow. "Prove it."

The Trickster thrust his nose into the air. "I do not have to! I am a God! My word is law!"

Flirt tilted her head. "Your word is bollocks, mate."

With a loud huff, The Trickster abruptly hurled all his cards into the air, watching as they tumbled like a blizzard around them. "I do not want such a slave as you anyway!" he exclaimed. "I grant you your freedom!"

As The Trickster stomped off, Fodder stepped past the sniggering Shoulders to Flirt's side. "Tread carefully, huh?" he said quietly.

Flirt glanced at him. "I was testing the water, wasn't I? Besides..."
She shrugged, her smile dry. "He was a pillock."

The Child was smiling at them rather wanly. "So here is your
reward, to be amongst the divine," he squeaked at them. "Be at liberty to
seek from us any truth you desire to knoweth until your companion
returneth."

"Yeah, we shalleth," Shoulders muttered as The Child skipped
disturbingly off. "What a bunch of nutters."

"I don't understand." Pleasance was gazing around the room in
confusion. "This is all they do, correct? Sit around here and practice
their skills, waiting for The Narrative? So, if they spend so much time
on these things, why are they so utterly bad at them?"

Flirt's expression turned from cynicism to a slight hint of pity.
"Because they *don't* practice, do they? They think they're Gods and that
these things will happen for them without having to try. They don't
practice because they don't realise they need to, do they? They can't
believe they can be God of something and be bad at it. They think it
should just come."

And perhaps that was the way in. The thought popped into Fodder's
brain. After all, The Messenger had been willing to accept Dullard's help,
albeit crediting himself for inspiring him. Perhaps if they offered to help
The Trickster improve his card tricks, helped The Mother save her
plants, sobered up The Merrymaker, and tuned The Muse's lyre, they
could make them see that they needed to work upon these things to
make them better, that they could be something without their precious
glory of the light. And maybe they would understand what had been
done to them, the dependence that had grown within their minds from
the Taskmaster's heavy-handed interference...

It had to be worth a try.

He glanced at the figures around them. The catatonic Merrymaker
was in no state to listen to anything, let alone a reasoned debate; and The
Trickster, engulfed by a cloud of miffed, was sitting on the steps bad-
temperedly flicking through his cards after his encounter with Flirt.
Neither felt the best place to start. The expressions on the faces of The
Siren and The Amour and the ongoing distraction they were causing in
Shoulders and, to some extent, with Fodder himself suggested they

would be a bad idea. The Father and The Warlord seemed absorbed in their game and probably wouldn't care for the interruption. The Child, in spite of his bizarre demeanour, had shown a flicker of awareness but the shattering of his illusions was likely to be amongst the more difficult and painful and was perhaps best left for the time being. And since he was now attempting to aid The Mother in the rescue of her plants, that left only The Muse.

"I'm going to try and talk to him." Fodder nodded towards The Muse. "See if I can wake him up a bit."

"Good idea." Shoulders's gaze had not strayed. "You do that, and I'll go and talk to the ladies…"

"Down, boy." Flirt's grab forestalled his first step in their direction. "It's the planting, isn't it?" She gestured to the sisters, The Siren with her sultry smile and intent stare and The Amour with her flirty giggle and beckoning fingers. "They think they're supposed to seduce mortal men, and you'd be the first so-called mortal they've had to play with for a while. It wouldn't be real, for you or for them. Is that what you want?"

Shoulders hardly even bothered to hesitate. "I'm prepared to make that sacrifice."

Pleasance rolled her eyes fervently. "Ask a foolish question…" she inserted acidly. "And while it would be quite amusing to watch that Siren reap terrible torture on what's left of you when she's done—as, in case you didn't know, dark Goddesses are prone to do—does it not occur to your panting, randy mongrel of a mind that you would be taking cruel advantage of two women who are unable to help themselves? Because that is what planting means. How they act is not their choice." She sniffed. "Do you think any woman would cast come-hither looks in your direction if it was?"

Shoulders's expression ploughed through a wild series of contortions, ranging from indignant fury through frustration to a flash of guilt, but although his mouth was working, no words settled on his tongue. At length, he managed a rampant "Fine!" and, shaking free of Flirt's grasp, he stormed away and slumped against a pillar not far from the slumbering Merrymaker. His arms were crossed. His face was unreadable.

Fodder nodded to the irritable-looking princess. "Thanks," he said quietly.

"I didn't do it for you or for him," was the snappish response. "I did it for those poor planted women. Nobody should be so deluded that they might find a headless weasel like him attractive."

Or a slobbering teenage Hero. The thought flashed through Fodder's mind, but he kept it to himself. "Well, we appreciate it," he said instead, glancing at Flirt. "And actually, you might be able to help us. Flirt and I are going to see if we can wake any of this lot up to what the Taskmaster's done to them and your help would be…"

But Pleasance was already rolling her eyes. "How many times do I have to say I have no interest in your little cause?" The words were firm but there was a slight hint of something else behind her eyes as she glanced around at the deluded array of Gods. If Fodder hadn't known better, he might have thought it to be pity. "I told you, I'm only in this for myself."

Fodder smiled. "That's funny. Because a minute ago, you were in it for those poor planted women."

Pleasance only glared. "Think what you like. Do what you like. But don't expect me to get involved."

And with a sweep of her skirts, the princess deposited herself on the topmost step, fingering her battered shoes as she stared out over the temple-scattered mountaintop. Her eyes strayed towards a certain tower teetering on the brink.

Flirt and Fodder exchanged a look. With a shared shrug, they turned and moved down towards The Muse.

The pallid young man with his mop of curly hair glanced up at their approach, his smile dreamy as he hummed tunelessly and strummed the lyre he was holding.

"Greetings, mortals," he said in a soft, distant voice. "Hast thou cometh to hear my heavenly music? I would gladly share it with thee."

"Ummm…" Fodder raised a quick hand to forestall any return to the tuneless twanging. "Actually, we thought we might help you out." He gestured to the lyre. "Would you, er, like us to help tune that thing for you?"

The young man's brow wrinkled. "Tune? What meanest thou?"

Fodder glanced at Flirt, but her expression indicated that this one was all his. "You know, *tune*. As in 'make sound in tune'?"

The Muse was frowning deeply now. "I know not what thou doth mean."

Yeah, we can hear that. Fodder sensibly kept this Shoulders-ish thought to himself. He sighed. "It's just, when an instrument is tuned, it sounds nice, yeah?" He smiled wanly. "And when it isn't, it...doesn't."

The Muse's expression shifted to faint curiosity. "My music is divine. It hath always been and shall be *nice*. Therefore, why needeth I this tuning of thine?"

Fodder took a deep breath in preparation for the step into danger-ous territory. "Because—and no offence, mate, I really am trying to help—your music? It's terrible."

The Muse's expression froze. His eyes stared long and hard for a moment at Fodder's earnest face. He blinked. And then, bizarrely, he smiled, a smile tinged with a distinct air of condescension.

"Poor mortal," he said, his dreamy tone suddenly taking a turn for the patronising. "I pity thee and thy poor, distorted ears."

Fodder had suffered loss and damage of a number of ears in his time, but he was fairly certain that his current set were both straight and true, which meant instead a fresh and happy delusion had cropped up in his path. He sighed.

"Sorry?" he said wearily.

The Muse smiled. It was the smile of a dog owner patting a dim but faithful hound upon the head. "I see what tragedy has befallen thee. Thou art despoiled by the lesser sounds thou hast endured in thine earthly realms. Thy mind is too mortal, too mundane to absorb the glories of mine art!"

Oh magnificent. "No, really, mate, my ears are fine." Fodder actu-ally saw his words bounce off the sheen of happy self-delusion that had engulfed The Muse like a shell. "Sorry, but I've heard drowned cats that are better than you. You can't sing and you can't play. You are awful."

The Muse reached out and patted him on the cheek. "Thou poor creature. Thou cannot comprehend my glory! It doth too far exceed the powers of thy simple mind!"

Something unpleasant was starting to bubble in the depths of Fodder's brain as he stared at the superior smile, listened to the patronising tone, and looked into a pair of eyes that bore no trace of a hint that anything he said would make the slightest difference to his self-opinion. He fought it down as best he could, but the edges of his words began to bow under the strain.

"So my opinion doesn't matter?" Heat was leaking into his words— he felt Flirt's hand on his arm, heard her softly say his name, but he took no notice. "Nothing I think is important to you because I'm only some worthless mortal who can't understand, is that it?"

"It is ever thus." The bubbles were coming to the boil as The Muse's smile widened. "Art it not beholden unto us to nurture thy poor, limited minds into more than thou art capable of without our divine touch? Thou knoweth so little beyond the cradle of our care. Thou art imperfect until our hands descend to mould thee. Thou existeth only to be guided by our wisdom and benefaction." The Muse nodded with condescending grace. "Thus, thou mortals should ever be grateful."

"Grateful." Boiling rage began to overflow the restraint of common sense. *"Grateful?* Why, you patronising..."

"Fodder." Hands, Flirt's hands, caught him sharply by the arms, yanking him away, stumbling up the steps, before he could finish his sentence. The Muse, his smile unchanging, stared distantly after him for a moment, before returning to his twanging as though the whole incident had been of no account.

But Fodder was steaming, burning with anger, his fists clenched and his face contorted as feelings he could barely articulate surged to overwhelm him. How dare he talk down to him like that? How dare he dismiss him and his opinion as worthless, just because he thought himself better, more superior? Why couldn't he understand, why couldn't he listen, why couldn't he...

"Oi!" Flirt's sharp exclamation was accompanied by a sharper smack against his shoulder. "What the bloody hell was that?"

Fodder was in no mood to be reprimanded. "Didn't you hear him?"

"I heard him, didn't I?" Flirt's stare was fierce. "I heard a planted, self-deluded nutjob who was unable to hear the truth because his head is such a mess. You should feel sorry for him, not bite his bloody head off!"

"But..." The words Fodder had intended to follow this exclamation vanished under a sudden surge of cold reason. Shame was not far behind it. He took a deep breath and then another as his shoulders heaved and the bubbling rage within him subsided to a simmer. Flirt hadn't stopped staring at him.

"Better," she said quietly. "Now, I'm asking again, aren't I? What the hell was that?"

And that was the question. The answer, simmering within his brain, finally cleared the steam and let itself be noticed.

"It's what you said earlier." Flirt frowned at Fodder's quiet statement. "About this being practice." Flirt's eyes widened with realisation but she did not interrupt. "Because this is it, isn't it? The way these so-called Gods look at us as mere mortals. Our opinions aren't worth hearing, because we're only mere mortals. Nothing we say can be right if they don't agree, because we are simply mere mortals. If they don't want to hear it, nothing we say will even penetrate! They think they can play with our lives and nothing we do matters without them. They think without their guidance and care, we have no value, that, if our opinions don't agree with theirs, *we* need to be corrected. They think of us as pets...no. As *toys*. And even if they are deluded as all hell and completely insane, they'll never hear the truth from us, because the *mere mortals* aren't worth listening to. We're *beneath* them." He shook his head. "And that's it. That's exactly it. That's how *the Taskmaster* sees us too."

Flirt's expression was sombre. "Fodder..."

"You know I'm right." Fodder breathed deeply once more. His brain was struggling to frame itself around an idea circling deep within, an idea so incomprehensibly huge that he couldn't quite bring it to bear. "I've always assumed the Taskmaster could see sense, could be reasoned with, that we could get that fair choice, that chance, if we got past the Courtiers and straight to the source. We had to, because the Taskmaster runs the world. But until we started this, and even after, I'd never really realised—look at how we're treated. We're planted with characters, subverted into something we're not, used, ruined and discarded after, chucked away to cope with what's left of ourselves without any fix or help. Planting is evil, Flirt. Look at the state of these people!" He gestured to the sad clumps of Gods scattered beneath the dome. "What kind of a fair chance, of a choice, can they have when they can't even think for themselves? Does the Taskmaster know or care what's been done to them? And if the Taskmaster does understand, is there any point to what we're doing? What's the point in a fair shot at a good character if we're not ourselves when it's over?" He shook his head. "Why is the whole world scrambling for the Taskmaster's approval, when I don't even think it's worth having? Being disdained and ignored just because I won't put up with the crappy lot I was born to? The world is a mess and the Taskmaster did it and we've every reason to believe nothing we say about it will make a difference, because if the Taskmaster is even a bit like *them*..." He felt himself gasping for breath as the huge edge of something burned at him. "So maybe... Haven't you ever wondered?" The enormous, terrifying thought strained against his mind, blocking his words as he struggled to get it out. "Don't you think maybe...it might be better— *we* might be better—if..."

He couldn't finish it—he barely wanted to think it, for the thought tugged at the very sensibilities of his soul. But Flirt's expression and the slow shake of her head implied he didn't need to say any more.

"Fodder..." she said softly. "Look, I see what you're getting at, don't I?" She sighed, closing her eyes for an instant. "You're ahead of yourself, aren't you?" she managed after a pause. "We can cross that *monster* of a bridge if it comes to it. But we don't know that the Taskmaster is like them, do we? Maybe the Taskmaster doesn't know or understand what's being done here—isn't that what we assumed when we started this? We started this for a fair chance. Maybe we can also bring some reason."

Fodder's hands were shaking. "And if the Taskmaster won't listen?"

Flirt gave a wan smile. "Then we *try harder*. And if we do..." It was her turn for a deep breath. "The Taskmaster broke these people, Fodder. Maybe the Taskmaster is the only one who can fix them. After all..." She shrugged. "They don't want to hear it from anyone else, do they?"

Try harder. The words, the hope of them, replaced the turbulence loose in Fodder's brain with a new edge of tempered steel.

"Or maybe we don't need the Taskmaster," he said. *If I can turn them, if I can help them, without having to go begging to some conde-scending...* "Maybe I can still do it."

In spite of her inspirational words, Flirt failed to hide the flash of cynicism that crossed her face. "Are you sure that's a good idea? We're outnumbered, aren't we, and if we upset them too much, it's a long way down."

Fodder gave her a steely look. "Whatever happened to *try harder*? We need to help these people. Who's going to do it if we don't?"

Flirt sighed. "I know but...you know me, Fodder. I say what I see, don't I? And from what I've seen here, there's more to do than can be done by us, even if we had time to do it. I'm happy to fight when it's needed and talk when we're dealing with sensible folk. But these people aren't right in the head, are they? Fixing them will take more time than we can spare right now, if it's not beyond us altogether. I'm trying to be practical."

"Well, you're being more like Shoulders." Flirt's expression suggested to Fodder this had not been a wise statement. "You want to leave them to see if the Taskmaster can be bothered to help them?"

Flirt looked sorrowful but shrugged. "Not really, but I don't see what else we can do, do I? We can't get in their heads like the Taskmaster can."

"And isn't that what did the damage?" Fodder's mind flashed back to Humble Village, to the Archetypal Inn and a life-changing conversation. "Wasn't it you who first asked why we have to obey the Taskmaster at all?"

Flirt cocked an eyebrow. "Not obeying doesn't mean you have to clean the house up on the Taskmaster's behalf, do you? Point out the mess and let the Taskmaster do the tidying. I thought that's what this was all about, didn't I?"

But Fodder shook his head. Let the Taskmaster do the tidying just because that's who made the mess? Did she think the Taskmaster would do any more than sweep it under the rug and move on?

No, there were people under those walking balls of delusion that called themselves Gods. If he could help them without pleading with the...*thing* that had made them that way in the first place, he would. It was only right.

"I have to try." Ignoring Flirt's reproachful, if slightly respectful, shake of the head, he turned to the scattering of Gods and braced himself.

"Hello!" It was an inauspicious beginning, but his call did turn a few Godly heads and get him some attention. "Look, I need to talk to you all, yeah?"

The Father glared at him out of the depths of his hair and beard. "Thou art intruding upon our game! The fate of thy very world hangs upon our motions!"

Fodder sighed. "It doesn't," he said bluntly. He hated to be callous, but it seemed the only way to penetrate the mass of self-delusion. "That figure you're holding, Sir Kyrtin?" He pointed to the lumpy mass of clay in The Father's hands, before gesturing to the form of Pleasance, settled upon a step nearby and looking rather perturbed at being drawn into whatever was afoot. "That's her brother-in-law. And whatever you reckon you've been sending him off to do, he's actually been sitting around a palace, living it up with his wife and going bog all of nowhere. He's retired."

The Father stared at the figure. He stared at Pleasance. He stared at Fodder.

"Why doth thou speaketh such bizarre untruths?" he rumbled angrily.

"His mind art unhinged by the limits of its mortality," The Muse piped up, to Fodder's irritation. "He comprehendeth not the divine glories that surroundeth him and salves his struggling thoughts by the belief we Gods art as mundane as he." He smiled distantly. "He claimeth even that my divine music art terrible."

The Warlord came to his feet in a surge of muscles and rage. "Thou speaketh thus to thy God?" he roared.

Oh great. Well, in for a groat, in for a sovereign, Fodder supposed. "No," he said wearily, braced for pain. "I speaketh thus to someone who can't play the ruddy lyre."

As The Warlord clenched his fists in anger, Fodder ploughed hastily on. "Look, The Messenger told me how you live up here, okay? He said you remember the power you had in what he called the glory of the light and how different it feels without it." The variety of twitches that crossed the various would-be Gods' expressions told Fodder he'd hit closer to the mark. "He even suggested you struggle with things you found easy in the light. His flying, for example, and The Trickster's card tricks? The Muse's music? The Mother's plants?" He gestured to the very-much-dead begonia that The Mother, even with The Child's help, had failed to rescue. "Because without the light, these things don't work anymore." He swallowed hard and took the plunge. "Haven't any of you ever wondered *why?*"

There was a long silence that Fodder took as an affirmative.

"So, let me tell you," he continued softly. "Let me tell you about your glory of the light, because we have it too, us mere mortals. It changes us too, gives us powers, talents, thoughts we wouldn't have without it. And when it's gone, those powers leave us, like yours do. The only thing is, most of us know it doesn't last, that it wasn't real. You don't seem to." He looked from face to face, searching for understanding, even for an inkling of suspicion that he was telling them something they'd known all along. "When the light comes, you are Gods, I'll give you that, because it makes you so. But without it, I'm sorry, but you're as mortal as the rest of us."

"Mortal?" The Trickster drawled the word like a curse. "Thou darest to call us mortal?"

Fodder risked a slight smile. "Mate, if I stabbed you with my sword right now, you'd bleed just like I would. The power the light gave you has messed with your heads, made you believe what it gave you was real. You need to remember how the world really works again and—"

"And thou wouldst tell us?" The Warlord cut in sharply, his muscles bulging almost as much as his red face. "Thou, a mere mortal, wouldst dare to preach to thy Gods about the workings of a world they designed?"

That wasn't good. "You didn't design it," Fodder emphasised. "Can't you see what's happened to you? Playing terrible music, killing plants, keeling over drunk, and doing card tricks an infant could see through! Do you really think these are the acts of divinity?"

The Child squeaked into the debate. "But when the glory of the light cometh…"

"The glory of the light is minutes of your life! It's not more important than the rest of it!"

The Father thundered to his feet. "The glory of the light art our truth!"

"No, it isn't!" Fodder was gesticulating wildly as he struggled to drag the conversation back to sanity before it lurched out of control once more. He could feel the anxious eyes of Flirt, Pleasance, and Shoulders, all gathered by the pillar above and watching in curious concern. "The glory of the light is what uses you! You're pawns, like the rest of us. Pawns to the one who sent it and messed you up, the one that you should really be angry with. You need to listen because it's the Task—"

"Another?" The Warlord's bellow drowned the rest of his sentence like a tidal wave. "You darest impugn our divinity and claim us pawns to a divinity yet greater? We are Gods! We have the power, we have the glory—"

"But only in your precious bloody light!" Fodder took a quick gulp of breath to calm himself, rooting in his pouch as a sudden idea took hold. "Look!"

With an awkward yank, he untangled the Ring of Anthiphion from the drawstrings of its leather home and held it up. "You see this ring? Only a piece of costume jewellery, right? No power, no nothing! But when your precious glory of the light comes, this thing turns into the most powerful object of magic in the world! It can slay armies and bring down the sun! But right now, it's nothing more than…more than…"

His voice tailed off. It felt prudent given the sudden, hungry circle of eyes that had fixed, without exception, on the glittering Ring he was holding.

"What?" he said nervously.

"Thy ring art magic?" There was an alarming appetite to The Father's tone.

Fodder closed the Ring abruptly into his fist, sensing that without knowing how, he'd made a big mistake. "Not exactly."

"Thou said it was thus." The Trickster was on his feet, crouched, his expression wild and cunning. He thrust out his hand. "Thou wilt surrender it unto us."

"He bloody won't." Fodder was more relieved than he cared to admit at Flirt's appearance at his shoulder. "What's it to you?"

The Gods had all risen, were all approaching, slowly but with intent, every eye fixed upon Fodder's closed fist.

"Thou holdeth a piece of magic blessed in the glory of the light." The

Siren's voice was a seductive hiss. "We have waited long for such an object!"

"Why?" Pleasance hadn't moved from the pillar where she and Shoulders were waiting, but both were eyeing the exit with a certain degree of interest. Her question seemed to emerge accidentally.

"We have long suspected that an object, such as thou holdeth, may be the key to our restoration." The Father's eyes appeared to glow from his mass of white hair. "That a touch of magic art all we doth require to call forth the glory of the light once more!"

Fodder was backing up the steps, Flirt's hand on his shoulder. He heard the steely clatter as she drew her sword. "But I told you, it's simply a ring here!" he emphasised desperately. "It doesn't work outside the light!"

"In your hands perhaps, mortal!" The Trickster was capering up the steps towards them. "But inspired by the touch of divinity..."

"Oh bugger," Fodder heard Shoulders mutter. "Leg it?"

Staring round a final time at the sea of hungry faces, at the utter lack of understanding, Fodder felt a combined surge of pity, rage, and a slight niggle of fear. Shoulders had a point. These weren't faces to be reasoned with.

Bollocks.

"Yep," he said. "Leg..."

But Shoulders was already a disappearing blur. With an irritated huff, Flirt shoved past Fodder, swinging her sword in broad arcs to ward off the advancing Gods, but belief in their own invincible divinity meant that they didn't so much as flinch as they closed in. With a squeal of alarm, Pleasance scrambled her skirts out of the way and also took to her heels as Fodder caught Flirt's arm.

"Wound one!" he hissed.

Flirt gave him a sharp glance. "What?"

"Wound one of them!" he exclaimed. "Make them bleed! Show them they're ruddy mortal!"

"Thou willst hold!" The Warlord's enormous muscles flexed—his hands outstretched, he charged forwards past his brethren with a roar. Flirt, who had been staring at Fodder with an unreadable expression, switched instantly to action mode. Her sword lashed out, not in a deadly arch but in a controlled one, missing assorted vital organs and limbs as she slashed her blade instead across The Warlord's reaching hands.

And he flinched. Pain registered on his face as he staggered to a halt, twisting his hands and staring at the two red lines that snaked across his palms. A drop of blood welled in the crevice of his skin.

He blinked. His fellow Gods hesitated around him, staring down at the red speck with a mixture of confusion and incredulity.

"I bleedeth," The Warlord muttered, his bellowing voice softened by shock as the drop seeped into a trickle. "Dost thou seeth my blood, my brethren?"

"I seeth blood." The gravelly voice of The Siren was full of amazement. "How canst this be?"

Yes, yes, yes. Fodder stepped up to Flirt's shoulder once more. "I told you," he said as gently as he could. "You're mortal. Now do you believe me?"

But not one God so much as looked round at the sound of his voice. Other than the slobbering, inert form of The Merrymaker, they turned as one to stare at the white-bearded form of The Father.

"Master of all wisdom." The Muse spoke beseechingly. "Enlighten our shadowed minds. What meanest this madness?"

"I just told you..." Fodder started, but the booming voice of The Father rolled over his milder words and cut him off.

"I seeth only one solution to this tangled mystery," he intoned. "One possible reason for this. This hath been wrought by the power of that *ring!*"

No, no, no! Fodder grimaced at Flirt's distinct I-told-you-so look. How deep was this delusion embedded that they would go to such lengths to preserve it?

The Warlord gasped. "Truly, the power of the Ring art astounding!"

The Trickster, however, was already rubbing his hands together. "Imagine, my brethren! Our powers restored! Wielded by mine hand, it shall—"

"*Thy* hand?" The Father snapped. "Thou art a child besideth me! I shall wield it!"

"But my flowers!" The Mother implored. "Please, they have but little time!"

"I must spreadeth my music!"

"I must spreadeth my love!"

"I must fight again!"

"I must seduce again!"

Snort! "Not pished! Pop goes the weaseeellll…"

The clamour of voices swelled in an argumentative cacophony. Flirt glanced at Fodder.

"You know what you suggested earlier?"

"You mean legging it?"

"Yep. Good time, you think?"

"I reckon so."

Flirt turned and bounded up the marble steps. Hot on her heels, Fodder wheeled, hurtled up two steps, and then went flying as the flailing legs of the semi-conscious Merrymaker slapped against his ankles.

"Oof!" Marble step met face. Fodder scrambled himself free of the lump that had tripped him, but any chance of a discreet exit was blown.

"The mortals flee!" Even as he staggered upright, a hand slapped down upon his shoulder—instinctively, he flailed a wild fist backwards. Stumbling free, he caught a glimpse of The Trickster staggering back, clutching his nose.

"You think I enchanted my fist too?" It was a final, plaintive shot in the dark, but the angry ring of divine faces were well past listening and with a mixture of frustration and sorrow, he turned and bolted after Flirt.

"Foul, defiant mortals! Thou willst return!"

Bloody willst not! Fodder surged through the marble pillars and out onto the windy, rocky roof of the Mountain of the Gods. At once he spotted Flirt, slowing, searching over her shoulder for him, her face showing a flattering amount of relief as he emerged. And beyond her, to his surprise—for he'd thought him long gone by now—he spotted Shoulders, yanking and hammering at the golden gates that were failing to open for him. Beside him, an angry-looking Pleasance was waving her pointed shoes at him in an equally pointed manner.

"Will you forget the damnable gate?" Her piercing voice echoed across the mountaintop. "We can't just leave! What about Dullard?"

Shoulders snorted. "What about him?"

Pleasance's porcelain face flushed with red-hot rage. "How dare you! Run if you like, you pathetic coward, but I'm not leaving without him!"

Shoulders did not even turn from his manic rattling as he tried and utterly failed to get purchase to climb over the slippery, vertical golden bars. "Fine by me! Have a nice plunge!"

Pleasance gave a furious huff. Stamping one foot, she paused for the necessary register of pain that the absence of her shoes caused, before turning hurriedly and wrestling her unruly clothes in the direction of The Messenger's tower.

Oh bollocks. One glance over Fodder's shoulder told him that this was not a good time to be split up. The Warlord had charged out of the marble dome, his bleeding fists clenched and his eyes burning with vengeance, and a yard behind, the bloody-nosed Trickster cavorted at his heels with The Muse bearing his lyre like a club at his shoulders. Fodder redoubled his pace, much to the objections of knees and muscles still sore from the long slog up the mountain that made their presence very much felt with seeping achiness and bursts of roaring pain. If there was one thing Fodder would admit he missed about The Narrative, it was the ability to walk and run for miles without a single twinge. In that respect, real life stank.

He focused on the gates. Flirt had joined Shoulders but she too had failed to find whatever trick The Child had known to part them—the Portal of Divinity remained firmly stuck. The clatter of divine footsteps behind, not to mention the sweetly called-out promises of one hell of a good time from The Siren and The Amour, were closing fast. There was no more time.

"Head to the tower!"

Shoulders reeled around to face him. "You what?"

"Can you...open...that gate?" Fodder roared between desperate gasps for air.

Shoulders grimaced. "Not yet but—"

"Then tower!"

Flirt pulled a face but grabbed Shoulders by the arm and hauled him, protesting as ever, in the direction of The Messenger's tower. Fodder huffed on aching limbs alongside them. A bottle, presumably yanked from the slumbering hands of The Merrymaker, hurtled past to smash on the rock beside them as they puffed and scrambled their way towards the edge of the mountain. The tower loomed before them, its arched wooden door, apparently already yanked open by Pleasance, gaping before them.

Through the arch as they staggered forwards, Fodder spotted a motionless blond lump in a toga lying on a polished marble floor.

"Are you sure that was necessary?" Dullard's plaintive voice drifted out of the entrance Fodder plunged through, noting the imprint of a pointy shoe on The Messenger's unmoving forehead. "I'm certain he would have let me leave after a bit of reasoning and...Fodder?"

Flirt and Shoulders stumbled through the door as Fodder spun round, slammed the heavy wooden door, and fixed the latch in place. Flirt had already grabbed a nearby table, hauling it across the room and jamming it in front of the door; and Shoulders, making himself unexpectedly useful, did the same with a heavy-looking throne-like chair carved with a motif of wings. As the hammering and the increasingly explicit offers began from the far side of the door, the Disposable turned to Fodder with an expectant expression.

"Now what?" he rasped, his head wobbling violently.

Fodder gave a wan grin. "Dunno. Any ideas?"

Shoulders's expression of hope melted like a dying candle. "But you said to run here! I thought you had a plan!"

Fodder shrugged. "It was a place to run to. I didn't get any further!"

Beyond the door, The Warlord was hammering with his meaty fists as he issued blood-curdling threats about what he would do to their fragile mortal bodies. The Father was intoning some manner of command as The Mother tried to encourage a strand of scrubby grass to grow into a vine and wind its way inside to tie them up. The Muse was trying to use his music to crumble the walls, which Fodder had to admit was probably possible, whilst the offers from The Siren and The Amour were becoming downright indecent. And The Child...

"I am but lithe and small in size. I shall fitteth easily through yonder gap beneath this door and charmeth them into the Ring's surrender!"

A set of chubby fingers inched painfully under the gap beneath the chair and table. They jammed immediately.

Dullard was staring at the door with pensive resignation. "I take it there's been some manner of falling-out?"

"They think the Ring of Anthiphion will restore their lost godlike powers, don't they?" Flirt sighed as she stepped over the supine Messenger to join him at the foot of the winding staircase. "And they won't take 'that's bollocks' for an answer."

"Oh dear." Dullard frowned. "I'm sorry I wasn't there to help, but I'm afraid until Pleasance arrived, I had no idea there was a problem. I was quite occupied working on The Messenger's glider..."

Glider.

A part of Fodder's brain prodded him sharply, bringing up the image of The Messenger dangling in a tree surrounded by broken bits of wood and cloth. The other part, however, was glancing at Flirt and seeing the same battle between common sense and desperation in her eyes.

"This glider." Flirt was the first to risk it. "Big, is it?"

"Bigger than his previous effort, yes," Dullard remarked, smiling at the sudden interest shown in something academic. "And a great deal more stable since I added a tail to it for counterbalance. You see..."

Fodder, rather aptly, was next to take the plunge. "Will it carry five?"

Shoulders's eyes went saucer wide. *"No."*

Pleasance settled for turning pale. "Are you out of your bashed-up mind?"

With a crunch and splintering of wood, a part of the door buckled. A bloodstained fist strained in the crack.

Fodder got to the point. "You want to stay here?" There was an alarmed silence. Fodder turned to Dullard once more. "Will it carry five?"

Dullard winced. "Maybe. But I can't make any guarantees about—"

"Sod guarantees." A second plank of wood splintered under The Warlord's assault. "I'm taking the maybe."

"You're not going along with this?" Pleasance was staring at Dullard with outright horror.

The prince stared at the slowly shattering doors and sighed. "We can't lose that Ring," he said with resignation. "I'm not sure we have a great deal of choice."

"But a fall from this height?" The princess was almost white. "We'll be smashed to pieces!"

"I'm not sure it'll be that bad." The uncertainty in Dullard's tone made Fodder really wish the prince was a better liar in real-life situations. "Come on, it's this way."

"No way!" In lieu of a head to shake, Shoulders was waving his hands. "No way are you getting me—hey!"

There was a violent snapping of leather knots as Flirt ungraciously yanked Shoulders's head free of the bindings holding it to his neck. He gaped in fury as she tucked his head under her arm, his body flailing madly as it tried to reach her. She batted his hands off easily and trotted up the stairs.

"Your head's coming, isn't it?" she informed him matter-of-factly. "Want me to bring the body too?"

Things moved quicker after that. The run up the stairs, with the two halves of Shoulders acting, with much protest, under Flirt's guidance, added further pain to Fodder's aching knees. He wished he could assure them that the pain was nearly over but when he saw the glider perched on the roof, he had a nasty feeling it was just beginning.

"Are those silk bedsheets?" Pleasance was staring, aghast, at the contraption of wood and, yes, silk bedsheets, to which their lives were about to be entrusted. Fodder could only be grateful that evening twilight was now setting in, so he had merely a vague view of the landscape they were about to plummet into.

"Never mind that!" Over increasingly muffled protests, Flirt stowed Shoulders's head in her pack before, with Dullard's help, tangling his body into the leather straps. Unfortunately, since the glider was built for a single pilot, that did leave the rest of them unsecured.

Below them, wood shattered and the sound of a table being shoved across a marble floor rent the air.

"Quick!" Dullard was looping his climbing rope around the frame as securely as time allowed. "Tie yourselves in!"

"How?" Pleasance's screech at this prospect of menial work led to Dullard knotting her in, himself—by the time he was done, Flirt and Fodder too had attached themselves to the rope as best they could. The frame gave an alarming creak as Dullard himself clambered aboard, the bedsheets flapping in the wind. Fodder tried to tighten the rope around his arms and body only to find it didn't.

He stared out over a landscape of mountains and forests washed in the last faint traces of the sun's light. And everything he saw was pointy.

Except...

Was that a glint?

Yes!

"Dullard!" The prince looked up as he grasped the wooden upright, ready to push off. Angry-sounding feet battered the staircase beneath them. "Aim for that lake!"

Dullard pulled an awkward face. *"Aim?* Ummm..."

The door behind them burst open. Even as Fodder's hopes of a soft landing plunged, Dullard gritted his teeth and shoved.

And then his hope wasn't the only thing plunging....

* * *

"You *lost* it?"

It had to be said. It needed to be said. Perhaps there might have been better moments for the admonishment; Fodder was prepared to admit that. He dragged himself free of the disintegrating remains of silk and wood floating in the dark waters of the mountain tarn that—whether by luck, accident, or design—their tumbling glider had plunged into after a terrifying, swooping strafe through the pointed, jagged peaks of the Most Savage Mountains.

Indeed, as he struggled through the weeds, wading his way towards the rocky shore as best he could in the last dregs of twilight, a part of his mind was occupying itself by having a silent scream at the memory of looming rock and battering winds, sharpened ridges rising out of swelling darkness, a rip of silk, a hint of treetops, a bottoming stomach, and a wailing, fading screech before dark water surrounded him, filling his mouth and nose, swamping his ears as he spluttered and fought through the tatters of their escape craft to the surface. And there, aching, wet, and vaguely traumatised, he had found a bedraggled Pleasance being helped free by Dullard; the headless body of Shoulders reeling and splashing in frantic, senseless circles in its bindings; and Flirt, holding her pack in her hands and staring down at its parted clasp with a distinct hint of alarm. And the part of his mind not having a hysterical breakdown registered the absence of a certain something that had been stowed there for safekeeping.

It had to be said. It really did. After all, misplacing a handkerchief or perhaps a drinking bottle would have been no great thing. Losing a friend's head in mid-air, however…

Flirt carried on staring at the pack, her expression shifting from alarm to shamefaced remorse. "I did it up in a rush, didn't I?" she muttered, half to herself. "I must have missed the buckle…"

Fodder could feel hysteria threatening to swamp the previously safe corners of his brain. "Do you know where you lost it?" he managed. His awareness of a vague discomfort, probably hastened by the plunge, was not helping matters.

"I think it was that last stoop, wasn't it?" Flirt struggled to give a matter-of-fact reply. "When the sheet ripped over the trees and we turned sideways?"

Fodder had been trying to forget that particular instance. He swallowed hard as he forced his mind kicking and screaming back to the stomach-churning instance when the glider had stuttered and he'd heard Shoulders's muffled, and then less muffled but more distant, voice give a keening, fading screech. Yes, and there had been trees in a valley below, and then the water…

"He dropped in the trees." That was something. They had some-where to look, a search radius, and if his helmet had stayed on, there was a good chance he wouldn't be too badly bashed-up. But Flirt was still staring at the empty pack.

"I should have left his head on him, shouldn't I?" she murmured guiltily. "But he wasn't moving, and they were coming."

Now was not the time for that. With a small shove, Flirt was sent wading in the direction of the shore as Fodder himself turned back and caught the flailing body of Shoulders by the joints for which it was named. It fought to loosen the ropes that bound it to the glider at the direction of its currently absent and probably eager-to-be-retrieved head.

"Shoulders!" Fodder hissed, but the wriggling continued unabated, growing increasingly frantic as though he hadn't...

Heard him. Oh for pity's sake...

Of course. No ears.

And at the touch, Shoulders's body went nuts.

Logically, Fodder could understand it. He couldn't see or hear a thing without his head—he had no way of knowing whether the fingers that had seized him belonged to friend or foe, although he was clearly panicking, given friend was far more likely under the circumstances. It was difficult to be considerate of this, however, whilst being repeatedly and violently knee-butted in the thigh, especially given this was not helping his own certain need.

Magnificent. As if it wasn't hard enough to calm Shoulders down at the best of times...

Well, he'd just have to do something no enemy would even think of. He'd have to make sure Shoulders got the message that he was in safe hands.

It wasn't easy to draw a sword out of its scabbard whilst tangled in the wreckage of a sinking glider whilst being knee-butted, but Fodder eventually managed it. By the time he'd succeeded, a slightly more coherent-looking Flirt had dumped her pack and waded back out into the dark water to help.

"Here," she said firmly. "Let me. I'll grab him and you cut."

Grasping Shoulders's contorting arms, she pressed them down against her chain-mailed body as Fodder reached down with his sword and slashed.

The ropes fell away. Shoulders's body froze.

There. What do you make of that?

There was a pause. With his newly liberated hands, Shoulders's body pressed curiously down upon the ripped, damp surcoat and battered mail of Flirt's stomach. Quite deliberately and, in Fodder's opinion, vaguely suicidally, one hand drifted upwards.

Flirt considerately allowed him a half-second to establish that yes, indeed, there was something unusually shapely to be found beneath this particular soldier's uniform before she brought her palm down on his knuckles with a pointed smack. He yanked the hand away, but the thrashing stilled as well. The message had been received. He was in friendly hands.

Even if his friendly hands had apparently taken leave of their senses. Though that was possibly a fair assessment given four out of five of them were currently nowhere in the vicinity.

Flirt was glaring at the headless body. "I'll be having words with you about that, won't I?" she told him in a stern whisper, jabbing one pointed finger into his chest. Lack of ears or not, Fodder knew Flirt would feel it needed to be said.

Shoulders rubbed his concussed knuckles as, by the guidance of his friends, he waded awkwardly ashore between them. From the sheepish set of his frame, Fodder got the impression he'd received that message too.

But how to get the next message across? For how did one go about asking a man with no eyes or ears where his head was?

He knew he'd know. Of course he'd know. The head that was powering the body was the bit that would be aware of such things and a separated body and head had, in Fodder's personal experience, a strange, invisible attraction that allowed them to be drawn back together. The fact that he hadn't heard them talking to his body suggested he was nowhere within immediate earshot. But how was he going to ask him?

Well, they'd got this far based on sign language and groping...

On the darkened shore of the tarn, they found Pleasance slumped in a dripping, shaking heap, glaring at them with a fierceness that could have started a fire on an iceberg. There was, however, no sign of Dullard.

"Next time I suggest you are out of your bashed-up little mind?" the princess hissed venomously as they staggered out of the water to join her. "I suggest you listen!"

Fodder frowned at the lack of prince. "Where's Dullard?"

Pleasance sniffed as she drew the dampened remains of her cloak around her. "He thinks he saw a light as we passed over that valley and went to take a look. I certainly didn't—I had the common sense to keep my eyes shut."

"A light?" Fodder and Flirt exchanged an alarmed look. A light in the wooded valley where Shoulders's head had disappeared in a long spiral of down?

Pleasance was staring at the headless, reeling body of Shoulders with a certain hint of curiosity. "Not that I object in the slightest to its absence," she remarked, "but where's the rest of him?"

Flirt sighed wearily. "The buckle on my pack gave out," she said with resignation. "We lost his head mid-flight, didn't we?"

A broad, beautiful smile spread across the features of Pleasance that a moment before had been full of frown.

"And I thought this crash was going to be a total disaster!" she exclaimed with glee, clapping her hands together. "Thank you so much! You've made my night!"

It was Fodder's turn to sigh, battling the swell of discomfort he had earlier become aware of. Damn, this was not a good time! "Look, I know you two don't get on but he's our mate, okay? And now we have to go and find the rest of him!"

Pleasance gave a pout. "Must you? You've got the least annoying bit of him here and, personally, I like him better this way."

Flirt grimaced. "In a way, I see your point, don't I? But yes, sorry, we do need to find the rest of him."

"The rest of...oh dear." Shadowed in the onset of night, the slender silhouette of Dullard appeared out of the darkness close by. "Do you know where his head went?"

Fodder gestured back in the direction of their descent. "We think in that valley we passed over, just before the tarn."

The outline of Dullard's face dropped. "Oh dear," he repeated. "That might be a problem."

Flirt stepped forward, abandoning the job of securing Shoulders to Fodder. "Pleasance said you saw a light?"

"I did." Dullard nodded. "And when I took another look, I saw I wasn't mistaken. Not one light, but several down there in a clearing in the trees and I could see tents outlined against the glow. It looks like someone has made camp down there."

"It could be Trappers or Woodsmen," Fodder offered more with hope than any conviction, given their long-proven talent for stumbling into disaster was showing no signs of letting up. "They might not be hostile."

"I doubt it. Trappers rarely use pavilions." Fodder could see the edges of Dullard's wince. "You see, I know these mountains as well as anyone can from my geology studies, and I think I managed to follow our trajectory when we came down. I'm fairly sure where we are." He took a deep breath. "I believe this is the tarn up above Maw the Dragon's cave. I'm sorry, but we appear to have ended up right back where we started."

There was a lengthy pause. In the lack of light, Pleasance's pale skin turned distinctly paler.

"The Dragon?" she whispered.

"I know. I'm sorry." Dullard gave a wan smile. "But never fear, we certainly won't be letting him anywhere near you."

"You'd better not." The words were stern, but Fodder could not see enough of her expression to tell if she had passed the fear.

Dullard nodded. "But more to the point, as I recall, that valley has a hidden entrance into the Perilous Pass. In the absence of Pleasance, the crucial Dragon scene has still not come about, so it would make sense for them to make a camp nearby, out of sight, to make ready at short notice when the moment comes. I suspect that's what I saw."

Flirt rubbed one hand across her brow. "But if Shoulders's head is down there," she said, "we can't go looking for it, can we? If we search in daylight or by night with torches, they'll see us. If we call out for him or he calls out for us, they'll hear us. And if we look in the dark, it'll be like, well, looking for a missing head in a dark forest, won't it?"

"Maybe it's not down there at all." Even Dullard's usually relentless optimism sounded flat. "Perhaps we will be fortunate and find it landed close to the edge."

"Well, there's only one person who knows." Flirt turned back to Shoulders's rather limp-looking body. "Oi!" She tapped him firmly on the chest. "Pay attention." Her hand reached out and caught his, bringing it up to briefly touch her face before she reached out and rapped her own fingers against the side of his neck.

"Where's your head?" she added, apparently for her own emphasis. "Point!" She caught his hand and isolated his forefinger, hauling it back and forth melodramatically. "Where's your head, Shoulders?"

He shook his hand free. For an instant, Fodder wondered if they were about to witness the true horror of a silent paddy but yet again, it seemed, Flirt had managed to make herself understood. After a moment's contemplation, Shoulders's right hand reached out and pointed down in the direction of the valley.

Pleasance snorted. "So much for fortune! I suppose if I suggest we leave him—"

"We'll politely but firmly tell you to shut up," Flirt interrupted. "Tempting as it may be, we can't, can we? Aside from anything else, we can't forget we owe him for finding that trap at the beach."

Pleasance's mouth snapped shut. With a reluctant sigh, she pulled herself to her feet. "Don't expect me to scramble through brambles in the dark!" she exclaimed haughtily. "I don't even like him!"

"Really? I couldn't tell; you hide it so well, don't you?" Flirt was peering into the darkness, her practicality setting in. "Dullard, can you take us to where you saw the camp? I'd like to get a look myself."

It was a short walk up a slope of rock to the edge of the wooded valley below. And as Dullard had said, a cluster of pavilions illuminated by lantern and torchlight lay nestled in a small clearing right at its heart. White-robed Priests wandered in the light, bustling, carrying boxes and bundles of cloth in and out of the largest pavilion present. To Fodder's eyes, they looked remarkably busy for an evening in a camp in waiting. The reaction of Shoulders's body, his tapping on their shoulders and waving of hands, also suggested he too was aware they were not alone.

And around them, as true night set in, the trees shadowed all that lay beneath them into solid darkness.

Fodder sighed, his own dismay fighting the now pressing urge in his nether regions as he stared from the light to the darkness. An idea popped into his head.

"Tell you what," he said matter-of-factly. "I am absolutely dying for a ruddy pee. Why don't I nip in there to sort myself out and see how it is getting around while I'm at it? That way, we'll at least know if searching without light is practical."

In the dark, he couldn't clearly see Flirt's face, but he could feel the look she was giving him. "Not a bad plan," she said. "Even if it did come with too much information."

"I think it was the tarn that did it."

"Still too much."

"Plus the drink I had climbing the mountain…"

"Just get on with it, will you?"

Fodder did. And only a few steps into the forest told him that searching like this would not only be impractical, but near impossible. The slope of the forest floor towards the bottom of the valley was steep, the footing uneven, full of holes and roots and brambles, and the trees shaded even the hints of moonlight from view, as well as offering face-height branches as an incentive not to proceed. After travelling perhaps twenty yards into the murky woodland tangle, Fodder found himself resting against a tree, broken branches scattered at his feet as he found one brief, vaguely flat spot in which to take care of business. Fumbling downwards, he breathed out as a familiar trickling sound brought relief.

"That's better," he murmured.

"I know you like taking the piss, Fodder, but this is daft."

Fodder yelled. He couldn't help it; it came with the violent start and the rapid fumble to conceal certain aspects of his actions a moment before back in the safety of his trousers.

"Oi! Ssshhh!" The familiar-voiced reprimand came from above. "Don't you know there's a camp full of the enemy down there? Why do you think I didn't call out when I heard some great oaf crashing towards me?"

His dignity—what remained of it—safely retrieved, Fodder looked up, scarcely believing what he was hearing, for no, there was no way that they could get this lucky…

It was hard to see, barely a hint of moonlight skittering through the canopy. But yes, about three yards above his head, he could see a roundish shape dangling from leather strands where it had lodged in the grip of a branch. It appeared to be swinging gently back and forth.

"Shoulders?" he hissed. "Shoulders, is that you?"

There was an unmistakable huff. "No, it's Doom the bloody Dark Lord. Who d'you *think* it is?"

"Are you all right?"

"Let me see." There was an unmistakable edge to Shoulders's tone that told Fodder this had been the wrong question. "I had my head ripped off by a psychotic Barmaid, who shoved me in a pack and didn't bother to close it properly. My head then fell out of said pack and tumbled through mid-air at some speed where I whacked into some foliage and got stuck up a tree, with a twig jammed up my left nostril. And while you lot beat my body up and pushed it around, my head was left hanging from said tree by a few strips of leather right above a slope that, if I fall and my head rolls down, will see me land up right smack in the middle of an enemy camp. How do you ruddy *think* I am?" The words were a fierce hiss. *"Get me down."*

Fodder bent down. "Okay. Hang on."

"Are you trying to be bloody funny?"

Ignoring the retort, Fodder rooted at his feet until his hand fixed upon what felt like a broken branch. Fortunately, it wasn't very damp, a fact for which he could only be grateful.

"Here." He lofted the branch above his head and snaked it, as best he could in the darkness, towards his friend's dangling skull. "Can you get your teeth in this?"

"That depends if you peed on it."

"Course I didn't." Fodder couldn't be entirely certain this was true, but this was no time to quibble.

"Why don't you climb up and get me?"

"You're a long way out on that branch, mate. I don't think I could reach."

"Get Flirt or Dullard then! Someone who can climb?"

"You're not Flirt's favourite person after that grope, you know."

"And since she ripped my head off, she's not mine. Ow! That's the nose twig! Stop it!"

"Sshhh! They'll hear! Just get your teeth in!"

"The nose twig's in the way!"

"Stopping talking might help too. Get your teeth in it!"

"All right! Mmf!"

"Are you ready?"

"Mmmmmf!"

In hindsight, Fodder reflected, that had not been the best question to ask, given that *mmmmmf* could have as easily stood for *no* as well as *yes*. But hindsight was like that. It provided common sense when it was already too late.

"Here we go!" And Fodder yanked.

There was a desperate, muffled screech. The shape of the dangling head, nose twig and all, went catapulting off into the down-sloping darkness. A hint of something round and shiny bounced in the cradle of light that washed the clearing below.

Fodder paused. He stared at the dark branch. He stared down at the distant hint of clearing. He sighed.

That was the thing about having a talent for finding the worst in any situation. It never let you down.

* * *

Ow.

Root.

Ow.

Rock.

Ow.

Branch, definitely.

Ow.

Root again.

Owwwww!

Nose twig!

As a man not unused to finding his helmet-clad head hurled at a rate of knots through dark foliage, Shoulders was able to endure the dizzy, bouncing ride of his tumbling head with the resigned practicality of an experienced Disposable. And it did give him time to come up with a myriad of ways to beat up Fodder. The moment he was sure he was in range of his fists…

Teeth in the bloody stick! Pillock!

Ow.

Another root.

Ow.

Another branch.

O… Not ow.

Canvas? Light?

Bollocks.

His head was skidding, skimming his way across a slope not of rock but of material. Glimpses of white canvas and taut guy ropes intermingled with dark sky illuminated by a well of flickering torchlight. Hurriedly, he clicked his brain out of vengeful thoughts and took instant stock—canvas meant tent, tent meant camp, camp meant buggered. *Don't be seen.*

On tent roof. *Don't fall off.*

His head was going down, he could feel it, spinning over and over, down into the ball of light filled with bustling figures that would chuck his head in a locked box and store it under the biggest pile of junk they could find forevermore, if they had the chance. *Must stop fall, must stop fall, must stop fall...*

Teeth.

Lips touched rope. Shoulders bit down.

He stopped cold.

There was a breathless pause. Thankfully, somewhere along the line, he'd parted company with that ruddy nose twig, which made the necessity of breathing through his nostrils that bit easier. But it was difficult to take further stock given that his brain felt like someone had taken a whisk to it and his vision was a spinning blur of light and darkness, splashed with white canvas and a hint of treetops that undulated in front of his eyes...

Slowly, queasily, the world drifted back into focus. It tasted strongly of guy rope and looked mostly like canvas as the white roof and flickering pennant of a pavilion solidified before his eyes. Somewhere below and behind, he could hear voices, though thankfully no one was shouting "Look, a severed head's trying to eat our tent!" for the moment, at least. But the angle at which he had caught this fortuitous rope gave him almost no peripheral view of where the action sounded to be, and that, he felt, was likely to be a bit of a bugger.

He needed to know his situation. Could they see the back of his helmeted head if they happened to look up, or was he safe and snuggled out of view? It was times like this he really missed his neck. For how the hell was he supposed to turn his head without it?

Oh blimey. He'd have to adjust with his teeth.

Was it even possible? He'd never tried it. He knew his teeth to be reliable in such situations—he'd had to chew his way out of many a roadside bramble before now—but they weren't known for their manoeuvrable qualities. But he was potentially exposed and, thanks to Fodder's moment of stupid, alone again and he'd be buggered if he was going to hang here by his teeth and wait to get caught.

Right.

Don't let go the grip you've got. Just try and grip a bit higher...

Bloody hell! This is dental contortion!

Using only the corner of his mouth, Shoulders snapped at the guy rope, missing, slipping as he munched and chewed at it, and damn, it hurt, but yes! A grip!

His head shifted position. And there, in the extremes of his peripheral vision, he saw a blurry imprint of a torchlit clearing, of another pavilion as a white-robed figure with a great pile of something or other heaped in his arms staggered outside.

He was in full view. One glance up and it was box time.

Joy.

What else could go wrong?

Someday, somewhere, Shoulders was sure, someone would manage to say or think that toxic sentence and not end it in twice as much doo-doo as they started. But today was not that day.

For at that moment, his teeth, his good, strong teeth, straining under the painful pressure, decided they no longer had the will to hold on.

He tried to stop it, tried to gnash his way to new purchase, but it was too late. Suddenly, he was tumbling again, the world spiralling as he struck the edge of the pavilion and went spinning into empty air before landing—ow! Rope!—against one of the supporting lines. It twanged as he bounced against it and sent him twirling like a football over the dirt floor, spinning again—oh Gods, more spinning—and was that the inside of the tent looming towards him?

It was.

And apparently the flap was lifted a little, for he bounced unimpeded past the canvas wall onto the rug floor beyond—ow! Carpet burn!—rolling and tumbling in a blur of colour. Something hard struck his chin—ow! Wood!—and suddenly he was in shadow, spinning in a circle on the spot as he came to rest against canvas once more.

Oh bloody hell. Now where—?

"Did something fly in here?"

The female voice rolled through the air like a sharpened blade, every corner of every word crisp and precise and carved like an Artisan's craftsmanship, honed to perfection. It was a voice born to be heard by a Narrative, and from the rich unnaturalness of its tone, maybe already had.

"Dinna see, meself, Your Highness." The voice that replied, by contrast, was born to remain forever out of Narrative earshot. Shoulders wasn't entirely familiar with the specific speaker, but even if he hadn't caught the tang of pixie dust in the air, he knew a pixie voice when he heard one. "Could you please keep yon head of yours still for me? We dinna want any mistakes. Raising cheekbones ain't all that easy."

"If I must." There was an elegant sigh. "It feels most abominable to me to enter The Narrative using any face but my own, but the Taskmaster calls and, as ever, I shall answer."

"Aye, Your Highness. Now, if you dinna mind, I need yon face still. You can talk again when I work on yon hair of yours."

Another sigh, this one of melancholic resignation, followed. "I suppose, as needs must. But her hair too—it's so *wild*. I'm not sure how I shall cope with it."

"Your Highness, please?" There was an unmistakable plaintiveness to the pixie's tone. "I ain't done a full face job like this before, not to such a specific pattern. I need to concentrate."

"Very well." Silence finally fell. The air gleamed pink.

Once more, Shoulders's blurred vision began to congeal back into decent sight. Much to his immediate relief, he found the wooden item he had struck had been the leg of what seemed quite an elaborate bed and that he was nestled down in the shadows beneath it, against the tent's rear edge. The pavilion beyond it was brightly lit—he could not see but could only assume it was by lanterns hanging from the beams. On the opposite side of it, he could make out the legs and rim of what appeared to be a dressing table with a fancy-looking chair placed before it and a fancy-looking pair of very female legs wrapped loosely in a silk dressing gown that draped down to the rich rugs of the floor. Pink sparkles laced the air as a busy, winged shadow flitted across the floor, a marker of the pixie above.

Pink? The entirely unsafe memory of Flirt's pink-dusted, overinflated Narrative bosom flashed across Shoulders's mind. *Must be Urk, the one who does cosmetic stuff. Guess whoever she is needs a touch-up.*

Somewhere far above, Shoulders felt a hand land on his body. It felt more substantial than anything Flirt, Dullard, or Pleasance was likely to offer up and, as a result, Shoulders took great pleasure in lashing out with his fist.

Contact with something bruisable was definitely made. That was satisfying.

Bloody Fodder and his bloody stick...

But the poking was beginning again, the chopping at his neck, the request to guide them to the head Fodder had bloody lost, and so he pointed and then hands were hauling him down a slope and roots and brambles tangled round his sightless legs.

Oi! Careful, you buggers, don't rip me to shreds!

But they were on their way. Maybe, just maybe, a blazing miracle would occur and he'd get out of this unboxed...

Wait. This was them he was talking about. No chance.

Well, what could he do but sit here and wait? His jaw and teeth, the only possibilities for mobility, were off the ground and he had no chance of rocking himself over. Heaven help him, his friends were the only chance he had.

I'm doomed.

But at least I'm out of sight. Surely things can't get any—

"My Lady Vanity? May I come in?"

Someday. Someday I'll learn to stop thinking these things...

For there was no mistaking that voice. After recent events, the tones of Strut, the Taskmaster's taskmaster, were etched on his brain under *avoid at all costs.*

"Do come in." The distinctly regal voice, apparently the Lady Vanity, intoned.

There was a pixie sigh. "Your *Highness.* I said *don't move.*"

Strut's stick-thin legs came into view beyond the edge of the bed. "How goes it?"

"It would go better if yon Highness would *stop moving.*" There was an openly tetchy edge to the pixie's voice.

"You only have a few more hours before the scene." Strut's riposte was like a sword thrust. "Work faster."

"This be difficult and delicate work!" was the irritable response. "Constructing a full new face from a rough sketch..."

"That sketch was painted by the finest Artisan artist before this Quest began." There was a steely edge to Strut's languid voice. "Alas, it was never designed to be perfect, but it is all we have. And believe me, if I could drag the original in here for you to work from, I would. Unfortunately, she isn't...available." The brittleness of his tone melted into syrup. "And we must show our gratitude to the Lady Vanity for so willingly stepping into the breach yet again in our hour of need."

"I am always ready and willing to do my Narrative duty." Lady Vanity's crisp tone rang with smug. "And whilst this role may prove rather more challenging than my previous ones, I'm sure I can rise to it admirably."

"I am aware, of course, that this may prove...difficult for you." There was a catch in Strut's tone. "Fulfilling your Narrative duty in a romantic capacity whilst a married woman, especially given the gulf in your relative maturity..."

"I'm sure I can manage. And my husband understands, as all of true blood do, that Narrative needs must come first." Lady Vanity sniffed. "I will confess, though, when you came to me with this plan, I was surprised you hadn't chosen one of those eager little princesses-in-waiting we have around the palace. They would have made a closer match in age."

"I considered it," Strut conceded stiffly. "But the necessity of facial reconstruction would not have sat as well with them, whilst with you, it should hopefully take care of any overt signs that you are older, if you'll forgive me, than perhaps you should be. Besides..." Shoulders saw one heel of his elaborate shoes dig furiously into the carpet. "Under the circumstances, I felt it prudent to place a more experienced hand at the wheel in case of...interference."

"Is that likely?" Lady Vanity's tone sounded professionally curious.

"It's possible." There was a hint, just a hint of acid beneath Strut's tone. "Although, the last we saw of them"—with this word, the hint of acid became a surge—"they were some distance from here and unaware that we have found a way to continue without what they've taken. But, with the crucial importance of the Dragon rescue to the plot, we must be ready for anything."

The Dragon rescue? Shoulders felt a surge of alarm as a bell rang in the back of his head. *That was the scene that was so important, wasn't it, their chance to put things right and ours to wreck it properly? But I thought they couldn't do it without the princess.*

"Oops!" There was a flutter of wings as a piece of paper slipped from where it had apparently been resting on the dressing table, coming to rest on the carpet not far from the bed. Shoulders caught only a quick glimpse of the words WEDDING NOTICE and a pair of rough sketches of what were recognisably the faces of Prince Dullard and Princess Pleasance, before a knobbly, winged little figure swooped down and scooped it back up out of sight. And Shoulders recognised it at once, for hadn't the kingdom been plastered with them, notices announcing the wedding of Princess Islaine to Tretaptus of Mond, as a setup to The Narrative?

Uh. Oh.

The alarm bells in Shoulders's head were ringing up a cacophony. For unless, for some sick reason, they were grafting Dullard's features onto an elegant ex-Heroine...

They're replacing the princess. They're slapping her face on some other posh bitch and sending her out to snog Bumpkin instead!

But why would they do that? Maybe Pleasance was making all the right noises to his friends and that gullible sap Dullard, but Shoulders was so sure she'd go running back if The Narrative called, that she was playing them and surely Strut would know that...

Unless—and it was a tough thought to settle into his suspicious brain—she'd been telling the *truth*.

Oh, bloody hell. That was a prospect that would take some getting used to.

And as for why he'd have to...

A part of Shoulders was chuckling inwardly at the thought of Pleasance, with her airs and graces and sense of her own irreplaceable superiority, being shunted unceremoniously out of the picture by a lookalike. But at the same time, with the Ring neutered by whatever

Magus had done, the princess was the only bargaining tool they had, the only thing keeping them safe from Narrative slaughter if the worst came to the worst. And if, as she'd claimed—yep, definitely going to be a tough thought, that one—she'd been outed as a traitor to Strut, he'd know she'd be a danger to The Narrative rather than an asset. If the Taskmaster didn't need her anymore...

Okay. Now we're all buggered. Screwed. Doomed. Arse-over-tit. Up the bleeding sewer and down the creek of shi—

"Out of curiosity," the precise tones of the Lady Vanity cut into Shoulders's doom-laden musing. "If they do show themselves, what do you plan on doing with them?"

This was a question that Shoulders was eager to hear answered. He strained his ears for Strut's reply.

And when it came, the alarm bells rang another echoing peal; for Strut, for all his tight control and professional distance, spoke with a near-terrifying undertone of relish.

"I have pondered that for quite some time. We are clearly far beyond simple dungeons, and with word spreading of their abominable actions, it has been decided our response must act as a deterrent to any possibility of a repeat." Shoulders could almost hear his teeth grinding. "I am also aware that my brethren and I are not employed for our imagination." He spoke it like a curse word. "So I have taken advice from a different source." He chuckled, the sound unnatural on his lips. "Poniard the Assassin may be a lunatic, but he is a lunatic with some very inventive ideas. An example will be made, a fate so terrible and permanent that no one will even contemplate defying the instructions and the Taskmaster again." The relish dripped from his voice. "I will make certain of it."

Oh. Shit.

Oh shit, oh shit, oh shitty, shittity, shit...

It would have been nice to tremble a bit. Even a good, neck-length gulp would have helped. But alas, such things were beyond a lone head, and his less-distant-than-it-had-been body, though trembling decently enough, was unable to give it the beans due to the sudden, concerned pokes of his friends.

You want to know why I'm trembling out there, you four? Because we're going to be a ruddy example, that's why! An inventive, permanent fate courtesy of a trained killer we earlier pissed off! And it's all of your bloody faults but mine!!!

"That sounds perfectly acceptable." Lady Vanity's tone was one of cool detachment. "How go the preparations for my first scene?"

"My colleague Primp is taking care of coaching Maw the Dragon. It does tend to take some time." Strut's tone was weary—clearly, like Shoulders, he'd talked to the dim ball of scales in the past. "And The Narrative has been summoned. In fact, I had best go to meet them soon. They cannot be far away."

"Of course." Lady Vanity's voice was pure dismissal. "You run along and, I suppose, we had better finish turning me into my cousin. Even the hair. Urk?"

"Aye, Your Highness?" The resigned tone was one of a pixie trying to pretend he hadn't been hovering for the last few minutes waiting for her to shut up so he could get on.

"Proceed, if you would be so good. We don't have much time until The Narrative will join us."

"Aye, Your Highness." Shoulders could tell that Urk was giving serious consideration to putting her ears on backwards. It was a shame he wasn't likely to go through with it.

"I will return soon, my lady," Strut's voice declared. "And it is a pleasure to work again with such a *professional.*"

"You're most welcome." At Urk's tut, he received a harsher one in return, but Vanity made no further noise. The scent of pixie dust filled the air.

Against the wellspring of vivid panic that was filling Shoulders's brain, he became aware that somewhere, not that far away by the feel of it, something with bark on it was being tapped against his hands.

Is that a branch? They're going to try to get me with a branch again? Is Fodder taking the piss?

He could feel Flirt's familiar poke for directions once more and automatically his fingers obliged by pointing. His hands were being placed over the apparent branch, and he could feel it being slid through his fingers, pushed forwards and then, just to his left, in the corner of his eye, the canvas edge of the tent bowed slightly.

More taps. Approval to go ahead, it seemed. *Yeah, fine, but to head righ...*

Sign language received, he saw the bow of the tent move clo closer until it stopped at his tap beside his head. A branch s carefully under the canvas and edged its way under the bed.

If he's peed on this, I swear...

Bark brushed past his nose. With a grimace, he dug his teeth in with his own hands pulled. His chin snagged for a moment on the can but after a bit of wriggling, his head slipped under the loosely-pegg side of the tent and out into the night. And Shoulders knew as his head clinging by its teeth to the branch, bumped along the dusty earth to the rear of the pavilion towards the shadowy figures in the deep, dark trees, that the following conversation was going to be less than fun. But one thing he was certain of.

He was going to start it with "I told you so."

* * *

"Vanity? *Vanity?*"

Voices were shushing her. Dimly, Pleasance could hear them, but the swelling fury of her indignant rage drowned out any desire she might have had to pay the slightest bit of attention.

"They dare...they *dare...*" The words were an infuriated splutter. "They dare to take my princess, my character, and give her to *Vanity?*"

"Pleasance, please." She was peripherally aware that Dullard had scurried over from where he had, a moment before, been making the finishing touches to re-securing Shoulders's head to his body. His voice was hushed and full of concern. "The camp and Maw's cave aren't that far away, and your voice does carry, rather..."

"I don't care if it does!" She could feel her nails digging into the skin of her palms. "I want her to hear me! I want her to see me! I want her to know it's me when I slap her fake, monstrous cheekbones right off her *smug face!*" She took a gasping breath. "I mean, *Vanity!* That self-satisfied, superior, cold-hearted bitch with her perfect locks that never tangle and her smouldering eyes and her bewitching smile! Twice! *Twice* she's been the glory girl, twice a Heroine while the rest of us sat waiting for her to clear her perfectly rounded backside out of our way so we could have our chance! And now, when it's my story and my glory, here she comes again, strutting in to steal my face and my plot for glory strike number three!" She gave a wild laugh. "*I* created Islaine! I worked on her, I honed her, I took what The Narrative gave me in that first moment and I made it real! She doesn't have that! What, does she think she can merely walk in there and…and…and busk?" She could feel the fury burning in the depths of her soul like wildfire because how dare she, she couldn't, she *couldn't, she couldn't!* "She'll *ruin* her! I told Strut and I'll tell her too, the selfish, thieving usurper! They can't take this away from me! *I* am the Heroine of this Quest! Islaine is *mine!*"

The words rang in the air for a moment, vibrating like an oncoming storm. She could feel her own body locked in a ball of furious tension, her fists screaming, her shoulders taut, her teeth clenched, and her eyes narrowed so as to focus the burning rage that shimmered out from behind them. And from beyond the circle of her anger, she could feel four incredulous stares fixed upon her.

"Wow." It was the irritant Shoulders, bringer of the foul tidings, who broke the ensuing silence. "And you lot reckon *I've* got issues?"

"Pleasance?" Oh damn and blast it, why did Dullard have to get involved? She *wanted* to be angry; with every fibre of her being, she wanted to rage and scream and throw the greatest tantrum known to man at the unfairness of it all, but she knew, she just knew that the moment Prince Dullard opened that ridiculous mouth of his, he was going to be all *reasonable* at her and she'd end up calming down. Couldn't he ever understand that sometimes she didn't want to be calm and reasonable?

"What?" she hissed. "And you'd better make it quick. I have a cousin to smack."

"It's only…" And he was doing the blasted eyes too. Why did he have to do those eyes? "I thought, from what you said to Strut, you didn't *want* to be Islaine anymore?"

And there it was. Sweet, unwavering reason. *Bastard.*

"Of course I don't want her!" she snapped in return, as much annoyed by the seeping away of her anger as by the question. "But that doesn't mean that *Vanity* can have her!" She swallowed hard, clinging to the dregs of her tirade, but she could feel the tension leaking from her body. Damn him. "When Strut threatened me, he said that I wasn't irreplaceable, but I won't accept that, I won't! And just because I don't want to be Islaine doesn't mean they can simply take her away and give her to someone else! They can't merely trot out someone wearing my face and pretend that everything will work perfectly! Islaine's *my* character and whether I use her or not is up to me! It's *my* choice to make! Not theirs!" She let out a loud huff of annoyance, irritated by the plaintive note that had slipped into her voice. "I will not be treated like I'm nothing! I will not be thrown aside as if I don't matter. I will not be used and discarded like I'm...*I'm...*"

"Disposable?" Fodder's voice was quiet but somehow the power behind it stopped her rant in its tracks.

And she stared at him. Stared at this plain-faced man in shabby armour, who was staring back at her with eyes filled to the brim with the very same emotions that were coursing through her veins: the same frustration, the same sense of injustice, the same helpless fury in the face of a choice ripped away and a life not lived as it deserved to have been. And for the first time, the very first time since that appalling Disposable had knocked her unconscious and dragged her into his mess, Pleasance felt the tiniest inkling of why it was he'd done it.

A hand came gently to rest against her shoulder. Dullard's. Of course it was.

"Now do you see?" he said softly.

Oh, he had to rub it in, didn't he? And he always had to do it so nicely. If he was smug about it, she had the comfort of resenting him without the guilt, but no, he always had to be reasonable.

She *hated* reasonable. It was the ruin of a good tantrum.

As was a well-placed inkling. Damn.

"Well, if the princess is done." It was Flirt who wallowed into the thickening silence. "Maybe we can decide what happens next, can't we?"

Fodder was staring down at the floor, his unremarkable features knotted in thought. "We can't let them replace the princess," he stated the remarkably obvious. "Shoulders was right. We'd be buggered."

"If we act, we have to act soon, don't we?" Flirt's chosen location for her thoughtful glare was the sky glittering darkly above the top of the wooded slope by which they stood. Her eyes broke off to scan the horizon. "Shoulders, did you say The Narrative is on its way?"

The damaged Disposable tried to nod, jerking his head sideways. He huffed and pushed it back. "Yep. Strut went off to meet it right before you pulled me out. He said the scene was due in a couple of hours."

"They'll probably be acting it out at Maw's cave," Dullard added. "Due to his limited intellect, they do tend to try and keep him to familiar locations where possible. Otherwise accidents might happen." He tutted. "Apparently, he sat on a castle once. The Artisans were most annoyed. They'd spent a lot of time on those battlements."

"This might not be so bad, you know." The Barmaid was tapping her lips in thought. "I mean, our original plan back in the Wild Forest was to ruin the Dragon scene, wasn't it? Maybe this is our chance to go back at that plan from another direction."

Fodder, unlike his friend, was successful in nodding his head. "That's not a bad idea. And I think I have a plan. I wonder how The Narrative would cope if it had *two* Islaines to choose from?"

Rampant alarm surged through Pleasance's body. Shaking free of Dullard's lingering hand, she stepped forward.

"No."

Shoulders the irritant fixed her with a look of disdain. "Do you ever say anything else?"

There was no way she would allow that to pass. "Hark who's talking!"

"Not now." Fodder sounded impatient as he intervened. "Pleasance, why not?"

How could these people possibly go through life being so dense? "I can't go into The Narrative." She spoke the words with mordant emphasis. "If I catch Bumpkin's eye, I'll be in love with him, and you promised me when I agreed to help you that you wouldn't let that happen!"

"Yeah, and much ruddy help you've been..." Shoulders muttered, but to Pleasance's secret glee, he cut off sharply when he saw her fists clench.

"*Shoulders.*" It was Flirt who cut in this time.

"Well, it's true." The pointless oaf didn't meet her eye. "What's she ever done for us, eh? She's more useless now than she was as a prisoner!"

"Surely even an idiot like you can understand this!" Pleasance fixed him with her best look of death; he flinched in a satisfactory manner, but his bullish expression did not retreat. "If I enter The Narrative, I risk becoming Islaine. And if I become Islaine, in spite of your clumsy efforts to stop it, the Quest can be completed."

Shoulders gave her a sarcastic glare. "I thought Islaine was *yours,*" he drawled. "Your precious bloody character? Why so scared of her?"

Pleasance fought to conceal the shiver of fear that ran through her blood by redoubling her menacing stare. Dullard's hand reappeared on her shoulder. How did he do it? How did he always know? "Islaine may be mine, but if I step into The Narrative, I'll be *hers.* And she belongs to Bumpkin. One loving look and I'll be lost."

"Yeah, but why would they want you?" Shoulders spread his hands. "They've got Vanity the professional to play Islaine." Dullard's hand tightened on her shoulder as her muscles tensed at the mention of that hated fact. "She's the one pillock-boy's going to be casting soppy looks at, not you. They probably won't even bother with you at all."

Pleasance couldn't quite decide what made her want to slap him more—the scarcely concealed reference that she had outlived her usefulness to both sides or the casual way he dismissed the greatest fear in her life. "You think I want to take that chance?" she retorted venomously. It was time for a more personal jab in return. "Do you want to go back into The Narrative? Given your ample success there thus far..."

Shoulders's face contorted with resentment. "At least I try," he snapped back. "And at least I've come up with some good ideas to get us out of this mess, even if you had to go all change-of-heart and scupper them! In fact..." His words broke off as a sudden look of realisation flashed over his face like a breaking dawn. Slowly, he began to smile.

"Oh yes," he whispered. "Oh yes, that's it."

Fodder and Flirt exchanged a look that reflected the confusion Pleasance was feeling. She exchanged a glance of her own with Dullard.

"Shoulders?" It was Fodder who spoke up first. "Shoulders, what...?"

The Disposable's eyes, when they fixed on his friend, were gleaming. "I've got it!" he exclaimed. "I know what we can do! Why do we need another plan at all? The one we had before works just as well." He beamed beatifically. "Let's feed a princess to the Dragon! Let's get the Heroine killed!"

It took a couple of seconds, over the swell of fear, indignation, and rage rising in Pleasance's chest, for her to realise exactly what the appalling man was saying. And it took Dullard a few moments longer.

"Shoulders," he admonished, as sternly as he ever could. "We have an agreement with Pleasance and..."

"Oh, not her!" Shoulders waved a dismissive hand. "She's been replaced, what does she matter?" Even over the slowly growing hint of gleeful satisfaction, Pleasance allowed herself a snap of rage at this slight. But the foul Disposable ignored her glare and plugged on. "No, I mean we knock off the *new* Heroine. We take down *Vanity.*" His grin was malicious, but in this case, Pleasance found it forgivable. "Think about it. The Quest loses its Heroine, Bumpkin loses his love interest, and The Narrative loses the plot. I get the great pleasure of seeing a princess get mashed up and we don't break Dullard's precious ruddy deal with the princess we've got." He stuck both thumbs into the air. "It's win-win!"

Mental images rampaged through Pleasance's head: happy, happy pictures of Vanity, selfish, smug, over-exposed Vanity the experienced Heroine of choice getting stomped on, battered, and chewed by the Dragon they had once threatened to set on her. She had to admit, it was an image to savour.

The death of a princess. The death of the Heroine. The death of Islaine.

Islaine would be gone. Her perfect princess, her character, her chance, destroyed forever, never to be known in the way she knew her, never to live in the way she'd planned. *I will never be Islaine.*

A part of her felt relief. But another, deeper part wanted to scream and keep on screaming.

I will never be Islaine. I will never be Islaine. I will never be Islaine. I will never be Bumpkin's.

Stop it!

Internally, she gave herself a firm slap. Bumpkin was the price she'd pay for Islaine to live. Her life would be with him. Forever.

No. She didn't want Islaine. She didn't. She'd said so. She *didn't want Islaine.*

Did she?

Dullard's hand against her shoulder seemed to burn.

"Are you all right?" he whispered.

Her fists had clenched again. She hadn't even noticed.

She did not look at him. "Fine," she retorted. But the feel of his eyes against her face told her he hadn't been fooled.

"I know this will be hard for you." Why, oh why, was he still speaking? "It'll be the end of a childhood's worth of dreams. But it will be worth it." She sensed his smile. "You'll be *free.*"

Free. Her breath rasped in her throat. *Free?*

Abandoning all that she'd ever wanted was being free?

Can I do that? Am I ready?

But echoing in the silence of her mind, there was no answer.

"I hate to admit it, don't I?" Beyond Pleasance's bubble of mental maelstrom, the conversation was moving on without her. Flirt spoke up. "But that's not a bad idea. Even if we can't get the Dragon to do it, they're bound to have her trapped or trussed up or something so Bumpkin can rescue her. If we get in quick, one of us could quickly knock her off ourselves."

"It needs to be irreversible," Fodder reminded her. "Stab wounds can be healed. And it'll be risky. We don't know if we can rely on the Ring to escape after what happened at the Place of the Quickening."

"That was cheating," Dullard reiterated. His hand remained clamped to Pleasance's shoulder, a disconcerting comfort. "They shouldn't have been able to do it and deep inside, I imagine they know that. If we can shake their belief enough, make them realise they can't stop you, I think you can get use of the Ring back."

Shoulders blew out, puffing his cheeks and jerking his head slightly sideways. "That's a bugger of a thing to try out on the fly."

"Do we have a choice?" Flirt pointed out. "The Narrative isn't far off, is it? We don't have time to set up anything elaborate."

Fodder nodded. "Let's get over to Maw's cave and take a look around. Maybe we'll get a chance to talk to Maw again."

"Do you have a sledgehammer?" Shoulders said mordantly. "Because that's what it'll take to hammer a new idea into that scaly pillock's head in the time we have left."

"We'll work something out, won't we?" Flirt shouldered her pack. "Come on. Let's get moving."

Dullard's hand remained on Pleasance's shoulder, guiding her round as she absently followed her companions towards the dreaded Dragon's lair. But this time, it wasn't she who was in danger. It was Vanity. It was Islaine.

Islaine was going to die.

And there, nagging at the back of her mind more than ever before, lurked the question, the question that had plagued her since she'd bitten Dullard on the nose and faced her own fears in a ruined city, since she had struck a deal of protection with her kidnappers and faced Strut on that beach, the question she lived in both anticipation and terror of knowing the answer to.

If Islaine is gone, what happens when it's only me?

And the most frightening thing of all was she could almost see an answer.

* * *

"So, what do you think Strut meant by 'inventive' and 'permanent'?"

Fodder had to admit that the most alarming part of Flirt's sentence was the undertone of uncertainty. It wasn't something he associated with his practical, confident friend. And if he were honest, he had been avoiding thinking about that particular aspect of Shoulders's revelation that the stakes had, in some mysterious fashion, been upped. It wasn't the kind of prospect one wanted on one's mind on the eve of a potentially defenceless face-off with The Narrative.

"It depends, I guess." He rested his head against the rock behind which they had crouched. They were waiting quietly for Dullard to return from his scouting mission along the edge of the cliff top that separated the tarn they had landed in from the head of the Perilous Pass, trying to get a look at Maw the Dragon and his cave. A little way away, visible in the light of the newly risen and presumably needed moon,

Pleasance was staring up at the starry sky with a notable absence. Nearby, Shoulders was fiddling with the leather bindings on his reattached head. "If it's from Poniard, I guess it must be something...physical." His mind baulked from a plethora of possibilities. "Some kind of lifelong torture maybe?" He sighed. "But that seems stupid. Everyone knows about us, and something like that would horrify everybody. Would people stand for it?"

"Depends how much we've upset them, doesn't it?" Flirt's expression was grimly wry by the pale moonlight. "And how scared they are of joining us. Strut did say it was a deterrent, didn't he?"

Fodder felt an odd glow of emotion, part pride, part satisfaction, and part raw, unfiltered terror in the centre of his heart. "That's one thing to be pleased about. If they've had to come up with a special punishment for us, we must have the Taskmaster scared."

"The Taskmaster's scared. *Whoop-de-do.*" Shoulders's sardonic voice drifted into their conversation. "When I'm being tortured in terrible, permanent agony, I'll take that as a comfort, shall I?"

"Shoulders—" Flirt started, but the Disposable cut her off sharply.

"No, you can sod off with your dismissive tone!" he retorted harshly. "I never wanted to get involved in this crud in the first place but no, you two said it'll be fine! As long as people find out what we're doing and why, you said, they can't touch us! But now look! People know and because they know, we're not safe at all, are we? We're going to be a bloody *example.*" He shifted himself awkwardly round so he could glare at them. "All you've done is make things worse!"

"If you wish to change your underpants, please find another rock to do it behind." Pleasance's voice was terse. "I have no wish to bear witness."

"Mock all you like," Shoulders retorted as he dropped back against the rock, directing his comments as best he could in her direction. "But you remember, miss high-and-mighty, you've been replaced; you're not standing on that safe Principal high ground anymore, you're down in the dirt with the rest of us! What they do to us, they'll probably do to you too!"

Pleasance's head whipped sharply round as she stared at him. Her eyes filled with horror. "But...they wouldn't dare!" she stammered. "I'm a princess, I'm Royalty, I'm—"

"Fired?" Shoulders said the word with relish.

"It's not going to happen, is it?" Fodder was grateful for Flirt's firm intervention. "Because we're going to kill off that new princess, ruin the Quest, and get our point across. They can't touch us after that."

"Or we'll kill off the new princess, ruin the Quest, and be arrested and hauled off for punishment," Shoulders replied with grim fervour. "You really think the Taskmaster's going to care about a bloody thing we have to say after we've ruined the precious Quest? For all we know, this punishment thing might be coming straight down from on high!"

There was an ominous silence. The unpleasant doubts that had surged through Fodder's mind after his encounter with the Gods returned in a rush. What if Shoulders and his own suspicions were right? What if the Taskmaster simply didn't care? What were they supposed to do then, other than give up and take their punishment? For without the Taskmaster's agreement to change, what hope was there?

Fodder felt his jaw tighten as he saw flash across his mind's eye the deluded faces of the planted Gods, Preen's dismissive treatment of him and his friends, Gruffly's battle with himself and the ignorance of his kindred and the fear written on Pleasance's face when she realised that for all her privileged existence, she was as disposable as the rest of them.

No. It wasn't fair.

And he would be damned if he was going to give up because they'd been threatened, for the first time, with a fate worse than boredom. There were so many people who didn't even know or understand the horror of what had been done to them—how could he stop before he'd found a way to help? He'd come this far, and while he still had hope, he would try. If he had to force the Taskmaster to listen to him, he would find a way. And even if he had to go down, he wouldn't go without a fight; he would take this damned Quest down with him...

Oh yes. He'd give them an *example*.

Because maybe they'd been able to hush up whatever strange disaster had occurred within *The Chalice of Quickening*, to hide that away, suppress it, and make everyone but the traumatised Courtiers forget. But he'd make certain that, for whatever reason, no one would ever forget *The Ring of Anthiphion*.

Determination flooded through him to the depths of his bones. He was going to do this. He was going to do it. He *was*.

And all he needed now was one chance and...

"Fodder!"

Fodder started as Dullard appeared beside him, his sword drawn and his face flushed in the silver light. Flirt was half-up in an instant at these signs of combat, her own hand flying to her sword hilt.

"It's fine!" Dullard was quick to whisper a hurried reassurance, his hands, including the sword-bearing one, held out in a placatory fashion. "There was a little trouble, but I've taken care of it. In fact..." He beamed. "We may have had a piece of good fortune. Come and see!"

They did. At Dullard's instigation, they kept their heads low as they followed him across the rugged, scrubby terrain towards the cliff edge below where, Fodder presumed, Maw's cave must be located.

"Over here!" Dullard waved them towards a nearby clump of rock. "You see, I was scouting to try and find Maw, as we said, but unfortunately I could see my uncle Primp was with him and doesn't look likely to leave until The Narrative comes. I think they've learned their lesson there." He glanced over his shoulder as he dropped into the shadow of the outcrop. "I was about to leave when I came across *these* gentlemen."

Gentlemen? Even as Fodder opened his mouth to ask, his eyes focused on a shadowy lump he had taken for further rock and found instead a moon-washed huddle of four figures: three bulkier ones in chain mail and one, more slender, wearing a dark scruffy wig and a dreadful doublet-and-ruff arrangement that even Bard the Minstrel would think twice about. As a collective, they seemed groggy, bound firmly with a length of chain and gagged securely with the ripped remains of their own surcoats, their battered livery the familiar colours of Sleiss. They also wore the sheepish look of men who had seen Dullard's gangly limbs, effusive manner, and polite smile and taken him for a pushover. Fodder knew the look well; he'd once worn it himself.

And as he stared at their outfits, at their build, at the bad wig, a suspicion began to form in the back of his mind. *I think I see where this is going...*

Dullard continued smiling. "Don't worry, nobody saw or heard us fighting—I waited until Maw was practising his roaring before I made myself known. And it didn't take long. They don't appear to be fully trained Disposables—I suspect Strut merely grabbed the nearest four persons of suitable size and shape that he could find."

Fodder stared down at them, his suspicions hardening by the second. "Where'd you find them? And where did you get the chain from?"

"Do you recall that crevice we hid in the last time we were here? The one the Merry Band chased us up?"

Fodder did. Vividly. Most particularly, he remembered the moment when his foot had stepped into empty air and sent him plunging into the nothingness of the dwarf tunnel.

"Yeah," he replied with great restraint.

Dullard nodded obliviously. "Well, it's over there and that's where they were waiting. They had the chain with them, and I took advantage of it once I'd knocked them out. Presumably it was to enhance their role."

"Their role?" Shoulders was squinting down at the foursome with a distinct air of alarm. "Who're they supposed to be?"

Dullard shrugged. "I would have thought that was obvious. They're meant to be us."

Fodder's suspicions scurried into fact. Flirt's expression darkened. "One of those beefy lads is meant to be *me*? That's flattering, isn't it?"

Shoulders's face, however, took on an edge of alarm. "They've replaced us? What, are they going to send out some second-rate substitutes to knock us off?"

Pleasance gave him a sharp glance. "Not a nice feeling, is it? Being *replaced.*"

Luckily, Dullard intervened before the inevitable snipe match could commence. "That wouldn't be practical. Aside from the fact they aren't much of a likeness, I imagine Strut would know killing us off would only make it worse for the credibility of the Quest when we make our inevitable reappearance. They can pass a spare Islaine off as a fake if Pleasance is seen, but all of us? No." He tapped his chin. "I suspect they are simply meant to be the back of our heads, fleeing like cowards out of Narrative as we abandon the lovely and helplessly chained-up new Islaine to a dragon's jaws." He hefted his sword. "And I don't know about you, but I think I fancy playing my own role."

It was a way in. Fodder knew that Dullard was right. They were expected to be there, and no one would look too carefully at the faces until it was too late, not with a princess to rescue…

Perfect.

"How long have we got?" he said.

"Not long." It was Flirt who answered, gesturing back towards the Perilous Pass. "Look what's coming."

It was a sense rather than something visible, an area of blackness somehow blacker, its stars brighter as it rumbled its way towards them. The Narrative had arrived.

"Let's move." Fodder turned to where Pleasance was watching. It was odd, but just for a moment, against the backdrop of the Narrative sky, with her pale, moonlit face, she looked somehow smaller than she had before. "I assume you don't want to come with us?"

She nodded. "You assume right."

"Okay." Fodder glanced at the prisoners for a moment before shifting his gaze to where Shoulders was staring down at his counterfeit with a look on his face that only an old friend would recognise. "Shoulders, you stay here too."

The look on his fellow Disposable's face flashed briefly past relief before settling on indignation. "You're making me stay with *her*?"

There was a game to be played here and Fodder was prepared, in lieu of his friend's still-unclaimed smug, to give him the dignified escape from this Narrative encounter that his eyes were yearning for. "Someone has to," he replied brusquely. "No offence, princess, but I don't think we want to be leaving you alone at the moment; and no offence, Shoulders, but I'm going to need Dullard and Flirt. You two can take the packs and wait and watch in that crevice in case we need to make a quick run for it. Okay?"

Shoulders crossed his arms, but his expression wasn't as fierce as it could have been. "Are you saying I can't do it?"

"No, I'm saying I need you here." Kind as he was trying to be, Fodder only had so much time for ego-salving. "Shoulders, you pull Flirt's pack on and, Pleasance, you take Dullard's. That way if we have to run, we'll have our stuff."

"Oh! That reminds me!" Dullard sheathed his sword and rummaged in his belt pouch. "I only remembered after a near miss in the fight—I still have this!" Glittering in the moonlight, the crystal flower almost seemed to glow as he pulled it free. "I was going to put it in my pack but with climbing equipment and my books, there are so many hard edges that might damage it. Does anyone have anywhere soft where we could…"

"Here." With an odd look of irritation, Flirt snatched the crystal flower from his grasp and grabbed her pack back from Shoulders. After a moment's exploration, she pulled free a piece of brown cloth that looked vaguely familiar.

And Fodder wasn't the only one to think so. By the moonlight, Shoulders was squinting at it too. "Flirt," he said curiously. "Is that your apron?"

Flirt slowly wrapped up the flower, wearing an expression that implied this was a subject she had hoped would not come up. "Yes."

Shoulders's hint of a grin was risky. "You still have your apron?"

"Yes." This time the threat in Flirt's voice was not concealed. She pushed the apron-wrapped flower back inside and carefully secured the buckle.

But Shoulders foolishly pressed on. "Want to pull me a pint?"

Flirt's expression was deadly as she shoved the pack into Shoulders's waiting hands. "Shut up, Shoulders."

"The Narrative's almost here." Luckily, Dullard prevented the slaughter with his intervention. He fingered the dreadful ruff he had liberated from his impersonator and pulled it on with palpable reluctance. "We'd better hurry."

They moved as quickly as they dared down the dark crevice nearby, taking great care to avoid the open hole that had earlier provided a bruising downfall. Ahead, the plateau before Maw's cave opened out up the slope before them: they caught glimpses of scurrying Priests and Courtiers rushing out of sight as the air around them thickened. Maw himself, his expression one of intense concentration, was backing into his cave with Primp at his side; and ahead, at the plateau's centre, an up-thrusting spire of rock had been fashioned to which was chained, with a carefully arranged expression of terror on her face, a wistful, moon-washed Pleasance lookalike in artfully shredded robes.

"Ha!" Pleasance's expression was deeply indignant. "Look at her hamming it up. And she doesn't look a bit like me!"

Privately, Fodder had been reflecting it was a fairly close likeness, but he chose not to break it to the already furious princess. "You two get out of sight," he said to her and Shoulders instead. "In case someone—"

"Hey! Fake enemies! Where are you?"

Shoulders and Pleasance darted as one into the fortunately not-hole-shaped shadows behind the lump of rock that had concealed them the last time they had been there. A white-robed Priest, whose voice Fodder recognised as the one who had spoken to Thud in the dwarf tunnels, peeked his head around the crevice's edge. Dullard and Flirt both ducked their heads, recognising at once that Fodder's all-purpose face was far better for the job of Priest-repelling than their own, more distinctive offerings.

"We're here, mate," Fodder responded with appropriate ease. "Are we up?"

"Of course you are!" the Priest snapped. "The Narrative's almost here! Get out there and pretend to be chaining the princess!" He hesitated a moment, causing Fodder's nerves to flutter. He saw both Dullard and Flirt's hands edging for their swords. "Wait," he said curiously. "There should be four of you. Where's the other one?"

Fodder thought quickly, and recent events gave him what he needed. "Think he went for a piss, mate. He should be back in a minute, though, if—"

"We don't have a minute!" the Priest huffed, glancing anxiously over his shoulder at the thickening darkness. "We'll have to do it with just the three! Now move!"

The Priest vanished out of sight. Fodder glanced at Flirt and Dullard and nodded.

"Ready for this?"

They nodded in return. Fodder risked one glance back to where Pleasance and Shoulders were peering out from behind their rocky concealment and then, with the prince and Barmaid at his side, he stepped out of the crevice, up the slope, and into the open.

And it felt insane. He knew people would be watching—the Priests most likely, and certainly Strut—and he could feel The Narrative and the Merry Band it carried so close as to be tangible. Like his two friends, he kept his head ducked, but a part of him was waiting for the cry, the "That's them!" and hands rushing to stop them, but it didn't come. For, after all, as Fodder knew himself, when it came to a Quest, who ever looked closely at the little people?

You'd really think they'd learn.

The rock pinnacle loomed and as they got closer, Fodder could see a few subtle differences between Pleasance and her face-grafted cousin—a slightly fuller figure, a tad more height, and the odd slant of features that didn't quite sit comfortably. She glanced up from her nest of chains and glared at them.

"If you touch me," she drawled coolly, "I'll have you *skinned.*"

Fodder hid his wry grin. Some traits did run in the family.

Dullard ducked to the rear of the rock, his face too recognisable as his own to risk Vanity seeing it. Flirt and Fodder glanced at each other as they both reached up for the chains. Carefully, Fodder slipped his free hand into his pouch and pulled on the Ring of Anthiphion.

Maybe it'll work, maybe it won't. But it's at least worth a try.

The syrupy feel of The Narrative surged at their backs as the clatter of the Merry Band's hooves topped the plateau. Fodder took a deep breath.

"Well," he muttered. "Here it…"

Comes…

Islaine!

Erik felt a wild surge of horror as the scene, so terrible and plaintive from his earlier vision, unfolded before his eyes. For there she was, his beautiful, beloved, tormented Islaine, her clothes a ruin and her hair wild as she writhed, chained with ruthless efficiency to a pinnacle of rock thrusting up from the bright, white moonlit plateau that opened out before them. And surrounding her like spectral wraiths of purest evil, the ridiculous figure of insane Tretaptus and two of his henchmen—the Ring-thief man of Sleiss, who had worked the impossible magic in the woods before Elder's powers had thwarted him in the mountains, and the unnatural female dressed in armour. They were securing the last of her chains before, Erik was certain, their inevitable cowardly flight from the horror—his vision had told him—they had dragged Islaine here to summon.

For where was the faceless, monstrous beast of evil that had lingered on the edge of his vision like a scourge? Had it referred only to Tretaptus and his mad cohorts or was there something more?

"Help me!" Her beautiful voice rang out, echoing through the mountains like a golden bell to summon Erik to his destiny. "Oh please, please help me! Somebody, anybody, help me! They mean to kill me! Tretaptus says if I will not love him, he will see me love no other! Help me! Oh, help!"

"Blimey!" Erik heard the man of Sleiss exclaim. "You could carve that ham!"

Perhaps it was his imagination, but Erik could have sworn that Islaine fixed the guard with a deadly glare.

"You impudent fiend!" he heard her hiss. "How dare you?"

"We must save the princess!" Sir Roderick's hand was already at his sword hilt. "Those wretches, how dare they manhandle her thus?"

"Stay!" It was the whip of Elder's staff that blocked the path of both Erik and Sir Roderick, preventing both from hurtling forwards to her aid. Even as they stared in shock at the white-haired sorcerer, he fixed them with a fierce look in return. "There is worse here than this! Take care!"

And then they heard the roar.

It echoed like a peal of the deepest thunder from within the depths of the gaping maw of a huge cave at the plateau's edge, rolling with a tangible force through the silver-washed air as though to push it into darkness. It was a sound that drove terror, primal instinctive terror down to the very tips of Erik's nerves—he could feel the hairs on his hands and head teetering on end as they felt its hammer blow. It was a roar of vastness, a roar to rouse primeval fear, a roar that could petrify a man down to his very bones.

"The dragon of Eretra!" Erik heard Elder breathe, his voice filled with a horror which, in his mentor, was unfamiliar. "What madness must lie in that head to rouse such mindless evil out of petty revenge?"

Smoke, roiling and burning into the air, rolled out of the cave in waves of vivid heat. In the depths of the darkness, two yellow eyes glowed like blazing lanterns.

Erik felt fear wage war with terrible fury in his chest. For true, the sight and sound of the beast that lay within those shadows terrified him to his core but, for Islaine, chained, abandoned now by her cowardly, fleeing captors, desperately imperilled as she writhed and shrieked at the sight of her fate, he felt only anger and a desperate yearning to help her. And, as though she sensed his frantic gaze, her writhing stilled, her shrieking quietened, and her eyes, so brimmed with fear, turned slowly across the moonlit rocks to meet...

"Perhaps not!"

Erik started in shock as what appeared to be a lacy ruff slapped like a blindfold across his beloved's eyes, causing her to screech with indignation. Prince Tretaptus, he who, it had seemed to Erik, should have fled like a coward already, brushed his hands together with a vague look of satisfaction.

"Sorry to intrude on your magical meeting-of-eyes and all," he said cheerfully, his absurd face smiling up at Erik and his friends as the unnatural woman and guardsman of Sleiss appeared back at his side. "But trust me, it really wouldn't be a good idea. You see, vanity here has already abandoned one betrothed—poor defiant, it was a terrible business—in favour of a fresher loving connection with valiant and, well, though none of them are my favourite people, I'd hate to see the whole sorry thing play out again, especially if she left her husband for a teenage boy. The poor woman has been forced by narrative urges to be fickle enough already. It doesn't really seem right to me to go through the whole mess again. Don't you think?"

"What?" Slynder, his knives clenched in his fists, stared down at the mad prince with incredulous eyes. "What nonsense does he speak?"

"Ignore his blathering!" Elder hissed. "The dragon comes! We must hurry!"

"Oh!" The strangest look passed over the insane prince's face. He glanced at his two companions. "I've just had the oddest urge! I think the narrative wishes me to...cackle."

"Cackle?" The unnatural woman grinned. "What, you?"

"Yes. Yes, it definitely wants cackling." Tretaptus paused thoughtfully. "And possibly some manner of declaration about how if I can't have the princess's love, no one can? And yes...yes. A fist shake. Definitely a fist shake." One of the prince's hands gave a rather lame shudder nominally skywards. He pondered it a moment before shaking his head. "No, I do apologise, but that simply isn't me at all. Not to mention it's terribly undignified."

That was the last straw for Zahora. "Enough of this!" she screeched, whipping her swords out of their sheaths! "Get them!"

Only the frantic shaking of the ground stayed Zahora's rush as heavy, earth-shattering footsteps pounded within the cave. A vile stench of sulphur and rotting flesh drifted across the plateau.

"Oops!" Tretaptus and his two companions exchanged a glance. "Perhaps we'd better get on with this?"

"I've got it." The unnatural woman, her face fixed grimly, hefted her beautifully crafted sword high in the air. "Say goodbye to those vocal cords, princess!"

What? They were to behead her when they'd summoned the dragon? What impatient madness was this, what cruel insanity...

The sword was swinging. Erik's thoughts snapped back into place.

"NO!!!" he screamed at the top of his lungs.

And like the primal power of the dragon's roar, his voice carried like a surge of hurricane wind across the plateau, twisting the air, uprooting rocks as it rolled forth like a tidal wave. The pinnacle to which the princess was chained shattered away in a shower of rock behind her, dissolving the chains into flares of rust and sending Islaine, Tretaptus, and his two henchmen hurtling into heaps against the rocky floor. As the wave passed, Erik saw the princess, who in the quiet of his own mind, he knew he had somehow shielded from the worst, stagger to her feet, ripping the ruff blindfold from her eyes as she thrust away the circle of dust and smoke around her with a delicately waved palm and turned towards where Erik waited, yearning to delve into her eyes and...

"Oi!" Like a bolt from a crossbow, the man of Sleiss rocketed into the princess, tackling her to the floor with heartless malice as she gave a keening screech. "No looking!" His own face whipped round to stare up at the shocked cluster of companions twenty yards distant across the moon-washed rock. "You and your bloody cheating!" he roared angrily. "Blocking a Ring of infinite magic when you know it can't be blocked, mysterious bloody powers! Play to your own rules for once! And I am not a bloody henchman!"

Grabbing the struggling, screaming Islaine by the wrists, he hauled them both to their feet as Tretaptus and the woman staggered, dusty and bloodied, to aid him.

"It's dragon time!" The man of Sleiss bellowed the words with unpleasant relish. "Oi, maw! Time for a good stomping, mate! Drop your scaly trotters on this yellow-haired thing! Come and get squishing!" He laughed wildly. "We've even got you a boy of destiny!"

Islaine! Erik grabbed the reins of his horse, intending to dive forwards, but in that moment came a roar so massive and so terrible it set even Sir Roderick's bold warhorse bucking. And then, wreathed in garlands of smoke and sulphurous steam, the dragon of Eretra emerged.

By the silvery glow of the moonlight, its scarlet scales shimmered like icy fire as its towering, serpentine neck writhed like dancing flame in the darkness. Vast wings, leathery like a bat's, scratched at the air as they arced out of the barrel-like, muscular body, shadowing four twisted, powerful limbs crowned with enormous, spreading feet from which sprouted curving, terrible talons. A huge, sweeping tail thrashed like a mace, the ball of spikes at its tip carving vast chunks out of the edges of every rock face it touched. But what Erik gazed on with the greatest dread was the face, if such a thing could be called one, an elongated snout crowned with gaping nostrils and those dreadful yellow eyes burning deep within a bony mass of ridges, topped by a strangely delicate pair of crested, horn-like ears. But most terrible of all was the rancid, tooth-lined maw that parted to free its awful scream, fire burning in the depths of its throat as it stared out over the plateau at the little range of figures and ran its horrific tongue along the length of its teeth.

Islaine! No!

"To arms!" This time no force in the world would have prevented Erik and his companions from riding forth into the jaws of hell itself. "For the princess!"

"Incoming!" the unnatural woman cried out as she and her companions hauled the screaming, wriggling princess towards the terrible apparition before them. "Fodder!"

"Maw!" Yet again, the man of Sleiss, clearly as insane as his master, shouted inexplicably at the dragon's vast, scaly form. "Stomp! Down here! Stomp this princess! Or even a spit of fire'll do, incinerate her a bit! Come on, mate, do us a favour!"

But the dragon, its huge head tilted as the yellow eyes stared down upon its prey, neither spat fire nor crushed them with its dreadful feet or jaws. As Erik charged towards them, his sword raised and his heart filled with fervour, he might, had he not known the dragon to be a mindless, rampaging killer of ancient evil, have taken its expression as one of confusion.

With a tilt of its head, it appeared to make a decision. One foot towered above them, poised for a ruthless strike.

Islaine!

"No!"

Yet again, the power of Erik's yell, to his own ongoing confusion, was enough to cast the princess and her three captors backwards just in time to avoid the dragon's crushing foot. The evil band scattered, the man of Sleiss hurtling sideways, the unnatural woman scurrying beneath the dragon's very belly itself, and the treacherous Prince Tretaptus, clinging to the ruined sleeve of Islaine's gown, collapsing in a heap with her at the rock face behind the dragon's towering form.

Erik and his companions surged forwards. Dimly, beneath the storm of his fury, the young man could hear Elder muttering enchantments to thwart their foes, could hear the whistle of Slynder's daggers as they tore into the air, could hear Zahora's war cry, Svenheid's vengeful roar, and Sir Roderick's relentless charge. For with such companions, how could even the most evil monster stand in their way?

And then they struck.

The dragon screeched as a ball of maddening hornets hurtled from Elder's hands to fill its mouth and throat. Svenheid's vast axe blow dug deep into a tree-trunk-like leg, digging out a vast chunk of flesh down to the bone. Erik himself slashed and sliced at the other, desperate to clear a path past this monstrous impediment to his Islaine, who remained pinned by the rock wall as she struggled in Tretaptus's grasp. Sir Roderick, his visor lowered, took a wild swing at the man of Sleiss, who escaped his vengeance by only inches, even as one of Slynder's daggers bounced off his helmet. Agile Zahora vaulted from her horse in time to avoid the deadly, painful swing of the writhing dragon's tail as she rolled and leapt to her feet directly in the unnatural woman's path.

"Now you will answer for your crimes, foul wench!" she declared, swinging her twin swords in a deadly pair of arcs towards the woman's neck and surely no force on earth could…

The woman's sword whipped up, twisting around one blade and slapping it down into the other as she curled backwards. Her hand turned sharply, pushing the blades aside as from her lean, her head catapulted forwards like a boulder in flight.

"Wench?" she screamed.

The crashing impact of the headbutt echoed across the rocky plateau. Zahora staggered back and the woman, looking rather cross-eyed herself but still standing, lashed her free fist around and smashed it into the warrior woman's face. Her eyes glazing, Erik's companion dropped.

"Wench!" he heard the unnatural woman hiss. "When are you people going to get a new line?"

"A little *help?*" The man of Sleiss's plaintive cry drew his companion's attention—he too ducked insanely beneath the agonised, thrashing body of the dragon, so as to avoid the frantic strikes of Sir Roderick's sword and Svenheid's axe, even as Slynder, at Elder's sharp command, abandoned the pursuit to his friends and rushed to Zahora's aid. The chain-mailed woman dived under the scaly form while batting away Roderick's blow with irrational ease, going back-to-back with her fellow as they held their circling attackers at bay.

But Erik could see another way, a way to end all and clear the path he craved.

"Roderick!" he bellowed. "Svenheid! Stand clear!"

The two horse-backed men dived out of the way without question as

Erik charged forwards, his teeth gritted and his eyes wild as he clamped his hands around the hilt of his sword and prayed for every scrap of strength in his body. He saw the man of Sleiss and his female companion exchange one look.

"Run!" the woman screamed.

But it was too late. For Erik had already struck.

With all the might of his heart and soul, he thrust his sword into the dragon's breast.

And the dragon reared. Fire exploded from its body in a wild rush, as though waiting to be free, and it surged towards the chain-mailed pair of guards in a rolling ball, unstoppable and...

"Jump!" To Erik's astonishment, the woman grabbed her companion and threw him sideways as he thrust out one hand, the deadly flame missing them by inches, almost seeming to veer. How could it have missed them?

But there was no time to ponder it. His companions could take care of them. Islaine needed him.

And even as he sought a desperate glimpse of his beloved beyond the dragon's thrashing form, he saw the mace-like tail of the dying dragon carve a slice out of the rock face, sending chunks of razor-sharp rock raining down on where his lady and Tretaptus struggled. The pair dived apart as the rock crashed into the ground around them, but it was Islaine, his bold, beautiful Islaine, who was first upon her feet, snatching up a dagger-like shard of detritus as she hurled herself at her tormentor, makeshift weapon raised over his bleeding, half-stunned form.

"You will pay for what you have done to me!" she screamed, her voice both beautiful and terrible in its rage. "Die, Tretaptus!"

"No!!!" But this time it was not Erik's scream that burst across the air like a peal of thunder, but another, a familiar voice, so familiar, too familiar but how could it possibly be...

"I'm Islaine, you selfish, thieving bitch! And you're not touching him!"

Even as Islaine stared, another figure, a figure in tattered blue velvet just as she was, with wild blonde-red hair just like hers and a face, oh a face so alike as to be a twin appeared as if from nowhere from the rocks beyond. Her features compacted with rage, she charged like a dainty bull into the stunned form of her doppelganger. The two women collapsed to the ground kicking and fighting, and who was who not even Erik dared to guess. The Islaine beneath screeched as the Islaine above dropped her full weight onto her stomach, her fingers scratching at her face like a wild banshee as she slapped and screamed and tore.

"You take off my face this instant, vanity! It is not your turn, you hear me, you have no right! I'm Islaine! Me! Me, me, me!"

"You don't deserve her!" the Islaine beneath shrieked back. "You never did! You're a spoiled brat, a brat with no idea! Get off me!"

"But I'm still Islaine!" the Islaine on top screamed back. "I'm Islaine forever and you know it! The narrative knows it, everyone knows! This is my quest and my romance and my happy ending! I'm Islaine! Islaine is me!"

"Pleasance!" Battered and bloodied by a wound to his head, Tretaptus staggered over to the extraordinary battle with an inexplicable cry. "Let her go, we have to leave! Now! Get up now!"

But one wild hand slapped him away. "Unhand me, Tretaptus! This is no concern of yours! I must deal with this imposteress of yours!"

Tretaptus's eyes widened and then suddenly his expression hardened. Beneath the shadow of the thrashing dragon, his hands lashed out with unexpected firmness, grasping the Islaine above by the arms and dragging her off her lookalike.

"We are leaving now!" he exclaimed with coherent firmness. "Right now, pleasance!"

"No!" But Islaine was struggling in his grip. "Unhand me, you monster! Unhand me, you fiend! You have no right, Tretaptus! Let me go!"

"Never!" was the fervent response. "I will never let you go! Not while she's waiting!"

"Look out!" In view of the bizarre drama that had been unfolding, the battle had staggered to a halt. But nothing would stay the death throes of the tormented, brutally wounded dragon and in the midst of the chaos, it had stumbled towards the rock face, reeling and struggling, its huge form teetering on the verge of collapse. And like a mighty tree finally felled by one last stroke, it had begun to fall.

And below, the three figures lay directly in its path.

Except suddenly there were four. For the voice that had cried out had come from the rocks behind and suddenly the third of the three chain-mailed guards bolted into view, his helmet strangely crafted and bound with what appeared to be leather strips. He slammed into Tretaptus and the Islaine he clung to and hurled them stumbling backwards. Behind, in the shadow of the falling beast, the other Islaine had staggered to her knees, scrambling over herself, but even as she rose, one heel of her shoe jammed into the ruins of her dress and sent her tumbling to the floor. Even as one hand reached, yearningly towards where Erik was watching in helpless horror, a terrible scream of desperate pleading ripping from her lips, the full weight of the dragon's body smacked down on top of her and crushed her messily beneath.

With a final exhale, the dragon gave a last, rocking shudder sideways and lay still. The freshly exposed remains of one of the Islaines lay even stiller. There was no question that she was dead. Nothing that flat could really be alive.

"Yes!" The entirely inappropriate exclamation broke the horrified silence. Even as Erik turned his head, he saw the final guard pump one fist in a gleeful downwards motion. "Pulped princess!"

"A deception!" Elder's strangely relieved voice broke into the breathless silence. "They created a counterfeit princess to try and fool us, but the true one escaped her foul captor and came to expose it! We must save her!"

"Oh, bollocks!" The crude exclamation came from the man of Sleiss. "Run for it!"

The newly arrived guard staggered suddenly as though hit by a hammer blow. "Oh no," he whispered madly. "Oh no, no, no! It's after me!"

"So run!" The chain-mailed woman hurled herself to his side, grabbing him by the shoulders and bustling him forwards. "Go!"

"But the dragon's blocking the crevice!" was the man's plaintive response. "Go where?"

"Down the slope! Go!"

"But…" Tretaptus, who was hustling the strangely blank-faced true Islaine before him, turned in concern. But the guardsman of Sleiss shouted his master down.

"Just go!" he roared. "Below the horizon!"

"Hold, you fiends!" Slynder, who had put the now-conscious Zahora back in her saddle, whipped his horse in sudden pursuit. "You will not escape again! I will not—"

"Oh bog off!" The chain-mailed, unnatural woman wheeled swiftly, her sword swinging in a sweeping arc as she plunged it for the second time into Slynder's already wounded thigh. He screeched in pain and slipped sideways from his saddle with a thump.

"Slynder!" Even as his furious companions rushed to his aid, Erik saw the foul little band as they hustled the princess away down the slope into a darkness deeper than any that…

Goes…

The Narrative melted away as they plunged beneath the horizon and, in the shadow of the looming mountain, the silver light of the moon was abruptly gone. They scrabbled for decent footing, skidding and sliding on the steep scree slope. Dullard's voice, breathless and anxious, cut through the sound of clashing stones.

"We have to be careful!" he exclaimed. "I think there's a—"

Abruptly, the shadows ahead appeared to swell, expanding from a narrow blackness into a vast expanse of drop. With a cry of shock, Fodder scrambled to a halt, his feet slip-sliding on the loose stones as his hand reached out to grab a jut of rock. He heard Shoulders grunt as Flirt hauled him backwards, knocking them both off their feet in the nick of time. Dullard too managed to apply the brakes before a nasty plummet, grabbing handfuls of Pleasance's skirt as he dragged her back and swung her in a tumbling arc to thump with a thud into Fodder.

For a moment, they all lay stunned and shocked in the blackness. But then, Dullard's voice broke into Fodder's hearing once more.

"Ravine," he heard the prince breathe. "I thought so."

But the horizon above them was thickening, the vivid darkness creeping closer, and there was no time to be surprised.

"The ground's gone!" Pleasance exclaimed, and there was a note of panic in her voice, an edge of horror that seemed to touch on more than merely the drop. "The ground is gone! What do we do? What do we—?"

"Not all of it!" Flirt was back on her feet, hauling the disorientated Shoulders upright with a yank. "There's a ledge, look! Come on!"

"A ledge?" Shoulders's voice was rather high-pitched. "Hang on, where's the other end? How do we know it goes anywhere?"

"A narrow but traversable ledge within escaping distance of a Dragon's lair?" Dullard too was scrambling upright, his eyes brightening. "It will go somewhere, believe me. It wouldn't be a horrendous cliché if it didn't!"

But Fodder, his heart pounding in his ears from the wild scramble, could see the flaw at once. "We'll be horrifically exposed out there!" he declared anxiously. "One good burst of night vision and a quick landslide or avalanche…"

"And we aren't exposed here?" Pleasance's pale face was upturned towards the advancing horizon and all it implied. "Thank you, but I'll risk it!" One hand lashed out, wrapping around Dullard's wrist as she hauled the surprised prince hurriedly along behind her. A moment later, their shadows melded into the darkness of the ledge.

"For once, I'm with the princess!" Shoulders was next, head wobbling as he staggered past Fodder, grasping the cliff face for desperate support.

"They're right, aren't they?" Flirt too was edging out onto the narrow ledge a yard or two shy of Shoulders, as she beckoned to Fodder. "Get the Ring ready, Fodder, and if it gets us, use it! Don't doubt it! Now come on!"

The Ring. Could it be trusted? Fodder still wasn't sure—he hadn't been able to tell whether his attempt to block the ball of flame closing down on him and Flirt in The Narrative had been a success or a fluke. And besides, Elder's attention had been elsewhere, not on blocking him. It wouldn't be this time.

But they were cheating. It had to work. He had to *believe* it.

Following his friends, he too began to move into a rapid-but-careful creep along the—of course—crumbling, half-yard-wide traverse. If they could stay in the shadows and move quickly, if they could just keep out of sight of any kind of...

Light...

The flare of light from Elder's hand burst across the sky like a mighty comet, illuminating the slope that fell away in a rocky, uneven stumble before vanishing into a sharp plunge down into a deep, winding gully. For a moment, it appeared that this dead end had stolen away the fleeing figures impossibly, but then, with a cry, Erik saw them, five nervous silhouettes edging with swift care along a narrow, crumbling traverse along the cliff face. The three soldiers, their chain mail glinting in the vivid light of Elder's magic, were bringing up the rear—Erik recognised the rearmost as the man of Sleiss. Beyond him, his new companion who had taken such glee in the death of the fake Islaine was clinging on as he flailed and tripped and stumbled his way along the treacherous path, saved from a terrible plunge only by the quick reflexes of the unnatural female as she grasped his careening body and all but pinned him to the cliff. But there in front—oh yes!—was the blonde hair of beautiful Islaine, true Islaine, her face turned almost frantically away from them as she was pushed and manhandled along the treacherous ledge by the madman Prince Tretaptus. And rage began to course through his veins like vivid poison that she should be so endangered, that this delicate flower of womanhood should be treated in such an impertinent manner...

"Why do they play such games with us?" Over the rising tide of his anger, Erik heard Sir Roderick declare, "Why replace my noble princess?"

"Never mind that!" Slynder exclaimed, twitching his freshly wounded leg awkwardly. "That guard still has the Ring!"

"He shall make no escape this time!" Elder drew himself up straight in the saddle, his arms raised as white light danced across his fingertips. "The enchantments I have laid will keep him from using the Ring in such a manner again! They can disappear nowhere! They are trapped!"

From out on the ledge, distinct swearing could be heard and the words "Get us out!" "...it's still blocked!" and "...bloody cheating!" drifted to Erik's ears. But he did not care, for the anger growing in his breast was so vast, so immense, that it could not be contained. It swelled like an aquifer within him, bubbling to the surface and yearning to burst free. In his mind's eye, he saw the three soldiers and Tretaptus obliterated against the rock, saw noble, brave, beautiful Islaine left safe but alone to drift as if by magic to the safety and relief of his arms and he wanted it to be true so strongly, so badly, that he was helpless against the force of it. He felt his arms extend of their own volition, felt the surge of power within his chest and behind his eyes roaring as, with a frantic cry, he let it rip free into the illuminated night.

"Oh shi—"

The Ring-bearing guard thrust out one hand and gold glittered there, but against such an awesome surge, there was surely nothing he could do. Tretaptus was yelling as he bustled the shaking Islaine along before him and the woman in mail could only grit her teeth as she froze, trying to keep her unbalanced companion pinned against the rock face. The epic energy tumbled towards them like a tornado blast and there would be no holding it back, no stopping it from smashing into the cliff and obliterating them like...

"No!"

In the strange half-light of Elder's spell, the Ring glowed scarlet. But it would be too little too late, for how could anything halt the overwhelming power of Erik's will? There was no way that it would...

The power struck the glowing barrier and the world seemed to explode.

The light seared at Erik's eyeballs, forcing him to turn away. Far in the distance, he heard a voice screaming "You lot, run!" but as his vision cleared, he could see the vast chunk of mountain that his deflected, accidental spell had carved sheer from the rock as it shattered and tumbled in a terrible surge towards the five stranded on the cliff face. And then, with a thunderous roar, it struck.

Tretaptus and Islaine vanished, lost on the far side of the waterfall of rocks that crashed down the cliff face as they stumbled desperately out of view. The new guard and his female companion were not so lucky, as the boulders smashed away the ledge on which they stood, sending both tumbling and twisting through the air as they plummeted towards certain death in the dark gully below. And as he disappeared in a hail of massive stone, it felt inevitable that the thief of the Ring would be lost too, torn away from the secure embrace of rock to face the crashing fall. But as the landslide of rocks diminished, incredibly, the guard appeared, shrouded in red as he clung to the last, shredded outcrop of the ledge onto which he had ventured. He stared up at Erik and his companions and the boy could see the fear that gleamed within his eyes.

For he knew that, at last, there was no escape. He had lost all his allies and, with the traverse destroyed on both sides of his feet, there was nowhere left to run. The kidnapper of Islaine, the Sleiss troublemaker, the thief of the Ring of Anthiphion was trapped. And now it was time to meet his fate....

TO BE CONTINUED ...

TRAPPED BY CRIME. FREED BY MAGIC.

When Skate tries to burgle a shut-in's home, she gets caught by the owner—a powerful undead wizard. He makes a deal with her. Now, she'd better find out exactly where her loyalties lie.

Skate the Thief
by Jeff Ayers

TRUE LOVE. ANCIENT CURSES.

Theodora is determined to unravel the mysterious Seth Adler's secrets. No matter how many thousands of years old.

Painter of the Dead
by Catherine Butzen

RIDICULOUSLY MAGICAL & MAGICALLY RIDICULOUS

Crafted as a slave to serve Time, the clockwork man escapes to seek out his imagination, his purpose, and his name.

The Land of the Purple Ring
by Deborah J. Natelson

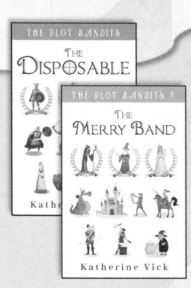

IT'S TIME TO TAKE OVER

Fodder of Humble Village is a soldier for the plot of each new story, and, frankly, he's really sick and tired of getting speared, disembowelled, and decapitated so the good guys can look glorious. In fact, he's not going to take it anymore.

The Disposable and
The Merry Band
by Katherine Vick

AND YOU THOUGHT COLLEGE WAS TOUGH BEFORE

Try getting bitten by a werewolf. And being hunted by madmen. And being stalked by a very suspicious secret organization.

Hunter's Moon by Sarah M. Awa

THE CLOCK IS TICKING

Plans seldom survive contact with the enemy, a truth thrown at Mercedes when an ordinary trip turns into a battle for survival.

Bargaining Power
by Deborah J. Natelson

About the Author

Katherine Vick was born in the middle bit of England longer ago than she'd care to admit (1979, if you must know. Aren't you nosy?). She studied geography at the University of Wales, Aberystwyth, writing her dissertation on the role of landscape and culture in fantasy novels. She then moved on to a master's degree in literary studies and creative writing at the University of Central England, where she wrote the dissertation that inspired the creation of Fodder, so she hopes you'll feel she put her education to good use. She flirted briefly with fast food and retail work before settling down as a college administrator. She spends occasional weekends on historic battlefields in her capacity as a rather clumsy late-medieval reenactor. She (mis)spent a part of her youth writing stories based around other people's literary and media creations. She likes to read and watch fantasy, history, and science fiction—frankly, anything that gets her away from the real world, which is far too much trouble. Occasionally she even gets around to writing stuff.

You can visit Katherine at
https://realmofkatherinevick.blogspot.com/